WHAT THE CRITICS SAY ABOUT THE NOVELS OF MARSHALL GOLDBERG, M.D.

"Fascinating, exciting, emotion-packed!"[1]

"Captivating!"[2]

"Only a physician could have written this!"[3]

"As busy as a Saturday night emergency room...medicine at its most graphic!"[4]

"The tension is terrific...a super thriller!"[5]

[1] *Detroit News* review of "The Anatomy Lesson"
[2] *Los Angeles Times* review of "The Anatomy Lesson"
[3] *West Coast Review of Books* review of "Skeletons"
[4] *Publishers Weekly* review of "Critical List"
[5] *Publishers Weekly* review of "The Karamanov Equations"

We will send you a free catalog on request. Any titles not in your local book store can be purchased by mail. Send the price of the book plus 50¢ shipping charge to Tower Books, P.O. Box 270, Norwalk, Connecticut 06852.

Titles currently in print are available for industrial and sales promotion at reduced rates. Address inquiries to Tower Publications, Inc., Two Park Avenue, New York, New York 10016, Attention: Premium Sales Department.

DISPOSABLE PEOPLE

Marshall Goldberg, M.D.
and
Kenneth Kay

TOWER BOOKS NEW YORK CITY

*This book is for
Nancy, Elizabeth, Alice, Ariane, and Kenneth.*

For background information on the legal rights of prisoners the authors are indebted to Judge Hardy C. Dillard of the University of Virginia School of Law and to the librarians of the Arthur J. Morris Law Library of the University of Virginia.

A TOWER BOOK

Published by

Tower Publications, Inc.
Two Park Avenue
New York, N.Y. 10016

Copyright © 1980 by E. Marshall Goldberg & Kenneth Kay

This is a work of fiction, and all characters (with the exception of public figures) are fictitious. Any similarity between these characters and real people in name, description, occupation, or background is purely coincidental.

Chapter 1

BETHESDA, MARYLAND
9 September

The somber-faced man in green stood at a lectern on the small stage, throat mike looped under his chin, watching the audience file in. There were about thirty men and half a dozen women, all wearing ordinary street clothes except for a sprinkling of military uniforms, and all with tense and solemn expressions. After they were seated the only sound in the auditorium was a whisper of chilled, filtered air being pumped six stories underground.

The man on stage spoke abruptly. "First slide, please."

The auditorium dimmed to twilight. A projection screen brightened at the back of the stage. Block letters flashed upon it:

CONSOLVO'S ULCERATION[1]

"Next slide," said the man tonelessly.

A blow-up of a color photo taken at close range appeared: the tanned, heavy-muscled forearm of a man who had worked hard outdoors. Between elbow and wrist the underside of the arm lay open in a ragged, suppurating, black-edged slash four inches long.

"The first known case," said the speaker. "The victim was a sixty-eight-year-old rancher in New Mexico. He died with the unhappy distinction of giving his name to a previously unknown disease. Here is another photograph of Howard Consolvo's forearm, taken six hours after the first."

In the second slide the gaping wound was visibly wider and deeper and had lengthened into the crook of the elbow. A scarlet rash with white pinpoint pustules spread out on both sides. "Next slide," said the speaker in the same flat monotone.

The third photograph was of the whole arm from wrist to shoulder. From bicep down it was a shapeless stump of festering tissue, black and streaky-red with onion-pale blisters glistening with a yellowish exudation. Someone in the audience stifled a sound of disgust. "This picture," entoned the speaker, "was taken ten minutes before the patient went into the operating room for amputation of his arm at the shoulder. The operation achieved nothing. Two hours later the same evidence of advanced putridity had appeared on his upper torso, and death followed. Like all the other victims of this disease so far, Howard Consolvo simply rotted away from the point of initial infection until his vital functions were so impaired that he ceased to live. That's enough pictures, I think. Last slide, please, Harrison."

On the screen there appeared:

SPECIAL BULLETIN
Morbidity and Mortality Report
Federal Center for Disease Control

CONSOLVO'S ULCERATION: A putrescent inflammation of the epidermis characterized in early stages by acute burning sensations and the formation of vesicle-like blisters containing a highly contagious serum. Usually accompanied by subnormal body temperature, around 92° to 94° F.; low white corpuscle count; jaundice; acute mental depression. Etiology uncertain. Causative organism not yet isolated; may be microbic or viral. Primary means of contagion not yet determined although physical contact involving mucous membrane areas or broken skin appears likely. Vector unknown: causative agent may be transmitted by animal parasites or insect life, or be airborne. Earliest symptoms bear a superficial resemblance to *Melaney's Ulcer*, but unlike it, amputation of affected members of a subject's body does not arrest spread of infection. This disease progresses with great rapidity from point of original infection, apparently consuming and thriving on keratin, in the process producing an unknown enzyme on which it further feeds. The flesh of a victim literally "rots" away, emitting a stench so nauseating as to complicate the tasks of attending medical personnel. Pain is exquisite; the most powerful analgesics, including opiates, provide little relief. To this must be added the mental agony of the victim who remains fully conscious of his probable doom until *extremis*. Fatality rate on known cases has been 100%. From initial symptoms until death, elapsed time has ranged from less than seventy-two hours to as long as ten days. WARNING: This is an extremely dangerous new disease which, unless controlled, could lead to an epidemic of major proportions.

After the audience had time to read and absorb it, the slide went off, the projection screen darkened, the auditorium lights went up. The man in green scanned the house. "Questions? Yes, Admiral Graybar."

"Ah, yes," said a silver-haired man with shoulder boards on his white uniform. "One question. Even though a full week has passed since the first victim was observed, we have made no progress towards finding a causative agent?"

"I'm afraid that's correct."

The admiral looked deeply troubled. "We're still totally in the dark? No clues at all?"

"That's the situation, sir."

"Thank you." The admiral sank into his chair, shaking his head. Behind him a woman's hand went up.

"Yes, Dr. Riddle?"

"But as I understand it, the only part of the country seriously affected so far is the Southwest. Is that right?"

"So far, yes, Doctor, depending on what you mean by the word 'seriously.'"

7

"I'll rephrase it. So far it hasn't moved out of the Arizona-New Mexico-West Texas area in epidemic proportions?"

"Add Las Vegas, Nevada, and, yes, we can say that."

"Then there is hope that we may have time enough to isolate the organism—the whatever-it-is—before epidemic sweeps the nation?"

"Every private and government medical research laboratory in the country is working round-the-clock, Dr. Riddle, on the basis of just that hope. But so far hope is all."

"Thank you." Biting her lower lip, the woman sat down. A man in a brown suit stood up.

"But it is spreading, isn't it—east and west?"

"Unhappily, yes, Dr. Smalley. Salem, Oregon; San Diego—you see how erratically it jumps around? St. Louis, Gary, Nashville, Panama City, the Florida panhandle—one or two cases in all of them."

"So it's on its way? And no way to treat it? No way to vaccinate against it? And quarantine infeasible?"

"That's correct, Dr. Smalley."

"Then God help us," said Smalley, collapsing into his chair.

"Any more questions?" Suddenly the man on stage looked as weary as if he too might collapse. "If not, thank you for coming. I'll report again as soon as there is something to report. Meantime, I can only echo Dr. Smalley's statement. God help us. God help us all. God help the United States."

Chapter 2

The President was too agitated to stay behind his desk. He kept pacing about, pounding his fist and shooting questions at the only three men in the world he now believed he could rely on, questions nobody could answer. As he paced, he sent anguished glances outside at the bright September day as if hoping for help out there. Nothing he saw reassured him—the wilted rose garden, the lawn long brown since the gardeners had fled and the city water pressure had dropped too low for the sprinklers, rolls of barbed wire the army had piled up inside the iron fence along Pennsylvania Avenue, and four soldiers in jump boots guarding a gate. Like the gardeners, the White House police had fled except for a stalwart few still manning posts inside. Not just White House police either. All Washington and its suburbs were being guarded by Eighty-second Airborne troops through a tenuous chain of command from Fort Bragg, North Carolina, to Fort Monroe, Virginia, to Readiness Command in Tampa, up to the Pentagon, and back across the Potomac to the gaunt person of Lloyd P. Dobson striding back and forth in his White House office. Like another Illinois president a hundred and fifteen years before, Dobson was trying to keep a nation from falling to pieces from inside a garrisoned city.

"Less than ten days," he was saying. "Barely a week. And already Albuquerque and El Paso and Las Vegas practically shut down. Watts and Harlem and half of Detroit and St. Louis and the Chicago southside burned out. Even cities where nobody's sick yet are closing down. It's worse than those nuclear-strike briefings Charley's people are always scaring me to death with over at the Department of Defense."

"Oh, I wouldn't say it was that bad, Mr. President," said Charles Cohane, Secretary of Defense. "It's not nearly as bad as a nuclear attack. And there's no rioting since you declared martial law, not even in the ethnic minority hot spots. Maybe the worst is behind us."

"I'm glad you think so, Charley," said the President. "I certainly can't. I don't think we've seen anything yet. I think this is the well-known 'lull.' And not to take credit from the regular army, you've got to admit that one reason the mobs have vanished is that people have gotten scared of crowds—of catching this disease."

"I suggested federalizing the National Guard," said Cohane. "I think it's a misuse of regular troops."

"Now, now, Charley," said Dobson. "If there's one thing we've learned from history, it's that militia is unreliable against civil unrest. Hiram, you haven't said a word since you sat down."

Hiram Cawthorp, the attorney general, sucked his cold pipe. "The reason for that, Mr. President," he said in his courtly Valley of Virginia manner, "is that so far no questions of constitutional law—law of any kind—have come up. So far, a tragic number of citizens are dying for reasons the medical professionals seem unsure about, but the deaths are presumably from natural, which is to say, legal causes. Sooner or later, though, Mr. President, questions of law *will* arise. They always do. Until then, these problems lie outside my domain. I pass, sir."

And that was that, thought Dobson, irritably. Nobody

budged Hiram Cawthorp, not even the President of the United States. They called it integrity, precisely why he had wanted the stiff-necked old Charlottesville aristocrat in his cabinet. It was also damned annoying when he needed counsel so desperately. Lloyd Dobson, a contented chairman of humanities at an Illinois university named for his grandfather before the politicians dragooned him into the statehouse, faced the window to hide his anxiety. He wondered if Lincoln had ever had to conceal his panic from his cabinet members. He stared at the astonishing sight of downtown Washington totally free of traffic, and breathed the sweet untainted air—the single blessing of this calamity. On the sidewalk beyond the barbed wire ten or fifteen men and women dressed in the obligatory Army Surplus, social-protest garb stared at the White House, wondering, perhaps, what wisdom for this crisis was being generated inside the anachronistic nineteenth-century mansion. Precious little, if only they knew, thought Dobson, fear coiling in his intestines like a snake.

Behind a jeep with a machine gun poking across the hood, army trucks rumbled around a corner, carrying rations to a distribution point in the black Inner City where fear of infection had quelled rioting. Wincing from the image of a beleaguered city, Dobson began musing aloud.

"Who of our people will be sacrificed for this disaster, Gentlemen?" the President began again. Wars and pestilence always take the young, strong, and most promising, and in the end the nation suffers. France bred runts for a hundred years after Napoleon's tall grenadiers were killed off. That could be bad genetics, but it illustrates my meaning. Two world wars reduced England to a third-rate power. Historical imperatives may have helped end her empire, but I maintain that it was Ypres and Dunkirk that bled the vigor out of England."

Hiram Cawthorp sighed. He respected Dobson—would not have left his Wall Street practice for a cabinet post otherwise—but he was beginning to wonder if the man realized just how serious a threat this southwestern epidemic posed. He himself was terrified for the nation, though he would never show it, but all Dobson was doing was airing this preposterous notion about eugenics. In the far chair Charley Cohane, who, on six years of Texas grade-school learning, had worked up from a Burkburnette oil rig roughneck to Board Chairman of Consolidated Petroleum, scowled at his burly right fist. He hated it when Lloyd Dobson got on one of his lecture-hall kicks. But you couldn't ask the President to kindly shut up.

Dr. Simon Green, the third man, who had never been in the White House before, stared at the rug and wondered if these men were really sane. An uncontrollable disease spreading fast out of the Southwest that killed everybody who caught it and that no doctor understood—didn't they comprehend? What was all this foolish talk about the English empire?

"Wars kill off the best," said the President, "because of an insane logic that makes us send our best against the enemy's best. The human race would be better perhaps if the old-time kings had sent their feeble-minded and inept and feckless to war and kept the best home for seed stock. But that would be too sensible. Take the pestilence now. You might think epidemics would cull out the unfit as Arctic wolves cull cripples out of the caribou herds. But nature isn't any more sensible than kings. Epidemics take the best too, just like war. The 1918 flu epidemic that killed upwards of twenty million people around the world hit hardest at America's healthiest—the young men in army camps and on navy ships, Pershing's troops in France. It nearly put this country out of the war."

Cohane and Cawthorp, not the most congenial of men, exchanged impatient glances. Cohane drew a deep breath and bulled ahead. "Chief, DOD and JCS are waiting for guidance from you. Anything you want the military to do, they're ready. But you've got to tell us, sir. Until you do,

12

goddamn it—!" He slashed the air with his fist. "Excuse me, but goddamn it anyway! Until you do, they're stymied. This thing's out of their line. It's not something you can shoot a gun or missile at or drop a bomb on."

"I know, Charley," said Dobson. "I'm not criticizing the military. Now just let me keep on exploring this line of thought a minute longer. I want you to know how my thoughts are running. To start with, I'm basically optimistic. I believe we'll bring this epidemic under control. I don't believe this is the American *Götterdämmerung*. I don't believe God is ready for the United States to die yet."

Simon Green fidgeted. Whatever he had expected when they summoned him to this office, it had not been to hear the President speak of the Deity so familiarly. Hiram Cawthorp sent him a reassuring wink, but Simon was still uncomfortable.

"I believe," the President went on, "that America will survive this crisis as she has all her previous crises, through the help of God and by the unique genius of the American system. But that's enough rumination for now. Let's get down to the pragmatic. Dr. Green, my attorney general refuses me legal counsel. The defense establishment has no new schemes of maneuver to propose. How about some medical advice?"

Simon Green, M.D., former director of the National Institutes of Health and now assistant secretary of health and scientific affairs, stared at this perplexing president and wished, not for the first time, that he had gone straight home to Rocky Mount, North Carolina, after medical school forty years before and set up as a country doctor. As he pondered, the folds of his fat sixty-five-year-old face worked so earnestly that Hiram Cawthorp was reminded of a troubled old English bulldog. "Mr. President," Simon began unhappily, "the trouble with epidemics is that even when you know what they are, say encephalitis or hepatitis or maybe typhoid, they're still awfully hard to get under control. When it's something

13

brand new and unheard of like this Consolvo's Ulceration, why, we don't know where to start. The public health departments, the university labs, the pharmaceutical houses, all the National Institutes of Health—right now they're all trying to isolate the causative agent—"

The President interrupted him. "That was an unfair question, Dr. Green. I'd forgotten that this was your first meeting with us."

"Yes, sir," said Green. "That's right. It is my first meeting." Which was Birdie Bellanca's fault, he was thinking. The gravelly voiced New Jersey ex-congresswoman whom the liberal pressure groups had forced on the President as health secretary had always insisted on attending before. And like old Harry Truman used to say, Birdie didn't know any more about epidemics than a hog does Sunday.

"Then, to keep you from having to waste your valuable time covering ground I'm already familiar with, Dr. Green, let me sum up what I know."

"*Your* valuable time, sir," said Green politely.

"Thank you. Now. Although I can't put it in technical language, I know that Consolvo's Ulceration is a hitherto unknown disease, and so far one hundred percent fatal. Also contagious, although we don't know how. No treatment is effective against it. We don't know if it is caused by a bacterium or by a virus or by some kind of weird cross, which I understand is at least theoretically possible. I understand how the U.S. Public Health Service and the Center for Disease Control send task forces out when an epidemic starts. I know that your old organization in Bethesda—the National Institutes of Health—is spending millions on research. I know all these things in broad, lay terms. But that's all I know."

"Mr. President," said Simon, "I hate to admit it, but that's all anybody knows. I could fancy it up with medical lingo, but it wouldn't mean a thing more."

"An honest man," said Dobson. "Regard him and marvel, Hi and Charley. One more question, Dr. Green.

14

Would all this elaborate Public Health Service epidemic-fighting apparatus work faster if we pumped emergency funds into it?"

"You mean, could we speed things up if you gave us four or five million extra dollars? No sir. NIH spends over a billion a year on research already. Trouble is, more money couldn't buy more labs or doctors or medical technicians. Those take time and training. I don't expect I'm telling you anything you don't know, though, Mr. President."

"That's how I saw it," said Dobson. "Thank you for your corroboration. One vital element, though, is lacking in all that medical machinery. Do you know what it is?"

"Not offhand, sir."

"This is a war," said Dobson. "Before we win it—and we *will* win it—we could lose a lot of battles. Lincoln nearly lost his war before he finally found Grant. Franklin Roosevelt needed George Catlett Marshall. For this war, Dr. Green, I've got to have my own Grant/Marshall—a doctor, obviously, to run everything from the last eyeball peering through a microscope in a California medical lab to quarantine-officers dynamiting contaminated oyster beds in Chesapeake Bay, if that's what it comes to. This doctor will have absolute authority over everyone and everything—*my* authority as commander-in-chief—in this fight. What he says will go. He'll report to me directly, outside of channels. He will run my war against this epidemic."

"I can see the tabloid headlines now," murmured Hiram Cawthorp. "PREZ PICKS PLAGUE CZAR."

"Probably," said Dobson. "Actually 'Plague Czar' is a fairly descriptive title for what I want. My Grant/Marshall is going to be the most powerful doctor with the most sweeping authority in American history. Dr. Green, I want you to be my Plague Czar."

Simon's heart sank. "Mr. President, this is the most overwhelming—" He gulped and went on. "Mr. President, I'd do anything in the world to control this epidemic—I mean that—and this is the finest compliment I've ever received. But, sir, I'm twenty years too old and fifty pounds too heavy. The man you want—he's got to be somebody who can dash around the country and work thirty-six hours at a clip. Mr. President, it shames me, but I'm too old and fat and out of breath and my heart's not so good either."

From his angular height, eyes glittering under his shaggy brows, bold nose jutting from his seamed, craggy face, Lloyd Dobson stared down at Simon Green. Dobson's resemblance to Lincoln, not least of the political assets that had put him in the White House, was disconcerting. Simon Green, who had never shrunk from a man in his life, knew a flutter of apprehension. Then the ugly presidential face smiled. "Dr. Green, you're not only an honest man but also a modest one. Very well. If you're not qualified, who is? I've already ruled out all the physicians holding senior military or civilian rank in the government. I need someone free from entanglement and parochial loyalties. I don't really know the top men in academic or private medicine. Who would you suggest as coming closest to being you if you were—" Dobson's smile widened—"twenty years younger and, as you suggest, a few pounds lighter?"

"I know the man," said Simon whose mind had been sorting through dozens of candidates for Dobson's Plague Czar. "I hate to admit it, but he's even better for what you need, Mr. President, than I would ever have been for at least one good reason. Don't you gentlemen let my wife know I said this or I'll put sand in your soup, but for some jobs it's better to hire a bachelor and Noah Blanchard has never been married."

"We're all married men here," said Dobson good-humoredly. "Nobody's going to peach on you. Who is Noah Blanchard?"

"*Dr.* Noah Blanchard, Mr. President. He's so right for what you want I can't think of anybody who would even come close."

16

"That's encouraging. Tell us about him."

"Well, sir, he used to be a Public Health Service epidemiologist—with just exactly the background you need now—switched to the Air Force which used him all over Europe and Asia as a trouble-shooting flight surgeon—he's an inactive reserve colonel now—and since he got out of uniform he's been chief of infectious diseases at Cook County General Hospital."

"Chicago?" said Dobson.

"Yes, sir. It's his home. Noah's from a pioneer Chicago family. It's the only thing I ever heard him brag about."

"Old Chicago family," murmured the President. "That's a mark in his favor."

"Yes, sir," said Simons noncommittally, catching another of Hiram Cawthorp's winks.

"Tell us about him as a person," said Cawthorp. "His character, temperament—the kind of man he is. Do you know him well enough to say?"

"Yes, sir. Noah's kind of a protegé of mine. I've known him nearly fifteen years, know him right well. To start with he's his own man, hardheaded, stubborn. Unless he thinks something is right, nobody can push him into it. And he's brave and venturesome—did dangerous work for the CIA in Asia, hunted big game in Alaska and Africa; fought oyster pirates in a typhoid epidemic in Texas; qualified as a parachutist in the Service. He looks and moves like a basketball player—he's lean, quick, and six-and-a-half feet tall. Noah's had as varied a career as any doctor I know—tried nearly everything but private practice where he could get rich. Money's not very high on his priority list."

"How old is this paragon?" said Cohane.

"Well, let me see," said Simon. "Getting on towards forty, I guess. My goodness, how the years pile up."

"And never married?" said the secretary of defense.

Green chuckled. "If I catch any implication there, Mr. Secretary, I expect I could round up fifty or a hundred nurses and women doctors and various assorted females

17

who would happily testify you got no grounds for suspicion of Noah Blanchard. Yes, sir, I know him that well. I wouldn't say Noah's like a son to me but we're close. One late night at my house over a jug of Virginia whiskey he talked freely as I ever heard him. He was back from the Congo on a State Department mission and feeling pretty depressed. Or maybe just tired. He got to talking finally about feeling guilty for not being mature enough to pick a good wife and settle down. He just didn't have time to find one, he said, and anyway the kind of life he'd chosen it wasn't fair to ask a woman to share. He was melancholy that night and speaking from the heart. No, sir, Noah ain't any what we used to call fairy in my day. Not that it matters like it used to, though I'm old-fashioned."

"What do you think, Hiram?" said Dobson. The attorney general nodded. "Charley?" Cohane shrugged and the President said, "Well, I'm sold. Now we've got to invest him with the authority to do this job. He's a reserve Air Force Medical Corps colonel, you say? How about if I give him a spot promotion to flag-rank? Say, three stars. Those top military doctors are only two stars, aren't they? Major General? Rear Admiral? That right, Cohane?"

"Jesus Christ!" sputtered Cohane. "Mr. President! I haven't been in this defense racket very long, but one thing I've damn well learned is that those career officers look at rank as the most important single mark of distinction and accomplishment in their world. You go jumping some bird colonel not even in uniform over two-star generals and admirals and you're going to risk mutiny. You think your epidemic means trouble—you wait and see what trouble is!"

"He's right, you know," said Cawthorp gently. "But it's no great problem. American military men certainly are rank-conscious, which is nothing to criticize, but they have no hesitation at all in deferring to civilian authority. Never have. That's why we never had to worry about a military coup in the United States. The crustiest four- or five-star officer who ever lived—well, since George McClellan and maybe MacArthur—instantly accepts the authority of the lowliest civil servant representing the executive or legislative branch. That's a fact. So all you have to do is appoint yourself a—let's see—cabinet or semi-cabinet rank ought to be sufficient for our Dr. Blanchard. Suppose he was your deputy, Dr. Green? The President could appoint him deputy assistant secretary for health and scientific affairs. That sounds impressive enough for any purpose. And simply forget Dr. Blanchard's reserve commission. What do you think?"

"It would have to be a tentative appointment," said Cohane, "awaiting Senate confirmation—but what the hell."

"Fair enough," said Dobson. "Now then. Where is this medical marvel I've just made the most powerful sawbones in the world since Papa Doc Duvalier? Chicago?"

"No, sir," said Simon Green, feeling slightly stunned. *Noah's going to kill me, he thought, when he finds out I had a hand in sticking him with this.* "No, sir." He managed a wry smile. "Along with everything I told you about Noah Blanchard, I forgot to mention his instinct for being where trouble is. Would you believe that he was on the exact spot when Consolvo's Ulceration was discovered—actually examined the original Consolvo himself? That's the honest truth. Noah's right down where this epidemic started—in Albuquerque, New Mexico."

Chapter 3

The worst August heat wave in Chicago history and a spate of critically ill patients in Cook County General's Intensive Care Unit had left Dr. Noah Blanchard wilted to the marrow. When he finally got to the airport, four hours late, he felt as if people had been beating him with baseball bats and that he had been breathing nothing for days but traffic fumes and hospital disinfectant. But once aboard the Albuquerque flight, after missing an earlier one, and settled in first class,—his seventy-eight-inch frame made extra legroom a necessity no matter what income-tax auditors thought—he began to feel better. Though a former air force flight surgeon with hundreds of hours in a dozen kinds of airplanes, he still had to strain nerve and muscle to help the unseen pilot up forward get his DC-10 down the runway and through lift-off and wheels-and-flaps up, but once they were seven miles high and leveled out, Noah relaxed. He slipped off his shoes, opened his attaché case on the seat beside him, ordered a martini on the rocks, and began leafing through *The New England Journal of Medicine.* By the time they were crossing far above the Upper Mississippi, he had his nose in a mix of ice, vermouth, and gin that dispelled the hospital reek from his nostrils. When he finished, he told the stewardess not to wake him before Albuquerque and tipped his seat back. The stewardess, a newly divorced brassy blonde with improbably jutting breasts and a heart of perennial hope, was disappointed. The redheaded, towering Noah had looked exciting bending under the overhead down the aisle, and the other men in first class were all about seventy. After seeing to their needs, the stewardess went aft to pose in the archway to the coach section for the benefit of two army majors sitting behind the bulkhead.

When the airplane started a letdown east of Tucumcari, Noah woke up. He looked out the window at dun-colored desert far below and felt a sudden sense of holiday expectancy. He hadn't especially wanted to attend this Albuquerque medical convention—it was mainly an excuse to get away from the hospital for a few days—but now that he was here, he meant to enjoy it: bake his hide by the hotel swimming pool, listen to colleagues read papers, go out for drinks and Mexican food with old friends, maybe meet some nice woman.

The plane came in pretty damn fast at Albuquerque, Noah thought in some alarm, but the pilot greased her onto the runway prettily, made his turn and taxied back. Once down the ramp, Noah was blinded by the desert sunlight and felt hot tarmac burn through his shoe soles. He slipped dark glasses on and strode towards the terminal building with his old flight bag bumping his leg, the glare and heat and alkali desert-smell reminding him of air force times, of landing at forlorn NATO fighter strips in the bleached Turkish badlands. It was a pleasantly nostalgic sensation that made him feel footloose and carefree and even carried him through the monotonous wait at the luggage pick-up.

As he hunted a taxi stand in the crowded terminal building, some woman kept getting in his way. Whenever he moved, she seemed to move to block him. He gave up and, taking his sunglasses off, blinked down at her. She was a very tall and attractive brunette of perhaps thirty,

21

wearing a button-down white linen dress. He muttered an apology and tried to step around her, but she put her palm on his lapel. "You're Dr. Blanchard, aren't you?" she said, flashing a smile. "Kate Petrakis. I've been waiting for you. Come on. I'll drive you to the Conquistador."

"That's nice of you," said Noah, remembering his secretary writing "Conquistador Motor Hotel" on the envelope with his ticket and reservations. Genuine southwest hospitality—their sending a car for him this way. "I expected to take a cab. Here, you carry this one. It's the lightest."

As she took his attaché case, looking slightly surprised, he realized how handsome she was in a vaguely foreign way. He could not place it, something Levantine or Aegean about her looks—perhaps the pallor of her skin or the Grecian knot her dead-black hair was twisted up in. Petrakis sounded Greek at that. He was reminded of the elegant women with jeweled coiffeurs he had seen in expensive Istanbul and Beirut nightclubs. She was a promising start to his holiday in any case, and with luck he meant to know Miss Petrakis intimately. When she walked away with his attaché case, he followed along, admiring the rhythmic swing of her hips and her shapely calves.

In the hot sun of the parking lot she unlocked both doors to a green Buick and let them stand open. "Don't get in until it blows out," she said. "Chicago was a steambath, but my God, this New Mexican sun will fry you. What happened? Did you get held up at the hospital? You were supposed to be on the noon plane."

He wondered how she knew. "I hope you haven't been waiting all this time." He threw the suitcase in the back seat.

"Oh, no. When you weren't aboard, I went and checked in. Checked you in too. A good thing. I don't know how long they'll hold a reservation at the Conquistador, so many people clamoring for rooms. Not just doctors. Half the silly organizations in the country seem to be having conventions. I got you a nice corner room, though."

"Just a minute," said Noah, bewildered. "It's dawning on me. The hotel didn't send you, did it?"

"Send me?" She looked as baffled as he felt. For the first time he realized what astonishing green eyes she had, long and almond-shaped. "Send me—who? I'm sorry, Doctor, but you threw that one past me."

"I'm an idiot," said Noah. "For some crazy reason I thought you were a driver from the hotel—a friendly New Mexican gesture, I thought. I did think you were too damned good-looking for a chauffeur, and not dressed like one either."

"The dear Lord." Over her green eyes, bushy jet brows knitted. Then she chuckled. "Well I've been called lots of things, but never chauffeur. And thanks for the left-handed compliment. I'm the foolish one, Dr. Blanchard. I assumed you knew who I was. I assumed your secretary told you."

"Miss Petrakis," groaned Noah, "I'm floundering deeper by the minute. What on earth was Mrs. Ragusa—my secretary—supposed to tell me?"

"Oh boy. I better go back to Chicago and start all over." Kate Petrakis gave him a rueful smile. It was as if a circuit had been closed, sending a massive electrical charge to his groin. It was almost like being nineteen again on his first trip abroad when the Roman contessa picked him up on the Via Veneto. Or like his doomed love affair as an intern with Mary Frances MacLaughlin, the student nurse whose freckled Scotch face still haunted his dreams. This Kate is some woman, thought Noah. A woman worth going after. So approach her softly, he warned himself. Don't flush a bird out of range.

Her bubbling laugh made him tingle. "Wait till Maury Murray finds out you took me for a hotel driver. Oh boy. Dr. Blanchard, I'm a TV investigative reporter, with General Broadcasting Company in Chicago. I followed you down here—got here ahead of you, actually—

23

because I'm after a story. I want to interview a lot of doctors at this convention of yours, but you're the one I want to talk to most. I've been trying to for a week, but your secretary kept blocking me out."

"I'm sorry about that," said Noah. "She was just following orders. The only people she's supposed to let in are those referred as patients. Otherwise I'd never get anything done. If you'd been sick now—" He grinned at her as she leaned on an open car door, lithe and graceful. "But one look at you and anybody can see you don't need a doctor, Miss Petrakis."

She made a mock curtsy. "Thank you again, Doctor. You're full of compliments. And you might as well call me Kate, the way I mean to pick your brains. That's no big deal, either. Everybody from my cleaning lady to Fred Williams calls me Kate."

"Who's he?"

"President of GBC. Not that I call him Fred. Back to what I was saying, I work for Maury Murray, anchorman of 'Get With It.'" Her face fell at his expression. "You mean you don't know our show? I thought everybody, at least everybody in Chicago, did. It's GBC's latest challenge to CBS's '60 Minutes,' and a lot better, you ask me. And if you don't know what '60 Minutes' is either, this is going to take more explaining than I expected, Doctor."

"If I get to call you Kate," said Noah easily, "then you have to call me Noah. Why don't we get in out of the sun? Your car's blown out by now." What on earth, he wondered, could she want from him for a television show?

"Why not?" said Kate. "I'll tell you about it on the way to the hotel."

A few blocks from the airport they turned north on an elevated interstate highway. Noah began to crane his neck, looking about for landmarks he remembered from his last trip to Albuquerque, half-a-dozen years before. He had a sense for terrain strong as an infantryman's and felt uneasy in a place until he was oriented. As they sped north in swift traffic, Kate lane-changing with masterly skill, memories of the city's salient features began coming together for him. Somewhere to his right must lie the state university with its tawny, pueblo-style buildings; off west, the Rio Grande winding green and shallow through the arid land. Near it lay Old Town, the restored plaza from Spanish colonial days with its fountain and ancient adobe mansions converted to gift shops and restaurants. Maybe he would take Kate there tonight. Margaritas and guitar music and one of those elaborate seven-course Mexican dinners should put her in a melting mood. Except for a few new high-rise buildings sticking up at random intervals, it seemed to be the same raunchy Albuquerque he remembered—sleepy Indian-Spanish heritage mixed with raw cow-town.

"It's not easy, being a woman trying to get ahead in my game," said Kate. "Oh, there's Barbara, of course, and Jane and all, but it's still male-dominated. The only way I'll get a break, working for Maury, is to come up with a show idea so strong the bosses will make him let me do it and give me the credit. He'll never help me on his own; he hates women. But he is one fireball investigative reporter and there's nobody in the business I could have learned so much from. I'm grateful to Maury. He's got an instinct for smelling out a story, and when he does he bores in, regardless. We're really an exposé show, you know—I forgot, you *don't* know—the best on the air, even if the ratings aren't up yet. One reason is that Maury's almost too good, digs up stuff too hot to report. Don't tell me there's no censorship in America. You wouldn't believe how the public is kept in the dark. They put it out that a freeze killed the coffee crop and sent prices soaring, but Maury found out it was actually a CIA defoliation scheme against guerrillas hiding in the Colombian jungles that started the blight. And don't think the speculators on the inside didn't make a bundle. Then there was the cosmonaut killed in space because NASA was experimenting with laser-beam communication. Maury dug that one out, too, but of course the execs wouldn't let us use it."

Noah looked at Kate doubtfully. Could television programming be that bizarre? "You mean people actually believe stories like that?" he said.

"You better believe they believe. And they better. It's horrible the things that get hushed up. I never dreamed until Maury began to tell me things. The stuff that gets out, like the Allende thing and those Korean bribes—they're nothing. It really blows your mind to find out how systematically Americans are being deceived."

Noah made a noncommittal noise. A vague question about this good-looking woman's emotional stability began to trouble him. Of course, a little nuttiness in a dame could be overlooked—most people were screwy on some subject—but even so, some of the edge had been knocked off his delight in her.

Scarcely slowing down, Kate exited from the Interstate and sped east along a main arterial boulevard into the city. They passed a Holiday Inn and two cut-rate chain motels, fast-food franchise houses, identical with thousands across the country, tire stores and used-car lots and standardized shopping malls. It could have been a main traveled avenue on the fringe of any city from Bangor to Sacramento. The only thing distinctively New Mexican was the wrinkled brown face of a long barren mountain rising straight up miles ahead. They called it Sandia Peak and it looked dry and lifeless as a moonscape, but Noah had been on top of it and knew better. Up there, two miles high, wet sea winds sustained a climate like Labrador's. On the far side grew an evergreen and aspen forest, and in winter snow lay deep on the ski trails. The mountain was deceptive in other ways, too. Even though this desert plateau looked as unmarked by man as any upthrust of the earth's surface, there was a secret city of tunnels and offices and shops deep inside it. Noah had been there for a special-weapons briefing once. Not that it was such a secret. Technicians who worked for the Air Force Special Weapons Center lived openly among civilian neighbors in Albuquerque. Not that everything inside the mountain was general knowledge. Noah's briefing had been for senior officers with Cosmic Top Secret and Need to Know clearance, and he was pretty sure they hadn't told him everything about the mountain. Which was nothing for anybody to worry about except War Plans officers in the Kremlin maybe.

Kate's next remark startled him. "What do you know about Legionnaires' disease?"

"I've done the necessary reading," he said cautiously. "Why?"

"Because that's what I've been wanting to talk to you about. Here's our hotel. Isn't it ghastly?"

In a glittering sea of parked automobiles an imitation Castilian castle soared up, all battlements and fluttering pennants. A twenty-foot silhouette of a fifteenth-century Spanish soldier leaning on a lance guarded the entryway. A sign read CONQUISTADOR MOTOR HOTEL AND CONVENTION CENTER and in smaller letters below, *Welcome Doctors*.

"I don't believe it," said Noah.

Kate laughed. "It really isn't so bad when you get inside." She stopped the car in the shade of the porte-cochere at the hotel entrance, cut the ignition, and turned sideways to face him. "I wanted to do an interview with you—a major segment of a whole show even— because, whether you know it or not, you've a rare reputation with media people. You're supposed to be one doctor who hasn't sold out, who'll tell the truth about medicine no matter whose toes you step on."

"Hey, now," said Noah. "Don't make me some kind of saint."

"I'm not. I just think you're an honest doctor, one who won't cover up."

"What's to cover up?" he said, trying to keep it light,

27

growing increasingly uncomfortable at the course the conversation was taking. "Nothing about Legionnaires' disease that I know of."

Her green eyes hardened. "I don't agree. I happen to think it's been the worst cover-up since Watergate."

"Come on, Kate. That's pretty strong."

"I mean it. I've studied the evidence, as much of it as they've let out, and it's obviously not what they're saying at all. It's a deadly menace to the American public, if only they knew, and with the right kind of testimony from experts—starting with you—I can let them know. I'm not being wholly selfish either even though a show like that would knock the ratings for a loop; it's that it's wrong for the authorities to deceive the public this way about a deadly disease."

"Well, now, before we get to any sort of commitment," said Noah, wondering who had been selling this woman a bill of goods, "why don't you tell me all you really know about Legionnaires' disease, Kate. As a disease."

"Sure I'll tell you," she said. Her voice tightened with some fierce, suppressed emotion. "Or I'll tell you what they tell me. Oh, I've interviewed the doctors all right, lots of them. And they all say the same thing, that it's just an old strain of pneumonia bacterium, nothing new at all, and the only reason those old vets in Philadelphia got sick was that they were exposed to it some way and must have been taking some kind of medicines for other illnesses that made them susceptible. That's what they *say*, those doctors I've interviewed. But that explanation won't cut it with me. Because people keep on catching it and dying of it all these months later. Only last month, in towns as far apart as Poughkeepsie and Omaha, I read about people dying of it. *Dying*, Noah, and being buried in the ground, with nothing all your miraculous modern medicine could do to save them. So the truth is being hidden. I don't know why; I'm not sure by whom. But I want to find out and tell the people."

Noah whistled silently. "And that's why you flew down

here? To interview doctors at the convention for this show you plan?"

"That's exactly right." She put her hand on his thigh. He couldn't help himself. The response was immediate and powerful. Oh, Lord, he thought. It would be so easy. A few ambiguous answers, a little medical double talk, and this dizzy, ambitious woman would be so grateful, I could have anything. "That's just what I intend," Kate went on. "I know I could get some of them to talk to me. Especially if you led it off. We could tape it through our local affiliate station, and there you'd be—with me on national network primetime!"

Noah reached over the back of the seat for his baggage. Why did things have to turn out bad so often? "Thank you for the ride, Kate," he said. "I suppose I could give you an interview, although I'm really not much for personal publicity. But it would have to be on a worthwhile subject that I was qualified to discuss and it couldn't be anything sensational. You see, your description of what causes Legionnaires' disease and how people contract it is absolutely correct. So far as we know. You always have to stipulate that in medicine. *So far as we know.* But there isn't any cover-up, any sinister conspiracy, any effort by anyone to deceive the public. And that's to the best of my knowledge, which I think is pretty complete, and it's certainly what I believe."

Kate's mouth sagged. She stared at him in a pathetic sort of way. "You can't say that. You can't put me off like that. I thought we were—starting to be friends."

"Friends, yes. But what you would want me to say simply wouldn't be true."

"You won't help me? You're refusing? Like all those others? When you know how important it is to me?"

He got out of the car with his bag and attaché case and stood on the entrance steps, looking down at her. "I wouldn't refuse you anything, Kate. Not if I could help it. But I would have to tell the truth and that wouldn't suit your purpose. I'm sorry."

She stared up at him. For an embarrassing moment he was afraid she was going to weep. Then fury filled her face. The Buick shot forward, tires screeching, leaving a cloud of blue exhaust. Depressed, disappointed, not a little angry, Noah turned, pushed open the double glass doors, and entered the lobby of the Conquistador. It was absolutely packed, men and women standing shoulder to shoulder, dribbling cocktail glasses in their hands, shouting party talk over the general din, milling about, shaking hands, and slapping backs. As Noah edged his way through to the reception desk, men he recognized waved at him: Eddie Stohlman from Houston General; Hal Chalmers from the Center for Disease Control in Atlanta; Mortimer Laskey from Seattle, dean of Pacific Northwest cardiologists—all with their wives, all in sporty holiday dress, all with highball glasses, and all obviously enjoying the convention. Doctors weren't the only conventioneers. As Noah turned and twisted through the noisy, milling throng, he saw name tags for Sertoma, the Rubber Foundation, and a hardware dealers group. The only placid people in the lobby were six Navajo women sitting on the floor with silver and turquoise jewelry spread for sale before them.

The desk clerks were turning away, but Dr. Blanchard, they assured him, was already registered and with his room key given a convention schedule and a telephone message in an envelope. Riding up the elevator, he scanned the schedule. Everything was over for the day except a Happy Hour open bar, obviously now in progress, to be followed by an outdoor ox roast. He was in no mood for either. Kate had spoiled his holiday spirit entirely. He put the schedule in his pocket and unlocked the door.

It was a much better room than he was expecting, a large corner room with an outside balcony and a wide two-angle view of Sandia Crest. He opened the envelope with the telephone message, expecting to find an invitation for drinks or dinner from some colleague or other for whom he had no heart. Instead he read, "Please phone Dr. Nelson Gutierrez at the Santa Rosa Clinic as soon as possible, any hour, no matter how late."

Noah's dark mood lightened instantly. Nelson Gutierrez! The best medical resident he'd ever trained! Noah chuckled, remembering the bantam Cuban in the feathered Tyrolean hats and high-heeled jodphur boots and his ceaseless pursuit of many a rich, tall *señorita* in Chicago's Spanish-American community, the taller the better. But what in the world was he doing in Albuquerque? All the time he trained at Cook County General, he talked mainly about returning to Miami to practice among the Cuban refugees there. Well, one way to find out. Noah telephoned, and a moment after the Santa Rosa switchboard operator responded, Nelson Gutierrez's distinctive voice, a blend of singsongy Cuban and cracker drawl, came on.

"You sawed-off *habanero* Casanova!" cried Noah joyfully. "Do you still wear those elevator heels and Bavarian hats to fool the *señoritas* with?"

"*Rojo!* Big Red! How the hell are you? How is cruddy old Chicago? No, down here I wear sombreros and cowboy boots. Same effect. It is good to hear your voice, Doctor."

"Yours too, Doctor. What are you doing in New Mexico? What happened to Miami?"

"Oh, Miami's crawling with Cuban doctors, all getting rich on Medicare. Down here I can bring the wonders of modern medicine to the *pobrecitos*, the poor Mexicans and *Indios*. No, what really happened was I took some more training in St. Louis after Chicago, met a girl from here, and fell in love with her."

"You're always falling in love. Twice a day sometimes. Usually with six-foot-tall Spanish brunettes."

"Don't tell Jeanie that. My bride's a four-foot-ten honey blonde straight out of a German fairy tale and the best damn pediatrician west of the Pecos to boot. Maybe east of it too. She's anxious to meet you, says you're all I

31

ever talk about, which is ridiculous exaggeration, of course, my old mentor. So how about you get your ass over here, *amigo*, let me show you around our clinic, and then the three of us will go out to dinner. Goddamn! It's been too long."

"Whoa," said Noah. "Slow down. You mean you're married? To a lady doctor? You run your own clinic? Sure I'll come. You couldn't pay me to stay away. Give me a minute to change shirts. Oh, how do I get there?"

"I'll send a car for you. See you then."

Noah changed quickly into a blue pullover and light jacket and rode the elevator down. The lobby was even more packed, and as he squeezed through, hands plucked at him, voices importuned him to stop for a drink, go out to eat, listen to this story. Noah brushed past good-humoredly and made his way outside into slanting afternoon sunlight. A white station wagon pulled forward instantly and a dark boy reached over from the wheel to open the passenger door. "Hop in, Dr. Blanchard."

"How did you know?" said Noah, getting in.

"No question at all, Doctor. Doc Nelson said look for an Anglo redhead tall as a church. I'm Juan Otero, third-assistant pill-roller at Santa Rosa."

"Glad to know you, Juan. What's a third-assistant pill-roller?"

"I'm a university freshman, want to study pharmacy. So they let me hand out vitamin pills to the new mothers, and like that. Mostly I sweep up and run errands and drive VIPs. Like now." He grinned, revealing strong, healthy white teeth. "Do whatever Dr. Jean or Doc Nelson says to do."

"Tell me about the clinic," said Noah, admiring the boy's skill in maneuvering the big automobile through rush-hour traffic. Kate Petrakis had handled a car with that same smooth command. He wondered if he would see her again. A woman like that. What a damned waste. He felt a stab of remorse. But there was nothing else he could have done. What a crazy world she must live in to make her do and think such things.

"What do you want to know, Doctor?"

"Anything you want to tell me. I'm ignorant. I thought Nelson Gutierrez was practicing medicine in Florida."

"Oh no, sir. He's been with us over a year, ever since Dr. Jean, Dr. Fenstermacher's daughter, you know, met him at that St. Louis hospital she was taking a course at and they got married. Old Doctor was way past eighty, you know, and everybody was tickled pink when Dr. Jean brought home a doctor husband to keep the clinic going."

"Then it was her father, this Dr. Fenstermacher, whose clinic it was?"

"Oh yes, sir. Of course he practiced medicine long before there was any clinic, out of his hat and satchel, like my grandpa says. Back then, fifty years ago, the Hispanic and Indian people around here were at the bottom of the heap, Dr. Blanchard, all poor and ignorant, and if they got sick, the old village women nursed them well or they died. Then one day this big green boy fresh out of some New England medical school came driving down the *arroyos* in a Model T to treat the sick people. Pay him in corn or beans or maybe some fresh venison—why, all right; pay him nothing—why, all right too. To my grandpa's people, Dr. Hugo Fenstermacher was an angel the Virgin sent, a funny big-footed angel who cussed in German and if a girl cut her eyes at him followed her into the brush, snorting and pawing. But an angel of mercy all the same. When Old Doctor died every little church in the valley burned candles for his soul."

"Sounds like what a doctor is supposed to be," said Noah. "But where did he ever get money to build a clinic?"

"Nickels and dimes people saved up to give him. It started out just a two-room shack; now it's forty beds and two wards—one maternity, one for sick children—and rooms for special patients. Most of the money came from Mr. Howard Consolvo after he made his uranium strike,

33

out east of town. He was just another small rancher till then, poor as anybody, and Dr. Fenstermacher took care of him and his family like he did everybody. So when Mr. Howie got rich, he built a clinic for Old Doctor, and to this day it's the only place he'll go for doctoring no matter what's ailing him. He's in there now—picked up this infection in his arm I think Dr. Nelson's pretty worried about. Howard Consolvo could go anywhere he wanted to—Mayo Clinic, shoot, he could buy it!—but Santa Rosa's the place he trusts."

Suddenly Juan made a daring turn across two lanes of oncoming traffic and suddenly they were in a quiet street of stucco bungalows, many of them the vivid green and pink colors of Mexican architecture and standing in bare dirt lots where kids and dogs romped under cottonwood trees. In the third block they turned abruptly under an ironwork arch and up a graveled driveway to a square two-story building of red brick. Letters painted on the portico over the entrance read SANTA ROSA MEDI-CAL CLINIC. Before the station wagon had stopped, the front doors flew open and Nelson Gutierrez in a hospital frock came trotting down the steps, beside him a blonde girl also in hospital whites whose head just reached his ear.

Noah had to meet four Mexican nurses, two nurses' aides, a mute Navajo janitor, and a Spanish office doyenne in old-fashioned purple bombazine before Nelson ran out of people. Then they toured a ward full of mothers nursing black-eyed babies. At last, to Noah's relief, the three of them sat down in a dingy office where a shy Indonesian from the kitchen staff served coffee. Nelson was charged with enthusiasm for the work of the clinic and for his growing outside practice in internal medicine. He leaned back in a swivel chair—with his feet, shod in elegant high-heeled El Paso cowboy boots, on a desk top—and expatiated at length. To Noah it was obvious that his old friend and protégé was totally happy with his life, his labors, his Dresden-doll wife. She was no fragile decoration, though. The tour through the ward had shown her to be a forceful, authoritative pediatrician regarded with awe by patients and staff. Noah approved of her as a woman and as a doctor.

This had been her father's office, she said in the contralto that issued startlingly from her dainty frame. A huge oil painting hung above the rolltop desk: young Dr. Hugo Fenstermacher in lace-up boots and peaked cavalry hat, glaring over a Kaiser Bill mustache. Behind him stood the legendary Model T touring car and behind it, a surrealistic range of jagged New Mexican mountains. The painter was supposed to be some half-mad tubercular drifter whose life her father had prolonged. It was terrible art, of course, but even so the history museum wanted it. It was certainly the only surviving picture of him from those early days. And constituted the most substantial fee any patient had paid up until that time.

Depended, though, on how you defined substantial, said Nelson, winking at Noah. According to the oldtimers, Jean had older brothers and sisters in every river village between Socorro and Barnalillo. Jean wrinkled her nose, said even if it was true, which it wasn't, her father, you had to remember, had been fifty before he could afford a wife. Nelson said he was sure glad he wasn't that poor and Jean's smile made Noah envy both of them.

Somewhere a telephone rang and after a minute the dowager in purple bombazine put her head in the door. Dr. Heim from the university was calling on Nelson's phone. "I expect he's got the preliminary lab reports on Howie," said Nelson. "Pray God they give us a clue as to how to proceed. Excuse me, Noah."

When he was gone, Jean said, "We've got this rather special patient in Isolation. He really ought to be in a big, fully equipped hospital, but he's a stubborn old rancher my father took care of all his life, and he won't go anywhere else."

"That the patient with the infected arm your boy Juan mentioned?"

35

"Trust Juan! Gossips like an old woman. It's all right, of course. Howard Consolvo. I call him Uncle Howie. Way back when he and Aunt Rosa—the clinic's named for her—were dirt-poor, their children got diphtheria, nearly always fatal then, but Papa pulled them through. Uncle Howie and Aunt Rosa thought the sun rose in Papa after that, and when they found uranium on the ranch after the war and began getting rich, they helped Papa build the clinic he'd always wanted, a place for babies to be born in and where sick children could get well. Since Aunt Rosa died, Uncle Howie's added two wings and every year sends us an enormous check. We get HEW grants now, but it was Uncle Howie who made it all possible. So you see how we feel about him and how much we want to cure this awful thing."

"What sort of infection does he have?"

"That's just it. Nobody seems to know. Leo Heim on the phone now, he's the best dermatologist at the university—Nelson got him and Dewey Jamison too, the top pathologist in the whole state, to examine Uncle Howie. They'd neither one of them ever seen anything like it. Dewey was so perplexed he got a clinical photographer to take pictures of it. Said they might want to see them at the national health archives. He keeps coming back, this photographer, to snap pictures on a regular schedule."

"Well, tell me what the symptoms are."

"Well it ought not be anything. Uncle Howie's just scratched the inside of his arm on barbed wire, an everyday occupational hazard for a rancher. Not that he does any real ranching anymore—keeps a few head so those three old broken-down cowhands he's had on the payroll all these years won't get bored. A scratch—that hardly broke the skin—that he sloshed kerosene on, that sovereign ranch remedy, you know. But the scratch didn't get well. It got worse, horribly worse, and we're terribly worried."

Nelson returned, his forehead furrowed. "Leo was no help except that it's not *Melaney's Ulcer*, which we'd

36

about ruled out already. Neither the skin tissue culture nor the blood chemistry shows anything useful."

"Poor Uncle Howie. And he's in such pain. I wish you'd persuade him to let us transfer him."

"Me? You try. Besides, until we know what to treat him for, what could a hospital do that we aren't doing? Trying to keep him comfortable is about all. Not that the morphine he's on helps much. This is a pretty important patient we're talking about, Noah."

"Jean told me. How deep was the laceration?"

"Hard to tell, the flesh has deteriorated so. He says it was just a scratch he didn't give a thought to until it started burning. It must have hurt like hell to bring him to town. Howard Consolvo's a tough old party and he hates to have to come down from that ranch of his." Nelson hesitated, then added, "I know you're on vacation, but would you look at him for me?"

Noah spun his empty coffee cup with a forefinger. "Skin disease is a little out of my line, you know."

"It's right down Leo Heim's line and he's as good as anybody in the Southwest and he's stumped. I thought maybe in your exotic wanderings you might have seen something like it somewhere." He turned to his wife. "This fellow's been places most people never heard of, Jeanie."

"So you've told me about two hundred times," she said, smiling at Noah. "But I agree. Would you examine Uncle Howie—just a quick look—and maybe come up with a guess?"

"Well, of course, if you two want it. But don't expect anything."

"You never can tell. Look, I don't know if this thing is contagious, of course, but I wish you'd wear a mask and gloves. I do."

"Well, I don't," said Jean. "Oh, a mask, yes, but not gloves. Not for Uncle Howie. Nelson, don't you think you'd better warn him?"

"You're right. Noah, this could be a little embarrassing

if you don't know what to expect. Not for you, for old Howie. The plain fact is, his arm stinks like nothing I ever smelled before. Howie's a fastidious old gentleman and to exude an odor like that—well, it's downright mortifying to him."

"You mean I shouldn't go in holding my nose," said Noah dryly.

"Come on now. Don't be hard on me. I have to consider the man's feelings. I had to warn you. This is the most revolting stench I ever smelled. Those masks we put on, they really don't help."

"I helped cut the bodies out of a C-130 once that had crashed on Mount Ararat," said Noah. "An old Crash Recovery tech sergeant showed us how to rub gasoline on our upper lips. The sun had been cooking those poor guys in that fuselage for a month, but we couldn't smell a thing. Gasoline freezes the olfactory nerves. It also makes blisters, but it was worth it."

"Yech," said Jean. "No more travel stories please."

"The nose," said Noah sententiously, "is an invaluable diagnostic tool, Nelson. And if this sounds like a travelogue, you brought it on yourself. Way up the Brahmaputra in Assam, an old British medical missionary left over from Empire days took me into a Naga tribe that had the plague. Not many American doctors nowadays have actually seen the plague. You know what one distinctive characteristic is? The stench. A pungent, rotten stench you never forget."

"Howard Consolvo hasn't got the plague," said Nelson. "It may be rare, but there was an outbreak in New Mexico last year and Dewey Jamison saw some of the victims. He knows the plague and he examined Howard and that, at least, we know Howard hasn't got."

"I didn't suggest it. I just wanted to remind you that odors can be very useful in diagnosis. So let's suit up and look at your patient. If you're sure you want me to."

"Of course I'm sure," said Nelson and, smirking at Jean, added, "teacher."

Chapter 4

All his professional life Noah Blanchard had watched sick people die. He still could not resign himself to the inevitability of death. The passing of a human life filled him with awe, outrage, and a sense of deep mystery. When it was a patient of his own who died, his anguish was inexpressible. Between a patient fighting for life and the doctor fighting for him, an intimacy intense as that of lovers can develop. To lose such a patient was worse than losing a beloved woman to a hated rival, and when it happened Noah despised himself and his profession.

The moment he saw Howard Consolvo he resented the death of a human being this valuable. The professional instinct that told him Consolvo was dying and no one could prevent it also told him the world would be poorer for the loss of this bronzed, white-haired man in the high hospital bed.

"Hey, Howie," said Nelson jovially. "I brought somebody to meet you. Big-shot Chicago doctor and an old friend, Dr. Noah Blanchard. He wants to take a peek at that arm of yours."

Consolvo hitched himself up on his pillow with the help of his left arm. The right one was swathed in bandages and lay upturned on a white enamel table beside the bed. Even though pain glazed his squinting outdoorsman's eyes he managed a lopsided grin. He was nearly seventy, but his stocky physique, not at all the rangy figure Noah had somehow expected of a New Mexican rancher, was hard and healthy. Except, of course, for the arm rotting on the table. Through the betadyne sprinkled gauze mask he wore Noah could smell it.

"Thank you kindly for dropping by, Doctor," said Consolvo. "Any little hint you might drop about what to do for this damn arm, by God, would sure be appreciated."

At a nod from Nelson the nurse who had come with them to the Isolation Ward, actually a bay with two other beds, both empty, began to unwrap Consolvo's arm. An almost palpable stench rolled up. Noah gagged and heard Jean catch her breath. "Jesus God," groaned Consolvo. "I stink like buzzard puke. Jeanie, honey, you don't have to stay here. Gentlemen, how can you stand being in the same room with me?"

"It's not as bad as you think, Mr. Consolvo," said Noah, steeling himself to bend over the injury. It was like nothing he had seen before. The muscular underbelly of Consolvo's forearm lay open in a blood-oozing, blackened cleft between wrist and elbow, the original barbed-wire scratch long eaten away with the surrounding tissue. Noah had seen lesions of leprosy in Louisiana, ruptured Plague buboes among Naga tribesmen, but horrid as they were none approached the horror of this. Nor, he thought, stunk so. It seemed to sting his eyes, and the urge to vomit kept welling in his throat. Here was the ultimate obscenity of death. Howard Consolvo's arm was a putrid corpse and soon the rest of him would be too. As Noah looked at it, the red upper end of the wound seemed to wriggle like something alive. It might have been an optical illusion, but he did not think so.

"What's your verdict there, Dr. Blanchard?" said Consolvo, laboring for joviality. "You got any good guesses what to do about that stinking mess?"

Noah smiled at him, thinking, how can I tell this doomed mortal that I haven't the faintest idea what his disease is? To Nelson's unspoken question he gave a quick negative headshake. "Mr. Consolvo," he said, detesting the unctuous sound of his voice, "Dr. Gutierrez's treatment is exactly what I would recommend. Of course new lab test reports might suggest changing antibiotics. It depends on what kind of bug they find is causing the infection."

"I been thinking," said Consolvo, clearly undeceived, "maybe there ain't no medicine for this thing. I don't like to holler, but fact is, Jeanie honey and Nelson, it's hurting about so bad I can't hardly stand it. And I don't expect my hand's ever going to be much use anymore either. See, I can't even make my fingers wiggle. So I been studying it over—I know it's a hell of a note, being my check-writing hand and all—but shoo, here I am nearly seventy and anybody that old ought to make it on down the line with only one fist. So goddamn it, Nelson, let's quit fooling around. Let's chop the son-of-a-bitch off. 'Scuse me, Jeanie, I'm upset. But go on, take her off. Right there clean at the elbow. Higher up if you got to. Go on now."

The three doctors looked at each other. The nurse stared impassively into distance. "Hey, now, Howie," said Nelson. "Let's not go jumping the gun. As Dr. Blanchard told you these new lab tests we're waiting on might put us onto a whole new line of medication. So let's hold off on anything so radical as amputation. You agree, don't you, Noah?"

"Oh, absolutely," said Noah, watching the oozing red fissure. It was no optical illusion. The ghastly thing was working its way into the crook of Consolvo's elbow. He took the chart from the foot of the bed. At noon the wound had been seven and a half centimeters long, by three o'clock had reached nine, by now was nearer twelve. If amputation was actually justified, time could be running out. He wondered if Nelson had a surgeon on call. He wondered what good such an amputation would be if, as he thought probable, the unknown tissue-eating organism was free-floating in Consolvo's bloodstream. The man's dying, he thought. Nothing can save him. Why butcher the poor bastard? "My suggestion," he said, "would be to give Mr. Consolvo more relief from discomfort while we go after those reports."

"I concur," said Nelson, and leaning on the nightstand scribbled an order to the nurse for a morphine injection so massive that Noah, reading over his shoulder, raised his eyebrows. Nelson had no more illusions about Consolvo's chances than he did. "All right, Howie," said Nelson heartily, "Mrs. Pagosa's going to give you a little shot now that ought to make you feel a lot better. We'll check those tests and be back."

Jean blew a kiss at Consolvo. "You try to get some rest now, Uncle Howie. We won't be long."

The Spanish lady was still at her desk when they entered, even though the antiquated Western Union clock on the wall showed half-past six. Noah wondered what hours the Santa Rosa staff worked. As if to answer him the Spanish lady stood up and pinned a stiff black straw hat to the top of her high-piled coiffeur. Dr. Heim wanted Nelson to phone him and, she added, she had to go cook her husband supper now but would gladly return.

"No thanks, Clarissa," said Nelson wearily. "Nice of you, but no need for it."

"I thought perhaps with Señor Consolvo so sick I could help some way. How is he?"

"I'm afraid not good, Clarissa," said Jean. "But maybe Dr. Heim has come up with something." She dialed a telephone number.

Clarissa crossed her impressive purple bosom. "I will stop by the church and ask Father Miguel to say a prayer for Señor Consolvo." With a dignified nod she departed.

"I hope Father Miguel knows some potent prayers," said Nelson gloomily. "I hope Leo's come up with some new ideas. God knows I can't think of any. Thanks, hon."

He took the telephone from Jean and began talking. When he hung up he shook his head. Along with the staph and strep microbes swarming in Consolvo's blood that they already knew about, Heim said there now seemed to be a curious toxic abnormality of the white blood cells unfamiliar to the hematology techs and unlike anything in the literature. But what that signified, or if it had any significance, or what different medication it might suggest Leo had no notion. He was apologetic, but that was the size of it. Rage contorted Nelson's features and he burst into Spanish obscenities.

"Hush, darling," said Jean. "That won't help. What do you think we should do now?"

"Jesus. How do I know? Call Ben Lingenfelder, I suppose. Tell them to get the operating room ready."

"Dr. Lingenfelder's our surgeon," Jean said to Noah. "He usually operates at Community Hospital, but if a patient is too weak to move or for any other reason, he doesn't mind operating here. Not if it's anything terribly complex, of course. And not that we do much surgery."

"Nelson," said Noah reluctantly, "do you really think amputation is indicated?"

"Christ, no!" cried Nelson furiously. "But what else can I do with all that infection in his blood that the antibiotics don't seem to faze? Not that there's any necessary connection between them and this flesh-rot that's killing him. Heim's baffled and so is Dewey Jamison and all the people they've consulted and they're the best in the whole goddamn state of New Mexico. So being the stupid kind of doctor I am, all I can think of is to cut off his fucking arm! Sorry, Jean. But maybe that will arrest the infection."

"Which you don't believe for a moment," said Noah.

"Which I don't believe for a moment." Fury drained from Nelson's face, leaving it haggard. "Give me a cigarette, goddamn it."

"I quit them."

"Me too. A year ago. Now I want one."

"No, you don't," said Jean sadly. "You just think you do."

"Well a drink then. There's some bourbon in the file cabinet."

"Not if you're going to assist in the operating room."

"Well, get *her*," said Nelson with a wretched smile. "Keeper of my conscience. What would I do without you, Jean? What did I do before I found you? Noah, don't you say a word."

"I already know," said Jean, with a forlorn smile. "You brag in your sleep." Her face changed and she grabbed her left shoulder. "Ouch!"

"What's the matter, hon?"

"Nothing, I guess. Sort of a quick biting burn there for an instant, but it's gone. Well my goodness, Shorty and Pecos! Did you come down to check up on how Howie is?"

They were two aging cowhands, the one Jean called Shorty, a gangling six-footer with a lock of white hair down his forehead and Pecos, a swarthy wide-shouldered runt with Mexico in his features. "Dr. Blanchard," said Nelson, "shake hands with Shorty Tibbs and Pecos Alvarez from Howie's Bar H-C ranch. Last time I saw this pair they were in jail for beating up four Texas rodeo riders."

"Aw, that was after calving-time," said Shorty. "We didn't come down to do no drinking this trip. Thing is, we all got to wondering about the Boss, so me and Pecos and Big Foot and Wang drawed straws and we got elected. Reckon we could see how he is?"

"Of course you could," said Jean, before Nelson could speak. "It would do him good to see you boys. But only for a minute. Howie needs his rest. I'll take you back to him. You don't mind tying on a couple of silly operating room masks, do you?"

"Just a couple of minutes," called Nelson, as Jean led the two men down a corridor. He turned then and looked at Noah glumly. There did not seem to be anything for either to say. Away ⟨ the maternity ward an infant squalled briefly. They heard a snatch of a Johnny Cash song on some patient's radio and the measured diction of Walter Cronkite relating the news. Outdoors a dog barked and a bird whistled with piercing shrillness.

"I know why you're going ahead with this," said Noah finally. "Not that it's my business. He's not my patient and you didn't ask my opinion. Would you rather I didn't talk about it?"

"Of course I want you to. You're about the only person I do want to. Or that I want to talk to about it. Except Jean of course, and that's different. Only I don't know what to say to you."

"Well the first thing you could say is that from a medical point of view amputation is totally defensible. This mysterious infection is obviously going to kill him unless it's arrested. Medication isn't helping. If it were gangrene you wouldn't hesitate. Nobody is going to criticize you for cutting. Conceivably it could save his life."

"Don't kid me." Nelson grimaced. "The odds against it are a thousand to one and you know it. Weak as he is, this persistent low-grade fever he's running, the effect of continuous pain on his nervous system—odds are he'll die from the shock of operation."

"You can't be certain of that."

"Let's cut out the horseshit. You know the score. The man's my friend and Jean loves him. He's in unspeakable agony that gets progressively worse. I keep upping the analgesic dosages. There's a limit to that. If I can't save him, maybe I can spare him some agony."

"The surgeon has to agree. Will he, do you think?"

"Ben Lingenfelder's a good man. We've never had any trouble working together. Why are you putting me through this interrogation?"

"You're putting yourself through it. I'm just verbalizing the questions. You know you have to touch all the bases first. Whether anybody blames you afterwards or not, you have to. You know it and I know it."

"What base haven't I touched?"

"Come on, Nelson. You know perfectly well. And not to disparage them, all excellent men no doubt, these doctors you've consulted, they're all local men. Ten minutes from here at that convention the Conquistador Hotel is packed with the top men in virtually every medical specialty you can think of. Don't you believe we ought to invite a couple of them to look at this patient with this mystifying, unheard-of disease before you go and saw his arm off?"

"You think that would do any good?"

"That's not for me to think. You either. All we know is that the opportunity exists and that's a base you haven't touched."

Nelson bit his lip. "You think you could get them to come over?"

"I'm sure I could."

"Who would you want?"

Noah ticked them off on his fingers. "First I'd want Quint Hasbrouck, the Kettering Institute dermatologist; then Penner from Wisconsin for pathology; then either Cameron from Mass General or Aaron Perlman from Columbia for internal medicine. Any three of the four would represent seventy years of practice, study, experience equal to any in the world. Don't you think your friend deserves that? And to be absolutely on the safe side I would also ask Hal Chalmers from the CDC."

"The Center for Disease Control?" Nelson looked uneasy. "Does that mean you think this thing's contagious? Jesus! Anyway you're as competent an epidemiologist as anyone. Why call Chalmers?"

"Thanks for the compliment. No, I'm not saying it's contagious. I don't know. Neither do you. But if there's a risk of it spreading, the sooner the CDC is cranked in the better."

"My God," breathed Nelson. "And it had to start here.

It's a good thing you came to town, I guess. I guess I guess. So phone your experts. They're probably all half-drunk by now, though."

"Not these fellows," said Noah. "And if they were, that convention is full of back-up talent. Here comes Jean, in a hurry, like something was vrong."

"What is it, hon?" said Nelson. "Is Howard worse? Where did you leave the two old guys? Not back there with Howard, I hope. You know they don't understand hospital procedure."

"Hush!" she said sharply. "Shut up a minute, Nelson!" Her pretty face was frightened and she was rubbing her shoulder nervously. "They're in the coffee bar. Uncle Howie was too dopey from that last shot, so we went for coffee. Nelson, it's scary. Shorty was limping, and when I asked why, he showed me this sore where his boot-top rubbed his leg. It's a nasty, oozing ulceration, half-dollar size. Shorty said he never noticed it until part way to town when his leg started burning. I'm scared, Nelson, really scared. It looks just like Uncle Howie's arm did at first."

"Contagious?" said Noah grimly. "What do you think now? What's the phone number of the Conquistador, anybody know? Where's your phone book? Nelson, you better go look at that leg. With mask and gloves on, damn it!"

"You bet your ass!" said Nelson savagely. "Jeanie, call Lingenfelder and fill him in, then Dewey or Leo, better yet, both of them. And it might be wise to call the County Public Health Office. See if there's a duty officer. If not, call the head guy at home—you know him, that Jim Gentry. Let's not panic, but for God's sake let's get on top of this damn thing before it decides to get worse."

Instead of a festive dinner to celebrate reunion, Nelson and Noah ate sandwiches at ten o'clock in the clinic kitchen where Clarissa Delgado, Juan Otero, and two girl volunteers Juan had recruited from his freshman class were slicing ham and frying eggs and keeping the big coffee urns bubbling in a night-long short-order service.

They had a steady stream of customers: the four doctors Noah had telephoned and half a dozen others drawn from the convention by curiosity; a telephone technician because Hal Chalmers and Jim Gentry, the county public health service doctor, wanted open lines to the CDC in Atlanta and other PHS offices in the Southwest and because the local phone company manager was Leo Heim's private patient; Dr. Benjamin Lingenfelder preparing to amputate Howard Consolvo's arm and looking highly dubious about it; Heim and Jamison and two assistants they kept chasing back to the university medical laboratory with blood and tissue samples; night nurses and two city policemen the mayor ordered over after Dr. Gentry told His Honor that he might have an epidemic of some sort on his hands and that a little Law and Order could be useful.

Coffee drinking was about all the visiting doctors could do either, after they had examined Consolvo's arm and Shorty Tibbs's leg and consulted with one another, but deep in all of them gnawed the same unspoken fear: unless sombody found a treatment pretty damn quick for this mysterious contagion that Hasbrouck, the Ohio skin specialist, was calling, "This ulceration of Consolvo's," the consequences would be too ghastly to contemplate. Two hours after midnight they gathered in the clinic's small surgery and watched respectfully while Ben Lingenfelder, commanding the largest audience of his career, removed Howard Consolvo's arm at the shoulder with superb technique. Not that it did any good. Even in deepest anaesthesia and after the severing of key nerves, Howard Consolvo continued to thrash and scream as infection ate the flesh from his upper torso. Shortly before dawn he expired, either drowning on fluids in his pleural cavities or because his overstrained heart simply gave up. No one would be sure until after the autopsy; no one cared; they were just grateful that he had stopped screaming.

As gray dawn first began to pale the clinic windows,

Shorty Tibbs, survivor of fifty years of beans and bacon and bad whiskey, of being horse-kicked and cow-hooked and snakebit and froze-up and of three cases of clap, lay miserably alive and clearly doomed, his left leg fissured from ankle halfway to the kneecap by the now familiar black, red-oozing cleft. As dawn light crept into the office where the switchboard was, Chalmers and Gentry put down the telephones they had been calling long-distance on to stare at each other in dismay. Two positive cases of "Consolvo's Ulceration" had turned up in other places, one in El Paso, one in Santa Fe.

As the sun broke red over Sandia Crest, the Bar H-C stake-and-platform truck clattered into the Santa Rosa parking lot, Big Foot Johnson at the wheel, beside him Charley Wang, Howard Consolvo's cook for twenty years, grimacing and nursing his pot-stirring hand. A felon on Charley's thumb had erupted suddenly with pain so exquisite not even a stoical Cantonese Buddhist could endure it. That meant that nobody was left on the mountain to mind the ranch, but Pecos Alvarez was too shook up by Consolvo's death and Charley in the process of dying to even think about cussing Big Foot out. Even more stunned was Nelson. Unable to hide her agony from him any longer, Jean had revealed her entire left shoulder-blade, starting from a scratched mosquito bite, to be one vast patch of oozing red and black horror. Sedated to semi-consciousness, she lay in the Isolation Ward, Nelson sitting beside her, holding her hand and staring at nothing, incapable of action.

Gummy-eyed and yawning, despair in his belly like a lump of lead, knowing there was nothing he or anyone could do for Jean or Nelson, Noah left them. The corridors of the clinic were busy with traffic: Public Health Service technicians, nurses and aides and corpsmen trundling patients out the back way for transfer to hospitals away from this infection, more doctors from the Conquistador trying to hide their consternation as they button-holed anyone who seemed to know anything, city cops trying to help and getting in everybody's way. Grunting apologetically, Noah thrust through the traffic, wanting quiet and solitude. The anguish inside him was unbearable. He opened the front door of the clinic and, head-down and unseeing, walked out to the small porticoed stoop where scarcely twelve hours earlier Jean and Nelson had greeted him. His anguish for them sharpened. He would have wept if he could. Keeping his eyes closed, he turned his face to the brick exterior wall and held his forehead pressed against it. Gradually he became aware of a subdued murmur of people talking in low tones. He turned and saw what seemed to him an astonishing spectacle.

Out beyond the clinic parking lot, filled now with police cars and gray PHS vehicles and official city sedans, past the ornamental ironwork entrance, men and women, some holding children, were simply standing in the street staring in. They filled it from sidewalk to sidewalk, a quiet crowd, not hostile, not gesturing, simply watching, working people by their dress, some only partly dressed as if they had been called hastily from bed at this dawn hour. It occurred to Noah that it must be a neighborhood crowd, the people of these quiet streets for whom the benevolent clinic in their midst had suddenly become a mystifying menace.

Now the murmuring crowd began to part to let through a tangerine-yellow van with a man standing on top behind a camera—a television station van, Noah realized—shooting the scene. A senseless rage seized him. He went down the front steps with long strides, his fists knotting. From nowhere appeared a motorcycle policeman in boots and britches, blocking his way.

"Sorry, Mister. You got to have a pass to leave. They're putting this place under quarantine."

"Goddamn it, I'm not trying to leave!" roared Noah. "I want you to stop that circus out there."

The cop drew back. He was a head shorter than Noah and his eyes seemed to widen at the fury in Noah's face.

"Now just hold it, buddy," he began, but Noah cut him off.

"You don't understand." He was on top of his anger now, able to reason. "I'm a doctor, Dr. Blanchard from Chicago, there ar people dying in here, don't you understand? We can't have that kind of—that carnival thing, that yellow circus-wagon thing."

"Blanchard," said the cop, relieved to be given something he could deal with. He took a card from his shirt pocket and looked at it. "Right, got your name here. You're authorized. Sorry, sir. I didn't know. You can leave if you want to."

"But I don't *want* to leave, officer. What I want is for that carnival out there to stop. It's indecent."

The policeman looked at him uncertainly and back at the van. It had stopped just outside the entrance archway and the camera was panning on the upturned faces of the crowd, then on the parking lot, and would, Noah thought resentfully, zoom in on him next. Down in the street another cameraman was walking backwards, balancing a portable TV camera on his shoulder, taping a tall brunette in a lime-green pants suit as she interviewed people in the crowd, microphone in hand.

"Goddamn it!" stormed Noah. "That's what I mean. Turning this into some kind of Roman holiday. Make them knock that off."

"We can't do that," said the cop, sounding puzzled. "I mean, you know, Doctor, hell that's the media."

The woman in green turned their way and smiled delightedly. Beckoning the cameraman to follow, she started up the driveway. My God! thought Noah. It's Kate. Christ. She's *enjoying* this. He panicked and fled back inside.

Chapter 5

Almost sick for want of sleep, the man in green leaned on his lectern and watched the audience straggle into the underground auditorium at Bethesda. Dressed in the lab frocks and cotton jackets they'd been wearing at their various places of duty when he sent for them, they looked as exhausted as the man in green was feeling. There were only about twenty of them now, half as many as three days before, and no one was in military uniform. The four generals and their principal assistants had been rushed to epidemic trouble-points in the West. The night before, Admiral Graybar had flown to Norfolk, Virginia, where an invasion of Consolvo's Ulceration, leap-frogging half the continent unexpectedly, had knocked SACLANT's operational readiness into a cocked hat. Right now the Atlantic Sea frontier lay wide open to any possible seaborne attack. Which, thank God, was no responsibility of the man in green. He had all he could do trying to counter a deadly attack already launched inside national frontiers by an enemy none of these brilliant, dedicated people before him with all the scientific resources of a wealthy nation at their disposal were able to identify in their microscopes.

Summoning energy from somewhere, he began to

speak. "I'll be as brief as possible, ladies and gentlemen. I want you back in your laboratories as much as I'm sure you do. Many serious events have taken place since we last met and busy as you are you may have missed some of them. I've been instructed to bring you up to date. To be frank, most of them are bad news. But there is a glimmer of a possible hope. In the total darkness we've been groping in, I think you would agree that any glimmer is worthwhile. What it is, there is a chance, an outside chance, that we may have a lead to a possible carrier of Consolvo's Ulceration."

Excited murmurs ran through the audience. The man in green smiled faintly. "I thought that would wake you up—and with as little sleep as I imagine you've been getting, that might take some doing. But before I discuss our possible disease carrier and all the obvious new possibilities suggested by that, I have to fill you in on other occurrences. One that hits close to home and will grieve all of you—if you have not heard it yet—is that our friend and colleague, Dr. Mary Riddle, is in isolation at Walter Reed Army Medical Center with one of the first confirmed cases of Consolvo's Ulceration in the District. Prognosis is unfavorable—one hundred percent unfavorable."

The speaker paused and then by an almost visible act of will went on. "Next, I am to tell you that President Dobson is unsatisfied with our progress."

Another stir went through the audience. The man in green raised his hand. "I am to assure you," he said, "that this is not meant in any invidious way. I told my informant that we weren't satisfied either and welcomed any help we could get.

"Next. In the event that you've taken a moment from your investigations to look at a television screen, you've undoubtedly seen all the horror stories this damnable epidemic is causing across the nation. For a couple of days it looked to me as if we were about to cease existence as a nation—less from the epidemic than from the evils it's been releasing in human beings. For the most revealing evidence since Viet Nam combat films about the atrocities terrified people are capable of, Harrison up there in the projection booth has a series of slides and film strips he can show you of the burning of Denver and Tacoma, some low-level reconnaissance aircraft shots of what is left of the New Orleans French Quarter, and photos of a dozen other cities where fear and hate had civil war going for a while. Do you want to see them?"

After a moment a man in the second row spoke. "We'll take your word, Walter. Most of us glanced up from our lab work long enough to see some of those television news stories. I don't need any more convincing. I doubt if anybody else does either."

The murmur this time was of general assent. The man in green nodded. "As usual, Dr. Weinstein has expressed a consensus. So we'll pass on. But with one word of reminder. What kept the national fabric from being irreparably shredded wasn't any redeeming quality in people. Those Sioux and Blackfeet tribesmen who ransacked Rapid City, the blacks who invaded the Chicago north shore, and the Chicanos who took over San Antonio—no vengeful minority mob anywhere backed off or broke up the way they did because of some surge of human compassion. And it wasn't Christian charity that dissolved the white vigilante bands that were raiding the ghettoes of Denver and Memphis and Louisville, shooting up everything and everybody—men, women, and children—with their deer rifles and skeet guns. It was plain ugly selfish human animal fear. Somehow—thank God for it!—a rumor got out—that for all we know may even be medically sound—that the only way not to catch Consolvo's Ulceration is to avoid all physical contact with other people. That scattered everybody fast. Incidentally, this isn't just my personal analysis. It's the official White House position. Not that I don't agree."

54

Away in the back a woman raised her hand. "You were going to give us some good news."

"Yes. Thank you, Claudia. I'm ready to get to it unless someone has a further comment."

"Just one," said Dr. Weinstein. "That fear of physical contact—has anybody in the administration considered its long-term affect on the nation's population growth?"

"Not to my knowledge, Frank," said the man in green, sounding even more weary. "At least not so far. But I'm sure it will occur to somebody up there sooner or later. Now if that's all, this is what we know about a possible carrier of Consolvo's Ulceration. It's a bizarre story, maybe the most bizarre so far in this whole horrible epidemic scenario. It's also a heroic tale, about a brave doctor who sacrificed his life. So you see, not everything in human nature is base, which I guess we need to remind ourselves of now and then.

"This bizarre story is set in Las Vegas, Nevada, itself a bizarre place, if you have ever been there, a modern Sodom, if you'll pardon a scriptural reference, a citadel of lust, cupidity, organized crime, gambling fever, and what is called Show Biz. Proof is that two days after the appearance of Consolvo's Ulceration in Albuquerque had every other city in the Southwest in a state of panic, it was business as usual in Las Vegas: dice rolling, wheels spinning, slot machines working, all the big shows on the strip going full-blast. Why Dr. Victor Velour, a California dermatologist of the highest professional standing should have stopped off on his way home after attending a medical convention in Albuquerque for anything so frivolous as a Las Vegas television talk-show, we can only speculate. Perhaps his wife had tickets and insisted. Whatever made him do it cost his life and put us in his debt.

"It was one of those shows where the host interviews celebrities, the more outlandish and seldom-seen the better. This day they had a rare one indeed, about a man

55

who'd been living in total seclusion for fifty years in his private castle somewhere in the Nevada mountains with a couple of Japanese servants who'd never left there either. Some of you would have heard of him—I dimly remember his name—Monte Hethercote, a big film-star from silent movie days, who appeared with Mary Pickford and Douglas Fairbanks. Fabulously wealthy, too, the way those stars got to be on their huge salaries and with virtually no income tax. About the time the movies began to talk, Hethercote got religion of some strange variety, put on a robe and sandals, converted all his holdings into gold bullion—thereby neatly evading the upcoming stock-market crash—and vanished in the wilderness. I imagine most people, if they thought of him at all, thought he was dead, but something induced him to return to the world as a guest star on the show Dr. Velour saw. Who knows? Maybe after fifty years the old fellow got lonesome.

"This is how it was described. Hethercote was up there on the stage talking away and rubbing one bare dirty ankle, and suddenly he screamed in agony. Well, Velour came forward, recognized the symptom instantly—a sandal strap had chafed Hethercote's leg and suddenly the abrasion had turned into the distinctive black ulcer that Velour had seen in the original Albuquerque victim— Consolvo himself. Well the show broke up, naturally, but the news flashed on TV screens across the country. Consolvo's Ulceration spread to Las Vegas, so California, Arizona and Utah officials immediately sealed off their borders. Nobody in Nevada could fly out or walk out or drive out. So there was rioting in Las Vegas, but instead of shooting and looting as elsewhere, the mobs just took over the bars and gambling halls and gave over to orgiastic merriment until time ran out on them. Las Vegas is a dead city now. Oh, there are people there. They creep out when the trucks bring food in from Nellis Air Force Base, but then they scuttle back into hiding.

"Dr. Velour realized that the old man having been in absolute seclusion before coming to Las Vegas, old Monte Hethercote was a perfect control specimen. So knowing the risks, he stayed with Hethercote in the hospital until he died, cross-examining him about possible exposures. Sure enough, Hethercote remembered that two days before leaving his castle he had spent an afternoon with an investment counselor. Apparently the old miser wanted advice on how to get even richer. And that visitor was the first outside contact with another human being Hethercote had had in half a century. Well of course Velour telephoned the Center for Disease Control in Atlanta who recognized the value of the information. And Velour, one of those heroes nobody ever knows about, went back to his hotel and shot himself. Under his chin where he had scraped himself shaving was an oozing black eruption."

"Who was the visitor?" asked a man in the front row. "Who was this investment counselor? Does anybody know anything about him?"

"We know everything," said the man in green. "The CDC got on it at once. No problem. The Securities and Exchange Commission knows all about him. He's a registered investment counselor with a very small, highly exclusive clientele. He makes money in quiet, rigidly honest, extremely prudent ways for people who have lots of money already—like heirs to family corporations who don't want to bother with sordid business, or individuals who have come into fortunes and aren't accustomed to handling them. His name is Luis Olvera. He lives and has his office not ten miles from here in Annandale, Virginia. In a way he's a sort of mystery man; he never lets anyone, not even his small office staff, know what potential client he is trying to line up—never lets them know where he's going next when he's on business trips, only where he's been. So there is one little hitch in finding out if Luis Olvera is indeed a carrier of Consolvo's Ulceration.

Nobody knows where he is. Since the afternoon he left Monte Hethercote's hideaway in the Toiyabe National Forest, no one, not his ex-wife, not his secretary, none of his known clients has heard a word from or about Luis Olvera."

"He's vanished?" said Dr. Weinstein. "Well, I call that a pretty damn feeble glimmer of hope."

"True, true," said the man on stage. "But as long as he's out there somewhere, there is a glimmer. And you must concede one thing."

"What's that?"

"It's the only glimmer we have."

Chapter 6

So many people came to the double funeral mass for Jean Gutierrez and Howard Consolvo on Monday that some had to stand on the sidewalk outside Father Miguel's church. The procession to the cemetery afterwards was the longest the traffic policemen could remember, six blocks of limousines and family sedans and farm pickups loaded with kids in back.

On Thursday, when Charley Wang and Shorty Tibbs were buried, there was no church service or procession, not merely because Charley had been Buddhist and Shorty, by all reports, pure heathen, but also because by Thursday funerals were luxuries Albuquerque could no longer afford. The last coffin in town had been sold by Tuesday, and Charley and Shorty were simply rolled from an up-ended dump truck into a fresh-dug trench along with other bodies in plastic bags or mattress covers. While a bulldozer waited in the background, blade raised as in salute, prayers for the dead were read by a Methodist minister wearing a gauze mask, by a fat priest in both mask and rubber gloves, and by a rabbi with no visible protection. Afterwards the rabbi told Noah he kept a bottle of camphor ice in his pocket to rinse his hands with, a precaution his father had taken in the 1918 Spanish Flu epidemic, and he wondered what Dr. Blanchard's professional opinion was. Noah said it was undoubtedly as effective as any prophylactic and after walking away heard the rabbi arguing with the minister about it.

Pecos Alvarez and Big Foot Johnson were hunkered down between the stake-and-platform truck and Howard Consolvo's salmon-pink Continental Mark V they had driven out from the clinic. They looked as thoroughly played-out as Noah felt, all three having worked straight through since epidemic victims started pouring into the clinic. Years of helping mares foal and cows calve and treating sick stock had made natural nurses of the two cowhands, as good as any Noah had ever seen. Brave nurses too, unlike some of the RNs at the clinic, male and female, who had run away.

Pecos stood up and handed Noah some car keys.

"What's this for?"

"God almighty, Doc," said Big Foot. "You got to have wheels, ain't you? Ain't no cabs or buses or nothin' runnin' and me and Pecos got to get on back up the mountain, got stock to tend to. So you keep the Boss's car."

Noah yawned, so tired he couldn't think straight. "You're going back to the ranch?"

"Hell, Doc," said Pecos, "with Shorty and Charley Wang and the Boss all planted ain't nothing for us down here no more. You don't mind, do you? God, there ain't no more we can do for them poor bastards dying in that clinic."

Noah shook his head to clear it. "Of course I don't mind. You two ought to get medals for what you've done. I don't feel right about taking Mr. Consolvo's automobile, though."

"You don't, some sorry son-of-a-bitch will just steal it. You be doing us a favor, because we can't take it; got to have both the pickup and the truck here for ranch work."

"Shorty's right," said Pecos. "Take the pink bastard.

Just leave word where it is when you leave town so we can come in and pick it up."

"All right, if you fellows say so." Noah put the Lincoln keys in his pocket. "You know, I hadn't even thought about leaving, the way things have been. All I've thought about is the next poor victim they were bringing in down there. You're right. There isn't anything more any of us can do. Not until somebody comes up with a treatment for this thing."

"Screw it, Doc," said Shorty. "Why don't you come on and go back with us. Let this damn epidemic run out its string. You'd like it up on the mountain."

"Damn right," said Pecos. "We'd make a hand out of you in no time."

Noah laughed. He had been thinking momentarily of Nelson. He mustn't feel guilty about leaving him. Nelson was beyond help, his or anyone's. Nelson would either work himself to death in his grief, or catch this damn disease and die of it, or survive and in the end come to terms with having to live on as survivors always did. "It's got its points, I have to admit. You think I'd like it on your ranch?"

"God, yes, Doc," said Shorty earnestly. "Fellow like you, you'd purely love it. Ain't no sick people up on the Bar H–C, hell there ain't no people at all, just sky and mountains and cows and horses and now and then a deer strays in. Whole year goes by sometimes we don't see a soul from outside."

It was time he telephoned Chicago, Noah was thinking. For all they knew at Cook County General, he could be lying in that ditch the noisy bulldozer was pushing dirt into. "That's odd," he said. "When was the last time you had a stranger on the ranch?"

"Hell, I don't remember," said Pecos. "Why?"

"Well it's puzzling, that's why. If you were all that isolated up there now how did Howard Consolvo—or the cook either—get exposed to this contagion, whatever it is? Infections don't just come blowing in over the mountains, you know. You have to catch them. You sure nobody's been up there the last week or two except you five men?"

Big Foot frowned. "You ask that like it was important, Doc."

"It could be. Think hard now."

"Goddamn it, Big Foot," said Pecos, "there was. This dude come up to see the Boss last week, Monday, Tuesday, hell so much been happening I don't recollect. Some business dude the Boss had sent for."

"You're right for a fact," said Big Foot. "Thing is, Doc, me and Pecos was riding fence so we never seen him. Shorty did though, met him down the mountain and drove him up. Anybody don't know that road can get lost. Charley Wang seen him too. The Boss had him cook up a big feed and the dude tipped Charley ten dollars. I never seen him so puffed up about a thing, damn conceited Chinaman. He was a good cook at that, old Charley."

"Tell me all about this man," said Noah urgently. "His name, where he came from, where he went, what he was doing there, everything. Think hard. This could be more vital than you realize."

"Jesus, Doc," protested Big Foot. "We don't know all that. We never even seen him. He was long-gone, time we got back. But Charley Wang said him and the Boss talked investments and tax laws, how Howie could do better with money. Howie wasn't no money-hog and not any highbinder either, honest as the day, but he's got—had— kids and grandkids out in California he wanted to leave fixed as good as he could."

"Didn't the cook mention the man's name?" said Noah. An investment adviser of some sort, he was thinking. CDC could track him through the SEC if only they had a name to go on.

"It was a Spanish name," said Pecos cautiously. "I remember that. Around this country it's mostly ragged ass-working stiffs like me got the Spic names, not big-shot money dudes advising millionaires like the Boss what to do. So it struck me. Name was Ol—Ollie—something.... Big Foot, you said it reminded you of Los Angeles."

"Olvera! Damn right. Olvera Street in L.A. where they got the Mexican bars and mariachi music. I got drunk and laid and rolled there all in one night, the night I got out of the army. God almighty, gentlemen, I wasn't but twenty-two years old. Seems like last week."

Olvera, thought Noah. The SEC could track him down fast. Everybody was in a computer nowadays. "Boys," he said, "this could be the best day's work you ever did. Now the quicker I can get to a phone—if the damn things are working yet—the better. And listen, one of these days I will get up to that ranch. Maybe you can put me onto some trout fishing."

"Bet your ass, Doc," said Big Foot. "Any old time."

"Any time," echoed Pecos. "We don't need no notice from you, Doc." After exchanging crunching handshakes they climbed up in the GMC cab and went clattering off. Except for the bulldozer snorting along the ditchline the cemetery was deserted, the dumptrucks gone, the three men of the cloth driven away in a Navy gray PHS station wagon with an armed guard up front. A hawk circled in the pale sky and Sandia Crest rose sharp and bold in the distance. It seemed a lifetime since Noah had looked at it from his Conquistador bedroom window. He blinked his weary eyes and smelled his own stink. He had worn the same clothes for almost a week, yearned for a bath in a tub of soapy water, for fresh underwear and clean sheets. God, he could sleep for a week. But more important than anything was calling Hal Chalmers in Atlanta. The CDC had to know about Olvera, the possible carrier. There were telephones at the Conquistador....

He slid into the white leather upholstery of Howard Consolvo's automobile, found the power control that lifted the seat up and back for his long legs, turned the ignition key and shook his head in admiration. It was a

marvelous machine, an absurd symbol of opulence. Old
Howie Consolvo, the cowboy who struck it rich, must
have loved his preposterous chariot. The thought made
Noah sad. He touched the gas pedal and the two-ton
monster moved irresistibly ahead, smooth as silk, down
the rutty cemetery road.

The wide avenue leading into the city was utterly
deserted. As he entered the built-up section, he saw
evidence of the street fighting that had raged here for a
day and a half: burnt, overturned cars, shards of glass on
the pavement, burnt-out store buildings, and black,
smouldering rubble piles that had been places where
people worked and lived. He smelled charred wood and
scorched fabric and a molasses-candy sweetness from a
burned sugar warehouse. Once or twice he thought he
saw a head moving in an upper-story, apartment-house
window, but the avenue stretched out ahead, as endless
and empty of visible life as a nightmare symbol. Hideous
depression sank into Noah. It was like driving into one of
those 1945 film-clips of a bombed-out German city, only
worse. That had been the work of men at war; this was
God's work. A superstitious dread dating back to his
childhood with a Presbyterian grandmother crept into
Noah's mind. Wrathful Jehovah who reduced Gomorrah
to ashes was punishing gluttonous, slothful America. Oh,
come on! Noah said to himself. Knock it off. This isn't an
angry God. This is just some new or mutated organism we
haven't been able to isolate yet that's killing these people,
no more mysterious than a spirochete except that we
don't know what it is. But his sense of dread lingered on.

Ahead, two downed telephone poles lay in the street,
and it seemed prudent to turn at the first corner and go
around the block. But half a block down the side street he
came up short against a barricade of masonry rubble and
ripped-up asphalt chunks. As he began backing the car he
heard the spiteful snap of a .22 rifle, heard the bullet hit
the hood and ricochet singing away. Terror convulsed his

bowels. To die in a burnt-out slum street, ambushed with a toy gun! He slammed the back end of the car around and roared into the avenue, shifted down and made a racing turn around the telephone poles in the street. Suddenly an armored personnel carrier shot forward from an alley across his path. "Shit!" said Noah and hit his brakes.

The kid with the carbine and the gold bar pinned to his field fatigues collar who jumped down from the personnel carrier looked about nineteen. The helmeted soldiers who fingered weapons up in the vehicle looked no older and bore the unmistakable look of rank amateurs. Noah had seen too many real combat troops to be taken in.

"Yes sir, Lieutenant," he said as heartily as he could. The last thing he wanted was for any of these nervous kids to get trigger-happy. They were the New Mexico National Guard according to the markings on the vehicle.

"Don't you know this end of town's off-limits, Mister, under military control? You got any ID?"

"I know it now. This okay?"

The lieutenant read Noah's Air Force Reserve card and saluted clumsily. "Sorry, Colonel. Only, you know, it's not safe around these streets. Somebody might take a shot at you."

"Somebody already did. Don't salute me, son—I'm not on active duty—just an out-of-town doctor trying to get to the Conquistador Motor Hotel, if that's okay. Is it?"

"Well it's still open, sir. We've got a command post in it. I'll radio that you're coming in, if you want me to."

"That would be helpful, Lieutenant." Noah read his name tape. "Lieutenant Simpson. Where you boys from?"

"South, sir. Las Cruces, Socorro, in between there."

"What do you hear from down there?"

"About this sickness, sir?" The boy looked uneasy. "Well, thing is, we don't really know for sure. I think maybe it's starting to break out down there, too."

"Any of your bunch going AWOL?"

"Well, maybe one or two taking off after dark. They're good troops, sir, but you know, they get to worrying about their folks. . . ."

"I know." Noah shook his head. "It's asking a lot of you fellows to stay here and hold things down while all the time you're worrying about conditions at home. But I don't know who else we could count on."

"Thank you, sir." Simpson scratched his ear. "This thing. You know, it's not like what the field manuals tell you. They're no help. How do you fight this? Well, you're a doctor, so you know. Snipers now, they're bad, but you can hunt them down, get a bead on them. This epidemic. I just wish it was something we could *see*."

"So do the doctors, son," said Noah. "So do the doctors. That's what every medical laboratory in the country is working on right now, how to get a bead on this thing. And when we do, we'll lick it. Well, good luck. If I see your CO, I'll give him a good report."

"Thank you, Colonel." After another clumsy salute Simpson waved Noah ahead.

The big Conquistador parking lot was almost empty, half a dozen civilian cars, a scattering of olive-drab staff cars, some jeeps, three or four light GI trucks. Noah found a potentially shady place for Howard Consolvo's pink Continental and went in. A sentry inside the door checked his ID and saluted. All this saluting, Noah grumbled to himself. Might as well be back in Air Force blues. The big lobby was shadowy and humid, only a few floor lamps lit and the air-conditioning obviously off. Power shortage. Somewhere a gasoline generator racketed emergency power courtesy of the New Mexico National Guard, he presumed.

A Guard captain and a bald civilian were standing behind the reception desk. "Well, welcome back, Dr. Blanchard," said the civilian. "Higgins, assistant manager. They radioed you were coming in. God, isn't this the most horrible thing that ever happened?"

"Pretty bad," said Noah. "Pretty bad. Is it too much to hope that my stuff will still be in my room?"

"I don't see why not. Everything ought to be just as you left it. We haven't had a maid show up for work since Sunday, or hardly any other help either. Not many guests checking in, as you might imagine. Except the National Guard officers."

Noah nodded at the captain who stared coldly. "Any military objections to my having my room back, Captain?"

"Not from me. You won't be the only civilian. There's a bunch of you still here—got caught and couldn't get out of town I guess."

What was the matter with this surly clown? thought Noah, a little nettled. Maybe he was one of those Weekend Warriors who resent active duty. To test him, Noah said, "They federalized your unit yet, Captain?" putting a parade-ground snap into it.

The captain went pale. "Are they planning to do that?"

"Damned if I know. I'm just another civilian."

Higgins rushed in placatingly. "I don't know what we'd have done without them. Dr. Blanchard. They've been absolutely tremendous, helping in the kitchen, on the switchboard, taking out garbage, everything. You'll have to walk upstairs, not enough power to run the elevator. And there's only one light bulb in your room. It would help if you used it as little as possible."

"What's the water situation? I want a bath."

Higgins shook his head. "No hot water. It might be lukewarm, this time of day."

"Horrors of war," said Noah. He took his room key, nodded curtly to the captain, and turned towards the stairwell. He stopped. "One more thing. What's the telephone situation? Long distance, I mean. It's of absolutely the most urgent necessity for me to get a call through to Atlanta."

"Well, I don't know," said Higgins doubtfully. "The

phones have been spotty at best. And long distance, well, I haven't tried, but I doubt if you'll have much luck. But don't ask me. Come on around and ask our switchboard operator. We're lucky there. Our regulars never came in after Monday, so this woman volunteered."

"I'll do that," said Noah and, going around the end of the reception counter, walked into the back office. A woman with a telephone headset on her dark hair was sitting in front of the PBX switchboard, her back to him. "Excuse me, Miss," said Noah, "but what are the chances of getting a long-distance call through? Top priority, I assure you."

She swiveled her chair to face him. "You poor man!" she cried. "You look perfectly terrible. Why, you must be half-dead for sleep!"

Noah blinked in astonishment. Could this be the woman who had driven away in a spitting fury? "Well, Miss Petrakis," he said uncertainly, "we seem destined to keep meeting."

She gave him a rueful, gamine-like grin. "We do, don't we? And I always wind up looking like an unmitigated heel. Dr. Blanchard, I want to apologize. But truly, I had no idea last Saturday morning of the horrible situation at the Santa Rosa Clinic. I just thought I was on to a story—some mysterious goings-on they were covering up. All those doctors rushing over there all night from the convention, and the whispering. So I got a crew from our affiliate station here to cover it. You must have thought I was the most insensitive—" She broke off, shaking her head. "Well, that's me. Now what about a long-distance call, Doctor?"

Despite his reluctance, Noah found himself smiling at her. What a strange, mercurial personality she was. "You were calling me Noah last week, remember? By the way, where did you learn to run a switchboard?"

"Oh, Lord. That's just one of the things I did to pay my way through journalism school. Columbia, Missouri.

Maybe I should have stayed with Ma Bell, the way I keep screwing up trying to make it in television."

"Oh, I wouldn't say that, Kate," said Noah. Damn it, she was attractive. Nutty, but she was all female. "Now what I need is to get a call through to Dr. Hal Chalmers at the Center for Disease Control in Atlanta. As far as I know, nobody anywhere has a more important message for anybody than I do for Hal Chalmers. It's a wild shot at trying to head off this epidemic."

"Then we'd better do it," she said crisply. "But I kid you not, it won't be easy. The whole phone system seems to have collapsed, at least in the mountain states. I doubt if a trunk call has gotten in or out of Albuquerque in three days."

"You don't mean it's hopeless? My God, Kate, I don't need to tell you how critical this call is."

"I didn't say that. Let me think. I think the best shot would be to get the MARS radio station at the air base to try to contact a Ham operator close enough to Atlanta to work out a phone patch. I'll get started on that. It could take hours, so you go on up and do something about yourself. God, you look like death warmed over. It must have been hellish in that clinic all this time. Go on, Noah. I'll ring your room whenever I get through to Atlanta. Go on now. Leave it up to Kate."

"Nothing wrong with me that some soap and water and a razor won't heal," he said. "And maybe about ten hours sleep."

"Tell you what," said Kate, "after we get your call, I'll make sure nobody disturbs you—let you get some real rest. Okay?"

"Sounds like a winner," said Noah and left her, still marveling. Of all the unpredictable women he had known, this one ranked tops.

It was a long time before the call came through. Noah had scrubbed in a tub of tepid water, had scraped a week's accumulation of pink and gray whiskers off, leaving his face raw, and was dozing when the telephone rang. He reached for it on the nightstand, wondering what time it was. He had drawn the window drapes and didn't want to turn on a light to look at his watch.

"Hold on, please," said Kate's voice. "I think I've got him for you. Dr. Chalmers? Hold for Dr. Blanchard in Albuquerque, please."

"Hey, Hal," said Noah. "Christ, everything's gone to hell out here. I guess you know, though. How is it there?"

"Madhouse." Chalmers's voice sounded tinny and a long way off. "Everybody's going crazy."

"You mean the epidemic's moved that far?" The sound in Noah's ear kept fading and coming back.

"Sporadic outbreaks so far. Still mainly west of the Missouri. But it's coming. . . ." The sound began to die.

"Hal!" shouted Noah. "Listen hard. I think I've got a lead on a carrier. Last name, Olvera. That's spelled O–L–V–"

Chalmers cut in. "Luis Olvera was there too? That is highly significant. That might confirm that he is—do you know where he is?"

"Oh no. You mean you knew about him?"

"For four days or so. Everybody's hunting him. If you knew where he was—"

"I don't!" said Noah, feeling let down. "He's gone. I don't know where."

The sound began to die. ". . . office, nor his ex-wife . . ." said Chalmers, voice growing fainter. ". . . earth swallowed him . . ."

All sound ceased abruptly. The instrument in Noah's hand became a lump of dead, unresponsive plastic. Then it returned to life. "I'm afraid that's all we're going to be able to do," said Kate apologetically. "Everything just quit."

"It's all right," said Noah. "My news wasn't so novel after all. The hell with it."

"That's the way," said Kate. "You get some rest now. I'll see that you do."

"That's a deal," said Noah, yawning. "When I wake up, I'll buy you breakfast."

"We may have to cook it ourselves," she chuckled, "but I'll take you up on it. Sweet dreams."

Something woke him: the click of a door lock, a sharp scent of perfume—he was not sure. The room was black. As he struggled up from profound sleep, Kate, in a husky voice, said. "It's me." Her smooth, naked body slipped into bed with him.

Chapter 7

Leaning wearily against his lectern in the underground auditorium at Bethesda, the man in green watched his audience trail in. He blinked his burning eyes and nodded at the few who glanced up at him, wondering if so illustrious a collection of intellects had been gathered together anywhere since General Groves's Manhattan Project a generation earlier. Not even Groves had had so many Nobel laureates. From the stage he could count fourteen, including the three foreigners: Hasmin from Israel, Kopitsky, the Soviet chemist, Horner from Australia, whose generous governments had let them stay on in the United States to help out in this crisis. Or more likely, thought the man in green with gallows humor, their governments simply didn't want them coming home as possible carriers of Consolvo's Ulceration.

No military doctor had returned since the first meeting. Admiral Graybar was still in tidewater Virginia, where the epidemic had prostrated the Hampton Roads fleet; the Air Surgeon-General was in San Antonio; Mike Hanson of Walter Reed Army Medical Center was God knows where. Staring up at him from the front row were the Harvard scientists—battle-scarred veterans, all, of the gene-transplant confrontation with Cambridge's panicky politicians. Behind them sat the Cold Spring Harbor Lab gang with some of Berg's followers, all survivors of the knock-down-drag-out Recombinant DNA Molecule conference held at Asilomar in the heart of California's redwoods. Considering the nation's present peril, both conflicts seemed like childish tantrums now.

Sitting apart from the academic and government scientists in diffident companionship were Webster, Gay, and Goldblatt, the three pharmaceutical-company executive vice-presidents, ordinarily the fiercest of competitors. The women, too, tended to group—Hattie Manger, the Palo Alto microbiologist, and Sue Berne of the National Academy of Science in the same row as a dozen others of their professional sisterhood. Scattered about, some still in their stained lab jackets, sat the solid NIH workhorse researchers, whom the man in green valued as highly as he did the flashiest bearer of Nobel's laurels.

Up in the projection booth a yellow light blinked, Harrison's signal that the Marine guards had closed the doors. Down the aisle came Attorney General Hiram Cawthorp and Chief Justice Willoughby Judd, both attending for the first time, and mincing along, in their majestic wake, Clinton Sites, the Johns Hopkins mathematician.

It occurred to the man in green that the mean IQ of his audience must run close to 200 and that this admirable statistic guaranteed nothing admirable about the temperaments of its principals. Pleasant personalities though most of them were, they were all capable of intellectual rage. Before this meeting ended, he knew, fireworks would explode. Bracing himself mentally, he began to speak.

"Thank you again for coming. I know it isn't easy to leave your duties. But I have vital developments to report. Some you may know about, but not all of them and not all of you. First I'd like to—"

"What I want to know," interrupted Ben Russell, black-browed and scowling in the second row, "is if we've

73

got a line yet on this Olvera, this disease-carrier. I need that guy. They found him yet?"

The man in green willed his tired face to smile, thinking it must resemble *rictus sardonicus*, thinking that if Ben Russell hadn't been so able a virologist he would lower the boom on the loud-mouth. "I was going to get around to that, Ben," he said mildly. "The CDC has new evidence that almost certainly confirms Luis Olvera as a carrier. Two days before he met Hethercote, the old movie actor, in the Nevada mountains, it seems he was in contact with the original Howard Consolvo and two other early victims on an isolated ranch in New Mexico. We think that's pretty conclusive."

"So where is he? Anybody collared him yet?"

"No, Ben, sad to say. After Hethercote, Olvera simply vanished. There's an APB out on him all over the Southwest. Every agency still functioning—not many admittedly—from city cops to the Border Patrol are hunting him. So far no luck."

"Jesus!" said Russell. "Don't those yokels realize how important this guy is? Can't you get the Pentagon to turn out the goddamn army, comb out that country down there? Here we are working our asses off after a causative agent, with a known carrier running around loose that the dumb bastards can't even find."

"It's not that simple, Ben. Maybe you don't realize how chaotic things are in the Southwest—phones out, no TV or radio working, towns practically cut off from the world."

"Well, I still think it's disgraceful," grumbled Russell.

"Oh, why don't you pipe down?" said Hattie Manger. "The general said he had important developments to report. I for one want to hear them."

"Concur," said Michael Hargrave, a molecular biologist of the politically radical Science for the People group. "I didn't leave a critical test series to come listen to you blow off, Russell. Go on, General."

Well now, thought Major General Walter Burrows of the U.S. Army Medical Corps, this is support from an unexpected quarter. Mike Hargrave despises anything that smacks of uniformed authority. "Take it easy, everybody," he said. "We're all tired and frustrated and short of sleep and taking it out on each other. Dr. Russell is perfectly correct that to be able to examine and get a history on a known carrier of Consolvo's Ulceration would be highly desirable. Unfortunately, though, Luis Olvera could be in the bottom of a lime pit by now, one more unknown epidemic victim. But on the off chance he's still alive, we'll keep looking for him."

"Well, hell," said Russell, sounding aggrieved. "That's all I was asking for. What's everybody jumping on me for?"

Burrows swayed dizzily, catching the lectern to steady himself. No one noticed except Master Sergeant Chester Harrison in the projection booth who had served with Burrows since forward field hospital days long ago in the Viet Nam jungle. Now he called the President of the United States an epithet so filthy it would have justified court martial charges under the Uniform Code of Military Justice, had anyone heard him. Walt Burrows was killing himself on this epidemic, thought Harrison. In two weeks he had slept scarcely ten hours on the canvas cot behind his desk. And to show his gratitude, the President was putting in over his head some feather merchant. Who the hell was this Dr. Noah Blanchard? Well, at least the Old man might get a decent night's sleep for a change.

"Back to my agenda," said Burrows, squeezing his eyes against vertigo. "First a report on the status of the epidemic based on what sketchy and no doubt inaccurate data we have been able to feed into the computers. It's grim. Horribly grim. The disease has hit all the forty-eight contiguous states and spilled over into Mexico and Canada. The hardest hit places are west and southwest where in major metropolitan areas like Los Angeles, Denver, Albuquerque, Phoenix, Salt Lake City the casualty rate is running above twenty percent."

"God," groaned a UCLA geneticist, and beside him Rosemary Hamby of the National Health Archives, whose family lived in San Diego, began weeping softly. Burrows went on. "That translates into something like three million deaths already." His voice was flatly unemotional. Only Sergeant Harrison knew that his entire family of widowed sister, two small nephews, and elderly father, all living in Anaheim, had not been heard from since Labor Day. "Our computers predict that such a large number of casualties, if continuing at the rate at which this epidemic is spreading, will cause the United States in just three more weeks to cease to be a viable nation."

For ten endless seconds the auditorium was deadly quiet. Then the chairman of the biochemistry department of a Michigan university spoke. "If I may say so, General Burrows," he said respectfully, "I cannot believe you called us together merely for a doomsday pronouncement, especially in light of our two distinguished jurist visitors. I have to believe you have some positive information to pass on. Right?"

Burrows's head was clear again. He permitted himself a faint smile. "You are absolutely correct, Professor Craydon. But I was instructed to report that computer prediction first, not that I believe any of us needs to be reminded how serious the epidemic is. There has indeed been a positive development—one we have been praying for. The—the—organism, I have to call it, since it doesn't seem to be either a virus or a bacterium exactly—the apparent causative agent for Consolvo's Ulceration—has finally been seen. Electromicroscopically. Now wait a minute!"

He waved both hands for silence, but seconds passed before his voice could be heard. "It's not only been seen, it has been made to grow and reproduce in a human foreskin culture. It's been attenuated—now hold on! Please! Not all at once. Let me—listen now!—Let me—hold on and listen until I tell you. Then I'll take your questions. Please."

The uproar faded, although many in the audience continued to whisper excitedly from side to side and across the backs of their seats. Burrows held the throat mike that hung round his neck to his lips and shouted until the last of the hubbub died. "We held off telling you this," he said, "for obvious reasons—for fear the reports were premature and until we could be reasonably sure they were reliable. They seem to be. The same findings have been reported from three widely separate points. As so often happens—you know as well as I—discoveries were made simultaneously. Emory University researchers down in Atlanta reported it first, although I suppose the CDC people near the campus were in on it and deserve credit, too. And then the Collyer Foundation in Tampa came up with the same discovery and almost immediately after that the School of Medicine at Northwestern—"

"Hurray for old Burley!" someone shouted and was promptly shushed.

"That's right," said Burrows. "It was Dr. Artemus Burley who phoned it in. Actually I think he used short-wave radio, long-distance phone service being too uncertain, but no matter."

"God's sake, General," said Lambdin from Harvard, "get down to specifics. Tell us about this—this organism."

"I'll do better. I'll show you a picture—an artist's depiction of what the researchers isolated under their electron microscopes. Harrison, please."

As before, the lights darkened, a projection screen brightened at the back of the stage, and on it appeared a painting of a purplish, crystal-shaped object sprouting a growth of spicules dense as spines on a porcupine. It resembled nothing anyone there could call to mind. After a long moment General Burrows remarked: "Just look at that ugly son-of-a-bitch." The tightness in his voice

77

betrayed to Harrison at least the enormous tension he was under. "I'm sorry. That was uncouth. But when I think of the human misery that foul object—particle—creation—whatever you want to name it, has caused, I get—well, I get damned angry. Everybody looked at it long enough? Slide off, please, Harrison."

The picture vanished and the house lights went up. "Any questions, ladies and gentlemen?" said Burrows. "Not for now? All right. Here is what we know about this thing. Or think we know. The spicules, or spines—those needle-like stickers on it—are essential to the organism's virulence. I'll explain that. They are what it attaches itself to a human host with. It is something like the way certain burs and seed pods in the vegetable world propagate—blowing through the air until they catch their hooks in a host and start their reproductive cycle. The organism of Consolvo's Ulceration makes a lodgement in human skin tissue wherever a break in the skin surface—a scratch, some minor wound—admits it. And it hooks itself there with these spicules, and a devastating reaction results. How or why it happens we don't know, but a crucial enzyme is created on which the organism feeds and thrives as it simultaneously feeds and thrives on keratin—that is to say, on a fibrous protein substance in the skin. I am trying to describe this not-very-well-understood process in plain English. Not everyone here is trained in medical vocabulary."

"You are doing very well, sir," said Hiram Cawthorp in a strong, resonant voice. "I can follow you perfectly."

"Right on, General," said Clinton Sites, the Johns Hopkins mathematician. "No offense," he added hastily.

Major General Walter Burrows bent a long, studious stare at him, shrugged, and continued. "From the point of lodgement in the skin of a susceptible victim—not everyone exposed to it catches Consolvo's Ulceration, remember—the organism begins to reproduce with unbelievable rapidity, which is why the disease spreads so swiftly over a victim's body." Burrows paused a moment as if to collect his thoughts. "Now then," he resumed. "Having discovered it, the Atlanta researchers and later the ones in Tampa and Evanston, extracted the organism and put it in a test-tube culture where it flourished. Then they did everything to it they could think of—centrifuged it and precipitated it and radioactivated it and dumped every chemical compound in the pharmacopeia in it. Results negative. Until somebody had an inspired hunch. They started changing the atmosphere inside the test-tubes—altering the proportions of oxygen to nitrogen, changing the carbon dioxide content, ozonizing the mix, all sorts of things. And something extraordinary happened. Within a certain atmosphere—the formula is simple, the conditions easy to achieve, so much oxygen to so much nitrogen—the organism, this devilish crystal-shaped killer-organism that is neither virus nor bacterium that no one ever saw before, reproduced wildly, but with a significant difference. The spiculae disappeared. The thing became smooth-faced—had no spines to hook into tissue with. Result, no crucial enzyme produced, no keratin consumed, no human tissue eaten away. To put it in different language, cultivating the organism under controlled atmospheric conditions produces an altered, attenuated, non-virulent strain. And that, obviously, opens the way to—"

"A vaccine, by God!" shouted Lambdin, the Harvard immunologist who had been fingering the peace pendant dangling down his black turtleneck jersey as he followed Burrows intently. "That should make it possible to produce a vaccine!"

"Exactly," said General Burrows. "From the attenuated organism culture the researchers extracted a serum and injected it into human volunteers. The result was the classic reaction known since Jenner invented vaccination in 1796. The milder strain of organism stimulated lymphocytes to produce antibodies which apparently confer immunity to the disease."

At the back of the auditorium, Hiram Cawthorp and

79

Chief Justice Judd exchanged puzzled looks. They had expected a joyous outburst from the audience at Burrows's revelation. Instead, a sound of angry whispering filled the auditorium until the black-browed Irish-looking doctor whom the general had called "Ben" demanded loudly, "So what's the catch then? Can't they produce enough of the stuff?"

"No problem there, Dr. Russell," said Burrows. "They're turning it out by the bucketful. But yes, there's a catch. A hellish catch. The vaccine confers immunity on nine out of ten of the volunteers who've taken it, but the tenth develops Consolvo's Ulceration in its most virulent form within hours. For reasons we don't understand, the attenuated organism reverts to type in their bloodstream, grows back its spicules and produces the crucial enzyme."

"They tried to test it, I suppose, on lab animals?" said Russell.

"Naturally. But this is a disease animals seem to be immune to, even primates. Lab animals are useless."

"Every tenth one died?" said Rosemary Hamby shakily.

"Just about," said Burrows. "A few more than that in Tampa, a few less in Atlanta, about that at Northwestern. It averages out. For one of ten, vaccination is a horrible death sentence. And we don't know who that tenth is going to be. Moreover, some volunteers who died probably enjoyed natural immunity—considering the experience of the general population where the epidemic has been the worst—until we infected them."

"You keep saying 'volunteers,'" growled Hargrave, of the radical Science for the People group. "Who were these so-called volunteers? Ghetto blacks? Death Row inmates? Street bums? The feebleminded?"

"Volunteers is the precise word," said Burrows icily. "Brave, intelligent, altruistic volunteers who fully understood the risks, some of them university students, including medical students, from South Florida and Georgia Tech and Northwestern and Emory. Let me assure you—in light of the hostile implication of your questions—that nobody was dragooned, press-ganged, shanghaied or had his or her civil rights violated. And that specifically includes the poor, the helpless, the black, the brown, the yellow, any kind of minority. You don't know me very well, but it ought to be obvious from my color that I would never be party to such a thing!" The stars on General Burrows's massive green shoulders flashed silver as he strove to subdue his anger.

Hiram Cawthorp rose, a patrician, courtly figure. "If I might speak, sir. It was in anticipation of just such fears that President Dobson asked Chief Justice Judd and me to join you today. He is particularly anxious that you ladies and gentlemen of the life sciences, on whom the burden of protecting the nation weighs so heavily, understand his policy. The President told me, I quote verbatim, this is not Hitler's Germany and no matter how dire our national peril, it's not about to be, either. Even if he did not feel that way, a host of legal safeguards exists to prevent discrimination. The classes of people for whom you express alarm, sir—the poor, the socially disadvantaged, the ill, the institutionalized—believe me, you would be astonished by all the laws that protect them—that protect mankind as—to use legal jargon—'animals of necessity' in clinical investigation. The Chief Justice and I are prepared to discourse on this subject at length. But you might prefer to finish your own discussion first."

"All well and good, sir," said Lambdin of Harvard, squeezing his peace symbol with obvious agitation. "That's the same plausible kind of assurance the chemical warfare people gave Meselson and some of the rest of us about their experiments with anthrax. But by heaven we closed down Fort Detrick anyway! What you're giving us is Establishment talk, politicians' prattle. No offense intended personally, but I damned well don't buy it. I'm not worried about Hitler's Germany. That's history. I'm worried about the quality of thinking that gave us Nixon's

America, and before that Hiroshima, and now neutron bombs, and cruise missiles. That's worry enough for me."

"For me, too!" snarled the triple-chinned MIT molecular biologist, Paul Ruffec, who stood as far left of most Science for the People adherents, politically, as they did of Gay, Goldblatt, and Webster, the pharmaceutical house executives now scowling indignantly. Ruffec, thought Burrows, was one fat bastard he would suspect of offering aid and comfort to the enemy in time of war and, come to think of it, if fighting Consolvo's Epidemic wasn't war, what was? "I must protest," said Ruffec. "Everything I've heard here reeks of fascism and I refuse to prostitute *my* science to it."

A quavering, insistent voice interrupted. "Sir, sir! General Burrows, sir! Allow me to speak." On his feet, white locks falling about his tremulous head, stood the octogenarian physicist, Duval Badin, colleague of Lawrence at Berkeley in the birthing of the A-Bomb and proud of it. The battle lines are being drawn, thought Hiram Cawthorp. This assembly is about to blow wide open. He wondered what Kopitsky, the Russian, and Hasmin, the Israeli, talking in swift undertones, were making of scientific dialogue in a democracy. He considered what a magnificent document the Bill of Rights was and wondered if it would survive. He wondered if President Dobson had any idea what a volatile lot these scientists were.

"Please, everyone," said Burrows, clinking his water glass with a pencil. "Give Professor Badin the floor."

The auditorium grew quiet. Even those who detested Duval Badin's politics respected him as an elder statesman of science. "Colleagues," he said, his voice light and wispy, "this argumentation leads nowhere, generates heat, not light. The issue of who must serve the common good as Mr. Cawthorp's 'animals of necessity' is vital, but not paramount. The paramount issue is how we and other researchers can make this vaccine safe for all, in time to save the nation. If it cannot be made safe for all, how can

82

we identify those for whom it is not? I believe that sums it up. What instructions have you for us, General Burrows?"

"Summed up admirably, sir," said Burrows. "You are exactly right. The vaccine is our only hope. To make it safe—or to use it safely—we must vaccinate many more subjects and screen them medically, particularly those who die from it to find out what characteristics they had in common. Why does the vaccine in their veins revert to virulent form? Could a genetic or racial factor be responsible—as Chinese cannot be treated for tuberculosis with isoniazid in the ordinary way because their livers methylate the drug too fast? Could it be body chemistry, some sensitivity such as that of the one person in fifty thousand who dies of encephalitis when vaccinated for smallpox? Such a program in so short a time will be enormous, screening the thousands of antigens of the immune systems of all the unfortunate subjects who die. And who are the subjects going to be? We can't count on enough volunteers. Who should be picked? Where will they come from? How will we choose them? How many will we need? There's a question! Some of you may have wondered why Clinton Sites, of the Department of Mathematics at Johns Hopkins, is here. He came to answer that question. Professor Sites?"

"Thank you, General." There was nothing at all mincing about Sites now, standing erect in black-framed glasses, a black notebook open in his hand. "I will make it short and sweet, stripped of statistical jargon. Two days ago General Burrows's people laid down their requirements and provided my shop with what data they had. We fed them into the computers and have analyzed the findings. For ideal effectiveness of the program, postulating one subject in ten as a casualty to be screened with the utmost thoroughness within a time frame of ten days, adding a factor to cover attrition of medical screening facilities as the epidemic advances nationwide, you would need, in round figures, ten million people—a million a day to examine for ten days."

There was a kind of low collective gasp. Sites went on. "That being obviously unfeasible, the optimum figure we could arrive at came to a hundred thousand a day, for a total of a million subjects. Not ideal, but the best we can hope for." He snapped his notebook shut and sat down.

Michael Hargrave sprang to his feet, sputtering. "It's criminal, experimenting that way with human lives. You're condemning thousands to death."

"Come off it, man," said Ben Russell. "The epidemic is already killing twenty percent. Use your head. *Vaccinating cuts it in half.* That's a pretty fair gain."

"But it's God's twenty percent," wailed Rosemary Hamby. "Or Providence or blind chance or whatever you call it. *For doctors to inoculate innocent people, knowing every tenth must die—it's unthinkable!*"

"It's so thinkable!" squealed Ruffec, all chins wobbling. "It's too thinkable—it's classic fascism. First you pick the politically undesirable to vaccinate and next you pick—"

"Keep still, you home-grown Trotsky!" snapped Hattie Manger while beside her Sue Berne was saying in a wondering way, "Could we pick them by lottery?" and someone sneered that Shirley Jackson was dead while Craydon, in his pondering fashion, said, "A lottery is a sensible idea. Consider Selective Service. What's the difference? Casting lots to be sacrificed for the common good—that's an ancient cultural rite."

A fanatic-eyed cell biologist from Rockefeller University leaped up. "Why use Americans? We could buy people. From Bangladesh, from Paraguay, from Uganda. They'd sell us all we wanted. Or invite immigrants from Cambodia. They'd swarm in, regardless. Of course we'd have the problem of getting their medical dossiers, but—"

"Order!" yelled General Burrows, and pounded the lectern with a thick glass ashtray. Angry as he was, he still noticed the bewilderment of Kopitsky and Hasmin and the pained look on Horner's aloof features, and wondered how this meeting would be reported to Moscow and Tel

Aviv and Canberra. He saw the three pharmaceutical executives arguing with two Nobel winners, the shock on Chief Justice Judd's face, and Hiram Cawthorp covering his eyes as if in disbelief. "Order!" Burrows shouted again, thinking how much these yelling geniuses reminded him of children fighting in a schoolyard. Just below him the Viennese biochemist and former refugee, Ignatz Weinstraub, comfortably ensconced for forty years at Cal Tech, was dancing with rage, screeching: "Gas ovens they'll come to next. Science is not for killing!" while Frank Weinstein bellowed, "Shut your silly yap. What do you know from gas ovens? My whole family in Germany—"

"Shut up!" Burrows roared down at them. "Act your age." He hammered on the lectern and bellowed: "Order, order! Come to order!"

A sharp, sudden hissing filled the auditorium. A stench so vile it churned stomachs thickened the air. The scientists stopped shouting, looked about wildly, grabbed their noses and, like seasick deck passengers rushing for the rail, stormed up the two aisles, hands clapped to their mouths. On stage, fighting his own nausea, General Burrows watched them fight round the locked doors. At last he bent to the microphone that connected with the projection booth and gasped. "All right, Harrison, that's enough now."

"Sorry about that, General," said Harrison laconically. "Guess I hit the wrong button. Antidote coming up."

Fan blades whirred and a loud sucking noise sounded. Ears popped as waves of narcissus fragrance blew through, followed by puffs of pure, scentless air. With eyes streaming, the scientists—gasping, wiping their mouths with handkerchiefs, came back down the aisles to their seats, not one of them speaking. After a minute or two General Burrows spoke. "That was an accident. Harrison apologizes for causing you discomfort. You recognized the odor of course, most of you anyway. That's the odor given off by Consolvo's Ulceration in an advanced stage of putridity. Not the real thing, of course. That would be too dangerous. Our chemists synthesized this imitation for a briefing we gave down here in The Hole the other day to some senior HEW people. Quite authentic, wouldn't you say?"

Back in his front row seat, looking subdued and pale, Lambdin spoke. "I got the message, General. I guess I needed it. I forgot temporarily where the priorities lie."

"Here too," said Frank Weinstein, in a conciliatory manner. "I'd like to apologize for losing my temper. And if you don't have anything terribly important to keep us for, I'd like to get back and brief my people on this vaccine program coming up."

There was a general murmur of agreement. Even Paul Ruffec, leaning back ashy-faced as the woman in the next seat fanned him with a magazine, waved his fat hand in feeble assent. Duval Badin, looking daisy fresh and grinning like a white-haired imp, gave Burrows the A-OK sign.

"This was all I had," said Burrows, "and I want to thank all of you for your cooperation. I don't know if I will be with you again. The President has named a deputy to Dr. Simon Green to take charge of what he's calling his Epidemic Task Force, a Dr. Noah Blanchard from Cook County General Hospital. Some of you probably know him. I've read his curriculum vitae and he's a first-class man. So if I don't see you again, thank you for your help."

After the gathering had dispersed and the Marines had been dismissed, Burrows slumped in a chair backstage, tie pulled down, beribboned blouse unbuttoned. He sipped coffee tiredly. Sergeant Harrison watched him with worried blue eyes. "Look at it like this, sir. It could be a chance to take off, go see about your folks in California."

"That's a thought."

Minutes passed. Like an old married couple these two conversed elliptically. "It ain't like being relieved of command, sir."

"It rankles like it." Burrows scowled and then grinned a

little. "That was a hell of a trick you pulled. That was pure inspiration."

Harrison's eyes showed pleasure. "Ah, them goddamn feather merchants. Squabbling like babies. I couldn't think of no other way."

"It was exactly right. But don't underrate them. The principle they were arguing about is basically what's going to shape this country in the future—if it's got a future."

"I don't get you, sir."

"You will after you think about it. You've been ahead of me for years, ever since you hauled my ass out of that hospital cot when Charley got his mortar fire ranged in. Why me? Why not one of the white officers?"

Harrison was embarrassed. "Shit, sir, like I always try to explain, you was my company commander."

"You say that every time, but I think the reason goes deeper than either of us can understand. Look, even if this vaccination program works—a crash program like that, and we get everybody vaccinated—at ten percent that means killing twenty million people. Think about that a minute."

After a pause, Harrison said, "I can't. That's too many to think about."

"That's just it. Nobody can. Figure that size, it's an abstraction. Which is what a lot of those scientists—not just the left-wingers either—are scared to death of."

"You're still way ahead of me, General."

"How many times have I told you the story of my life, Harrison?"

"A couple of times." Harrison smiled. "First time was when you'd been operating all night and couldn't sleep and got into the prescription whiskey. Every time you got worn out, seems like."

"Well, you know how I feel about this country. My father and mother were minor government clerks in Washington. They couldn't have sent me to medical school any more than they could have flown. But the government did send me. Out of guilt for two hundred years of race discrimination maybe. Or because there was a president with a wife named Eleanor Roosevelt. For a lot of reasons. I'm grateful. Look at me, the highest ranking black doctor in the whole history of the regular American army. You think that doesn't make my old dad in Anaheim—God, I hope he's alive!—proud? His father was a livery stable hand and *his* father a Maryland slave. You think I don't love this country?"

"I know you do, sir." Harrison wondered if the general would consider a drink. It was past normal quitting time and he knew where the bottle was.

"But I'm worried. Not just about this epidemic. Even if we survive it. They booed Solzhenitsyn at Harvard when he said America had lost her moral courage, but a lot of people think he was right. I do, too. All those pacifists who opposed the Viet Nam War, as Solzhenitsyn said, did they hear the moaning of the thirty million victims of its aftermath? Did they realize they were guilty of complicity? You know better. This country is fat, soft, lawless, selfish, indolent, and increasingly illiterate. The only god it worships is material well-being. Maybe God is punishing it with this epidemic. I don't have the old-time religion, so I can't say that, except in a metaphorical way."

"How would you like a little bourbon and branch, General?"

"Sure. But let me lay this out first. It's been eating at me and I want to lay it out."

"Yes sir."

"People who believe that our only hope is to go back to the old frontier self-reliance, the Puritan ethics, all that—and there are lots of them—might view this disaster as a God-sent last chance to get the country back on the right track—to purge it of the criminal and indolent and wastrel elements of the population. Some of those people are racists and bigots and all kinds of fringe lunatics—Ku Kluxers and American Nazis and—if they had the power—Black Muslims and American Indian Movement followers and Chicanos who think they ought to have California back—all the nuts aren't white, you know. Suppose you had the political power to choose. And you've got a chance to get rid of trouble-makers and dissidents and welfare-cheaters and pot-smokers and hippy communes and Weathermen groups and convicted murderers and congenital idiots and so on. Who would you pick?"

Harrison said, "Sir, I just remembered. I promised my wife if I could get away, I'd take her to the store."

"Oh, go on. You don't need to listen to me."

"She still don't like it in Washington, sir. One of these days I got to take her back to Little Rock."

"Good. You offered me a drink, you know. Listen. I'm about done now. A lot of the President's closest advisors might just be thinking along those lines. My God, change my complexion and give me a New England or a Kansas or a Utah—somewhere where the old virtues still count—upbringing, decency, morality, and all that—and I might be thinking it too. That's what those scientists are worried about. Some. Some of them—like Shockley with his race theories—might think it's a good idea. For all I know, President Dobson—he might be thinking the same thing himself. Yeah, I'll have that drink now."

Chapter 8

From Thursday afternoon to Saturday, utterly ignorant
that he had been elevated to national prominence without
anyone bothering to consult him on the subject, Noah
Blanchard slept and half-woke and slept again in a
surrealistic depth of exhaustion. He would rouse dimly
and, finding Kate there, seize her in a dreamlike frenzy,
would wake later and, finding her gone, lie torpid in the
shadowy room, hearing the desert breeze rustle the drawn
drapes as he struggled for reality, wondering if she was
real or only a phantom of his imagination.

But at last and all of a sudden he came fully awake,
fresher and more alive than in months. His watch had
stopped but the slant of the sun between the drapes
suggested afternoon. He yawned profoundly, hitched
himself up the rumpled pillows, and gazed with admiring
disbelief down the naked length of his lanky, battered
body. A small, half-shamed grin came over his face.
Thirty-nine years old, he marveled, four days and nights
working without sleep in that pesthouse and, unless I
dreamed it, all a sexual performance little short of
phenomenal. I ought to write myself up for the medical
journals. My God, what a woman she is. He swung his
legs round and sat on the edge of the bed, and a punitive

ache stabbed him in the lumbar region. You earned that, my friend, he thought happily, and scratched his stubbled chin. My God, what a woman.

He heard a doorknob turn and saw the door to the adjoining room open. Kate backed in, carrying a covered tray that smelled of coffee and hot bacon. Noah salivated. "Good morning, Ms. Petrakis!" he said gaily and stopped an impulse to pull the bedsheet over his groin. "Hey, you really pulled a fast one last night. You were terrific. God, that smells good."

She put the tray on the nightstand. "Don't tell me I surprised you! You were great too. . . . Well, I knew you'd be hungry. I'm no cook, but it's bound to taste better than that leftover goop those soldier cooks in the kitchen had to offer."

She looked delicious, thought Noah, brown and barelegged in brief white shorts and red halter-top, touseled black hair tied in a red ribbon above her flushed face. It must be a sweatbox downstairs, no windows and the air-conditioning out. "I bet you're a wonderful cook. You want to throw me a shirt or something?"

Kate pulled a long-tailed yellow shirt from his suitcase, held it up for inspection, and tossed it over. "That ought to cover your modesty," she said and went to open the drapes. Bright sunlight flooded the room.

Noah fell hungrily to his breakfast—watery scrambled eggs, flabby toast, burnt bacon. He had never tasted anything better and said so.

"You're lying," said Kate contentedly, sitting down across the room from him. She pulled a pack of cigarettes from her halter-top and lit one. "I'm the world's champion bad cook. It's the only thing Otho DeBoyd and I ever really agreed on."

Noah pursued the last dab of runny egg with the last corner of flaccid toast. "You're a great cook," he assured her. "Who was Otho?"

"I do expect it tasted better than the stuff the National Guard offered—creamed chipped beef on toast. I won't tell you what the KPs called it. Otho was my first husband—veddy First Family of Virginia from Norfolk with Confederate ancestors hanging in the parlor. God how it frizzled their Shinto souls, Otho marrying a little Greek nobody whose father had run the picture show in Torrington, Connecticut."

"I'm an old soldier," said Noah. "I know what creamed chipped beef on toast is. Shit on a shingle. If you'll pardon the expression, that's what Otho's family was full of, if that's what they thought of you."

"Don't apologize. I'm a case-hardened old TV news-hen, remember. I know all the words."

Noah patted his stomach. "Thank you for my breakfast. It was just what I needed. Now I ought to shave, if there's a light in the bathroom."

"You don't need a light. I'll show you." Kate led him to the bathroom door, and opened and adjusted it carefully to the angle she wanted. The full-length mirror inside it caught and reflected sunlight from the windows at the mirror over the washbasin. "Neat, huh?" she said proudly. "I figured that out the other day in my room next door."

"Bravo," said Noah. "You must have a degree in Optics."

"Mass Comm," she reminded him. "From Missouri."

"That's right. I remember now. You worked on a switchboard." Noah dug out his toilet kit. "Look, while I shave, why don't you bring me up to date on what's been happening in the world since I passed out."

Kate went back and sat down. "Where do you want me to start?" She drew deeply on her cigarette.

Noah squirted shaving cream on his face. "Begin at the beginning, go on to the end, then stop."

"You've been reading *Alice*."

He grinned. He wondered what had happened to the petulant Lady Libber who had been so irritated with him, driving from the airport. Maybe Kate Petrakis was one of those happy souls who thrive on emergency and assume leadership in lifeboats and after car wrecks. He finished shaving in thoughtful deliberation and sluiced his face with stinging lotion. What a situation, he mused. No patients waiting for him, no classes to meet, no appointments to keep, no phones that could ring, alone in a motel room with this delightful, accommodating lady. Lady was the word, too, whatever the archaic term denoted. Whatever had made her slip into his bed— compassion, penitence, love, lust, the need to cling to another human being in a time of widespread dying, he was sure the reason wasn't sex for mere recreation.

"It's like living through a siege," said Kate hesitantly, "That's what I told Colonel Ryerson, the nice befuddled, middle-aged commander downstairs. He's terribly worried because his boys keep slipping away from patrol and running home. He's from Las Cruces—sells insurance there—and I think he'd like to slip off and run home too. We decided it was more like a siege than anything. But then I thought it was more like the *Decameron*, with those Florentine people holed up hiding from the plague. But Colonel Ryerson wasn't familiar with Boccaccio."

"The *Decameron* was hot, taboo reading when I was a Winnetka high-school kid."

"Winnetka. huh? One of those north shore aristocrats."

"Just bourgeois, Kate, plain old suburban bourgeois. Why do you call it a siege?"

"Well," she said doubtfully, "the Conquistador is kind of a sanctuary guarded by armed troops, and the civilians are out there in the city, and Colonel Ryerson sends his patrols in to keep the streets quiet and prevent arson and looting and protect the food when it arrives. I have this feeling that the people are sort of lurking out there, like hostile Indians around a fort. That's silly, of course. There's no reason they'd want to break in on us. But it's how I feel."

"How do you get along with the troops? Do any of them bother you? You know what I mean."

"Oh no. Not really. Mainly I get along fine. They

appreciate my helping in the dining room—chow line they call it—and running the switchboard, what few calls come in or go out. Anyway, they're just boys, homesick boys most of them, not my idea of real soldiers."

"They aren't," said Noah. "You said you got along fine 'mainly.' Somebody giving you a hard time?"

Kate shrugged. "Oh it's not anything I can't handle. Or go to Ryerson about, if I have to. I'd hate to do that though. It's just their adjutant, this captain, who breathes down my neck and makes innuendoes about how I ought to be nice to him, being a 'guest of the Guard,' as he puts it. You and I are the only civilians left, you know. All the others have vanished, even Higgins, the assistant manager.

"This adjutant," said Noah, nearly cutting himself, "is he a plump kind of middle-sized jerk with a fuzzy mustache?" He was astonished at the fury he felt.

"That's Freddy Wilmarth to a T," said Kate. "When did you meet him?"

"Oh, we had a halfway run-in. He's one of God's natural born jerks. So he thinks you ought to be nice to him, does he?" Really, thought Noah, I haven't felt this jealous about a woman since I can remember. What's the matter with me?

The edge in his voice seemed to startle Kate. "It isn't anything to worry about," she said. "He's just a pill. I've been handling his kind since I was fourteen years old."

Noah made a conscious effort to suppress his anger. "Is there a Lieutenant Simpson still around?" he asked. "A nice kid, looks about nineteen? I met him coming through town Thursday."

"Jeff Simpson? Oh, he's a love. I dote on Jeff. He's the one who's told me how scary it is in the city. Everyone hides until the food trucks arrive to unload at the ration points—and people creep out to grab their share and then scuttle back. It's horrible. It's not like America at all." Kate stubbed out her cigarette, stood up suddenly, and went to Noah. For the first time he saw past her easy, bantering manner. She was frightened. He could see it in her eyes. She clutched his shirt and stared up at him. "Horrible, just horrible. Oh, Noah, is there any hope? How is all this going to end?"

An immense tenderness welled up in him. "Hey, I don't want to get shaving cream on you." He finished shaving and patted aftershave lotion on his face, then drew her close and petted her. The way he felt was nothing like what he vaguely remembered of his earlier voracious passion. They had been in the closest physical intimacy, but now he did not know what words or touches would comfort her. He stroked her shoulders. "We'll make it," he repeated. "They'll come up with a vaccine soon. This isn't the Dark Ages."

"How do you *know*?" she moaned, clinging and shivering. "How can you be sure? Maybe we just wait until we all catch this sickness and die of it. Or maybe the food will stop coming first. I don't see any hope of help. We don't know what's going on anywhere else. We're cut off. It's worse than a siege. It's like being shipwrecked—marooned—on a desert island and no rescue coming."

"Hush, now, hush." He stroked her hair. "They'll find a vaccine. It's just a matter of time. Just a matter of holding out until they do."

She pulled back to stare up at him, tears glistening in her eyes. "You say that, but how do you *know*?"

"I don't *know* it. But you have to believe something. And the probabilities favor it. They've already found a carrier."

"And lost him." Kate pressed herself against Noah again, her damp lips moving against his bare chest. In some distant place he felt sexual urgency stirring. Under the circumstances, it was embarrassing, but there it was and it was growing. "They don't know where he is," murmured Kate.

"They'll find him. Or another. Or isolate the organism without him. Hush now. Hush, Kate. Hush, baby." His arms tightened around her, and like a child she turned her face up for a kiss. The kiss deepened, grew more urgent. He felt her breath quickening, her lips parting. Holding her close he began moving sideways towards his bed.

"No," she protested, pulling away as he pressed her. "No. Not—not—" It was half gasp, half laugh. "My room. My bed. Yours—all torn up. Please."

He threw a pair of pants on, and they moved blindly down the hall, kissing, caressing, tripping over their tangled feet towards her room. On the tufted bedspread, still kissing her, Noah slipped her halter-top free, unzipped the slide fastener of the white shorts while Kate, eyes closed, murmured softly between kisses.

Long afterwards, the day fading to dusk outside the draped windows, Noah lay in spent contentment, fondling Kate's body as she talked at first in fragments, then in sustained narrative, as if to justify herself. It was outwardly a banal enough biography. A pop sociologist would have summed it up in a paragraph—ambitious working woman on her own in late twentieth-century America.

A Flaubert or Tolstoy, on the other hand, might find the stuff of a novel in it. So far as Noah was concerned she was—if contradictory—simply the most exciting female he had met in years, and if he wasn't careful he might fall in love with her, a dangerous emotional state for a middle-aged bachelor.

Katherina Petrakis—the maiden name reclaimed after her second husband, a television writer and an alcoholic, plunged his car down a California mountainside—had spent an ordinary childhood in a Connecticut industrial town until television killed her father's neighborhood movie business and in the process killed him, too. Kate remembered boisterous, barrel-chested Nick Petrakis with grateful affection, but the ruling influence on her life had been her mother. Hannah Colter Petrakis was old Yankee stock gone to seed. The Colter family had produced clipper captains and Congregationalist ministers, Yale-trained missionaries and Transcendental philosophers, but by Hannah's generation had petered out to a single branch on an exhausted farm above the Naugatuck. When Nick Petrakis, the cobbler's son, home from the South Pacific as a decorated Marine Corps lance corporal, came courting, Hannah perhaps considered any marital chance better than her job on a Torrington assembly line. She could not forget her lofty origins, though, and when a daughter was born, last and brightest of her five children, she swore that Kate at least would not marry beneath herself. She did not use those words, but the meaning was clear. Kate would not throw her life away in the grime of a factory town, a drab slattern slaving for husband and kids. Kate would Be Somebody. She had Colter brains. She must go to college and Be Somebody. She must escape female servitude. All through Kate's adolescence Hannah preached incessantly—be independent, don't let a man waste your life. Although Nick's coronary and lingering death wiped out his savings, GI insurance, and the equity in the parking lot the movie theater had stood on, Hannah scraped up a few hundred dollars when Kate graduated as class valedictorian and Nick's old VFW post kicked in with a small scholarship grant. Together they got Kate from Torrington to the University of Missouri's famed school of journalism where she specialized in Television, her father's nemesis. Hannah had predicted that TV would be a whole new medium of communication in which women could rise as fast and high as men.

She sounds like a remarkable woman, said Noah, yawning. She was that all right, said Kate. Ma was certainly remarkable. Remarkably bitter, remarkably full of hate. For herself, her life, the world. I owe everything I am to her. Such as it is. It seemed an odd way to put it, but Noah was too sleepy to ask questions and when he opened his eyes again it was nighttime and she was gone. Back in his own room, he changed his clothes by the single lamp bulb and went downstairs.

The Conquistador lobby was dim-lit and empty,

soundless except for the distant pounding of the gasoline engine generator. From the shadowy reception desk someone spoke. "Miss Petrakis said you'd be coming down. I'm Colonel Ryerson, Dr. Blanchard. Supper's over but one of the cooks could fry you something."

"That's okay," said Noah. "Kate brought me a tray a while ago. Then I went back to sleep again."

"She said you'd been working day and night in a clinic in town. You two old friends back in Chicago, eh?"

"Well, more or less," said Noah. In the dim light Ryerson seemed to be about forty-five, a heavy man in rumpled suntans. "Where are all your troops, Colonel? On patrol?"

Ryerson grunted. "Mostly. What's left of them. Last week this was a battalion. Rate they're going over the hill, pretty soon I'll be down to a corporal's guard. Come on back and have some coffee."

"Coffee sounds good," said Noah, coming around the reception counter. A teletype machine clattered nearby.

"Great God," said Ryerson. "Don't tell me somebody's finally sending us a message."

The clatter stopped and a tech sergeant in fatigues appeared, a piece of TWX paper in his hand. "Another garble, Colonel," he said disgustedly. "Bunch of letters all run together. It's not code, not any code I ever heard of. No coding symbol either."

Ryerson read the paper aloud. "CGGG XYBLNSZXX BLN BLNCH RPT BLN YOTYPRTBLNC ZZOQ RPL URGNT RPT URGNY..." He shook his head. "Reply urgent? Reply what and who the hell to. But as least somebody's trying to tell us something. That beats the nothing we've been getting. Stay with it, Wheeler. Is Miss Petrakis on the switchboard?"

"I'm covering for her. She took off for coffee or to go to the can or something, a while back. Switchboard's dead anyway."

"Well, holler if a message comes through. As if I had to tell you. That TWX make any sense to you, Doctor?"

98

Noah shook his head. "Cryptology's out of my line."

"Mine too," said Ryerson. "Come on back to my office." In the first room a young soldier was reading a comic book. "If you can tear yourself away from that," said Ryerson, "you might bring us some coffee. How do you like yours, Doctor?"

"Black coffee, thanks."

"One black and white coming up," said the Charge of Quarters cheerily. "Anything else, Colonel? Piece of pie? Doughnuts?"

"You see Miss Petrakis in the kitchen, tell her Dr. Blanchard's up. Goddamn it, Manuel, you know I'm on a diet."

"Yes, sir," said the CQ grinning. Ryerson seemed to have a good rapport with his orderly room people, thought Noah. Must be a pretty good commander at that. In a panelled office Ryerson waved him to a couch and slumped behind a desk.

"What I'd like," said Noah after a long silence, "is a rundown on conditions. I've been asleep since Thursday. Far as I know, everybody in the country but us could be dead by now."

"I couldn't swear they aren't," said Ryerson gloomily. "Thanks, Manuel. You tell Miss Petrakis?"

The CQ put down two white coffee mugs. "Didn't see her, sir. Nobody knew where she was."

"Probably gone up to her room. Go on back to your comics, son." After the CQ left, Ryerson said, "Manuel's a good kid. They're mostly good kids, the ones that've stuck. But still kids—don't know their asses from deep center field. I could make soldiers out of them if I had time. I don't know how much time I got. I don't know a goddamn thing. Nobody sends me any orders. When this epidemic got out of control the governor sent us here to keep order. Since then I haven't heard a goddamn thing. From Santa Fe, or Washington or the National Guard Bureau or anybody. It's not easy trying to hold these kids together that want to go home where they're scared their

99

folks are all sick or dying. Hell, I'd like to go home, too. But I got this city to police, food trucks to convoy, burial details to provide. Every day I got fewer troops to do it with. They melt away. They go on patrol and some days don't half of 'em come back. Discipline's gone to hell. Some of my best men are beginning to crack. I'm running out of officers and noncoms. I'm not even sure I got an adjutant anymore—haven't laid eyes on that paper-pushing son-of-a-bitch all evening. And he don't even go out on patrol. Ah, screw it." He gave Noah a disarming grin. "Thanks for letting me blow off steam. Can't let my boys think the Old Man's worried. You want to know what I really think?"

"I've been waiting for you to get around to it."

"Yeah, I talk a lot. In Las Cruces, people buy insurance from me sometimes just to get me to shut up."

"What I want," said Noah, "is specific information about the state of the epidemic, how far it's spread, casualty rates, any instances of spontaneous remission, any progress towards a vaccine. What can you tell me along those lines?"

"I had a medical detachment last week," said Ryerson reflectively. "Two doctors and some corpsmen who could answer you, maybe. Now they're scattered all over Albuquerque, in hospitals and places, trying to help with this epidemic, the ones that haven't caught it and died. You know they're hauling dead people off in dumptrucks, bulldozing them into mass graves?"

"I saw it being done Thursday. Don't you have any solid information?"

"All I got is a strong suspicion that things are getting worse. I suspect I'm getting no orders from Santa Fe or Washington because nobody knows anything to tell me. I suspect they've written off Albuquerque—maybe the state, hell, the whole Southwest—and are concentrating on saving cities back east. Out here we can sink or swim, get well or die. That's my suspicion."

"That's pretty paranoid, Colonel."

"Yeah? Then why the hell don't we receive any TWX messages? Why don't we get any phone calls? All the hardware's intact—wires and antennas and communications satellites, right? My Signal people think so anyway. Either the communicators—the people that keep the phones and radios and TVs and telegraph and all that working—either they're all dead, or somebody's clamped down."

The teletype clattered, ceased, clattered and stopped again. Ryerson looked up expectantly, but no one came from the Message Center. Noah sipped his cooling coffee. "What's my best bet for getting back to Chicago?" he said.

Ryerson looked incredulous. "You haven't heard a word I said. Don't you understand? Albuquerque's cut off, no trains, planes, buses, anything. You try to drive out and somebody will shoot you for your car or you'll run out of gas and no gas stations are open. Doctor Blanchard, you're not going anywhere. Nobody is. We are cut off, O–F–F, off—WHAT THE HELL IS THAT?"

A pistol had fired upstairs. Ryerson spun out of his chair and through the door, Noah on his heels. He caromed off Manuel outside and pounded past Wheeler gaping at the reception desk. In the lobby, cooks and KPs were running out of the kitchen, and two sentries, rifles at high port, dashed in from outdoors. "Sound off!" snarled Ryerson. "What was that shot?"

Overhead a woman screamed and Noah darted for the stairwell. At the fourth floor he burst open the fire doors upon a three-figure tableau: Kate pressed to a corridor wall, face bruised and fixed for screaming, clutching to her breast the remnants of her torn red halter top; on his back on the floor a young soldier pressing his hands to his belly; another soldier, back to Noah, a revolver in his right hand shaking convulsively. The corridor smelled of gunpowder.

Without thinking, Noah threw himself at the soldier, clawing for the pistol. "Drop it!" he shouted, praying it wouldn't fire if it hit the floor, but then Ryerson was there, puffing and wheezing, to seize the gun by the barrel and twist it loose.

"Holy God," Kate said, disbelievingly. "He just shot him. He turned around and shot him in the stomach. Just like that. Like it was nothing at all."

The two sentries following Ryerson took hold of the soldier and pushed him back against a wall. Noah remembered him then—the petulant, puffy-faced adjutant, Captain Wilmarth. He looked on the verge of catatonic seizure, paper-white, spittle on his lips, eyes rolling, jerking in every limb. He probably did not even realize what was going on, Noah thought, but it was the wounded man who needed his help. He dropped to the floor beside him, recognizing the young lieutenant, Simpson. His teeth were chattering, his forehead was clammy, his pulse shallow and rapid. "Get him a blanket, somebody," said Noah over his shoulder, "and a couple of pillows to put his feet on. Take it easy, son. Remember me? Doctor Blanchard. Don't worry now. We're going to take care of you."

"Cold," whispered Simpson. "Freezing—sick."

A soldier knelt beside Noah and began tucking a blanket around Simpson's shoulders. "That's the way," said Noah. "Lift his feet now and put those pillows under them. Gently. Don't move his body. May I lift your hands away a minute, Lieutenant Simpson? Just long enough to take a look."

A quick examination showed little, but the little was enough. Simpson needed emergency surgery. Soon. Noah gave Ryerson a quick negative shake of the head. "What did he shoot him with?"

Ryerson scowled at the revolver he held. "Three-five-seven Combat Magnum. Smith. What the hell was Wilmarth doing with a cannon like—?"

"The round, damn it! What kind of bullet went in him?"

"Oh." Ryerson swung the cylinder out to spill

cartridges in his palm. "Thirty-eight Special, standard roundnose. How bad is it?"

Noah stood up and walked Ryerson down the corridor away from the growing crowd of soldiers. "About as bad as it could be. The round went through his belt buckle so along with a bellyful of perforated intestines he's got dirt, clothing shreds, and bits of broken brass in there. Infection probably one hundred percent. I could shoot him full of antibiotics if I had any, which I don't, and if I knew he wasn't allergic to them, which I don't either. I don't know if the slug's still in him or went on through, and the only way to find out is to roll him over which I'm not about to do. He shouldn't be moved, but he can't stay here. He's in shock, which could kill him, but when it wears off he'll start screaming with pain. The place for him is a hospital ER and damn fast. Any suggestions?"

Ryerson's expression was somber. "I've got no ambulance, no medics, not even a litter. Every hospital in town—if it's even functioning—is jammed with epidemic victims. All I can think of is to take a door down and slide him on it and drive him in the back of a weapons carrier out to the Air Base hospital. It could be jammed up too, but a military hospital would make room for him if any place would."

"Makes sense," said Noah. "If it doesn't kill him. But he'll die lying here. Get started then. I'll ride out with him. What are you going to do about the jolly lad who did this to him? He needs a hospital too—a mental ward."

"What that son-of-a-bitch needs," growled Ryerson, "is a rope around his neck. All I can think of is to hogtie him and take him along too. Let the Provost Marshal out there throw him in his stockade or whatever else they can do. What the hell you figure made him do a crazy thing like this?"

"You as much as predicted it," said Noah. "Untrained troops under this pressure. Some are bound to crack. Wilmarth probably couldn't tell you why himself. Just a basically unstable personality that some little thing triggered off. Yes, Kate. I'm sorry. I was going to check you."

She was plucking his sleeve, almost timorously, her bruised cheek even more livid, the torn halter top still clutched to her breast. "Oh my gosh, honey," said Ryerson in genuine distress. "I guess we forgot all about you."

"Give me a minute for Miss Petrakis, Colonel," said Noah, "and I'll be ready to ride out with Simpson. Make them keep him warm, his feet up, and don't let him have have anything—water or anything—by mouth." Taking Kate's elbow, he led her into her room and closed the door.

Inside she gripped his arms. "Oh thank you, thank you! I couldn't bear it any longer, all of them looking at me out there, thinking what they were thinking."

"Hush now," said Noah. "Let's check the physical damage." He tilted the lampshade to throw light on her face. "Wow. That's a beauty. You're going to have a real shiner. But I don't see any eye injury. What did he use, his fist?"

"Of course, his fist," said Kate with feeble spunk. "It wasn't the pistol. He kept that pointed right at my nose." She gulped, sobbed, put her face in her hands. The halter top fell, unnoticed by either of them. Noah soaked a washrag in cold water in the dark bathroom and pressed it to her eye. She took it from him. "Get me a blouse or something out of the closet there. I guess I gave them all a free show out there. You better go back to Jeff. He's dying, isn't he? For coming to help me. A nice boy like that, dying. Freddy Wilmarth must be plain crazy, insanely crazy. I came up to get some cigarettes and he jumped me from somewhere, just pounced on me, pushed me in and down on the bed, pointing that ugly big horrible black pistol—I kept thinking 'phallic symbol' like the psychiatric jargon—a big ugly black steel penis in my face. Ugh!"

"Don't talk about it if you don't want to," said Noah. "There's no reason you have to."

"Yes," she said. "I want to get it out, get rid of it. God. I've known guys that were rough, every girl does, but I could handle them. But not like this. It was pure rape. He didn't even really want—want—you know—it was like he wanted to hurt me mainly. He cursed me, crazy swearing, called me Jezebel and Messalina, tore my clothes and said that if I let *you* then I had to—had to—let him—"

Shame and loathing welled up in Noah. "Jesus," he said. "He must have seen us. I'm sorry, Kate."

"What for? Consenting adults." She laughed bitterly, a tinge of hysteria in it. "Free country. Woman's got a right. Because you like a man enough—that doesn't mean you have to with every—every son-of-a-bitch. That's when he hit me, when I called him that, and I yelled, I guess, scared as I was, and that was when Jeff pushed the door open. He hadn't even locked it. Jeff yelled for him to stop and Freddy—oh my God—he just stood up from me and zipped up his pants—oh yes, it was out, and he put it in calmly and zipped up his pants—and just like a robot or something he turned, backed him out of the room and into the hall, and shot. That's when I finally screamed out loud, really loud. And you know, from that instant, the instant he fired the pistol, from then on he never spoke or did anything. He just stood there and began shaking all over like someone starting an epileptic fit."

"Now look here. You clean up and change clothes and—I don't suppose you've got any liquor here."

"A miniature Scotch from the airplane," she said. "I didn't want it so I put it in my bag."

"Drink it," he said firmly. "That's a medical prescription. And when I get back from taking Lieutenant Simpson to the hospital, we'll decide what to do next."

"I don't want to leave this room," she said dully. "Ever again. Except to leave this place. You know what th— all thinking out there. Or will, after they have a—

talk it over. You know how men are. A woman raped, or almost raped, well, she had to do something to invite it."

"That's foolishness," lied Noah, knowing that it was not, knowing that it would be impossible to leave her here if he succeeded in getting away. He shook his head. Things seemed to be closing in. Someone knocked on the door, a sharp peremptory knock. Noah turned irritably. "Just hold it! I'm with a patient. Just hold it."

There was a second knock, even louder. "You've got to go," said Kate. "Something's probably happened to Jeff. He could be dying or something."

"Christ!" said Noah, and jerked the door open. There, his fist raised in the act of knocking, stood the shortest, angriest-looking Air Force brigadier general he had ever seen in his life. He was a full foot shorter than Noah, so short he had to tilt his head back to look up at him, which apparently infuriated him even more.

"Is your name Dr. Noah Blanchard?" he demanded. "From Chicago?"

"It is, sir!" snapped Noah, furiously aware that as a civilian no one-star pipsqueak could pull rank on him.

"I'm General Kimball from Kirtland Air Force Base. For your information, we've been looking all over for you."

"Sorry about that," said Noah curtly. "Excuse me, I've got a wounded man to attend to."

"Now just a minute, Doctor," said Kimball, but Noah stepped past him through a group of uneasy-looking Air Force officers to squat beside Simpson in the corridor. An Air Force colonel in a pale blue short-sleeved shirt and dark blue trousers was crouched down, examining him.

"I'm Blanchard," said Noah. "Cook County General."

"Glad to know you, Doctor. Greer. I've got the hospital group at the Base. General Kimball brought me along because the message about you had to do with this epidemic."

Wondering what message he meant, Noah said: "What's your opinion here?"

Dr. Greer shrugged. "No doubt the same as yours. Massive antibiotics, essential surgery in a hurry, and if the bullet went through or isn't lodged in his liver or pressed against his spinal column and if he's got a good enough constitution and a few other if's he might make it. If we hurry. Concur?"

"Concur," said Noah. "Can you get an ambulance for him?"

"Already sent for. We've got radio contact with the base."

"Outstanding," said Noah, slipping back into military slang. "What about the officer who shot him?"

Greer shrugged again. "I've got a Close Confinement Ward. It's damn near full of nuts since this epidemic got going good. One more won't matter. Listen, Doctor, I don't want to butt in, but General Kimball is a kind of short-fuse flyboy. I know he's nothing to you, but it might be smoother all around if you indulged him."

"As you say, Colonel," said Noah. "And many thanks for taking these two off my hands." He rose and with a pleasant smile said, "What can I do for you, General?"

Kimball gave him a hard stare followed by a hard, short laugh. Behind him the half-dozen Air Force officers and Colonel Ryerson winced visibly. "Do for me?" said Kimball. "What can you do for me? That's funny. That's funny as hell. Here I am trying to run an air base in the middle of this damned epidemic without any orders from anybody anywhere except to ground all my airplanes a week ago and since then not one word from anybody—until this evening when a personal message comes to me from the Secretary of the Air Force—Kimball Personal from the *Secretary* of the *Air Force*—to drop everything and make it my personal business to locate one Dr. Noah Blanchard from Chicago believed to be in the Albuquerque area."

"Excuse me," said Noah. "I'm not following you. The Secretary of the *Air Force*?"

"Oh hell," said Kimball. "He's way down the line. He's

just an errand boy. It's the President that wants you, the *President,* that's all. I got to find you and fly you to him first priority. You're deputy assistant secretary for health and scientific affairs, or something. That about it, Abrams?"

"Essentially, sir," said a slender young aide. "Here's a copy of the message."

"Give it to the doctor," said Kimball sourly. "Now what can we do for you, Mr. Secretary?"

Noah read and re-read the message. Gradually its full import sank in. His first reaction was resentment at Simon Green sticking him with this without even consulting him. His second was relief. Whatever Washington held, here at least was a ticket out of Albuquerque. "Do for me, General?" he said slowly. "Why I expect transportation to Washington, principally. The sooner the better."

"You got it," said Kimball. "There's a T-39 standing by that can have you at Andrews Air Force Base for breakfast. How soon do you want to take off?"

The preposterousness of it all suddenly struck Noah. He almost laughed. "Well, I could leave in fifteen minutes, General," he said. "But it takes a woman a little longer. Say an hour from now?"

"Woman?" Kimball frowned. "You lost me there, sir."

"My executive assistant," said Noah carelessly. "Ms. Petrakis. Came down from Chicago with me. I never travel without her."

Kimball shook his head. "Very well, Mr. Secretary. Whatever you say. My aide will arrange everything. Glad we could help out. If you'll excuse me, I ought to get back to my headquarters. Greer?"

"I'll stay with this wounded man, General," said the hospital commander.

Kimball turned to Ryerson. "We could use a little better liaison between our headquarters, Colonel. Abrams, see to that, too." With a nod, the diminutive general departed, his silent staff on his heels.

Kate was lying down when Noah opened her door, but started up in fright. "Hey, gal," he said. "Get your fanny up and start packing. We leave for Washington in thirty minutes."

"What? Me? Why?"

"Read this crazy message," he said, grinning. "I don't know what all it means either, except that it gets us out of here. And if anybody should ask, you've been my assistant or executive secretary or whatever fancy title suits you for quite a while—came down from Chicago to help me out here. You dig, as they say?"

She read and pondered the TWX. "My God," she said at last. "What a guy I seem to have latched on to. Okay, Chief. Mister Secretary Doctor, sir."

"Cut that out," said Noah. "Just get your tail in high gear. We leave in thirty minutes."

When he left, Kate sat pondering. At last, after a few false starts, she wrote a note, sealed it in a motel envelope and telephoned Sergeant Wheeler on the switchboard. By the time he knocked on the door she was packed. "Yeah, Kate?" he said. "I heard you were taking off, you and the Doc. Pretty soft, I call it."

"Government business," she said mysteriously. "Not many people knew it, but Dr. Blanchard and I are both connected with HEW. Listen, you said you knew Mel Arbor downtown at Channel Seven, didn't you?"

"Yeah," said Wheeler. "We worked in a TV station in Roswell together. Why?"

"Well, get this note to him after I leave. It's important. Kind of hush-hush, too. So keep your mouth shut about it, will you? There's fifty bucks in it for you. Okay?"

"Aw, you don't have to pay—*fifty*? Well, I could use it. Sure thing. I'll ride in with a patrol tomorrow; say I want to check on all the communications facilities in town. If Mel Arbor's still alive, I'll get your note to him."

"He'd better be," said Kate. "He'd damn well better be. Thank you, Phil." She gave Wheeler the envelope, two twenties and a ten, and a quick kiss and pushed him out.

An honorable man by his own lights, Sergeant Wheeler waited until enough hours had passed to make it certain that the T-39 in which Noah Blanchard and Kate Petrakis were escaping from the sealed-off pesthole Albuquerque would not turn back before he read the note.

"Dear Mel," it read. "For God's sake, get word somehow to the LA office or Maury Murray or *anybody* at top level at GBC that I have the absolute inside track on the new national epidemic task-force chief. You might call me a sleeping partner. Tell them to stand by for word from little Kate in Washington."

I wonder what the hell that means, thought Wheeler.

Chapter 9

Secretary of Defense Charles Cohane with his pink pugnacious Irish face and stocky hodcarrier physique reminded Noah of Mr. Jiggs in the old comic strip. Attorney General Hiram Cawthorp looked severely aloof as a history-book illustration of General Robert E. Lee. And President Dobson, behind a great desk cluttered with miniature flags and warship models, resembled an actor made up to play Abraham Lincoln. Noah distrusted all three. He was used to straightforward men: soldiers, scientists, doctors. These were devious political figures who commanded frightening power. They put him instinctively on guard.

"They taking good care of you, Dr. Blanchard?" Dobson's eyes searched him from under shaggy brows. "They giving you everything you need?"

It was an impossible question. "I'm not sure yet what I'm going to need, Mr. President," said Noah cautiously. "But so far everyone has done everything they could."

It was thirty hours since General Kimball's airplane had landed him at Washington National Airport in a red-streaked dawn where Simon Green was waiting with an HEW limousine and carryall and two GS-15 assistants. He had wrung Noah's hand, accepted Kate with beaming approval and driven them away in the limousine, leaving the high-priced flunkies to follow glumly in the van. Even for that early morning hour the streets of Washington looked eerily deserted. Simon said the city was so paralyzed by the epidemic that he had had to lease a suite at the Fleur d'Or Hotel on Embassy Row where OPEC sheiks with harems usually stayed, to make sure Noah would have an office and a place to live.

When they drove up to the canopied entrance of the hotel, a doorman and two pages in uniform and an assistant manager in a morning coat came out to bow them in. Simon dismissed his HEW aides and marched grandly in, Kate on his elbow, Noah following behind suspiciously. The suite was palatial: huge reception room and dining alcove with fireplace and parquet floor furnished in *Louis Quinze* rococo, five bedrooms and a butler's pantry where a French-speaking waiter immediately began serving breakfast of melon, truffled eggs, Georgia ham, Maryland shad roe, croissants and French-grind coffee. Kate and Simon fell to hungrily, but Noah merely sipped coffee, finally demanding an explanation for all this Lucullan extravagance.

Simon winked at Kate, his full-moon face creasing jovially. Why, it was simple, he said. President Dobson wanted his Plague Czar to have the best of everything, cost no object. Anything Noah wanted, by golly he could have. For instance, to set up an office for him, Kate, as his executive assistant, only needed to phone General Services and the HEW clerical pool to have office furniture and business machines and people to use them sent over. Not every government clerk had hidden from the epidemic, and Noah had priority over everything and everybody in Washington. Whatever was needed, just order it. Would that include personal necessities, asked Kate demurely, adding that she had been living out of a suitcase for days. Absolutely, beamed Simon. Phone any boutique in town and charge what you want to HEW. And don't worry about the price since HEW had the biggest slice of the budget of anybody, bigger even than the Defense Department.

Good God, Simon, said Noah, you'll bankrupt the country. But when he returned to the Fleur d'Or that evening, disheartened by ten exhausting hours of briefing in General Burrows's underground war room, Kate made a tempting sight at the dinner table in a brand new lace peignoir from Paris that revealed as much as it concealed. And she had achieved an amazing metamorphosis with the hotel suite, converting all but the dining section and a bedroom into an efficient office. Not that Noah was sure why he needed an office, Burrows's Bethesda layout having seemed totally adequate. But Kate was proud of her accomplishment and full of bright chatter about getting publicity for Noah's epidemic fight, and he was too tired to argue about it.

All that had been yesterday. Now here he sat under the baleful stare of the President of the United States. Like everything that had happened since he flew to Albuquerque—could that be only two weeks ago?—it had a phantasmagoric quality. His mind still reeled from the dimensions of the disaster unfolded by General Burrows's briefing teams, and he had a sick sensation that if he really comprehended its magnitude, he would give way to total despair.

There was a menacing edge in the President's voice. "They had better do everything they can for you. Dr. Blanchard. Anyone who doesn't, I want reported to me. When I assign a man responsibility, I give him the authority that goes with it. Do you understand?"

Noah blinked. "Yes, sir, Mr. President."

"About this army doctor, this General Burrows who's been coordinating the epidemic fight until now, what's your impression of him?"

Noah wondered what the President was getting at. "My impression?" he said warily. "It couldn't be better, sir. General Burrows struck me as first-class—a first-class doctor, scientist, administrator. He's on top of this thing as well as anybody could be. The one decision I've made so far is that I want to keep him on. I want him to stay as my chief of staff." He drew his breath and took the plunge. "Is there some reason, Mr. President, something I don't know about, why I shouldn't do that?"

Dobson glanced over at Cohane who leaned forward in his chair. "This is no time to worry about niceties, Dr. Blanchard," said the Secretary of Defense. "Too much is at stake. We are wondering if maybe General Burrows might harbor a little sneaking resentment of you being brought in like this over his head, an outsider, a civilian, most of all—let's be blunt—a white man. What do you think?"

Noah felt his face go hot with anger. "All I can say to that, Mr. Secretary, is that I don't think so. General Burrows and I talked a long time. I need what he knows. I need what he can do. I trust him thoroughly. In my opinion he's as good an American as anyone. I don't see that his color has anything to do with it."

Cohane scowled. "God knows it shouldn't, Doctor. It doesn't as far as I'm concerned, or the President either. Obviously it doesn't matter to you either. But it might to General Burrows."

"I don't think it does, Mr. Secretary. I certainly didn't get any hint of it."

"I must say," said Hiram Cawthorp smoothly, "that General Burrows impressed me favorably. The way he subdued that outbreak of unruly scientists in his underground sanctum was nothing short of masterly." He chuckled. "And I was a victim of his chemical warfare tactics at that. Dr. Blanchard, I agree with your opinion."

"Why, thank you, sir," said Noah, a little surprised.

"If that's your decision, Doctor," said Dobson, "it stands. Burrows stays and that's an end to it. When I give a man a job, I don't tell him how to do it or whom to pick to help him do it. I'm only interested in his results. Which brings up something else. I insist that you speak your mind with total candor, without any reservations of any kind. What is said in this office is heard only in this office. Nobody tapes conversations here for posterity or for any other reason. So speak out freely, frankly, honestly. Otherwise, what you say is of no value to me. Is that clear?"

Noah nodded. "Perfectly clear, sir. If—" He hesitated.

The ugly Lincolnesque face broke into an unexpectedly attractive smile. In spite of himself Noah warmed to the man.

"If you can only believe me, eh?" Dobson laughed. "Well, you just have to take me on trust. Or watch how these two egocentrics here speak to me with small regard for the dignity of my office or my personal sensibilities. That's the only way their advice is any good to me. It's what I want from you. No dissembling. No pulling your punches. The straight ungarbled truth as you see it. Dr. Blanchard, we're up against the gravest crisis in our history. Unless we get this epidemic under control quickly, it's going to destroy the nation. I don't know how to put it more forcefully. You are the man who has to tell me what to do to keep that from happening. So don't waste my time trying to spare my feelings. Speak out. Speak your mind, no matter whose toes you tread on. Is that clear? Have I convinced you? Do you believe me now?"

"Mr. President," said Noah, "I have to admit that I wasn't sure before, but now I guess I have to say I think I do."

Dobson laughed again. "And that's as positive a response as I'm going to get, eh? Well, I admire prudence. Enough of that. Let's get to specifics. You spent all day yesterday with General Burrows and his people, not nearly long enough, I'm sure, but time is a luxury we haven't got. Tell me what is the most urgent thing for me to do right now."

"That's easy, sir," said Noah. "Get this bogged-down vaccination program cranked up and going again."

"Right!" said Cohane. "Exactly what I've been saying."

"Exactly what we've all been saying, Charley," said Cawthorp wearily. "The question, though, is how? Nobody will take the risk anymore."

Cohane scowled. "How do you get soldiers to risk being shot at in a war? You draft them, unless you can get volunteers."

Cawthorp turned to Noah. "As I'm sure they told you, Dr. Blanchard, there were ample volunteers until it was realized that the vaccine was actually infecting every tenth person who took it. That's when the program broke down."

"Some people would still volunteer," grumbled Cohane. "Some people are still patriots enough to risk it."

"Now cut that out, Charley," said Dobson. "You know perfectly well I won't let you or Hi or the Joint Chiefs or any other principal advisor risk that vaccine. I can't afford to lose you fellows. How would I replace you? Not that you might not catch Consolvo's Ulceration anyway, but if you do, it won't be my fault at least."

Cohane snorted. "Please observe, Dr. Blanchard. The President concedes that he—the country—can afford to lose some people to this vaccination program better than some others. That's all I've been trying to say."

Hiram Cawthorp looked disgusted. "My God, Charley, how did you get to be board chairman of Consolidated Petroleum, reducing complex issues to such simplistic terms? Or maybe that's how it's done in the oil fields—that and being plain ruthless."

Cohane reddened furiously, but managed to grin. "Come on, Hi. Don't try to rile me. I'm not ruthless, just practical. Why is it more ruthless to draft people to stick with a needle than to send off to fight? This is a war, don't forget, a war for national survival, it looks like. If we have to use conscription to fight it, what's new about that? American presidents have fought wars with conscripts for over a century. The only thing radical I'm proposing is that we change the selective service criteria."

116

"Charley, Charley," groaned Cawthorp. "It's not the same thing at all. This is a nation of laws. There are laws against what you're proposing. I keep trying to explain that to you."

"Explain, hell!" Cohane's face had gone so crimson, Noah wondered about hypertension. He wondered how ethical it would be to question Cohane's physician. The President shouldn't be relying in a time of crisis on a cabinet officer in imminent peril of stroke. Forget it, thought Noah. That's not the kind of advice President Dobson wants from you. But it worried him all the same. "Damn it, Hi!" Cohane sputtered. "Let me speak my piece. I know about laws. Hell, I'm no lawyer, but I know about laws. And history. And presidents. Maybe I'm just an uneducated East Texas oil field Irishman, but, damn it, I read history. It's my hobby. And I tell you that what I'm proposing is no more illegal than things presidents—strong presidents—have done in emergencies before now. Sure, what I'm suggesting is technically illegal. But I think it's morally right. It's what is best for the country in the long run. Sure it could be politically disastrous, but President Dobson doesn't give a damn for that. It was nearly politically disastrous for Lincoln to issue the Emancipation Proclamation, but he did it because it was right and he got away with it. Wilson said he wouldn't declare war, but he did it. Because it was the right thing to do. Andy Jackson and FDR and Harry Truman—I could go on and on. When they thought something was right, they did it even if it meant flouting the law. Let's get back to the point—conscription. Lincoln drafted troops to save the Union. Wilson used the draft to raise the American Expeditionary Force. If FDR hadn't pushed through the draft in peacetime—and kept it going with one congressional vote!—Pearl Harbor would have caught the country even more flat-footed than it did. I'm not suggesting anything radical or ruthless. From FDR until the Viet Nam War every administration drafted Americans. It was what killed Lyndon Johnson's political

117

career, and don't think that savvy Texas politician didn't know it would, either. But he did it because he thought it was right, whether it was or not."

Fists clenched, flushed and sweating, Cohane turned from Cawthorp to Dobson. "Mr. President, I don't see how you've got any choice. You either draft subjects for this vaccine program or let the country go down the drain. Maybe it will anyway. But we've got to try to prevent it. Somebody has to be sacrificed. Actually we're only talking about ten percent anyway! And the epidemic is killing at least twenty percent. I'm only suggesting that for once we sacrifice some goats along with the sheep. Sure you'll have protests and riots. Johnson had Yippies and hippies and acidheads and campus slackers and leftwing lunatics. Look at all the nuts—right-wing and left—who howled against the New Deal. Look at the Civil War draft riots in New York." Cohane grinned suddenly, a wolfish gleam of white teeth in his flushed face. "The lousy rioting New York Irish. My folks. Unwashed, brawling, drunken, overbreeding immigrants from the potato famine that the old American stock like Hi's ancestors probably considered subhuman. My lowdown ancestors. Dregs of society. They rioted against Mr. Lincoln's draft. A rich man's war, a poor man's fight, they called the Civil War, and they rioted against being cannon fodder for it. Don't call me a bigot. When I say it's the dregs and misfits we ought to draft for this vaccine program I'm only saying that Mr. Lincoln was right. They were fit for nothing but cannon fodder, those ancestors of mine, and it was right for him to sacrifice cannon fodder to preserve the Union."

"Hear, hear," said Cawthorp mockingly. "What a speech. Charley, you ought to go back to Texas and run for office. My good friend, what you keep proposing is simply against the law. You simply can't force American citizens—not even disenfranchised felons—to submit to a one-to-ten lottery with death. It's simply against the law, a whole host of laws intended to prevent it. Laws for every category, even for those dregs and misfits—whoever they are—you keep referring to. To make it legal you'd have to amend the Constitution. You'd have to assemble a quorum on Capital Hill and God knows if you could, the way this epidemic has scattered the Congress, with half the House and Senate already flown the scene. You'd have to fight it through the Supreme Court. Then you'd have to sell it in principle to the doctors and medical technicians who would have to run the program and believe me that wouldn't be easy. Even if all those things were possible, you'd run out of time. Finally, if it matters, you'd have to get a new attorney general, because I'd resign before I became party to it."

Lloyd Dobson had been slumped in his chair, eyes hooded, listening. Now he sat up abruptly. "Give it a rest, Hi. Cool off, Charley. You've both made your points." He turned his hard gaze to Noah. "Perceive the quandary, Dr. Blanchard? My two most valued advisors taking diametrically opposed positions. The hellish thing is that they are both right. We are a government of laws, as Mr. Cawthorp says, not of men. To violate the rights of our citizens by forcing vaccination on them would in a very real way destroy what the country stands for. But when Mr. Cohane protests that I should be statesman enough—as other presidents have been—to rise above laws for the sake of the nation's long-range wellbeing, he is equally persuasive. What always sticks in my craw is that in war we sacrifice our best and brightest people, the very ones we ought to save for the future. Now for once—in a different sort of war for national survival—we have a chance to do that. We have a chance to preserve at least part of the nation's best and brightest at the expense of at least some others who are not quite in that category. Don't misunderstand Mr. Cohane. He's not proposing genocide or class extermination, singling out particular racial or ethnic or economic groups for the vaccine program. He is simply saying that we ought not to risk our most valuable citizens if there are others less valuable the nation could better afford to dispose of. Who would these disposable people be, you ask? Some seem obvious—those whose lives are already forfeited, for instance Death Row prisoners awaiting execution, and victims of fatal diseases wasting away in hospital beds. Then there are people who by any sane criteria have no moral right to live whether the law has condemned them or not—pimps and drug traffickers who prey on children; known, but untouchable leaders of syndicated crime who corrupt the nation's moral fiber; terrorists and anarchists; and lunatic killers such as the Manson Family a decade or so ago. Then there are the criminally insane, the psychopaths, hopeless drug addicts, imbeciles—I could go on and on. I'm sure you could add categories of your own."

For a moment Noah could hardly speak. Then he swallowed his rage and managed a tight smile. "Sure, Mr. President. How about incompetent or drunk or drug-addicted doctors—maybe five percent of the profession—who kill or maim patients that the local health boards never do anything about? Or drunk drivers—or neurotically reckless or stoned drivers—who kill people on the highways and only get their licenses suspended? How about back-alley button-hook abortionists, who kill girls and babies? Or if you want to talk about social burdens, what about infants who are defective or deformed at birth, who can never support themselves? Or welfare cheaters who take money that belongs to the real poor? Or street gangs of adolescents who won't go to school or work at the only jobs they are fit for and who prowl the cities like wolf packs? You want me to go on? There's an old Gilbert and Sullivan opera, Mr. President, with a song called 'I've Got a Little List,' naming all the people the character thinks would never be missed. With all respect, Mr. President, that's what you remind me of."

Lloyd Dobson smiled grimly. "You are precisely correct, Dr. Blanchard. That's the trouble with Charley's proposal. It makes sense until you think about the specifics of trying to apply it. If this government starts choosing certain people to stick deadly needles into—no matter how loathsome or worthless those people are—it's no longer a government of free people. It's no different from the governments of Stalin or Hitler. I suppose when Stalin purged his officers corps or Hitler decided to eliminate the *Untermenschen*—the Gypsies and Slavs and so on—their motives were high and pure, were for the long-range good of Russia and Germany, by their lights. I keep wondering about that. When I find myself wondering which people it might be best to test the vaccine on, I wonder if I'm not thinking like a tyrant."

I misjudged this man, thought Noah. Maybe I misjudged Cawthorp and Cohane too. I let prejudice color my judgment, came into this office hostile and on guard because of prejudice against men I knew nothing about. As he studied the President's lined face, it came to him that Dobson might be the loneliest man in the world. Military service had taught Noah that command is always lonely, but the weightiest command was probably nothing compared to the burden this man bore. Willing to help as Cawthorp and Cohane and the Joint Chiefs and the rest of them were, in the end they could only offer advice. The crushing weight was on Dobson and Dobson alone. A sense of humility came over Noah. Whatever he could do to ease this man's enormous burden he must do. He began speaking slowly, picking words with care.

"No one would ever call you a tyrant, Mr. President. Not if they knew you. Not even if you had to act like one. But that's beside the point. The point is that arguments about which people to sacrifice are simply—I have to be blunt—simply irrelevant. It can't be done that way. You can't just choose certain categories to vaccinate. We simply don't know why it's fatal to ten percent, although it's probably genetic factors. But that's only a guess. The factors could be environmental. To find out, we have to test the vaccine on people of every class and category—by blood type, by ancestry, by all the weird mixtures of ancestry in this melting-pot nation of ours, by occupations and age groups and economic status and by what kinds of food people eat and what their medical histories are and what other kinds of sickness they might be having and—there's no end to the ways of dividing and categorizing people. A vaccine-testing program to be realistic has to include samples of people from every conceivable—even inconceivable—classification. A job that monumental—assuming it could be accomplished—well, there's not the time or place or any practical way of applying any eugenic theories, not matter how noble the motives for them might be. I'm sorry, Mrs. President, but that's the way it is. You told me to be honest."

Dobson contemplated Noah soberly. "So I did, Doctor, so I did. And I believe you. If I didn't think you knew your business, I wouldn't want you advising me. Still, of course, you could be wrong. Maybe events will show that you are. Or maybe that's just my old bad habit of wishful wishing. But you are correct that the arguments are irrelevant, although not for your reasons primarily. The primary reason, as Charley was complaining, is that most people refuse to be vaccinated. They're too scared. No matter what we do to try to persuade them. Public Health Service vaccination terms—more like expeditions actually—have gone out to towns and villages and into ethnic enclaves of cities, using every persuasive device the psychologists and Madison Avenue advertising tycoons could dream up. They appealed to religious and patriotic and political motives, to racial and national pride, even used ethnic cooking for bait which I consider barbarous, the way people are starving, but they argued that the end would justify the means. They used tactics that would have been absurd, Doctor, if they hadn't been tragic! Caravans rolling into Kosciusko Street in Chicago with a soundtruck blaring polka tunes and a priest exhorting people in three Slavic languages to come get vaccinated, and bringing up the rear an Army field kitchen cooking Polish sausage and Hungarian goulash; invading Harlem with hamhocks and cornbread and collard greens on the stove and the soundtruck alternating Marian Anderson

122

and soul rock records and at the mike Black Muslim and Old Time Religion preachers taking turns to urge the people out; going into German and Italian and Jewish and every kind of neighborhood, including lily-white suburban middle-class, with their music and flags and speeches and free food. And they struck out, Doctor. All those teams, wherever they went. People hid from them."

"General Burrows showed me a film clip of one team," said Noah, "that went to a Maryland coal mine town called Wansmere. It was pretty grim, what happened there."

The film clip had opened with an establishing shot from a helicopter of trucks and vans winding into Wansmere, a huddle of miners' shacks around two brick business blocks in the bottom of a mountain ravine. Under the fluttering sound of the rotor blades, the Sousa marches and Country Western tunes that the soundtruck played were tinny and distant. Outside the Town Hall on the main street the caravan halted and set up for business: white-smocked women technicians unfolding chairs and tables beside the laboratory vans, camera crews finding angles they wanted to shoot from, the computer van for screening medical histories pulling up behind the lab van, and in the parking lot Army cooks firing up field ranges to fry ham and flapjacks. When the music stopped, the District congressman, brought along from Washington, stepped to the mike to implore the good folks of Wansmere to come roll up their sleeves for the President's fight against this terrible epidemic and get some good free country cooking to boot.

But nothing happened. Nobody appeared. Beneath the black mountainsides where tipples and slag piles stood and mine mouths yawned, Wansmere was as still as a ghost town. Then the lab girls played a trump card. They broke open big cardboard cartons and began munching Baby Ruth and Milky Way candy bars, letting the paper wrappers fly. By twos and and threes towheaded children came stealing forth from hiding, but as the first child reached for candy a rifle fired, the flat smack of the shot followed by a fusillade. The children scattered, mothers rushed from hiding to seize them, and the technicians and cooks and the congressman dove for cover. Only the cameramen stood their ground, filming away. But a crowd of miners rushed them, swinging pick and axe handles, smashing the cameras, and knocking the cameramen down. Then, as swiftly as it had all happened, the population of Wansmere melted from sight. As the cameramen picked themselves up, a man with a bullhorn started speaking from an upstairs window of the town hall.

"All right now," he bellowed. "You listen to me. This here's the chief of police. You all pack up your traps and get on back where you came from, you hear? We don't want you. We ain't got no sickness here and we don't aim to have nobody a-bringing it to us either. Just pack up your poison needles and cookstoves and get on back to Baltimore or Washington or wherever you come from. Go stick them needles in somebody else, some of them welfare niggers and foreign trash you got down there. Don't come back here messing around with hard-working white folks or next time these boys won't aim their deer rifles to miss."

"That was the most incredible part," said Noah, describing the Wansmere film clip. "That venomous class—and race—hatred. I thought that stuff had gone out of style."

Dobson shook his head. "Unhappily no, Doctor. This epidemic has made it all too clear. Right here in Washington, near the Kennedy Stadium, snipers fired on a vaccination team, accusing it of genocide, of wanting to infect black people with Consolvo's Ulceration. And everybody on that vaccination team was black! Doctors and technicians and drivers. The crowd called them Oreos. How's that for irrational hate?"

"Panic breeds irrationality," said Cawthorp, "and not just among uneducated coal miners and slum blacks. I live in Falls Church, Virginia, where the education and income level must be in the top ten percent nationally, but the reaction to the vaccination team that went there was equally paranoic. I don't mean they opened fire—it's too civilized and law-abiding a suburb for that—but they were just as hysterical. This was in a shopping mall and instead of snipers there were groups marching with signs—League of Women Voters, Jewish liberal groups, PTA's—the very people you would expect sanity from. But no. Test the vaccine on welfare cheaters and hoodlums and derelicts, these signs read, not on honest upright citizens. By which they meant themselves, people with a little money living in low-crime neighborhoods among nice, white-skinned neighbors. Exceptions to that last, of course, since some prosperous Washington blacks have moved to the Virginia suburbs, although most of them prefer the Maryland side."

"One trouble," said Dobson, "is that your melting-pot America, Dr. Blanchard, never existed. It's pure myth. The divergent population elements of our country never really melded. We're a nation divided into an uncountable variety of classes and distinctions of people who, openly or covertly, despise, envy, and fear each other. I wouldn't have believed that a month ago. It took this epidemic to show me."

"So back to Square One," growled Cohane. "*How do we get the necessary cross-section of the population to line up for vaccinations?* Roust them out at bayonet point? Do we have enough bayonets? Would this, as Hiram and others like him insist, destroy the country? But if we don't do it, Dr. Blanchard, how long can the United States survive? What's your prognosis?"

Noah stared at Cohane, the enormity of the disaster that loomed over them finally sinking in. He shook his head savagely, as if to rid it of turmoil. "I assumed you knew the answer to that, Mr. Secretary. According to General Burrows's computers and the best estimates of his experts, at the rate the epidemic is spreading and the rate of progressive deterioration of essential public services and assuming the weather doesn't suddenly turn cold and start freezing people to death, why—two or three weeks. At the very outside, three weeks."

"Three weeks," repeated Cohane, his eyes boring in. "Then what, Doctor?"

Rage at the helplessness he felt made Noah's voice break. "Then chaos," he said. "Mass starvation. Fighting for food in the streets. Looting and murder. Outbreaks of new epidemics from garbage rotting and sewers backing up and malnutrition and exposure and contaminated food and water and—my God! from all sorts of causes. Hospitals swamped. Doctors and nurses dying. Ambulance and emergency rescue crews gone and no police forces and—I'm a doctor, not a novelist or historian or movie director. I don't have the imagination to paint that doomsday picture. All I can say is that nothing that ever happened—nothing since the Black Death six hundred years ago—would come close to it."

"Doomsday," said Cohane softly. "The end of our world. And my good friend Hi here quibbles about breaking a few laws to vaccinate people. Faugh! Doctor, for your information, we may not have three weeks. We may not have three days. Mr. President, isn't it time we informed the doctor of the juiciest aspect of our dilemma—the foreign threat?"

The silence in the office was absolute. Cawthorp sat with his chin on his chest, a man plunged in blackest gloom. President Dobson touched his seamed forehead as if to stroke away pain. For the first time Noah perceived the fine trembling of his fingers. "Why not, Charley?" murmured the President. "Even if it's not a medical aspect. Go ahead and brief him."

Cohane grunted. "Dr. Blanchard, when the Joint Chiefs give me briefings they always start with what they call an Intelligence Estimate of the Situation. You know what that means?"

"I went to the War College," said Noah, a little sullenly. "I remember the gist of it."

"God's sake, Charley," protested Cawthorp, "don't drag it out. Get on with it, man."

"In a minute," said Cohane. "In a minute. Then you remember, Doctor, that an Intelligence Estimate only tells you what the staff thinks the enemy is capable of doing. It doesn't predict what it's going to do."

"That's the commander's decision," said Noah, puzzled. "At least according to American military doctrine. I think British staffs do it a different way. But I don't see what this has to do with—"

"With Consolvo's Ulceration?" said Cohane. "It does, Doctor, it damned well does. Because I'm talking about our enemy's intentions."

"Enemy?" Noah looked blank. "I'm confused. What enemy? Who's an enemy? Except the epidemic, if that's what you mean. Who else is an enemy?"

"Every nation in the world is our enemy," said Cohane softly. "Every country everywhere. Because we've got them scared to death of us. Why do you think, assuming you realize it, that not one government anywhere has called home a single member of its diplomatic corps from the United States? Why do you suppose all the United Nations delegations are still here, even though the UN hasn't met in two weeks? If they had any sense, wouldn't those foreigners get the hell out of this plague-stricken country? Wouldn't they haul-ass for home like our yellow-bellied Congressmen did? You want to know why, Doctor? Because their governments won't let them. They're scared they'll bring the infection with them."

"I didn't know any of that," said Noah. "Not that it occurred to me to wonder about it. But it doesn't make them our enemies. Those countries are simply taking intelligent precautions, it seems to me. In effect, they're putting the United States under quarantine."

Cawthorp sat up abruptly. "That's more civilized

language than the kind their newspapers and radical politicians are using."

"You can say that again." Cohane grimaced. "According to *Pravda,* the U.S. is a running sore in the side of humanity. The Albanians call us a purulent abscess that needs cauterizing if anybody cares about Albania. Peking drops discreet hints that America should be purified, manner not stipulated. Even among our allies they're getting off some venomous stuff: Labor MPs insisting the Prime Minister take action against the abominable Yankee plague; Communist party members in the Chamber of Deputies demanding that France impose sanctions; similar agitation in Rome and Bonn and Athens; everywhere, even in usually quiet Scandinavia. You could write it off as bombast except that American officers in the various NATO headquarters report an ominous tension, an air of secret conspiracy they're excluded from. A host of covert indications convince us that something drastic is brewing; that if we don't bring this damned epidemic under control, soon a consortium of friends and adversaries alike intend to do it for us."

"How could they do that?" Noah looked puzzled. "Nobody knows more about epidemic fighting than Americans. We've got the best public health system in the world. What do those clowns think they—?" He stopped abruptly. "You don't mean that. Surely not. You couldn't. I refuse to believe it."

"I don't want to believe it myself," said Cawthorp. "It's repugnant to my instincts, to everything I stand for. And yet . . ." He shook his head. "In a horrible way it is only simple logic for them to do it."

"I wouldn't believe it at first either," said Dobson. "But now I think we must accept it as an all-too-likely possibility. One so likely we don't dare ignore it, one we must take preventive measures against."

"The *British*?" said Noah incredulously. "With our common heritage, our close history, our language—with

128

Canada across the border and no earthly way to keep fallout—?"

"Canada's infected too," said Cawthorp. "Don't forget that. Consolvo's Ulceration is in Toronto. A few cases. In the west it's worse. Whole sections of Victoria quarantined. Outbreaks in Calgary. So far Quebec seems free, but then upstate New York and Maine are relatively free too. No, I don't think the proximity of Canada can matter much to a British decision."

A horror he had not dreamed of came over Noah. "Oh, my God," he whispered. "R.A.F. bombers targeting us? The French *Force de Frappe*? I could believe those Russian bastards using the epidemic to justify a preemptive strike in the eyes of the world, but the *French*? the *English*? And what about our allies without a nuke or long-range nuke delivery capability? West Germany? Taiwan? Japan? Where do they fit in? The whole idea is simply—" His words faltered.

"Simply unthinkable," said Dobson. "Is that what you were going to say, Doctor? But it's all too thinkable, once you accept a basic premise. Put yourself in the position of a foreign government, however friendly. Consider it from the point of view of Downing Street. A deadly epidemic is raging out of control in the most technologically advanced nation in the world. If American medicine can't arrest it, how can it be arrested anywhere? The most elementary tactic in fighting an epidemic is—what? Isolate and destroy the source of infection? What would you expect Downing Street—no doubt with the heaviest of hearts—to be thinking? If this unknown, unstoppable disease leaps the ocean by airplane, aboard ship, blown by jetstream—in whatever way—to gain a foothold on the Eurasian landmass that in turn is separated by the narrowest of waterways from the vast continent of Africa, then what? The entire human race will face extinction, or at least a death rate so heavy it might usher in a new Dark Age. And you can help prevent it by cauterizing the

129

source of infection with a single massive assault. . . . Aided and abetted and with the moral support of all other nations. . . . What would you do? What is the only realistic, intelligent course of action? Face facts, Dr. Blanchard. We too shared your incredulity until we faced the facts. Suppose the situation were reversed. Suppose the infection were confined to England. What would you recommend—reluctantly and with a heavy heart of course—with the survival of both the United States and most of the rest of humanity at stake?"

"You actually have reliable intelligence—" Noah shook his head furiously—"You have solid strategic intelligence that NATO forces are actually going to...*strike*...with nuclear bombs?"

"Not hard evidence, Doctor," said Dobson. "I doubt if that is possible. But enough evidence to persuade us of its very great and imminent likelihood."

"How—how soon, sir?"

"Best estimates are four to six days. Unless we forestall it some way. Which would mean, as the most desirable of all ways, our arresting the epidemic. But if we can't, we must do something else. Incidentally, Doctor, you realize that all this is of the highest order of classification. Including we four, not ten men in the world know about our awareness of this threat."

Fury seemed to explode in Noah's head. "Those bastards! Those treacherous bastards! After all we've done for them, those double-crossing ungrateful—! Well, obviously there's only one thing for us to do."

"What's that, Doctor?" said Cohane.

Noah swung towards him in blind rage. "Hit the bastards! Hit first!" It was relief to have a tangible target for his anger. "We know their strike bases. Hell, we helped build them. We've got the Russkies plotted too. Down cold. The Navy tracks their subs. We've got all their ground-launch sites in our computers. Best of all, our fighter-bombers with nukes available are stationed from

130

Greece to Norway. Hit the bastards! Turn loose SAC and Polaris and the new Trident—"

"Wipe them all off the face of the earth, eh?" Cohane's chuckle sounded cold as steel. "Eradicate the bastards. You're a man after my own heart, Doctor. One great preemptive global nuclear assault before they can do it to us. Oh fine. Then what? Back to business as usual? Back to bringing our epidemic under control? In the midst of our own radioactive rubble? Because *some* of their retaliatory weapons would be bound to get through, regardless, just as ours would, in a reverse situation. As I know you are perfectly well aware."

"I'm a fool," said Noah, his rage draining away. "You're perfectly right, Mr. Secretary. That's no answer. A holocaust—it would be insane. But look here, they aren't insane either, London, and Paris, and Moscow. They're at least as sane as we are. Doesn't that suggest something?"

"Such as what, Doctor?" said Dobson.

"Well, sir, military intelligence is out of my line, but it just struck me that—Look here. This inferential evidence that you interpret as a massive all-out nuclear assault in preparation, couldn't it equally well be interpreted as preparation for something less—something not quite so insane?"

"I repeat, Doctor, such as what?"

"It's crazy, I admit it," said Noah eagerly, "but putting myself in their shoes here is what I might think. Here is America, ravaged by an epidemic that threatens mankind. There is a vaccine which works. It kills too, but it's ninety percent effective. Only thing is, Americans are scared to take it and for reasons that may not make much sense to a European government, certainly not a totalitarian government, and the President of the United States is unable to make them take it."

"I expect that does have them baffled in Moscow," murmured Cohane.

"Let me finish," said Noah. "As we said already, the primary tactic against an epidemic is to isolate and destroy the source. We don't know the source of Consolvo's Ulceration, but it must be in the Southwest, most likely not far from Albuquerque. So our friends and foes get together for mutual moral support and launch their strike—not against the whole United States!—but against that single probable source of the epidemic. As they see it, most of the local population out there is doomed already anyway."

"But wait," objected Cawthorp. "Even if they wiped out the source, the—ah—causative organism, I think that's the term they were using at General Burrows's underground conference—it's loose now, it could be everywhere—probably is."

"You know that," said Noah. "I know that. So do the European powers. But they could ignore it. Don't you see, it's an *ostensible* justification. What they would really be doing—"

"By Jove!" said Dobson. "Doctor Blanchard, you have a Machiavellian imagination. They would be justifying an enforced vaccination program by us of the most ruthless sort."

"I don't follow," said Cohane.

"I do," said Cawthorp. "It's preposterous. It's ridiculous. I refuse to consider it as remotely possible. On the other hand, I can perceive a fiendish logic in it."

"Especially," Noah went on, "if they *warned* us the strike was on its way and why—oh sadly and sorrowfully and with the heaviest of hearts—they had resorted for the brotherhood and survival of mankind to this draconian measure. It was for our own good, they would explain. And if President Dobson didn't get his act together, they would feel compelled to follow up with another selective, surgical strike against another doomed plague spot: El Paso next time, or Denver, or..."

"This time I have to side with Hi," said Cohane. "I can't buy it."

132

"I didn't say it was so," said Noah, suddenly abashed. "I just said that something of the sort was at least as credible as the insanity of a massive strike nobody could survive."

"He is correct in that," said Dobson thoughtfully. "It is a totally mad scenario, but let's just contemplate it a moment. I have the warning. I have the ultimatum. I see Albuquerque gone in radioactive dust. My choices? All-out war or rooting folk out of hiding at bayonet point, as Charley is fond of expressing it, for forced vaccination. Doctor, I can't say that we are any nearer a solution than we were before, but you have certainly set my imagination off on a different tangent."

"I don't believe it either," said Noah defensively. "But then I can't believe—after reflecting on it—that the Europeans would gang up on us the way you're suggesting for an all-out strike. Not until every hope of stopping the epidemic has been exhausted. And we aren't that far along yet. And I believe that my postulation, wild as it is, is as logical, based on the evidence, as yours. Finally I believe . . ." He floundered. "My God, sir, I don't know what I believe any more. I'm at my wit's end. Temporarily."

"So are we all," said Dobson sadly. A buzzer droned and he spoke inaudibly into a telephone. When he hung it up he said, "That was a reminder that the British and French ambassadors are joining me in a private dinner. Why am I reminded of FDR and the Japanese emissaries on the eve of the Pearl Harbor attack? Gentlemen, I have to meet with the National Security Council at ten in the morning. I would like you here at eight. With more ideas." He smiled at Noah. "No matter how preposterous."

Chapter 10

"You, by God, better believe it, Turner," said Farley Balfour through the cell door at Fairburn Penitentiary. He had finished his hundred push-ups and was hunkered down, breathing easily, one foot tucked under in the way Montagnard tribesmen had taught him. "You better, by God. They gonna barge in here and test that vaccine on us any day. Them laws against prisoners being guinea pigs you talked about, they don't mean shit now. Don't you know what's going on? Don't you listen to the news? Everything gone to hell out there, people hiding and shooting at doctors trying to vaccinate them. Cons like us, we're the onliest people left they can make hold still, long enough to vaccinate."

"If the government wants to, ain't any way we can stop 'em," said Turner Hornbow, a half-Huron. As usual he was squatting on the floor of his cell where for five years he had waited for the State of Indiana—the irony of the name not lost on him—to make up its mind to kill him. He and Farley Balfour and Olin Rodgers, who had been the first black quarterback in the history of the Chicago Bisons, were the sole inmates of Fairburn Penitentiary's Death Row. Rodgers had been there a year, Balfour nearly two, and execution dates for all three had been set repeatedly. Invariably last-minute reprieves had been phoned in from the governor's office, never for any clear reason. The uncertainty they lived by was enough to crack the strongest mind.

Although he had almost no education outside Green Beret infantryman training, Farley Balfour had figured out a way to keep from going crazy—by concentrating on a rigid regimen of physical development. Hour after hour every day he chinned and ran in place and twisted and strained every muscle of his body until by now his stocky plowboy torso was ridged with hard sinew and his shoulders grown wide as a door. Squat and broad, blunt-faced with slate-cold eyes, he looked as menacing as a tank. Actually Farley Balfour was an easy-going Hoosier unless pushed beyond endurance. The sadistic policeman in Logansport who had taken him in on a drunk-driving charge one night and tried to bounce him around an empty cell with his blackjack had discovered it to his mortal cost. Now Farley Balfour sat in Fairburn Pen, puzzled about justice, waiting for the State to get up the courage to electrocute him.

By any ordinary standard Olin Rodgers was probably no longer sane. Through the endless days he sat crouched on his cell cot, his tan, aquiline face—with the handsome corsair beard—buried in his hands, as he moaned softly, reliving the past. Only the year before he had walked the earth like a conqueror. Now he sat friendless and solitary, waiting like a sack of garbage to be thrown away. Only a year before, he had led the Bisons to their first playoff victory, their first shot at a Superbowl. Black fans in Gary, that almost totally black city south of Chicago, had laid on a mighty celebration in his honor; rented a whole downtown hotel for a party. How could he have known it would be a drug scene? How could he know that the armed men bursting in at midnight were narcs on a drug bust? One single blurred instant he could hardly remember now had dashed his life to ruins. Over and over, crouched on his cot, Olin Rodgers relived the night in his mind. If only he could somehow turn back time, undo his fatal act. So he sat, moaning, as indrawn as an autistic child.

Turner Hornbow, in the center of the three cells, had no difficulty keeping sane. Mainly he concentrated on his dreams. For Balfour he felt the unspecified hate he felt for all white men; for Rodgers, his vague contempt for all blacks who had once been slaves. But he was too shrewd to reveal it. When Farley, who was given to country garrulity, wanted to talk, Turner was affable. On rare moments when Rodgers seemed to realize where he was, Turner made casual pleasantries. But principally he lived to himself. Much of the time he was hardly conscious of imprisonment. Being of half-Huron blood, he had two souls, sometimes three, and in his half-Huron soul, guided by the *okie* of the medicine bag worn since his boyhood on a St. Lawrence River reservation, he took far-ranging dream journeys to visit his ancestors sitting in shadowy council in smoky winter ledges. Despite his white education—he had been a law student in Bloomington on a HEW grant for Indian students before his disastrous shooting accident—he had implicit faith in the revelations of his Huron soul. The Mohawk soul, for its quarter-strain of wild Iroquoian blood, could not be trusted. An enraged Mohawk soul demands blood-spilling. It was his Mohawk soul that had put him in prison. As for his sometime third soul, the one for his quarter-strain of Irish blood, it was a puny, stunted thing, hardly a soul at all. His Huron grandfather had often wondered if white men actually had souls.

When Pusgut Morgan, the day-shift C.O., came waddling down Death Row, what he saw in their solitary cells were black Olin Rodgers moaning on his cot with his eyes closed, muscle-bulging Farley Balfour chinning on the bars, and Turner Hornbow, red headband round his lank, black hair, squatting impassive as a block of carved wood. In Pusgut's vocabulary they were Crazy Nigger, Redneck Jocker, Staring Indian. But he was an easy old

136

screw in his last year before retiring and glad to be on Death Row because murderers were the least troublesome of all cons. For an occasional carton of commissary cigarettes he was glad to fetch Hornbow lawbooks from the library and smuggle out his letters to old Red Power cronies from campus days. They were scattered now and few answered, although he had been their hero once, on trial for his life. But Turner could be sure of answers from James Pigeonblood, the half-Apache head of a radical underground American Indian Movement group in Indianapolis. His replies, phrased cryptically to pass prison censors, were as filled with the old revolutionary fervor as ever.

Turner heard from another old campus crony too, Ross Cutnose, the Choctaw star of the University of Indiana basketball team. Ross had been the wildest and most rabid of them all, a roaring drunkard and the noisiest member of the courtroom claque that probably irritated the jury into throwing the book at Turner. At odd intervals during the year—the anniversaries of the Custer victory, of Osceola's death, of the Sand Creek Massacre, always for Columbus Day, Ross sent dry, ironic greetings to Turner. He was a thoroughly respectable Chicagoan now, coach of an all-black championship high-school basketball team in the heart of the all-black Southside.

Pusgut Morgan would have been happy to do favors for Farley Balfour and Olin Rodgers too—for the same reasonable price—but neither ever asked for anything.

"You really serious about this notion you got, Farley?" asked Turner. "You really figure they're going to come busting in here and pin us down and test that vaccine on us? Right in our cells?"

"Goddamn right," said Farley. "Why they got to, Turner, if they want to stop this epidemic. They got no choice."

Hornbow's mind raced. Ordinarily he paid little heed to anything Balfour had to say, but in a recent dream his shadow ancestors had predicted that the White Man's hegemony over the land would soon expire. An ill-smelling wind out of the west, they said, would sicken him and lay waste his cities. Soon Indians would reclaim their ancient birthright. It certainly sounded like this stinking epidemic, from what Turner had heard. Maybe Balfour was on to something he could twist around to help hasten that longed-for consummation.

"How can you be so certain?" he said. "You know all the laws against it. I explained them to you."

"Listen," said Balfour, "you can forget about the law. They got their backs to the wall out there. Jesus, there ain't nobody left to test that vaccine on but us. Oh, folks in hospitals, but they want healthy people. And they can't get no healthy volunteers. Whole damn country's in a panic. Don't you know what's going on? Don't you listen to the radio?"

"I broke my headphones," lied Turner. Actually he had slammed them against the wall in Mohawk fury at news of the FBI shooting Indians on the Red Bud reservation. "Anyway I've had other things on my mind."

"I know what you mean," said Farley. It was barely two weeks since Turner's last stay of execution. "It's hell, coming back from the edge like that. My last time, I almost wished they'd gone ahead and got it over with."

Turner grimaced and changed the subject. As a Huron he could steel himself for death, but to be snatched back repeatedly was torture too exquisite for even an Iroquois to stand. "How bad is it out there? Tell me."

"Ask old Pusgut," said Farley. "You wonder why we got no night C.O.? Why no bedding change and no chow but pork and beans? No epidemic at Fairburn yet, but just the threat's practically stopped the joint from running. Half the C.O.'s are hiding at home and cons won't turn out for work. Laundry's shut down and kitchen damn near. Pusgut said the warden's scared of a mass break-out, but that's all crap. Cons feel safer in than out. Outside—whoee! News I get, it sounds like Saigon when

138

the GI's pulled out and left the Gooks to sink or swim. I ever tell you what that was like, buddy? They goddamn well sunk, too, right before your eyes. Whole damn country dissolved: army melted, cops and firemen took off, refugees filled up the streets, shooting and looting and cars and houses on fire. That was Saigon at the last; what you'd expect of a lot of ignorant Gooks. Sounds now like our country is going the same way—coming unstuck over a goddamn epidemic. Ain't that a kick? Our country all tore to shreds. Americans acting like a bunch of Gooks!" Farley's voice seemed to break. Then he laughed mockingly. "So, regardless of laws or anything, old buddy, they got to grab themselves some human guinea pigs. And quick. They got to make that vaccine safe for people or else the whole frigging country's going down the toilet. All the fucking Russkies gonna have to do is walk in here afterwards and pick up the pieces. Guinea pigs, my boy, and nobody cares how many live and how many die. That means cons like us, U-S, us, my smart young lawyer Indian. And you better, by God, believe it because it's going to be your ass right along with mine."

Turner pondered. The chaos Farley was describing matched conditions in his dream. Being sacrificed as a laboratory specimen was an unthinkable fate, but in any event he had no time to think about it right now. The question was, how to exploit the chaos. What would his ancestors expect him to do to hasten the White Man's end? He said, casually, "My guess is you've figured some angle on this thing. You're not a guy to just go beating his gums for no reason. How about it?"

"Well, like they say, if you can't help getting screwed, relax and enjoy it. Yeah, I got an angle. Long as they gonna hold us down and stick them needles in us whether we like it or not, well now—why don't we jump the gun on them? Why don't we volunteer for it?"

"That's an angle? What kind of crazy angle is that?"

"Don't you see? If we got word to the warden that he had some noble-minded prisoners volunteering to sacrifice themselves for the public good and wanting him to get permission from the governor to be taken out and vaccinated, how do you think it would go down? Wouldn't that make us heroes? Like them soldiers in Cuba they tested that Yellow Fever on I saw in a movie once. Wouldn't that make the governor grateful to us? Maybe even the President, old Lloyd Dobson himself?"

"I thought you had an angle," said Turner. "Two of us wouldn't cut any ice. To test that vaccine they need hundreds and hundreds of people. Even I know that much."

"Two of us, shit! You think I'm that dumb? The idea is to go on TV or radio and talk other cons into volunteering with us. You know how many like us are rotting in this country on Death Row? Hundreds! And thousands of lifers without no hope of parole for forty or fifty years."

"Wait a minute!" said Turner. "Farley, I get your drift. You're a genius. All we got to do is get the governor to listen to us. With conditions bad as you saw, we could convince him that in return for concessions—shortening prison sentences, maybe some paroles even—a lot of cons might volunteer for this vaccine. He'd go for that. I bet the President would too."

"Oh sure," said Farley ironically. "Probably even make us two national heroes, like astronauts or something."

"Why not?" said Turner, lightly. It would be a way out, he thought—that was the first big thing. And it would put him on television—or anyway in a radio station—which was the second. "Why not?" he repeated. "Even grant us full pardons with apologies."

"Or at least give us a hot meal before they poison us with their vaccinations," said Farley. "I'm all for it. All the way. After all, it was my idea. So what do you figure's the best way to go about it? Time's a-wasting."

Some romantic people who saw Fairburn Penitentiary rising from the flat Indiana prairie considered it as picturesque as a medieval fortress. It was not picturesque at all, just a utilitarian structure meant to make malefactors penitent and keep them locked up. In ninety years a few had managed to escape with the connivance of bribed guards, but none ever from Death Row. Short of blowing the place up with dynamite or by armed invasion, there was hardly any imaginable means. Death Row was in the dank windowless top of the innermost of five granite buildings inside a twenty-foot wall guarded with machine guns. No one had ever left it except to die; by rope in early days, by electrocution since the 1920s.

The three Death Row inmates at Fairburn—white man, black man, red man—belonged to the most exclusive club in America, that of The Condemned. There were about five hundred of them, mostly poor, mostly black, most in Texas, Alabama, Georgia, and Florida prisons, all waiting to die. For ten years, because of a Supreme Court decision and a growing national taboo against taking human life, none was executed. Every day for ten years was a day of reprieve, a day longer to live, a day that strengthened the fragile hope that somehow they would be spared.

But in 1977 the taboo was shattered. Convicted murderer Gary Gilmore—who called himself unfit to live and derided the state of Utah for cowardice when legal maneuvers by the NAACP Legal Defense Fund and similar groups postponed his execution—finally went before the firing squad. That broke the spell. Within two years Florida had executed John Spenkelink. More would follow.

What all condemned prisoners—except a freak like Gilmore—had in common was the conviction that they did not deserve to die. Their crimes, if they admitted to crimes, were never their fault. The fault lay elsewhere. They were victims of social injustice, of political persecution, of some horrible misunderstanding, of simple bad luck.

In Olin Rodgers's case it was all frame-up, bad luck, horrible misunderstanding. One minute he had been happy-drunk on champagne cocktails in a rain of confetti

141

on a ballroom bandstand, orchestra playing, folks cheering. Then the lights winked out and there was screaming and shooting and people surging past him for the exits. He felt a hand in his pocket just before hard-faced white men with guns grabbed him. Scared, bewildered, Olin struck back and by chance drove his fist into a throat. It turned out to be a federal narcotics agent whose trachea he'd crushed, and when they handcuffed and searched him, a packet of heroin, street value a hundred thousand dollars, was in his pocket.

Any other time a popular sports figure like Olin might have got off with no worse than a manslaughter charge. But the Chicago newspapers happened to be crusading against drug traffic connections with professional athletes and howled for his blood. Some small-time Gary pushers fingered him in return for reduced sentences, and in the end clean-living Scrambling Grambling Olin was convicted of possession and trafficking and of murder in the commission of a felony. All a horrible misunderstanding and miscarriage of justice.

To Turner Hornbow it was political persecution pure and simple that put him on Death Row. Had Native Americans been respected as sovereign peoples on their own soil, students at Indiana would not have formed a Red Power protest group. That dinky suburban Tecumseh National Bank would not have advertised itself with an insulting cartoon figure of a feathered Indian in a breech-clout. Turner would not have led the Red Power students into the bank in protest; the cops wouldn't have thrown them all in jail; the municipal judge wouldn't have put them on probation. None of that would have happened with proper political respect for Indians.

They weren't about to let it drop with that—Turner and Ross Cutnose and James Pigeonblood. They got drunk and Turner made a fiery speech in the Student Union and they staggered off to have it out with that banker. Only Ross and James got too drunk to walk, and Turner stumbled in by himself, leaving them on the curbstone across the street. Then it was all kind of a blur: the fat bank guard with his wobbling gun pushing him and the women tellers screaming, and the banker rushing out, and the gun going off. Turner never meant to shoot anybody. He was completely flabbergasted at the explosion and the bank president sinking to his knees with red blood spreading on his shirt-front. It was pure accident, not anybody's fault. But the prosecutor said Turner had made threats in the Student Union and that it was premeditated murder. If Turner had been a white student, not an Indian, the prosecutor couldn't have made it stick. Pure political persecution, nothing else.

Farley Balfour considered himself the victim of bad luck and injustice. As he tried to explain to the Logansport jury, over objections by his Public Defender, when he killed Gooks in the jungle they gave him medals. This cop Kleinert now, who'd pulled him in and was hitting him on the head with a sap, why, killing him was an accident—self-defense—but they were calling it murder. It didn't make no sense. But even though Kleinert was notorious in his department for brutality, cops stuck together and none would testify. The jury looked at squat Farley Balfour with his piggy, killer's eyes and decided he was a murderous thug who deserved to die. All plain bad luck.

So for two years now Farley had shivered in winter and sweltered in summer, doing his methodical body-building exercises to keep from losing his mind. And in between, while he rested, he would remember the three parts of his life: growing up on a one-mule farm in the hickory ridges south of French Lick; the soldier years at Benning and in Nam; then yellow-headed, soft-bellied Millie in their Logansport basement apartment, where he was the super of the building and everything was swell until he got beered up and ran a red light and that fucking Kleinert pulled him in and started beating lumps on his head. Millie gone now like everything else—run off to Indianapolis with some jerk that was always sucking

143

around her down at Kalbach's Corner Bar. Which he couldn't blame her for. No future with Farley anymore.

Farley thought about the three parts of his life. He tried not to think about what it was going to be like when they came for him the last time to shave his head and strap him in to Old Sparkey. Suddenly now he had something new to think about—how if Turner Hornbow wrote the governor in Indianapolis about volunteering to test this vaccine, something wonderful might come of it. Farley thought about it from every angle. He couldn't write a good letter, but Turner could. Then it came to him that Turner had to get the black football player in on it too. A white man, a black man, an Indian—the governor would have to go for that.

Chapter 11

Simon Green parked the Government motor pool Chevy in front of the Annandale Trust Company Building, boarded-up and empty-looking like all the buildings in the riot-blighted street, and with the Air Force issue revolver hidden under his coat walked over broken glass to the side door, watching anxiously for possible assailants. Actually any mugger who tried to jump the fat, sixty-five-year-old doctor would have been in for a terrible surprise. Forty years before, Simon had been one of Patton's pistol-packing regimental surgeons in the Third Army's race across France, and by fair light and at short range he could still hit the buttons on your vest.

Even so, it was a foolhardy thing to do, giving his Secret Service escort the slip and sneaking off this way. But Simon had a stubborn streak, and having tracked down Olga Dalrymple on his own, he wasn't about to let anybody else in on this investigation until it produced positive results. Besides, he was a little miffed by the way Blanchard and Burrows were excluding him from their sessions and more than half-convinced they were on the wrong course anyway. Even if they succeeded in making the vaccine safe, it would probably be too late.

He found the hidden doorbell where she had told him

to look, pressed it, heard a buzz, and saw the side door spring ajar. Pulling it locked behind him, Simon climbed the stairs to a frosted-glass office door that bore the legend *Olvera and Son* in discreet black lettering. A woman's voice answered his knock. "Simon Green, ma'am," he called. "I phoned you."

There was another buzz and the snap of a doorbolt throwing. Simon entered a small, opulently furnished reception office. The red rug was antique Persian, the chairs antique or expensive reproductions, and the two blue-green seascapes glowing on the magenta walls unmistakably Oliver Owens Sturdevant originals worth a fortune. It was a décor intended to make old money—or new money wanting to become old—feel safe, respected, and at home. But none of this registered on Simon at first. What riveted his attention was the light double-barreled shotgun pointed at his middle by a seventy-year-old woman in plain black sitting at a desk behind a mahogany balustrade.

Simon swallowed. "That's a mighty nice-looking fowling-piece, Miss Dalrymple," he said in broadest North Carolinian. "Looks English-made. You wouldn't mind aiming it away from me, would you?"

"Show me some ID first." Old as she was, she cracked the order out like a drill sergeant. Meekly, Simon laid down his driver's license, physician's certificate, and HEW pass, studying the worn face under fine white upswept hair, the high, bony shoulders, and the long, thin hands. Behind rimless glasses Olga Dalrymple's eyes were the reddish-brown hue that went with auburn hair and freckly skin. In her youth, he would bet, this old dragon had been a handsome filly, one of those sorrel-top leggy tomboy gals fun to take on picnics but prone to give their hearts too quickly.

"Thank you, Doctor." Miss Dalrymple stood the shotgun behind her. "I have to be careful, you know. It could be anybody coming up those stairs. Not that anyone has tried, so far as I know. I expect everybody

146

thinks the building's evacuated. Come around and have a seat. Yes, the gun's English, one of a matched pair Mr. Felipe had made over there years ago. Luis doesn't like guns, but he keeps these on the wall out of respect."

"Not loaded, I hope."

"I know how to load them," she said crisply. "And shoot them. When Luis was a toddler, Mr. Felipe used to invite me to his Fairfax place Saturdays to shoot clay pigeons, he and Carlotta—Mrs. Olvera, she died, poor thing—and me."

"I see I don't have to ask if you've worked here long."

"Since 1931. Mr. Felipe hired me straight out of the Colmar School of Business in Alexandria. He was just getting established then, had just emigrated from Barcelona. He used to joke that he sensed the Spanish Civil War coming five years ahead and got out in time to save his skin. He was astute enough to do it too, Mr. Felipe was. I've been here ever since—not right here, we were in the old Brashear Block until they tore it down in forty-seven—but with the House of Olvera."

Half a century of loyalty to a man and his son, Simon reflected. Women were incredible. "Thank you for agreeing to meet me here, Miss Dalrymple. It was a risky thing to do. Is somebody going to pick you up afterwards? I didn't see your car in the street."

"I didn't have to come anywhere, Doctor. I've been here all along."

"Good God! All through—you mean—you never went home?"

"Home?" She said the word dryly. "My so-called home, Doctor, is a room at the Martha Washington Hotel for Women. Has been for years. Why would I go to that place? Everything I need is here. Old women don't need much. I heat soup and make coffee on Luis's alcohol stove. I've got his camp lantern if the power goes off at night. He has a closet full of canned goods and outdoor gear from when he used to take his little boys camping, before his wife left him and took them to her folks in

147

Oregon. Poor Luis. They weren't right for each other, but you can't tell people. No, Doctor, this is my home, where my duties lie, not that Martha Washington sanctum for broken-down females. Olvera and Son end their fiscal year next month and I have to get annual statements out to our clients. It's important that Olvera and Son continue to operate, no matter what. Or to be honest, maybe that's what I tell myself as an excuse to go on living."

"Forgive a stranger's familiarity, Miss Dalrymple," said Simon, "but I think that shows you to be a loyal woman. My compliments."

"Stuff! Don't get mawkish, Doctor. You're old enough to understand wanting to feel useful. You're no chicken either."

"Perfectly right, ma'am. So let's start being useful. Did you look up that information I asked you about?"

Her eyeglasses glittered in the light. "What makes you think Luis Olvera is alive, Doctor?"

Simon was taken aback. "What makes you think he isn't."

"I didn't say I did."

"Nor did I say I thought he was alive either. Not in so many words."

Olga Dalrymple sat perfectly still. "Stop fencing with me, Doctor. Tell me again—exactly and in detail—why I should open up Olvera and Son's confidential files to you."

"My goodness." Simon reached under his coat for the .38 Smith and Wesson digging into his stomach and placed it on the floor. "There. That's a relief. Would you believe that the President of the United States makes me tote this ugly thing around? It's awful what folks have to do nowadays, ain't it? Miss Dalrymple, I'm not foolish enough to tell you your boss is alive. We don't hardly know anything about conditions in the Southwest where he was last heard of except that they're awful bad, worse than anywhere else, with thousands and thousands of

148

folks dead. But from what little I know about Luis Olvera's movements and what I know about communicable disease, I'm willing to bet one thing—if he's dead it's not from Consolvo's Ulceration. My bet is that he is one of those lucky people with a natural immunity."

"Oh dear." She rose abruptly and vanished into an inner office, taking Simon by surprise. But she left him with two distinct impressions—she was crying and she limped. Her right leg was shortened and she wore a built-up shoe, probably the legacy of early polio. Simon suddenly felt that he understood everything there was to know about Olga Dalrymple—the bright, pretty young woman with the loving heart, denied womanly fulfillment because—hell, Jack, face it—what man wants to be tied down to a cripple? He ached for her, he despised all his sex.

She returned shortly, her eyes faintly red, a manila file folder in her hand. "I believe," she said briskly, "that you are primarily interested in Luis's movements for the several days before he saw the two potential clients whose names you know and if possible where he was going after he left them. Is that it, Dr. Green?"

"Short, to the point, and accurate, ma'am."

She hesitated. "You assure me that your reasons for this justify my violating the pledge of confidentiality I made many years ago?"

"Ma'am," said Simon earnestly, "if I don't find what I want, I'll forget everything else you show me. I don't understand high finance anyway. But if I do find it, all I can say is that it might be the saving of just about everything. That's the best I can tell you."

She pondered. She nodded. "All right, Doctor. Mr. Felipe always said integrity and trust were the keys to success. I take you at your word. Now let me explain how the House of Olvera operates, so you can understand what I tell you and why I can't tell you more.

"Mr. Felipe had certain inflexible rules: never to have more than thirty clients—whose holdings were to be

149

neither too large nor too small, adjusted for inflation, currently two to ten million dollars in reasonably liquid assets—clients he found personally congenial, who shared his belief in responsible, enlightened capitalism as the best hope for a humane, progressive civilization. Greedy men, arrogant men, stupid or deceitful men got short shrift. In return, the House of Olvera, for a very modest management fee, earned for its clients year in and year out never less than twenty percent appreciation of capital. And that included depression and recession years, Doctor."

Simon whistled. "I guess you don't have any trouble lining up clients."

"More applicants than we ever had room for." She smiled frostily. "Half the rich people in this country would give anything for Olvera and Son to manage their money. But Mr. Felipe—until his death five years ago, and now Luis—was choosy. He had to personally interview every potential client to be sure they measured up. Luis was in the Southwest because two of our oldest clients had died last summer and several of our applicants lived down there. We've never had a client there. Mr. Felipe liked his clients spread out geographically—said it led to cross-fertilization—and Luis believed the Southwest was due for economic expansion."

"So he interviewed that unfortunate New Mexican rancher who gave his name to this epidemic. And a few days later, an old-time Hollywood actor living in seclusion in Utah." Simon was grim.

"Monte Hethercote." Olga Dalrymple shook her head. "Oh my. I confess to a girlish flutter when Luis phoned me he had seen him. Like millions of girls, I idolized that conceited, posturing old fool once. Of course Luis turned him down. Which is something I would not ordinarily know, Doctor."

"Oh? Why is that?"

"Because rigid confidentiality on behalf of both clients and would-be clients was something Mr. Felipe insisted on. He explained that being known as a House of Olvera rejectee could seriously damage a person's business reputation. Whatever the reasons, people would automatically suspect the worst, and he considered that unfair. So nobody ever knew except Mr. Felipe—and since his death, Luis—who our would-be clients were. Oh, now and then I found out, inevitably, but no one else, none of our secretaries, not anyone. I only knew about Hethercote because Luis wanted to tease me."

"You also knew about Howard Consolvo."

"Oh. Well, yes. Because Luis had accepted him. I had to be told that. Luis was highly enthusiastic about Mr. Consolvo. He measured up well."

"Poor guy," said Simon. "And a few days later he was dying from a scratched arm. That's why I'm convinced Luis is immune, you see?"

"No, I don't. I don't understand that at all."

"Well, it's really simple, a matter of a time fix. We know what the incubation period for Consolvo's Ulceration is, pretty well. We know when Luis saw Consolvo, when he first exhibited symptoms, and we know when Luis met Hethercote. If he were normally susceptible, he would have revealed symptoms himself by the time he telephoned you to twit you about turning down your old matinee idol."

"Oh, not quite that, Doctor."

"No matter. What matters is that the time schedule suggests something potentially more important—something which may offend you, though it shouldn't. You should pray that it's true, and pray we find Luis alive. I mean, of course, that there's a good chance he is a carrier of this thing."

"A—You mean like Typhoid Mary? That's horrible, Doctor!"

"Actually, wonderful. It would mean—if we could find him—being able to interrogate and examine a known carrier. Nothing could be more important. So where had Luis Olvera been before he saw Howard Consolvo and

151

where was he going after he left Monte Hethercote?"

Olga Dalrymple bit her lip. She opened the file folder, fingered the papers in it, shook her head. "But that's just what I don't know, Doctor. It was a secret."

"No hints—no clues? Nothing in that file? You made notes of his phone calls surely."

"Nothing—" She almost wailed the word. "Just confirmation of motel reservations—of a car rental at the Denver airport—a—"

"Car rental!" Simon sat straight up. "Oh, my dear Miss Dalrymple! A car? Could you possibly get—is there any way—a line on the car? Color, make, license—?"

She looked blank. Suddenly she became efficient. "Of course. I talked to the Avis girl. He was fussy about cars, Luis, especially for driving long distances. Nothing but the most luxurious. I remember something else too. He mentioned getting liability insurance, to drive across the border."

"Mexico! He was headed for Mexico! Miss Dalrymple, you and I and that file folder are leaving here and we are going to feed every scrap of information you have into a computer. Miss Dalrymple, this could be the best day's work either of us ever put in."

Chapter 12

General Burrows's underground war room—the heart, brain, nerve center (Noah Blanchard could not decide which description fit best) of the Epidemic Task Force headquarters deep in the Maryland earth—was a marvel of electronics technology. Banks of closed-circuit TV screens for summoning into conference epidemiologists in laboratories hundreds of miles apart circled the walls and ghostly quiet teletypewriters printed out in luminous green letters what scant news the wire services had collected from a nation at a standstill. There were computers able to work any calculation, computers that held in storage virtually all knowledge, and one special computer that accumulated the rising total of Consolvo's Ulceration cases from the Center for Disease Control's Morbidity and Mortality Reports and flashed crimson warnings when one broke out in some new place. To survey this array of electronic wizardry from the command dais in the middle of the room was stupefying to the imagination. As a doctor trained in science, Noah could grasp the general principles by which it worked, but medicine was also part art and the artist in him was appalled by the portent of this harnessing of primal forces and whirling electrons. In the end, though, his common sense rallied to assure him that, for all its flash and dazzle, the war room simply functioned as a cross between military message center and corporation boardroom. In the end human brains had to shift and weigh the information and evidence it assembled to arrive at answers in the same old human way.

And there were still no answers.

By now Consolvo's Ulceration had spread to every state except Alaska and Hawaii and crossed into lower Canada and upper Mexico. Cities west of the Mississippi were hardest hit, but even where the epidemic was statistically light, as in Chicago and Washington D.C., and New York, the streets were deserted and essential services almost totally halted. Warm weather still blanketed the nation, but October was at hand and soon people in northern states would be freezing, unless, as Noah remarked gloomily to Walter Burrows, all the people were dead by then.

Every nation had closed its ports against travel from North America, and stranded foreigners had to do the best they could. According to Burrows, who managed to keep track of such matters while working eighteen-hour days, of the three foreign scientists at his major briefing, Horner, the Australian, was in Ottawa; the Israeli, Hasmin, had found sanctuary with the Chemistry Department at Brandeis; and Kopitsky's body had been discovered by the Washington police in an alley off Embassy Row, head caved in and pockets turned out. *Pravda* thundered about murderous American hooliganism, but there was a hollow ring to it, and State Department people assumed that Kopitsky had become a nuisance about returning to Moscow and so been liquidated by Russian agents. But with everything that was going on around the country the affair was too insignificant to merit more than passing notice.

Hour by hour, day after day, the teletypewriters and TV screens reported melancholy and bizarre events across the sick nation. Strange cults formed small communes in

154

the countryside that waged war with farmers whose land they squatted on and whose property they despoiled. Strange prophets touted strange cures and prophylactics, some dating back to the Great Plague of London. A retired naturopath in Norfolk, Nebraska urged people to steep their socks and underwear in spirits of turpentine; a chiropractor in Gorham, Maine, suggested asafetida bags round the neck; there were promotions of radium springs, electric shock therapy, and Yoga exercises. Rumors swept the land: the epidemic came from spores sown in the desert by extraterrestrials aboard flying saucers; it had mutated from a pesticide derived from DDT; it was insidious biological warfare by the Russians that the emasculated CIA had not foreseen; it was spread like infectious hepatitis by the drug and needle culture; carbon monoxide from automobile exhaust caused it; a Defense Department chemical experiment had backfired. It was popular to call it God's wrath and different ways to propitiate Him were proposed. The ministers of Laurel, Mississippi, a city which the epidemic had miraculously passed by, organized a day of thanksgiving and forty-eight hours later six cases of Consolvo's Ulceration appeared. In New Orleans and Mobile and Ybor City the Dream Book stores did a lively trade in jujus, and in New York City some Harlem streets were pungent with the odor of burning chicken feathers.

The famous Texas faith-healer, Reverend Billy Bob Hohenwald, started a week of prayer and gospel-singing in the Astrodome after exposing himself to Consolvo's Ulceration in the epidemic wards of Houston General Hospital. Thousands of earnest believers overcame their dread of contagion to hear him, and for thirty sweating hours under the TV lights Billy Bob exhorted and harangued from a pulpit setup on the Oilers' fifty-yard line. Midway of the second afternoon, about normal incubation period for the disease, he stopped, stared at his hand, cried out and fainted. A cat scratch on his thumb had suddenly erupted in the familiar red-oozing black

155

stigmata of Consolvo's Ulceration, and hundreds of people were trampled trying to get out of the stadium.

But crowds like that in the Astrodome were rare. Most Americans hid at home, venturing out only for the rations the Quartermaster General managed to distribute by a miracle of logistics. Public Health Service teams still went to shopping malls and rural courthouses, but few volunteers for vaccination turned out. The epidemic continued to widen, infecting two of every ten, most fatally. A few lucky people who got hyperbaric oxygen therapy recovered, but there were not nearly enough hyperbaric oxygen chambers. What the epidemic-fighters found both hopeful and frustrating were persistent reports of spontaneous remissions. For no known reason the infection simply dried up after a day or two in certain victims and their eroded tissue began to restore itself, leaving only minor scars. There were only a few such reports, but too many and from too many different places to be discounted as errors of diagnosis. What frustrated the doctors was that no common denominator could be found in these fortunate survivors—no similarity of age, sex, racial background, occupation, condition of previous health, anything.

"My guess," said Noah, "is that it's some mysterious enzyme their blood cells manufacture."

"How do you figure?" Slumped beside him on the command dais, uniform necktie pulled loose, huge shoulders sagging, General Burrows looked utterly exhausted. They had been together since dawn—monitoring electronic conferences between epidemiologists scattered across four time zones, evaluating new data as it was recorded, and racking their minds for hint of a breakthrough. Watching Burrows with anxious, narrowed eyes, Sergeant Harrison stood by, natty as always in crisp, fresh suntans.

"It has to be an enzyme," said Noah. "Process of elimination rules out anything else." He yawned deeply, as short of sleep as Burrows who for a week had only catnapped in his office when Harrison insisted. Noah went to his hotel every night—Kate demanded that—but it was never for long. And part of his fatigue came from having to brief the President every afternoon at six. Dobson refused to let anyone else be present, not even Cawthorp or Cohane, and he was becoming increasingly hard to satisfy. For that matter Noah was increasingly dissatisfied himself.

"You're probably right," said Burrows. "For whatever good it is. There are those rare types—maybe half a dozen in the world—whose blood produces antibodies against practically any infection. Used to be one in Washington who had a contract with some plasma producing house—sold his blood for two thousand dollars a pint or some such astronomical sum."

"I remember," said Noah. "The IRS came down on him for taking a depletion allowance, and he got mad and wouldn't sell it any more. That the fellow?"

"A rugged individualist," yawned Burrows. "If your theory is right, maybe we could figure some way to pass that enzyme-making capability on to epidemic victims. Any ideas? They tried transfusions—that was in Des Moines, I think—but no luck."

"I wouldn't even have a guess as to who to put onto a project like that. Would you?"

"Vincent Craigie," said Burrows. "If only he were alive."

Noah sat up and stared at him. "You amazing guy. Where did you ever know Craigie? Did you study under him too?"

"Me?" Burrows gave Noah a mocking grin. Like soldiers under fire together, the two had arrived at total mutual respect. In all his life Noah had never liked a man more. "Hey, Doc, I got my M.D. down in Alabama, remember? We had an OK faculty, but not any geniuses like Craigie. He was reserved for your rich white-boy doctor schools. Naw, I've only read about Craigie."

"Don't jive me," said Noah easily. "You had damn

157

good training, Doctor. Didn't he, Sergeant Harrison?"

"Yezzir," said Harrison noncommittally. He still wouldn't accept Noah as Burrows's superior and he was a little offended by the way the two kidded each other. It didn't strike Harrison as fitting somehow. "He's a right good doctor."

"I told you, see?" said Noah.

"Yeah, and it was free, too," said Burrows. "You studied under Craigie?"

"I took a course of his at Johns Hopkins once. He was everything they say, even more. What a teacher. What a doctor. He knew more about more things, about cell biochemistry, about the electron-transport chain! Why that man never won a Nobel Prize, God only knows."

"I wondered about that, too. Maybe he just died too soon. When did he die?"

"Oh, I don't know. Come to think of it, must have been six—seven—well, I had my course with him ten or eleven years ago. For the next few years he was—government projects, it sticks in my mind. Then—it's odd, when you think about it. A scientist of Craigie's stature. He wouldn't simply die and nobody take any notice of it. But for the life of me I don't remember."

"Easy enough to find out. Harrison?"

"Yes sir, General."

"How about having them run a quick check for us. Find out when and where Dr. Vincent Craigie died. Tell them he was at Johns Hopkins ten or eleven years ago."

"They shouldn't have any trouble finding a record of him," said Noah. "My God, Craigie was an advisor to half the projects the National Institutes sponsored for years. He advised everybody—Defense, National Science Foundation, you name it."

"Yes, sir," said Harrison. "That fellow Martin coming on shift now, I'll have him stick it in his computer. Won't take but a few minutes, General."

Noah glanced at his wristwatch. "Damn. Nearly time to go take my lumps."

Burrows said, "What are you going to tell him today?"

"More like what he's going to tell me, Walt. But God, I don't know. For all the progress we're able to report, he better get somebody else."

"Who, for God's sake? Nobody could do better than you are. It's an impossible situation."

"Well, thanks for the compliment." Noah gulped another shuddering yawn. "You want me back here afterwards?"

"Not unless the President has some brilliant idea for us. I'll call you at the Fleur d'Or if anything turns up here. Try and get some sleep, Noah."

"Okay, Walt." Noah pushed a console button and, when the receptionist four floors above answered, said: "Jeanie? Doctor Blanchard. Have my driver bring the car around, please. Time I got to the White House."

"Yes, sir, Dr. Blanchard."

"Don't forget your raincoat," said Burrows. "Harrison told me it was beginning to drizzle outside. Cold front coming through."

"That could be bad news. An early cold snap is just what we don't need."

"General," said Sergeant Harrison, walking back, "Martin says there isn't any record of any Dr. Craigie's death."

"That's impossible," said Burrows. "There has to be."

"Martin says not, sir. He checked every way—by the name, by profession, by time span. No doctor named Vincent Craigie died anywhere in the United States anywhere in the last ten years."

Burrows shot Noah a puzzled glance. "You suppose he could have died overseas somewhere?"

Noah frowned. "Anything's possible. But what I knew of Vincent Craigie, he was so immersed in his work he wouldn't take time to go away for the weekend, much less to a foreign country."

"No doctor named that died anywhere this side of the iron or bamboo curtains—or inside them either," said

159

Harrison. "I figured you'd ask that, so I made Martin run it that way, too. If he's dead don't nobody know it."

"Then," said Noah slowly, "it has to follow that the man is alive. But where? And why would he simply vanish? Look, it's probably not anything important, but if the computer operator has time, what do you say we track it down?"

"Hell, yes," said Burrows. "My curiosity's aroused too. Harrison, take care of it, will you?"

"Yezzir."

"I'll let you know if the President has any brainstorms to pass along, Walt," said Noah, putting on the white raincoat that made him feel like a B-movie spy. Kate had bought it for him their first rainy day in Washington. He hated it but he wouldn't hurt her feelings.

"Okay, buddy," said General Burrows. "I'm not going anywhere."

"Be better if you did once in a while." Noah gave him half a salute and went to the elevator.

According to historians, the Civil War aged Abraham Lincoln twenty years and, thought Noah, four years of Matthew Brady photographs proved it. It seemed to Noah, alone with the President in the Oval Office, that Lloyd Dobson had aged that much in a week. His rawboned farmer hands trembled visibly on his desk, his temples were sunken, circles darkened his eyes. His face reminded Noah of another doomed president in a famous photograph—the dying Franklin Roosevelt, shawl round his shoulders, strong features haggard, sitting between Churchill and Stalin at Yalta. If this man sitting across this desk from me were referred to me as a patient, thought Noah, and I did not know his real problem, I would prescribe complete rest, mild sedation, a change of scene and, perhaps, occupation. Which shows how far off the mark medical diagnosis can fly.

Deep in their shadowy sockets Dobson's eyes held a desperate gleam. "Dr. Blanchard," he began, "in the last three hours three unhappy men sat by turn in that chair

160

you're in—the French, British, and Russian ambassadors. I don't know if they colluded first, but they all said the same thing. Unless our epidemic is contained soon, their governments will be compelled to take self-protective action of the most drastic sort. There were no details, but it was clear that nuclear weapons were implied. Our epidemic, they said, was a threat to all mankind. It had to be stopped at all costs. At *all* costs. Doctor, those were not bellicose ultimatums in the classic sense. These men were not rattling sabers. Don't give way to patriotic outrage. They were sober, sorrowful statements of fact by men of good will—even Ambassador Popovitch—whose own lives and own families' lives are at stake too. They are not going home, any of them. Whatever awful fate comes to Washington—by mischance, if my own worst fears are realized and the nuclear powers are insane enough to loose the holocaust, or by some other possibility that does not even occur to me—they must bear the brunt of it with us. They are not going home. Their governments aren't about to risk importing our infection. So what should I have told those anguished men, Doctor? Defied their governments? Roared back? Warned that at the slightest evidence we would strike first?"

Despair sank through Noah. "No, sir. That would simply be lashing out senselessly, like a dying scorpion."

"I'm glad you still feel that way. I do too. Perhaps the finest compliment that could be paid us was the confidence expressed by Sir Charles and by Monsieur Ortelly and even by that Yankeephobe Dmitri Popovitch that America is too civilized for such an act. I did not concede it—you never show your hole card in these games, but I'm proud we enjoy that reputation."

"For all the good it does us," muttered Noah.

"For all the good," echoed Dobson. "Which is not much. Now where do we stand since yesterday, Doctor? Any new developments? Any hopes? Any daylight at all?"

Hot anger, the product of frustration and helplessness,

began to glow inside Noah. He chose his words carefully. "Nothing significant, sir. The epidemic is moving at the same rate of advance, has reached three new towns in New England. The vaccination program is still stagnant, stuck on dead center. On the bright side, four new cases of spontaneous remission have been reported at widely separated points. That would be wonderful except that we don't understand it. My guess is that it's some mysterious enzyme, but that means nothing useful. With enough time researchers might conceivably track it down—find out why and how the blood cells of certain patients manufacture this unknown enzyme and how we might induce a similar protective process in other patients. Assuming it is an enzyme, which of course it may not be."

"How much time for research?"

"Oh lord. Who knows? Weeks. Months. Maybe never."

"So this is just a line of speculation? Nothing of solid value?"

"I'm afraid not, Mr. President."

"Then we're back to the vaccine program. It or nothing. How do we revive it? And how soon will it pay off?"

Noah's suppressed anger exploded. "How do we revive it? You tell me, sir! You set the priorities. You have to call out the troops! Because that's the only way—root people out with bayonets and hold them down and stick needles in them. We can't persuade them, we have to use force. And who do we force first—the easy ones? The ones we can spare best? The slum and ghetto poor and useless, like Mr. Cohane wants? Well, why not? I'm about ready to, if that's what it takes. You tell me, sir. You give the orders. Start with the people we can dispose of at the least cost—street thugs and addicts and pimps and pushers and welfare cheats and wetbacks and illiterates and feeble-minded—people Mr. Cohane and maybe most of us, if we were honest enough to admit it, lump together as niggers and spics and other worthless riffraff. Vaccinate them!

See which ones die. After that we can turn to the nice people, the respectable, tax-paying, more or less law-abiding white people. But let's cut out the cant and hypocrisy. If that's our philosophy, let's get it out in the open. Damn the risk of mutiny and race-riot. We whites still outnumber them. You tell me, sir. If I'm your Czar, give me guidance. Who do we vaccinate first? How much time do we have? How long before our kindly allies and other well-wishers fry us with their ballistic missiles, pretending we're too humane and civilized to do it to them first? Tell me that, sir. Then I'll try to answer your questions. Meantime, I can't. Meantime I'm beginning to think I'm wrong for this job. You ought to pick General Burrows. He's a better man than I am. Plus that if he says go ahead and vaccinate blacks and Chicanos and Puerto Ricans first, why nobody can call him hypocrite. Because he's black himself. But I'm upper middle-class WASP. Maybe I'd better resign."

"You through, Doctor?" Dobson's voice was like ice. "You got it all off your chest now?"

Breathing hard, Noah pressed his palms to his face, feeling the sweat in them. Shame suffused him. "Yes, sir," he said. "I apologize, Mr. President. I—I guess this is just too much for me."

"It's too much for all of us," said Dobson. "But we still can't quit. I know how you feel. But let's have no more of it. As for resigning, you can't. I won't let you. And I don't give a damn what color General Burrows or any man is. Get that straight."

"I'm sorry, sir," said Noah, stiffly. "I was out of line."

"Forget it, Doctor. Now since you and your colleagues—no blame intended—remain frustrated, I have made a decision. I am going to destroy a dozen American cities."

"What?"

"Keep quiet and listen. You gave me the idea. That outrageous scenario you dreamed of, that planted the seed. So you're responsible in a way as much as I. You don't think I could hold still for foreign powers attacking our cities, do you? But on the other hand, suppose we did it to ourselves?"

"Sir, Mr. President, this is the most—most outrageous—"

"Simmer down, sir. Keep still. Hear me out. What is our very highest priority now? To gain time? To forestall action by the Europeans while you and your people find a solution?"

Noah bit his lip. "Yes, sir," he said. "But, sir—"

"Hush, Doctor. I took your inspired postulation and turned it around. I even embellished it. And I made a bargain with our foreign friends. If they will hold off and forbear, I will sacrifice a dozen of our western cities where the epidemic is worst to show our good faith. And I will ship them enough of our vaccine for them to inoculate a broad cross-section of their national populations. They can do it. They don't have our problem of popular resistance. For one thing, the disease is not there. Life goes on at more or less the normal pace from John o'Groats to Vladivostok. Moreover, European and Asiatic peoples—especially in Communist countries—are more docile than Americans. If their governments tell them to line up for vaccination they might grumble, but they'll fall in and roll up their sleeves. Oh, maybe the French wouldn't, but the French government doesn't share our passion for revealing the truth. They might well tell their citizens that the vaccine is for chicken pox. Besides, not all that large a part of the national populations have to be tested. Only a cross-section, as I said."

Noah's mind whirled. "I don't understand—What did you do to sell them on this, sir?"

"Well, they're not sold, not yet, but why shouldn't they agree? It's to their interest as much as ours to make the vaccine safe to use. The point is that they can—or ought to be able to—test out the stuff easier than we can. Assuming that sensitivity to the vaccine is hereditary, as

164

you fellows seem to think, why, over in Europe they can single out subjects of different blood lines: Magyar, say, or Norman French, or Basque, or Italian Tyrolean, or Georgian, and so on. We can't do that. Blood lines over here are simply too wildly mixed up. And if they discover, for instance, that people of Scottish or Polish or Armenian—or something—ancestry are peculiarly vulnerable, why it narrows down the field enormously. For them and for us too, once they report their findings back here. You're the medico, Doctor. Why am I having to explain this to you?"

"Yes, but wait," said Noah, dazedly. "If they're willing to do this, why do you say you have to destroy our cities?"

"My God, Doctor! It should be obvious. We're playing for the highest stakes in history. I have to put something valuable in the pot, don't you see? I have to prove that we are in earnest, prove that we are willing to make a sacrifice. Use your brains. Those cities are gone anyway. I'm talking about western cities where the epidemic is worst. What hope is there—be realistic now—for Albuquerque, Los Angeles, Denver, Salt Lake, El Paso, the rest? It's a miracle they've survived this long. How much longer can we keep sending in food? How long before their water-purification systems break down and typhoid and cholera begin to spread? Cold weather is coming and there won't be any heat or lights. How soon before starvation brings the rioters out of hiding to loot and kill? Doctor, to destroy these doomed pockets of plague is simply mercy-killing. It greatly lessens the moral justification of foreign nations to attack us. And for one final argument, it might be just the shock tactic to make Americans in the eastern part of the country submit to vaccination, seeing what we are willing to do to a city where the epidemic gets out of control. Doctor, I have no choice except this. Do you not understand the reasoning? Actually it's simply the principle of the backfire, which every school child understands. The nation is in the same plight as a city in a conflagration—like the great Chicago and San Francisco fires. To keep the flames from spreading further, the authorities dynamited blocks of buildings."

Noah stared at the ugly Lincolnesque face and the deep-socketed eyes, where it seemed to him a fanatic light gleamed. A sense of nausea went through him. He wondered if this were not how Hitler's generals felt in the dying days of the Third Reich, listening to the suicidal rant of the Fuehrer in his Berlin bunker. "The principle is clear enough, sir," he said nervously. "But this is pretty horribly drastic—Sir, I'm not sure you ought to be confiding such things to—well, any one person. Have you talked it over with—excuse me, but have you consulted Admiral Perrin lately?"

"Perrin?" The president's gnarled brows knitted. "For God's sake, man, I'm not sick! I almost wish I were, if that would change things. Are you suggesting that this is irrational? Please reflect. Actually it's the most rational, and most difficult, conclusion I have ever arrived at. I propose simply to sacrifice roughly a dozen cities—which are almost certainly doomed already—in the hope of saving the rest of the nation. I call that logical, not irrational. I might call it desperate, but not insane. If, when all this is over—if we live to *see* it over, Doctor—the Congress chooses to impeach me, if I have to stand trial for mass murder, well then, that is how it must be. Meantime, I am doing what I consider best for the country."

"But *how*, sir? You can't—I guess you mean nuclear weapons. But the fall-out. The prevailing westerlies—You'll contaminate everything east of—Mr. President! Please reconsider."

"That's what Weyland Evans said, too," said Dobson grimly. "Until I explained how to do it. He was here a while ago." He laughed, a harsh, flat sound. "If it makes you feel any better, Dr. Blanchard, he was as white-faced and horrified as you are. Maybe more so. After all, Evans comes from Oregon. But he understood why it had to be.

How it had to be. Cohane's going to blow his top when he finds out I went over his head to the Secretary of the Air Force, but now is no time for protocol. The fewer people who are in on this operation until it's consummated, the better. As for your worries about fall-out, there won't be any. The weapons used will be enhanced radiation devices delivered by fighter-bombers, the so-called infamous neutron bombs the Russians are so spooked about. No blast. No fall-out. No contamination. Just death. You didn't know we had those weapons in our inventory? Few people do. That information is part of the secret package of horrors every U.S. president passes on to his successors. Oh yes, we have them. Plenty of them. More than enough for this operation."

"But Mr. President!" cried Noah, agonized. "Maybe I'm being out of line here, but sir! How are you going to get American pilots to deliberately attack—? Sir, maybe I'm closer to the realities of this than you are. I'm a flight surgeon. I know how Air Force pilots think and feel. How can you or Secretary Evans or Mickey McDermott down at Langley Air Force Base or anybody in Tactical Air Command find American pilots who will bomb American cities?"

Lloyd Dobson moved a calendar pad from one point on his desk to another, his hands quivering as in a bad case of Parkinson's disease. But his voice stayed strong and steady. "A good question, Doctor. This is how. Tactical Air Command computers are already screening personnel for the task. Don't forget, we only need about fifteen—including three extra for aborts or other mission failures—two-man aircrews. The criteria are simple: men of eastern or southeastern birth who have never lived west of the Mississippi or have any close relatives there; men whose psychological profiles indicate strong loyalty, unquestioning obedience to orders, rigid self-discipline, and who are weak in imagination, abstract thinking, humanistic attitudes. Weyland Evans—he was the provost at Howland University, you know, before I talked him into joining my cabinet—has made a study of air-crew psychology. He tells me that those are the qualities the Air Force believes characterize officers who have operational command potential up to but not above Air Division level. And he assures me there is no shortage of them. Would you disagree with that? Don't you think our Air Force can muster fifteen fighter-bomber crews that fit that bill, Doctor?"

Noah's heart sank. "I'm afraid it can, Mr. President. Without any trouble. Now that you put it that way. And if TAC couldn't, the nearest Marine Corps Air Wing could. I take back what I said."

"So there you have it," said Dobson. "There is where we stand right at this moment. Not pretty, but at least things are moving. Unless you've got a question, that's it until your briefing tomorrow, when I certainly hope your people have come up with something progressive. Again, no reflection on anyone intended."

"Thank you, sir," said Noah feebly. "There is a question. How much time have we got? When do you plan to—to launch this strike? Any leeway at all? Have we got time to try to offer you some better alternative?"

Dobson bent a long, studied gaze at him. Again Noah remarked the ashy pockets under his eyes, the deep lines etched past his wide mouth, the telltale fluttering of his hands. "Dr. Blanchard," said the President, "you make it sound as if I were doing this for some evil edification of my own. Of course there is time. There is always time. However brief. It should be obvious to you that we will hold off until Moscow and London and Paris respond to my offer. I told their ambassadors that I would wait up to seventy-two hours. No longer."

Noah gulped. "And what if they turn you down, sir?"

"Then I would have to inform their ambassadors that at the slightest hint of preparations by them—the least strategic intelligence warning—for nuclear attack we will immediately launch our own preventive strike in self-defense."

"Would you really do it, sir?"

"What do you think, Doctor?"

Noah followed his blue-blazered, Secret Service escort down the White House corridor towards the side door where his car was waiting, so deeply preoccupied he did not at first notice when the President's personal physician fell into stride with him. "Could you spare me a moment, Dr. Blanchard?"

Noah stopped short and blinked down at the short, plump urologist. Admiral Perrin's pink, soft look contrasted oddly with his naval uniform, but Noah knew that his reputation in both general medicine and hospital administration was outstanding. "Wait for me down the hall, please," said Noah to his guard. "Yes sir, Admiral?"

"Damn it, Dr. Blanchard!" said Perrin. "This is irregular as all get-out, but the plain fact is that I have to have a consultation with you. You don't mind, do you?"

Noah was taken aback. "Consultation on what, Admiral?"

"On my patient, damn it!" Perrin sounded outraged. "I never even get to see him. It's none of my affair what you two are discussing, sir. I don't have any idea and I don't care. But you are a doctor and the man is my patient and his health worries me. What is your professional opinion of it, sir? That's what I want."

Noah hesitated. "Doctor, within limits I can tell you this. If he were my patient, I'd order bedrest. Not that I think it would do any good. In my opinion your patient has been driving himself on nervous tension and no sleep far too long. Does that help?"

Perrin nodded glumly. "Well, it confirms my judgment. If he were your patient, would you prescribe a sleeping potion?"

Noah laughed harshly. "How would you get it down him? But yes, certainly, by all means. If he were my patient."

"It would, of course," said Perrin reflectively, "be

169

grossly unethical to administer one surreptitiously—"

"Slip him a Mickey?" Noah grinned faintly.

"I have an accomplice," said Perrin, gazing away. "Mrs. Dobson, who is also my patient and who trusts me, I am happy to say, is equally worried. She also confides in me. The President has the old-fashioned habit when he goes to bed—usually about one in the morning and nowadays only to toss and turn until he rises at dawn—of taking a cup of hot cocoa. Mrs. Dobson makes it and brings it to him in bed—has for years. Now that's interesting information, isn't it?"

"And if by some well-meaning accident, someone happened to drop a Nembutal in that cocoa, the results might be salutary, you think?"

"It's an interesting speculation. Thank you for the consultation, Dr. Blanchard."

"A pleasure, Doctor."

It was therefore almost eleven the next morning before President Dobson, greatly refreshed by deep, unwonted sleep, could make himself available to the senior U.S. senator from Indiana. Senator Broadly, an elderly Republican, was virtually palpitant with astonishing information. Three Death Row inmates from a northwestern Indiana prison—one white, one black, one Indian—had volunteered to go on national network television to induce other condemned men and life-serving convicts to volunteer for testing the vaccine for Consolvo's Ulceration. With the consent of the state governor the warden had already sent them to the General Broadcasting Company's television studios in Chicago, forty miles away.

Jubilantly President Dobson telephoned Blanchard in Bethesda that the vaccination program might finally be getting off dead-center. He was a little put out when Noah said that he had already heard about it, and after Dobson hung up he wondered why his Plague Czar had sounded so depressed by the news.

170

Chapter 13

Maury Murray, originator and host of GBC's faltering Chicago-based "Get With It" rival of CBS's top-rated "Sixty Minutes," bragged that his mother was a descendant of Matthew Maury, famed hydrographer and Confederate naval officer, whose birthday was celebrated as a state holiday in Virginia. Actually Maury had no idea who his mother, or his father either, had been. She must have been a friendless, desperate girl, a sharecropper's daughter or millhand perhaps, to have abandoned her newborn infant, wrapped in a bloody towel, on a Baptist preacher's front porch in Columbia, Tennessee, in 1946. But whatever his antecedents, Maury was a born survivor who spent his first twelve years in the Maury County Orphanage (inspiration for the stage name he ultimately adopted) and two more in a Nashville home for runaways where bigger boys, enticed by his slight stature and girlish buttocks, sodomized him at will until he turned coquette and learned to play them against one another. At fifteen he was hustling pederasts along East Broadway, including an aging country music singer, who wangled him a spot backstage as a go-fer for Grand Old Opry performers. It was all the start shrewd Maury needed for a television career. Innovative, manipulative, ruthless, he learned where all the bodies were buried and never forgot an insult or forgave a favor. At WXYZ studios in Chicago his homespun show-host manner charmed viewers, while the sight of his diminutive, expensively tailored figure swaggering through the halls roused fear and loathing among underlings.

But Kate Petrakis was not afraid of him. She had the goods on Maury and he knew it. Walking through Lincoln Park one Saturday, she spotted him among loiterers around the men's toilet. Kate knew about T-Room assignations from her brief marriage to a switch-hitting Hollywood playboy, and more important, Maury realized she did. His consternation as she cut briskly away down a side path revealed it. Inversion didn't have to be fatal to a show-host career, but Maury yearned to move up to network management where the real money and power lay and where moral rules were as strait-laced, or at least as heterosexual, as in any executive suite. So Kate never mentioned the Lincoln Park encounter and Maury was always exceptionally cordial to her. Which was exactly how he sounded on the telephone at the Fleur d'Or after her office staff left that evening.

"Kate, baby! How the hell are you? Swell to hear your voice. Hey, I've had hell's own time reaching you."

She was cool. "I doubt that, Maury. I doubt that very much."

He bubbled laughter. "Come on, baby. It's been pure bedlam up here."

"It's like that everywhere. But you could have got me if you'd wanted to. Obviously you didn't need me. What is it now?"

"Kate, you sweet bitch, extract your knife from my back. I'm about to blow that Nielsen through the roof. And I want you in with me."

"Bullshit, Maury."

"Now, Kate, would I lie to you?"

It was her turn to laugh. "You son-of-a-bitch, Maury, I

172

sent you word from Albuquerque. You knew where to find me. So why do you need me now?"

"Because you're a natural for this thing, Kate. And it will make you, baby, absolutely make you. After prime-time tomorrow night every dumb bastard in the country will know who Kate Petrakis is. We're going to bust straight through those ratings, I promise you."

Kate was suddenly disgusted. "You are a contemptible little man, Maury. Don't you have the slightest sense of propriety? Chortling about ratings and prime-time! What's going on in Chicago? Rather, what isn't? Don't you know the score? If you were here where I am, reading daily death-tolls, watching doctors beat their brains out, knowing how really ghastly this thing is, you wouldn't—"

"Ho, ho, hold it, baby! That Blanchard's really stuck it into you, more than one way. Who the hell am I talking to, Florence Nightingale? Don't jive me, honey. This is Maury. I know you from way back. Hell, we're going to lick this epidemic. That's what I'm calling about. What's the big holdup? That people are scared to risk the vaccine, right? Shit, I'm scared to, too. Take my chances any day. But what if I told you that 'Get With It' has a great big explosive breakthrough for tomorrow night—the advertising's already out to all the affiliates—on how to get thousands of vaccine volunteers? My God, Kate, just listen! We'll blast them out of their seats. I've got the three wildest show guests coming you ever dreamed of. Three condemned murderers, Kate! Listen. You remember Olin Rodgers, the black Bisons quarterback that killed the narc? I got him! And a white Nam combat vet that killed an Indiana cop with his bare hands in a police station once and for Christ's sake an honest-to-God Indian—an American Indian that shot a white banker to death for making fun of Indians! Isn't that crazy? Isn't that the wildest thing you ever heard of? They'll all be coming to Chicago in chains, from an Indiana state pen under armed guard, coming on *our* show, Kate. For Christ's sake,

173

they're going to volunteer for this vaccine and they're going to beg other condemned guys on Death Row and lifers in pens everywhere to volunteer too! Talk about a once-in-a-lifetime show! My God, Kate, I've got to have you in on it."

"Are you making all this up, Maury?" Kate's pulse was beginning to thump. "Is this a bunch of press-agent garbage you've dreamed up?"

"God, no," wailed Maury. "Every word's the solemn truth."

"So why let me in on it? You're lots of things, Maury, but generous you're not. Why would you want to do this nice thing for me?"

"You stupid bitch!" shrilled Maury, and Kate suddenly realized he might be telling the truth. He really must need her. "Who else would I want on the show? For Christ's sake, you're the Plague Czar's private pussycat. Everybody knows—or will know. Who's been closer to this epidemic fight than you? Who has more inside information? We've got shots of Blanchard to blow up on the show—Jesus, he's a sexy guy in a dignified way—and everybody but a couple of morons in East Oshkosh will realize you've been screwing him and—Christ, Kate! It'll top every show of the year."

Her pulse was pounding now, but she kept a skeptical tone. "Assuming I buy this bill of goods, what's the deal?"

"Deal? *Deal?* Jesus Christ! Your contract's about to run out. What do you think you could renew it for, after this? For Christ sake, get your ass up here. The sooner the quicker. You'll be top dame in TV newscasting. I'll send a car to your hotel, have a charter plane waiting. Just say when."

She folded up. "It's too quick," said Kate feebly. "I have to think. What's the latest you can know?"

"Oh my God! Latest, she says. Don't blow this, Katie. I can do the show alone, but with you it will have extra dimension. And there's glory enough for both of us a hundred times over."

"How late can I tell you?"

"Good God! Take this phone number. It's a leased line to the studio. I'll be here. In fact, I live here now. We all do. Sweet Jesus. Call me, call me, don't put it off. I need you by morning."

She heard Noah's key in the door. "I'm hanging up," said Kate quickly, "but I'll call. One way or the other. It's not as easy as—oh, goodby. I'll call."

Seventy-two hours, thought Noah, as he rode away from the White House. There was no doubt that the President meant it. Three days from now, six twelve-hour shifts in the frantic research labs—a dozen western cities where millions of Americans lived would be rendered lifeless; every man, woman, child, dog, cat, rat, horse, chicken, rabbit, struck dead by enhanced radiation. Unless the researchers came up with a miracle first, and there was nothing in the medical textbooks about making miracles.

It was more than he could bear to think about. It was too monstrous. It was beyond comprehension. He shook his head and stared through the windshield wipers; rain lanced down, silver under the street lights. The streets of Washington were empty as usual. Noah glanced at the profile of his Secret Service driver. He would rather have driven himself, but the President would not stand for it. But Noah refused to sit in back, like the caricature of a lolling political fat cat.

"You got a wife, Gus?" It was the first thing that came into his mind and surprised him perhaps as much as it did Gus.

"Yes, sir. And two little boys."

Noah nodded. Considering how much time he spent with Gus it was surprising how little he knew about him. To the casual eye he resembled any ordinary middle-sized mild-mannered civilian of perhaps thirty-five, but Noah's knowledgeable eyes had remarked Gus's thick wrists and swift hands. He had reflexes like a fighter pilot. "Hard on them, I expect, you gone all the time driving me around like this."

"She's in Ocean City. I sent them to stay with her folks."

"I expect that was smart. The Maryland shore's pretty free of epidemic. I hope it stays that way."

"It will," said Gus stoutly. "It has to."

"Yes. Of course it does." If I had a wife, Noah wondered, would I send her away? Maybe, if we had kids. It occurred to him that many a worried married man would envy him his carefree domestic arrangements right now. Which reminded him, he had to do something about Kate. In her own way she was contributing as much to the epidemic control effort as the hardest-working lab technician anywhere. She was a marvel. Few women could have taken on a new, difficult task with no notice and performed so magnificently. Lem Akins, the White House press secretary, who considered public relations second only to medical research in importance, praised her daily. Even the Washington media corps, the most querulous in the land, was kept content by her news releases and the interviews she arranged with Task Force principals. Kate deserved a Freedom Medal when this was all over, probably a top journalism award as well. I'll talk to the President about her.

In his heart Noah knew that he was evading the real issue, what he ought to do about Kate personally. Things could not go on forever in this ambiguous way. She had become too important to him: housekeeper, chief of staff, companion in his brief intervals of relaxation, bedmate, and ever since the kitchen staff at the hotel ran away, his cook. An improving cook, always trying to come up with some new savory dish to titillate his taste buds when he dragged in, almost too weary for food. She'd come a long way since the first breakfast she'd cooked for him back in Albuquerque. It wasn't fair to Kate now, letting matters drift on in this undefined, unsatisfactory way.

Gus drew up to the canopied hotel entrance. It had a

forlorn, unexplainably seedy look about it. There was no doorman anymore, the potted palms that had flanked the door had vanished. Gus said, "Usual time in the morning, Doctor?"

"Unless something comes up, Gus."

"I'll be available. Any time. You want me to walk you in?"

"Hell no, Gus. I'm all right. Thanks though."

"Goodnight, Dr. Blanchard."

When the government sedan drove away in the rain, Noah stood a moment in the shelter of the canopy, watching until it turned the corner. Poor Gus. One more of millions of citizens hoping for a miracle to end this nightmare that had overtaken their lives. A miracle. Where is it coming from? I'm out of miracles, thought Noah, if I ever had any. Heavyhearted, thinking once more of the unspeakable horror that three more days might bring, he entered the lobby. Henri, the only waiter who had stuck it out, was sprawled in a lobby chair, smoking. There was no one else in sight. Except for the five hundred a day the government is paying for our suite, thought Noah, they would close this place down, I suppose. He hadn't seen another guest in days.

Henri jumped up. "*Bon soir,* Doctor. I fear you must walk up tonight. *L'ascenseur*—the lift—the elevator—she has ceased to march. A repair person was called for, but—" He let it got with a Gallic shrug.

"What's four flights of stairs? I can use the exercise."

"You are *gentil*," smiled Henri. "But the office ladies of Madame Petrakis complained indignantly when they departed."

"Next time tell them things are tough all over. Goodnight, Henri." As Noah started up the stairs he felt suddenly hungry, nothing to eat since dawn but two of Harrison's doughnuts. He could count on Kate having a tasty meal waiting. When the cooks disappeared, she and Henri had gone shopping and stocked the butler's pantry. Noah smiled on the staircase with the comfortable

177

assurance of a lover who knows that dinner will be ample, delicious, and on time.

That was a dangerous thought—as dangerous as dwelling on the solace of returning to Kate each evening. She was always there, always cheerful, eager to report her day's accomplishments and to listen to what he chose—or was allowed—to tell her of his day. God knows he couldn't tell her what was preying on the President's mind.

By the third flight of stairs Noah found himself out of breath. Disgusting. He had to quit this crazy living, had to get back to regular workouts in a gym. He would, as soon as this was all over. If ever it was. But it had to be. Anything else was not to be borne. Into his mind there swam the haunted expression on President Dobson's face—that seamed and contoured battle map of a countenance—and he knew with inexpressible horror that it was all too likely that he was wrong. This tiled staircase, the fifty-year-old brick and mortar and the steel beams of this eight-story building, Kate and I with them, could be atomized, scattered to our ultimate molecules, become part of the dusty air.

Which is why Kate deserves to know what I am beginning to think about, he argued to himself. Maybe she would laugh. But she has a right to know. It's indecent not to let her know. I don't love her, Noah brooded, whatever love is. Maybe I don't know what it means to be in love with a woman. Probably I am too old. But Kate is reliable, desirable, attractive, intelligent. We don't exchange endearments or any but the most comradely sort of casual caress outside of bed, but we're verbally affectionate. And in bed, my God! She matches my moods. She has more instinctive empathy than any woman I remember. I tell her things in the night I wouldn't tell anyone else. God knows her lovemaking—and she brings with it compassion as well as passion—is all I could possibly want for skill and variety.

What more could I possibly want in a woman? What is the least that I owe her? The offer. To know that I value

178

her this highly. Surely she is entitled to that. Besides, how could I do better—if we live through this thing—than to ask this congenial, educated, grown-up woman to legalize the arrangement? If, of course, she wants to.

From the stairwell he walked swiftly down the carpeted corridor and unlocked the suite door. As he shed his wet raincoat in the foyer, he could see Kate hanging up the telephone in the first sitting room. A smell of garlic simmering in tomato sauce hung deliciously in the air. Noah approached her with swift strides, letting the raincoat fall. "Kate," he said, "I've been doing a lot of hard thinking. About you. Us."

She met him, touched his cheek, bent for the raincoat, shook it out and hung it on a costumer. "Dinner's just ready. Your timing's perfect."

He reached for her. "I'm hungry as a cannibal, but it can wait. Kate, what would you say to our thinking about—"

"You come eat!" She turned lightly, just outside his reach. Well, hell, thought Noah, a little miffed. Then he sniffed the savory air again and felt better.

They hardly spoke at dinner, which consisted of a green salad, spaghetti with tomato sauce, and a half-bottle of a *Cotes de Rhône '49* from the hotel cellar. After Camembert cheese and Turkish coffee Kate summarized her day—a conversation with Lem Akins; a guardedly optimistic release to the press corps they had agreed on about the rising number of spontaneous remissions on the morbidity and mortality reports; and a request for Noah to speak at George Washington Medical School, at which he automatically shook his head, hardly listening to her. Something was bothering Kate. He could sense it. She jumped up and began stacking dishes nervously. "I told you about my day. Is there anything about yours I ought to know for tomorrow's press releases? I suppose you were at the White House? How was it?"

"Yes. And no. I mean, yes, I was at the White House.

179

Rough. Rougher than ever. But no, nothing I can tell you now."

Kate was efficient at everything. In no time the dishes were soaking in soapy water. Henri would do the washing and drying in the morning. She said, "You look terrible. I think you ought to get more sleep. When do you have to get up? Five as usual?"

"Walt Burrows gets along on a lot less sleep than I do," said Noah.

"Well, he ought to," said Kate, "he's a general." She shook her head. "I don't know why I said that. I thought it was time for a joke. You seem to be getting awfully serious all of a sudden."

"Well, the times they are serious," said Noah, but she still didn't smile. "Kate, damn it, I want to talk about something. We never said where all this might be leading us. We never considered the future."

"Future? What future? Is there one?" She avoided his eyes.

"How the hell do I know?" said Noah in sudden irritation. "Yes, I think there is. It's what I'm busting my ass trying to make sure of. I have to think there's a future. Otherwise, I'd quit and give up. Anybody who isn't in imminent peril of death has a future. I think plenty of people aren't about to die. Not just yet. I think that includes you and me."

"How did we get onto this morbid subject?" Shakily, Kate lighted a cigarette. It was the first time she had smoked in over a week. That was an odd thing about the epidemic. Under the threat of a new, horrible danger people tended to drink and smoke less. It was a manifestation of widespread terror the psychologists could not agree on reasons for. Kate puffed twice, made a face, and smashed out the cigarette. "I'm sorry." She waved the air around. "I know you detest the smell."

"It's all right. Kate, for Christ's sake, what's bugging you?"

"Do you want to go to bed? To make love?"

"Kate, Kate. What's the matter? God, yes, I'll take you to bed if you want to. Always. Any time. But I don't think that's what you want. What is it?"

She said, "You really have everything you want, don't you, Noah?"

The question surprised him. "Well, obviously I want what we all want—an end to this epidemic. That's not what you mean, though, is it?"

"No. I mean all you ever really wanted was to be a doctor, right? Your special kind of doctor. There aren't any mountains out there you ache to climb. No dreams that haunt you. You know what I mean."

He frowned. "I would have to think about it. But I suppose that's true. When you're kept busy doing what you want to do and consider yourself good at—you don't have time to dream of—well, unconquered mountains. Yes. I think you're probably right. That makes me sound complacent, doesn't it?"

"No. Just lucky. Just damned, damned lucky!" She said it fiercely. "God, what I would give—! You couldn't know. And really what I want is so cheap and so not worth having that I'm ashamed."

"What's that, Kate?" said Noah gently.

"I told you the first day. It's just cheap vulgar notoriety—popular commercial television notoriety. I want to be *known*. Isn't that petty? But it eats me like a cancer. Ever since I was little—as far back as I can remember. Kate Petrakis had to *be* somebody. Somebody special. And for me that means one thing only—my own TV show. It's revolting. But I can't help it."

Noah nodded, not surprised. Disappointed, though. But secretly relieved. Regretful, though. Hurt, too. In his vanity. "I think what you're saying is that no matter what you can do for me—with me—for any man, it's not enough. Is that right."

"Oh damn!" she said. "Why don't you shut up and take me to bed? Do you think I want to be like this, or to hear myself talk like this?"

"It's supposed to be the unforgivable insult to a woman," said Noah, "to offer herself to a man and not be taken up on it. Funny. If anything a woman can say that is apt to *dampen* ardor—there's a pretentious expression!— I expect it's just that. You want to go to bed? Sure. But first and foremost I think I ought to know what is going on here. I'm not angry, just puzzled. Because clearly something happened to you since I left this morning. You want to tell me about it?

"If I had any sense," said Kate, her teeth clenched. "But I don't have any sense. I'm not in love with you, Dr. Noah Blanchard, I never was, maybe I could be some day, but how can I know, and it doesn't matter. But I never liked a man more. I never knew one who was nicer to me, made me feel more important. There's just one thing lacking for me about us. It isn't a lack in you. It's in me. Yes. Something happened. Just a little while ago. I wish it hadn't. But it did. Maury phoned—Maury Murray. I told you about him. My boss. Anchorman of that show. In Chicago. He called from Chicago. He wants me there."

"I guessed it had to be something like that," said Noah. "What does he want you to do in Chicago?"

"You should know. You've got to know about it. Except for you I wouldn't be in it at all. Listen, there are these three convicts that want to go on TV to persuade other convicts to volunteer for vaccine testing. The governor of Indiana arranged it. All I know is what Maury said and he's such a liar you can't believe a tenth of—"

"Shut up," said Noah crisply. He was punching buttons in the red telephone he kept hidden in a wall cabinet. "Harrison? Blanchard. Put the general on. Top urgent. Right. Walt? Noah. Listen, Kate here is on to something. Have you heard anything about some convict volunteer scheme for the vaccine—? Up in Chicago— Indiana—Christ, I don't know any details, but Kate got a call—you *do*? Well, for Christ's sake. Governor Birdsall in Indianapolis said that? They're leaving when? They're—? What's your off-hand reaction? Does it sound

182

phony? You like it? Yeah, well listen, get more information and phone me back. Shit! Of course she's in on it. She's a TV pro, you know. See you, Walt."

"I'll come back, Noah," said Kate, twisting her hands together. "Right after the broadcast. I promise. If you—maybe you don't want me back."

"Sure, Kate," said Noah. "Of course you will. Of course I do." He took her in his arms, but he really wondered if she would.

Chapter 14

The three plenipotentiaries who met in an East German
farmhouse off the Berlin Access Road had been chosen
for inconspicuousness. No American intelligence opera-
tives were likely to notice that Boris Litovitch, a
second-level functionary in the Bureau of Agricultural
Affairs, had left Moscow; that Sir Henry Alford of the
Ministry of Petroleum Management was called home to
Coventry; that Jean-Marie Longlier was absent with *la
grippe* from his back-office desk at the Quai D'Orsay, the
French Foreigh Office. No West German spy in the
Magdeburg region was apt to remark three foreign
commercial travelers driving through: Litovitch in a
clumsy Lada, Alford in a battered Rover, Longlier in a
shiny Simca. The East German plain-clothes Volkspols
assigned to perimeter patrol of the farmstead had no idea
why and resented it. The French, British, and Russian
technicians, dressed as farm workers, who swept the
farmhouse electronically and pronounced it free of bugs,
particularly a small, lead-lined room in the cellar, did not
know why either, but were too professional to wonder.

There were no interpreters. Commonality of language—in this case English—had been another criterion
for selecting the plenipotentiaries. Lunch was served in

the whitewashed farm kitchen by the farmer and his wife—actually operators of an East German border listening post—at which the conversation dealt casually with chemical fertilizers and agricultural machinery. After lunch the three men submitted to body search and locked themselves in the lead-walled room in the cellar.

It was empty except for four straight chairs and a plain deal table supplied with pads and pencils, black-market American cigarettes, ashtrays, drinking glasses, and bottled spring water. The three men sat for a moment eyeing one another in silence. Then Henry Alford broke open a pack of Lucky Strikes, lit one with nervous fingers, blew smoke, and stubbed the cigarette out. "Well, chaps," he said, "we know why we're here. Either of you care to get the ball rolling?"

Litovitch, slight and swarthy, looking more like a Frenchman than the big-boned Norman-blond Longlier, spread his hands. "I'll start by asking a question—that okay with you guys?"

Wincing slightly at the Americanism, Alford said, "By all means, sir. Fire away."

"Well, about this Dobson bird? What do we know about him? I mean, as a man? What kind of fruitcake would offer to wipe out his own cities to show good faith? Is he crazy? Is he lying? I had six years in Washington, but I never heard of him."

Longlier said, "I can tell you this, our people are afraid of him." He spoke with a surprisingly soft voice for so hulking a man. "Ambassador Ortelly thinks he has fanatic qualities."

"That's odd," said Alford. "I thought he was a university don—a schoolmaster type—before he got into politics."

"Intellectuals often burn with fanatic fire," said Litovitch. "Consider the great anarchists. Our Ambassador Popovitch also believes that President Dobson is capable of the most drastic measures if put to the test."

"Well, if the fella's a fanatic," said Alford, "how can

185

one deal with him? Is he trustworthy in your judgment?"

Longlier said, "Remember, my friend, fanatic is not the same as madman. Not in this case certainly. Along with his respect for the President's strength of character Ambassador Ortelly has the highest regard for his intelligence, considers it perhaps the finest to occupy the White House in half a century. Certainly the most scholarly. But he still means what he says. He is not what the poker players call a four-flusher. Not according to Ambassador Ortelly."

"Nor Ambassador Popovitch," murmured Litovitch. "Well, my question was to find out what you thought, not what my government thought."

"And my response," said Alford, "was not to imply that Her Majesty's government was in doubt either. We might be wrong, of course, but our position is that when the man offers his cities in exchange for our risking his vaccine he means it. He will keep his word."

"Agreed," said Longlier.

"So stipulated," murmured Alford, writing on his notepad. "Now, then, what is at issue if we don't accept his proposal?"

"Obliteration," said Longlier somberly. "The issue is obliteration. For all. Debacle. Catastrophe. Cataclysm. *Finis.*"

"For you perhaps," said Litovitch truculently. "Russia would survive. Our defenses are so strong—" He cut his words short, smiled, wagged his head apologetically. "Forgive me. All that is beside the point. We, as much as you, want to avert the risk of any of us being put to the test."

"That would rule out our risking a first-strike. Do all concur?" Alford watched them keenly.

"Unless," said Litovitch, "one could be absolutely certain that the Americans could not detect the preparations in time and would launch their own massive preemptive strike. And I do not believe that is at all certain."

"Of course," said Longlier meditatively, "France has almost surely not been targeted by the United States for its ICBM or submarine-missile attack plan."

"Nor the U.K."

Litovitch smiled cheerily. "While my poor country is charted and targeted from border to border by Strategic Air Command and the American Navy, eh? Which makes you feel comfortable by comparison. Sir Henry, have there been unusual developments in recent days at the American fighter-bomber bases in your country? Any conditions of heightened alert for training purposes? Are outsiders temporarily excluded? And you, Monsieur Longlier, although France has tolerated no foreign forces on her sacred soil since the great De Gaulle evicted them, is she not ringed by American bases in Belgium, West Germany, Italy, Spain? Are not the aircraft on those bases capable of nuclear attack? Are not your major military installations—the sites of your V-Force, Sir Henry, your *Force de Frappe*, Monsieur Longlier, all your industrial centers—are they not known to those American pilots with their doomsday weapons?"

"He has us there," said Alford dismally. "We're all in the soup together."

"The *world* is, *mon ami*," said Longlier heavily. "The entire earth. Since childhood we have all lived with that knowledge. Never before, it occurs to me now, did I realize it quite this clearly."

"So our next assumption," said the Russian, "must be that a preemptive strike against America—to wipe out this epidemic—by us constituent members of the non-American long-range delivery nuclear club—what a term!—would be an unacceptable risk."

"Agreed again," said Alford glumly, and wrote on his pad.

"The next assumption, it seems to me," said Longlier, "is that this epidemic in America—unless quickly controlled—is a threat to the human race equal to that of nuclear warfare."

187

"Approximately," muttered Litovitch. "How do you compare such things?"

"So stipulated," said Alford, writing again.

"Now then," said Longlier, "we have been told of a vaccine American doctors have perfected. Can we trust the claims made for it? Let me mention hastily that I have been advised already by our epidemic specialists in Paris, but I would be grateful for your opinion."

"British health authorities," said Alford, "have absolute confidence in the Americans on this point. They accept American Disease Control bulletins unequivocally. They name names—Fundersen, Blanchard, Green, a dozen others, not all just with the Disease Control Center—as colleagues known, trusted, respected. Science, they assure me, certainly medical science, recognizes no international borders. If such men—not just men, they certainly include women—call the vaccine effective, then the British medical profession believes it."

"*Da,*" muttered Litovitch. "So, too, my sources. Americans may lie—do lie—all people lie. But not about this. Not their life scientists on professional issues. Never."

"So write that down as principle the second, eh?" said Longlier. "The vaccine, within its limitations, is reliable."

"And they offer it to us, freely and without conditions," said Alford. "But it has this limitation."

"Oh yes," said Longlier. "A famous limitation."

"How long," asked Litovitch, "do your epidemiologists estimate that Europe can be kept free of Consolvo's Ulceration?"

"It first appeared in the southwestern United States," said Longlier, "barely a month ago. The Spanish Influenza of 1918 swept round the world from the Arctic Circle to the South Pacific islands in under six months. I have been doing research," he added apologetically.

"They tell me that quarantine only works in restricted areas and only when the disease—its cause, its means of distribution—is well understood," said Alford. "How can you quarantine a continent?"

"About this famous limitation to the American vaccine," said Litovitch, "that along with conferring immunity, it unfortunately appears to infect every tenth subject with the disease. What does that signify to us?"

"That we are damned in any case," said Alford. "Sooner or later—who can say when?—the epidemic must reach Europe. Without the vaccine Europe is helpless. But if we use the vaccine, we deliberately introduce the disease immediately. And those unfortunates we infect with the vaccine instantly become infectious to all about them."

"Which is exactly why the American vaccination program lies in shambles," said Longlier. "The citizens refuse to risk it."

"Ours would not," said Litovitch. "Soviet citizens are not so unpatriotic."

Alford and Longlier smiled faintly. "I am sure you could vaccinate a goodly number before the rest rebelled," said Longlier. "No offense, ah—Boris."

Litovitch beamed. "None taken, Jean-Marie. I approve the familiarity. Men engaged in vital discussions should be informal. Would not Englishmen and Frenchmen be patriotic, too?"

Alford laughed. "My dear Boris. We can't even make the average English workingman agree to go to his job on time, much less stick a needle in his arm that might condemn him to death. On the other hand—I'm sure we could vaccinate a goodly portion of our population if we put it to them in the right way."

"We must find ways," said Longlier earnestly. "We simply must, all of us. There is no choice. No thinkable choice. Remember this vital fact. The vaccine *can* be used to control the epidemic. We need only learn to identify in advance the ten percent of mankind that is vulnerable to it. We must vaccinate subjects carefully and keep them in quarantine until time enough passes to prove them safe."

"And the luckless ten percent who catch it we keep isolated," said the Russian. "We keep in close quarantine until—"

"Until the poor sods die," said Alford. "Well, there's no help for that."

"I'm reluctant to bring it up," said Longlier. "It sounds so fanciful, but our ambassador reported a rumor that President Dobson was negotiating to buy human beings from an Asian country to test the vaccine on. Two hundred thousand from Bangladesh or Viet Nam. Did either of you hear anything of that sort?"

Litovitch snorted. "My country wouldn't have to consider anything like that. Our people are patriotic."

Alford chuckled. "I would question the validity of that rumor, friend Longlier. What a scandal in Washington, were it to get out! Not that the offer might not appeal to Hanoi. I could almost wish someone wanted to buy some of our troublesome types."

"The IRA?" said Litovitch, grinning.

Alford's eyebrows rose. "A consummation devoutly to be desired, what? I daresay you might not object to supplying a few guinea pigs yourself, were the price satisfactory. Say some Kurds or Mongols or Ukranians?"

Litovitch reddened. "I was joking."

"Oh, I too," said Alford airily.

"Look, you two," said Longlier. "This will take hours unless we keep on the track. I for one have to submit a recommendation to my government. And there is not much time."

"Hear, hear," said Alford. "Boris, what say we take a break, have that surly farmer bring us a spot of tea, and then buckle down to work. I would like to tell Downing Street something positive by tomorrow."

It was very late when the three left the farmhouse. They shook hands like survivors of an airplane crash who never expected to meet again but who had shared an experience so intense they felt as close as brothers. "I could wish," said Alford, "that some of those bloody-minded Admiralty and War Office types who frighten me to death could have listened to us this day."

Litovitch grunted. "And a Red Army marshal or two."

"My dear friends," said Longlier. "If we survive it, this crisis may yet prove a disguised blessing. I shall try to believe that. Very well. You both know what I intend to recommend to my government."

"And I the same."

"And from me, too," said Litovitch gruffly. Turning his coat collar up in the raw German air, he got in his Lada, cranked the four-cylinder engine, and, when it caught, drove slowly out of the brick-walled farmyard. As agreed, the others waited ten minutes before Longlier, after a quick Gallic shake of Alford's hand, got in his Simca and started up, and Alford, still musing, entered his Rover and rolled off in the opposite direction.

Chapter 15

Father always preached that the vital lubricant for business between gentlemen was courtesy—that even the least likely applicant deserved a sympathetic interview before the House of Olvera declined his account. The rule had pragmatic merit. Any man rich enough to apply was bound to have information worth knowing and some of it he might let slip. Nor was it dishonorable to use information gained that way except against the man who revealed it.

On this southwestern junket, mused Luis Olvera, he had not learned anything useful from the Bisbee copper king or the Pueblo smelter owner, or for that matter from old Clavering Washburn dreaming of lost glory in the ruins of his experimental, synthetic-fuel farm. Father would be saddened to hear how low the old titan had fallen. Clavering Washburn had been a figure of daring innovation to the chemical industry once—what Howard Hughes had been to flying and Henry Kaiser to shipbuilding. Forgotten now, disabled by stroke, there he sat in a wheelchair, tended by two old servants. It was too bad.

On the other hand, that posturing old fool of a silent movie star, Monte Hethercote, had let drop hints of labor strife brewing at Monarch Studios highly valuable to Olvera portfolios heavy in entertainment industry holdings. That was the quality of information Father welcomed.

He had done well on his trip. Father would be pleased. Particularly about signing up Howard Consolvo. There was a man Father would be sure to hit it off with. As Father also preached, any man who satisfied the stern criteria of the House of Olvera was worth having as a friend, not just as a client. And nothing could be more agreeable than a fiduciary relationship between trusting and trustworthy friends. Yes, Father was going to be delighted to have Howard Consolvo for a client.

From his dreamy musing Luis Olvera came startlingly and horribly awake, pain exploding in his skull so intensely he thought it would break. Reality returned. The noon sun blazing into the canyon pierced the palmetto frond screen over his hammock and struck his eyes a hammer blow. He turned his head and cried out at the crunching grind of broken bones. He shifted his buttocks and pain wracked his right ankle. Sweating and nauseated, Luis Olvera concentrated on a chameleon perched overhead, blowing his throat out in a vermillion bubble. Gradually, as the pain subsided, full comprehension returned. Father was dead, he remembered. Tears coursed weakly down his cheeks. He would never see Father again. He would never see anyone he knew again. He did not know what place this was. How could anyone find him here? He would die and no one would ever know. Merciful drowsiness crept over him. Then the sultry air seemed to stir and he knew Maria was coming. He smelt the tang of dry peppers that clung always to her fresh-washed cotton blouses and humid flesh. He smelt the hot soup she brought and he salivated like a dog.

"*Señor,*" murmured Maria, black Indian eyes kind in the fat brown face. She slid a huge arm underneath to lift him against her billowy breast and spooned soup into his mouth. It was greasy, unknown, unbelievably delicious.

He gulped greedily, strength flowing into him with every swallow. I won't die, thought Luis Olvera stubbornly. I refuse to die.

When she eased him back down he smiled. *"Gracias, muchas gracias, Maria."* It was almost all the Spanish he knew. He felt her calloused palm on his forehead testing for fever, and he wondered about her. She had three shy sons about twelve to fourteen who hoed corn in the canyon every day with the old men, but he had never seen her husband. There did not seem to be any husbands. There were many women—old and young—many children, a few old men. There were chickens, dogs, goats, a gray burro. Except for Maria who fed and nursed and kept him clean, no one ever came near. He saw the others only in the distance, only by turning his aching neck to watch. He wondered where the young men were. He wondered how long he had been here.

Maria adjusted his straw-mat pillow, touched his lips to enjoin sleep and left. He would not see her again until supper. He wondered what she did all afternoon. He lay as still as possible to prevent pain, listened to lizards rustling, hens clucking, the distant rush of water down the canyon that gave the village life. Dimly, as from a dream, he remembered hanging upside down in his crumpled automobile among granite boulders in the foaming dash and roar of rapids. He wondered who had brought him to the village.

Gradually he sank into shallow dreaming. He was on Consolvo's ranch, riding the high range in the old man's pickup truck, taking turns opening gates, admiring the Hereford steers that Consolvo said he raised just to look at, listening to him explain how he wanted his money handled—a little for his grown kids in California, but most of it to support a hospital named after his dead wife.

That was a happy day for Luis, made him feel like a boy again roaming the countryside with Father. They were much alike beneath superficial differences, courtly Spanish-bred Father and the rough New Mexican cowman, both men of rectitude and transparent honesty. Both enormously self-disciplined. When Consolvo jagged his arm on a wire fence, he laughed at it as Father would have done, shook off the blood, and would have let it go. It was Luis, fearing blood poisoning, who insisted on disinfecting and bandaging it with the first aid kit in the truck.

Just as deep sleep swallowed Luis, he leaped convulsively, seeing once again the green rattletrap Mexican bus clattering down upon him at breakneck speed on the wrong side of the road, running him off the cliff.

Maria's urgent voice penetrated his slumber. Her hands prodded him. Sluggishly he resisted waking. *"Señor, señor!"* she said. *"Dos hombres—Norteamericano—"* He felt his wrist gripped powerfully, a thumb dig for his pulse. Blurrily he looked up at a fat old man in glasses, wearing a battered Panama hat with drooping brim.

"Son," said a friendly voice, "we're mighty glad to find you. People been looking all over everywhere for you."

Luis started up. Agony made his head swim. "Hello, Father," he whispered. "I knew you'd come." He sank back, unconscious. Simon Green, sore from ten jolting miles up a mule trail in a jeep, rumpled and sweaty in seersucker, listened to his chest with a stethoscope. He nodded at the man beside him, swarthy and slender in a Mexican Public Health Service uniform.

"He'll come out of it. What do you know? Took me for his daddy. Poor fellow. His daddy's long dead."

"I hope he's the man we're looking for," said Dr. Alonzo Bernaldo. "I'd hate to have to take you on any more jeep rides."

"Me, too," said Simon. "Oh, he's Luis Olvera all right. His secretary showed me pictures. Well, Doctor, what do you think of our detective work? Bulletins out on this young fellow on both sides of the border and we find him like this."

"Ought to hang out shingles as private eyes, Doctor," said Bernaldo, who had acquired his English along with his M.D. at Michigan State. "Pretty slick, the way you figured it."

"Not me," said Simon. "It took you and your government."

It had been a neat job of detection, considering how far Simon was from the scene and all the difficulties he had faced. But using the rental car description and license that Olga Dalrymple supplied, he was able, with Dr. Bernaldo's help, to determine that Olvera had crossed the border at Agua Prieta, but failed to clear the customs office farther south. That narrowed the search instantly. Rural police were ordered to pursue rumors of a car wrecked in the wild Sierra de la Madera. In short order, that had brought the two doctors up a backbreaking trail by jeep convoy to this village. Now they stood looking down upon the unconscious form of the man they suspected of being the innocent cause of untold suffering to millions of people.

"One thing about him," said Bernaldo. "He must have an iron constitution to still be breathing. The sergeant of *Rurales* tells me this canyon is three hundred meters deep."

Olvera groaned and fluttered his eyes open. "Maria?" he murmured. He looked at the men. "Who are you? Where's Maria?"

"I'm Dr. Green from Washington," said Simon. "This is Dr. Bernaldo from Hermosillo. We came to fetch you out of here and get you to a hospital."

"You found me," whispered Olvera. "I had about given up—thank you."

"Thank Olga Dalrymple. She supplied the clues. And you can thank the Mexican border patrol and customs and policemen—a passel of good folks."

"Señor Olvera," said Bernaldo, "I am very glad we found you."

"Oh, my," said Luis weakly. "So am I, sir, so am I."

196

"Before we haul you down this mountain, son," said Green, "we need to check you over, see how bad off you are. I warn you, it might hurt some."

"I can take it." Luis tried to grin. "Anybody catch that green bus that ran me off the road? Maniac was driving on the wrong side."

"My friend," said Bernaldo, "maniacs driving buses on the wrong side are a bane of rural Mexico. We would never be able to identify yours. Excuse me, my colleague wants a consultation." He walked over to where Simon Green was standing in some shade.

"I was wondering," said Simon, "if maybe you ought to quarantine this place. All these people exposed to him, and if he is a carrier—?"

"Let me ask Maria some questions." Bernaldo talked in Spanish a few minutes and returned. "It's as I suspected. Except for her sons, who found and brought him in, she's the only person who's had any physical contact. That seems to be the custom in these backcountry villages. Could be a taboo handed down from tribal times that helped keep infections from spreading. Anyway, I don't think quarantine is justified."

"Probably not," agreed Simon. "Just thought I'd bring it up. Actually, the incubation period has passed and nobody got sick. That's good. Only thing is, I *want* him to be a carrier. So it's bad. That sound heartless?"

"Sounds like an epidemiologist to me. Well, let's look him over."

"You're willing to risk it?"

"After all the cases I've been on? I figure I'm immune."

"Me, too," said Simon. "Anyway, I'm so old, it doesn't matter."

"Nobody's that old. Well, let's see just how hurt the poor fellow is."

Mercifully, Olvera fainted when Simon tried to lift his right ankle, which made the rest of the examination easier on everyone. With only their fingers and eyesight the two doctors were limited, but the conclusion seemed inescapable: multiple fractures, too many to count, more than they could detect without X rays, possibly some extremely dangerous ones to his skull and vertebrae. He had suffered massive internal bleeding from a ruptured spleen or other organ. It was sheer madness to transport such a patient down a mountain by jeep. But they had no choice. The canyon was too narrow for the helicopters at Fronteras to land in, and time was running out. He would make it or he wouldn't.

"At least there's no sign of infection," said Bernaldo.

"Tribute to that constitution," said Green, "and Miss Maria's nursing."

Bernaldo repeated that in Spanish to Maria, who ducked her head and looked pleased. "She's the whole medical profession of the village," said Bernaldo, "midwife, apothecary, G.P. Mexico is too poor to give modern medicine to all her people."

"Looks to me like Maria does a fine job," said Simon. "All these folks look healthy to me. Think it would make this poor boy ride any easier to slap a couple of quick-set plaster casts on him?"

"We have to hurry," warned Bernaldo. "Darkness comes fast in these canyons."

When Luis Olvera came to, he discovered that he was tied to some sort of platform and looking up at the sky. His head was immobilized. His sore ankle and right arm were in plaster casts, and he could not move them. From head to toe he felt like one great screaming toothache. "Maria, where's Maria?" he asked.

"She's over here, waving goodby," said Simon. "We're going to fly you back home, son, fly you to Arizona and then to Washington. A whole bunch of doctors are waiting for you."

As pain leaped like a tongue of flame through his neck, Luis said, "What makes me that important?"

"Well, now," said Green, "not many men fall a thousand feet and live to tell about it. You're kind of a curiosity."

Another pain shot through Luis. "God," he groaned. "Maria. I want to do something for Maria."

"We have to start, Doctor," Bernaldo insisted. "Time is running out."

"My wallet," said Luis. "In my left hip pocket. Take the money and give it to her."

Green looked at Bernaldo and shrugged. "Why not?" He reached under, took out and opened the wallet. "You want her to have it all? Must be seven or eight hundred dollars here, son."

"She saved me," said Luis. "Give it to her."

"Of course," said Bernaldo. "I'll see to it." He took the wallet from Green and waved his hand. The forward jeep started its engine. Bernaldo got behind the wheel of the jeep that Olvera's litter was strapped across. Green climbed in beside him. They cranked up and started downhill. At the first rattling drop-off in the trail, Olvera cried out sharply. Green twisted around to look at him.

"Unconscious," he said. "Well, if he doesn't die on us, that's the best way for him to ride. Why didn't you want to give that girl the money, Doctor?"

Bernaldo concentrated on driving. It was a miserable descent: boulders on both sides, one rattling, bouncing, lurching drop after another. After a while he said, "You do not know these simple people, Doctor. That village is a handful of interrelated families of mixed Spanish and Indian blood, perhaps Pima, perhaps Yaqui, who can say? They have lived generations in their fertile narrow canyon. They live in unchanging ways. What do they need? They have goats, hens, perhaps fish from the stream, wild pig rarely, they grow corn, beans, peppers. Their men go out twice a year to work in the Arizona-Sonora citrus groves and melon farms—migrant workers—who bring home what money is needed. Not much. A few pesos for coffee, cloth, sugar, salt, a new hoe, a little candy for the children, a little wine for fiesta, perhaps a new figurine of the *virgen*.

"Our friend would have innundated Maria with an

unimaginable, inconceivable sudden shower of largesse. What would happen to her, her family, her village? This enormous unearned fortune. Remember, she nurses because that is her role in the village life, where everyone contributes according to his or her lot and talent. Nursing the ill is not something one grows rich from. What would such a bonanza mean? A roaring six-month drunk for Maria's husband and his friends instead of the one-night spree when they come home with a little wine? Jewels and finery for Maria? Would you confound their way of life, ruin their balanced economy, plant the seeds of envy, discontent, greed? No, Doctor. Return the money to our patient. I will keep out a little bit, enough for the storekeeper in Fronteras to send up enough red cloth for a skirt, a sack of candies, perhaps a gilt crucifix. That is enough."

"I see your point," said Simon, hanging on for dear life as the jeep lurched past a cliff-edge that seemed to fall away into a shadowy void. Night was closing fast.

"Sorry to lecture," said Bernaldo. "It's a sore point with me."

"No," said Simon, "there's a whole lot to what you say. Not just for folks in Mexico either."

Suddenly the trail twisted right, forded a shallow burbling stream, and struggled up from the arroyo. Then the jeep rolled smoothly again, and they were on the paved highway into Fronteras. At the airfield two Mexican government helicopters were waiting—a big Sikorsky to fly Green and his patient to Davis-Monthan at Tucson to meet a USAF Aeromedical Service evacuation airplane, and a small Bell to take Bernaldo back to Hermosillo.

Before the corpsmen, masked and gloved, lifted Olvera's litter into the large helicopter, they examined the unconscious man again. His heartbeat was shallow but regular, and he still had no fever. "This is one tough cookie, Doctor," said Bernaldo. "Anybody who could live through that mountain ride ought to live through anything."

"He's got to live," said Green. "We've absolutely got to keep him alive. Long enough, anyway."

"Assuming he is the carrier?"

"Assuming that. Which we still don't know for sure."

"And still no idea where he picked it up if he is."

"We have to find that out," said Green soberly. "The sooner this young man tells us where he was before he saw Consolvo, the sooner we might get a handle on this thing."

"You'll let me know?"

"You'll be the first, Doctor. I can't tell you how much I appreciate—"

"No need, sir. Mexico needs to stop this epidemic as much as the U.S."

"Everybody in the world does," said Simon. "Doctor, knowing you has been a privilege."

"Go with God, my friend."

Chapter 16

For the five years before Consolvo's Ulceration swept down on Washington, D.C., to turn St. Elizabeth's Hospital for the Mentally Ill into part pesthouse—as the epidemic did hospitals everywhere—its strangest but best-liked patient was the one who called himself Ambrose Alexander Noyes. Unlike the incontinent, unkempt, brooding manic-depressives and schizophrenics around him, he never gave trouble, kept himself immaculate, was cheerful, entertaining, agreeable, and versatile. He was a strapping, full-bearded man of at least seventy who waltzed indefatigably on dance nights with women patients and nurses, helped instruct therapeutic workshops in watercolors, lectured on the development of the English novel to the literary study group, regularly beat Henry Gault, chief of psychiatry, at chess, and after studying a copy of Goren lent him by Maurice Fleischman, the director of male admissions, won all the duplicate bridge tournaments.

Dr. Gault and Dr. Fleischman, who were not only colleagues but close friends, discussed him endlessly. In the customary sense there was nothing to justify patient-status for Ambrose Alexander Noyes. He needed no medication; psychiatric examination was futile; he showed none of the conventional signs of mania, depression, catatonia, or hebephrenia. To all appearances he was a perfectly normal, perfectly healthy elderly gentleman of cultivated tastes except for one small eccentricity: the unshakable conviction that it was 1895, Grover Cleveland was in the White House, and St. Elizabeth's was a genteel boarding establishment in which he was a guest while his family traveled abroad.

The psychiatric and psychological journals printed monographs about the curious fixation of Ambrose Alexander Noyes, and there was loose talk on the staff of another "Bridey Murphy" case until Henry Gault squelched it. Maurice Fleischman tried hypnosis to unlock Ambrose's identity, but he was one of those rare subjects who, although obliging, cannot be brought under. Besides, Ambrose Alexander Noyes knew perfectly well who he was and would gladly tell you. He was a Philadelphia-born retired Baltimore cigar factory owner whose wife and three daughters were taking the Grand Tour in Europe. He was a civil engineer from the University of Pennsylvania, had commanded a squadron for Sheridan, and for a few restless years after the war surveyed rights-of-way for railroads opening up the West. When he went home to settle down he married a Baltimore belle and had prospered. He made it all sound perfectly believable and absolutely ordinary. The history buffs who were brought in to hear him shook their heads and said that every detail of Civil War fighting and western exploration rang with authenticity.

But of course it was all impossible.

All the hospital could be sure of was that Ambrose Alexander Noyes—whoever he really was—had been picked up by the police strolling in his shirtsleeves one icy January midnight along the Potomac waterfront. He told them he had stepped out for a breath of air, leaving his coat, wallet, and identification in his Willard Hotel room. The trouble with that was that the Willard was an empty shell whose last guest had checked out ten years earlier.

Since he was sober and no Missing Persons Report fit, the cops took him to St. Elizabeth's where he remained in cheerful residence ever since.

As Fleischman said to Gault in one of their last discussions of Noyes, "The only way to describe him, unless you invent some new term, is 'acute paranoid schizophrenic.' Except of course—"

Gault finished it. "Except of course, that he isn't paranoid. Not in any way I ever saw before."

"Well," said Fleischman, "he is a little paranoid—if that's not too strong—about conceding the existence of modern phenomena. He won't look at TV—smiles and calls it a magic lantern—or out the window to see cars or an airplane overhead."

"Which suggests, of course, unwillingness to admit they exist."

"Or fear of what they represent."

"Which is?"

Fleishman chuckled. "We're getting in over our heads. What do automobiles, TV, jet airplanes represent? That is a question for philosophers, Henry. They represent conquest of time and distance. They represent the promise of an international community. They represent the poisoning of the atmosphere. They represent—"

"How many angels can stand on the head of a pin? Come off it, Morrie. They represent technology. They represent science. New science."

"So our cultivated, charming, civil engineer friend is afraid of science?"

"You wouldn't think a civil engineer—anyway, a man who says that is what he is—would be afraid of science."

"New science, maybe. Civil engineering—I'm no expert—but doesn't it mainly use old elementary scientific principles—simple mechanics, steam power, that sort of thing?"

"Nineteenth-century civil engineering certainly did. Tell me, what is so wonderful about 1895?"

"How do you mean?"

"All right. Here is an educated man hiding from new science. Where does he hide? In time. A time before modern science. When did modern science begin? How about the discovery of X rays? That was in 1895, in case you've forgotten. All right, all right, I looked it up."

"So what else about 1895 would make it an attractive year for a man to live in?"

"Depending on your position in American society, it was a good year or a bad one. Some ways a damn sight better time than now, what with worries about atomic weapons and drug addiction and Third World hunger and destruction of the environment, where four billion people in the world are screwing like crazy to make it five billion. If you were black or a factory hand or a western farmer, 1895 wasn't so swell: depression and strikes and Grover Cleveland tweaking John Bull's nose and the Jim Crow and Judge Lynch laws coming into their own. On the other hand, the country hadn't been at war for thirty years, the air was clean, labor was cheap, the oceans protected us from foreign enemies—"

"For a well-to-do Baltimore cigar-factory owner a comfortable uncomplicated time to be alive, eh? Well, it's a nice theory, but you couldn't publish it."

"Wouldn't want to," said Henry Gault cheerily. "This is just shop talk with a colleague. I expect Ambrose Noyes will remain a mystery wrapped in an enigma—isn't that a Churchill quote?—unless some extraordinary trauma jolts him back to reality."

"I wonder what it would take," mused Fleischman. "I wonder if I will ever know."

He did not live to. Consolvo's Ulceration arrived a week later, claiming Maurice Fleischman as an early victim. A tenth of the staff died with him, and others went into hiding, leaving the rest stunned, grief-stricken, and overworked. Like all hospitals, St. Elizabeth's made space for epidemic victims—consolidating wards, moving patients into halls, double-decking beds. One whole wing was converted to an epidemic ward and sealed off from

205

the mental patients, most of whom seemed little aware that anything irregular was going on. As the epidemic worsened, some complained about a vanished attendant or that the food was bad or that there was nothing on television any more but "Bonanza" and "Lucy" re-runs.

Ambrose Noyes, who did not believe that TV was real and was too polite to complain of anything, remained oblivious as long as anyone. But in late September, the same day the three European plenipotentiaries met in a farmhouse south of Magdeburg, he stopped Henry Gault, disheveled and harried-looking, in the main corridor.

"Excuse me, Doctor," he said with a courtly bow, "but has something happened to Dr. Fleischman? I haven't seen him for days."

"Fleischman?" Gault stared with red-rimmed eyes at the placid figure in robe, slippers, and pajamas. "Good God, man. Maurice is—" Remembering that this was a mental patient, he softened his tone. "I thought you knew, Mr. Noyes. Fleischman died some days ago."

"Died?" Noyes put his hand to the luxuriant gray beard he had grown in the hospital. "I am so sorry. I know what good friends you were. What happened, if I may ask?"

"But, Mr. Noyes. Dr. Morgenstern is dead too and Nurse Reynolds and others. You didn't notice they were missing? There's an epidemic, Mr. Noyes. A very serious epidemic."

"I didn't know," said Noyes, plucking his beard. "No one told me. This is terrible news."

Around them in the corridor, foot and wheelchair traffic streamed. Gault said, "I'm sorry, but I took it for granted you knew, I suppose. All the crowding and doubling-up and feeding in shifts—I thought you would have realized. It's an extremely dangerous epidemic. You'll have to excuse me, there are a thousand things I have to do, Mr. Noyes."

Ambrose Alexander Noyes drew himself taller. "If you're that busy," he said crisply, "you can use help. I've been in epidemics. I lived through two Yellow Jack epidemics, in Mobile and New Orleans. I can help. I'm not as young as I was, Dr. Gault, but I can carry litters, sweep floors, carry trays. Tell me what you need and I'll do it."

"That's very fine of you," said Gault. "We can use every hand." He reached and stopped an orderly hurrying by. "Perkins, get Mr. Noyes some work clothes and start him setting up beds with the East Wing crew. He's volunteered to help out. Tell Dr. Haveman I authorized it. Thank you, Mr. Noyes, more than I can say." When the two left, he wondered if other ambulatory patients would volunteer. The hospital was desperately short of help, and it could be good therapy. No psychological boost on earth like the sense of being needed. He made a note to look into it.

For forty-eight hours Ambrose Alexander Noyes wrestled bed frames and mattresses, cleared storerooms and lounges to make wards, pushed the clanking hot-meal cart up and down corridors, swept, mopped, lifted, moved whatever an endless succession of hoarse, faceless supervisors ordered him to. He grabbed bites of food when he could, usually standing, collapsed for brief catnaps on blankets piled in corners, forced his ancient physique to struggle on. As the mortality rate rose, they put him in gloves, a mask, protective overshoes, white impermeable coveralls, and set him on the emergency-entrance loading platform, bearing litters with new patients, carrying out plastic sacks with dead ones in them. Muscles aching, eyes burning, fighting nausea from the charnel stench, he unloaded ambulances and station wagons, filled dump trucks. Time, which had stopped moving for him for five years, became chaotic. Day and night ran together, he labored in bleary stupor. The chemical-soaked mask he mouth-breathed through made the miasmic stench of eroded, putrescent human tissues hanging in the air barely endurable. The work never let up. Statistically, Washington was treated lightly by the epidemic, but even a minuscule percent represented the dozens of thousands of human beings dying and dead, a monstrous tidal wave inundating the city's hospitals.

Except for grunted responses to orders, Ambrose Alexander Noyes made no sound there on the loading dock. What was going through his head could only be conjectured. After five years of steadfast refusal to acknowledge that he was in the late twentieth century, evidence of it was overwhelmingly and inescapably about him—hearses and trucks and ambulances backing to the platform, the transistor radios blaring rock music the other workmen carried as they stepped over and around the piled bagged bodies, and the strident chatter of news reports. Confusion and disorientation must have spread through his brain. Straightening finally, he shouted at the anonymous, masked partner he was throwing bodies with. "You know, I don't think this is Yellow Jack at all."

"Yellow what?"

"Fever. You know."

"You some kind of nut?" Over the smeared mask the partner glared. "They don't get no fever, way I heard. They just rot until they die."

"Oh?" said Noyes, weakly. It was all too confusing. He pressed one hand to his aching back. Of course it wasn't Yellow fever. What was he thinking of? Yellow fever like smallpox, was wiped out now. This was something new. He didn't like to ask, to show his ignorance. Keep quiet, he thought. Maybe you can figure it out from what these fellows say. Who are they, anyway? Where is this place? Not New Mexico. The trees look different. The air is not dry and prickly in your nose. This is damp air. It was all too confusing. It made his head hurt to think about it. He went on swinging heavy bagged bodies in rhythm with the other man off the platform into trucks.

After a while—time meant nothing—an hour, a day, who could say? he realized that someone was trying to speak to him. He stopped, wiped his wet forehead with his sleeve, blinked. The man was short, plump, worried-looking. He wore a white coat like a hospital Chief of Service. He wondered how he knew that.

"Mr. Noyes," the doctor said. "Are you feeling all

208

right? We're a little worried about you. You mustn't overdo it, you know. Maybe you ought to ease up, a man of your age. You're working these young fellows into the ground. Can you hear me, Mr. Noyes?"

Behind the chemical tasting mask Noyes licked his bearded lips. His eyes were like fire. He felt dizzy. "Who are you?" he said thickly. "Why are you talking to me like this?"

"Just friendly," said Henry Gault quickly. Perkins came up behind him, through the coveralled men on the platform, and stood watching warily. Perkins knew how to handle patients coming out of catatonia, swinging into mania. "Just being friendly, Ambrose Alexander Noyes," said Gault. "Just don't want you tiring yourself."

Noyes pulled his mask down. "Are you insane? Have you lost your mind? Who do you think I am? Who are you, anyway? For your information, sir, Ambrose Alexander Noyes died before I was born. He was my grandfather. What's the matter with you people? What is this place? What am I doing here?"

Perkins had moved almost unnoticeably to within arm's length, stood ready to seize and pinion him. All the work had stopped on the dock. The laborers gawked. The Sanitation Department dump-truck driver leaned out of his cab and stared back.

"That's all right, sir," said Perkins, smiling. "That's just fine. It's lunchtime, sir. Would you like to come and have some lunch? Nurse Gailey was asking where you were."

The man who had been Ambrose Alexander Noyes for five years swayed slightly, blinked, spoke softly. "This is nonsense. Or madness. Am I mad? Are you a doctor, sir? You're dressed as if you were. What place is this? A hospital? Where? Can't I get any sense out of you people?"

Henry Gault made a quick decision. "It's going to be fine, Perkins. The gentleman is just fine. Yes, sir, I'm a doctor—Henry Gault, a psychiatrist. You know me very well actually. This is St. Elizabeth's Hospital."

"In *Washington*? How did I get to Washington? Am I

your patient? In a *mental*—? Oh, God, help me. Doctor, my name is Vincent Craigie, M.D. Formerly of Johns Hopkins. The last I remember I was in New Mexico. Albuquerque. Believe me, Doctor. This is the truth. Help me. I need—well, I don't know what I need."

"Dr. Craigie? I know your reputation, sir. An honor. I thought—never mind. Perkins, it's fine. Don't worry. Get the men back to work, please. Dr. Craigie and I will be in my office. This way, Doctor. You might want to kick off those boots when we leave the platform."

Craigie? Gault was thinking. Vincent Craigie! But Craigie is dead. Been dead years. Everybody knows that. What is going on here? First he says I called him his grandfather, and now he claims to be a dead bacteriologist. What strange new delusion do we have now? "Come along, Dr. Craigie," he said. "We'll talk about it."

Noyes-Craigie did not move. He stared at the sky, the hospital facade, the dump truck, the bodies in their olive-drab plastic sacks piled on the platform. He seemed to shudder. "This stench. This foul stench. I know it from somewhere. This is an epidemic, I gather. What sort, Doctor? What irony! I appear to have been deprived of some vital part of my life. I return to life to find myself standing among corpses."

"It's a new kind of disease. Doctor. We don't really know much about it. Come along, sir. You know, in all the time you've been with us, we speculated about all sorts of theories. Amnesia, though. That one I don't remember."

It did not take too long for Henry Gault to persuade himself that Ambrose Alexander Noyes was indeed the eminent bacteriologist, Dr. Vincent Craigie. Everything checked out. There was even a picture of him in a medical journal from seven years back—no beard, but the same eyes and cut of forehead. None of the professional registers recorded a death date. They merely stopped mentioning him five or six years back. He had simply vanished from their pages as he had from the minds of his colleagues. No wonder he was assumed to be dead.

Weary and shaken though Craigie was, he insisted on talking. Five years of his life were lost. He was not willing to be put to bed and perhaps risk losing in sleep the life he had regained. Although he spoke with the calmness of a man with total self-discipline, Henry Gault's trained powers of observation detected the terrible tensions, the fear of falling back into limbo, that were eating inside him. Henry was deeply moved. For all his practice he never lost his awe of watching a soul find itself again. There was nothing at once so gratifying and pathetic.

Craigie kept talking, twisting his hands, shooting glances at Gault, talking to himself as much as to his psychiatrist. "I don't think amnesia's right. I'm not trained in the field, but doesn't that suggest total loss of identity? I didn't lose identity. I adopted a new one. For some reason—I'll get to the why of it—I decided to be someone else. It's as if I had been an informer for the FBI—one of those B-movie plot-devices—and they manufactured a new identity for me so I could hide in safety.

"I had a ready-made one. Look, this is hypothesis. I don't remember any of this. I can only postulate. Suppose you wanted to drop out of yourself, become another person. Think of all you would have to know about that person, from his birth on through life. Well, I had that. It was handed to me. On a plate. From my earliest memories I knew about Ambrose Alexander Noyes, my mother's father. He was all I heard for my first ten years. I knew every detail of his life. I envied him. I longed to be him, huddled for warmth, with my older brothers, round my mother in a Baltimore tenement after cabbage soup and day-old bread for supper. We were desperately poor, poor in a way nobody would conceive of nowadays, utterly penniless ever since my wastrel father squandered what the 1908 Panic had left of Mother's inheritance, and deserted. I don't remember him, don't know what happened to him. Nor do I know how we survived.

Mother did sewing, I remember, and my brothers caught crabs in the Bay and stole coal and vegetables from the open air markets. She might have accepted a little help from friends of better days, but no charity, not even if offered. She was too proud for that, shabby-genteel proud. That's what we lived on principally, Mother's pride and tales of lost luxury. We reveled in her stories: the ponies she rode, the big house with servants, the ball when she made·her debut, the Grand Tour when she met my fortune-hunting aristocratic Scottish father—rot him. But the central figure was dashing, romantic Ambrose Alexander Noyes, the Philadelphian who was a colonel under Sheridan, a hero of dime-novel western adventures after the Civil War, my gallant grandsire who made a fortune and lavished it on wife and daughters. She worshipped his memory. It was like Shinto. Over and over she related the story of his life until it was pounded into me, more real than my own, every detail and incident. So, Doctor, when I needed it, I had a ready-made new identity. That is, of course, conjecture. I don't remember."

"Certainly plausible," said Gault. "And it explains some of the mystery that had us stumped. But I wonder why you decided to live in the year 1895. In case you don't realize it, for five years you always insisted that was the date."

"All I can think of," said Craigie, "is that in 1895 my grandfather was the age I was when I—" He hesitated, a furtive expression, almost one of fear, passing over his face. "When, as it would appear," he said in a stronger voice, "my life was no longer bearable."

Henry Gault let seconds pass. He said quietly, "Would you like to go on with that thought, Dr. Craigie?"

Craigie pondered. "I'm not sure I would—or should. Leave that for the moment. Doctor, in your professional opinion what are the chances of my recovering those lost five years? Are they erased totally?"

"That is extremely difficult to form an opinion about,"

said Gault. He was far more worried that, unless Vincent Craigie confronted and came to terms with the demon he ran from five years before, he might without warning relapse into his schizoid second personality, become his grandfather once more. "My advice would be don't worry and they might come back." He smiled genially, watching the haunted look in Craigie's eyes. "Finally, considering how little happened in those five years, maybe they're not worth troubling about. Certainly not compared to all the productive years that preceded them."

"My productive years!" Craigie made a muffled sound of disgust. "Especially the last one. It was productive! Productive of error, doubt, tragedy."

"Want to tell me about it?"

Craigie bowed his head. "I'm not sure I can. Should. That it's safe to. Not until I know what changes five years have made in—things, conditions, security classifications. Doctor Gault, it could even be dangerous for you."

Good God, thought Henry Gault. And Maurice and I wondered if this man was really paranoid. "It's terribly late, Dr. Craigie," he said. "Let's pick it up after a good night's sleep."

"Or never, eh?" Craigie looked grim. "Once a schizo—always suspect. I don't blame you. But listen to this. This much and no more. Then I'll be a good boy, Doctor, and take to my little bed.

"Five, six years ago I was as satisfied with my accomplishments as any professional man in America. Pride goeth—My main field was bacteriology, but curiosity led me farther afield. I got interested in virology too. What we keep discovering about viruses is how little we know. How many diseases they may be responsible for; what their roles may be in the alteration of life forms; their possible—or at least not inconceivably possible— influences on the genetic codes of animal and vegetable life. The National Institutes of Health kept coming to me. Presidential commissions consulted me. More and more I ceased being a professor of medicine with a classroom and a laboratory; more and more I became a high-priced consultant high-flying from one government-sponsored project to another—kowtowed to, lionized on TV talk shows, all the heady dreck. I knew better, but it tickled my vanity. And my wife adored it, the first-class travel and hotels, the limousines, the celebrity stuff. And I adored my wife."

Henry Gault made a noncommittal noise. Vincent Craigie said impatiently, "A minute more. The last place I remember being before I came to on that platform full of corpses was Albuquerque. A hot day. A cheap motel room. I was hiding. From what, I can't remember. They found me. Who 'they' were, I don't know. Government men. I was in black grief. I still am, since I lost the five years that might have brought solace. My dear wife had just died unexpectedly. Perhaps that was the start of it going sour. They told me, these government agents, these—there were three or four. They came and went. Who? Don't ask. Who can keep them straight? CIA? FBI? For all I know, Treasury agents, since with his other enterprises Clavering was distilling unlicensed alcohol, or trying to, from bizarre sources on his mountain."

"Clavering? Who was Clavering?"

"Washburn," said Craigie impatiently. "Clavering Washburn. You know. Surely. Washburn Chemicals. On the Big Board. A maverick. Inventive. Maybe a scalawag. I don't know. He had a little trouble on his experimental station that I flew down to help with. Some new virus or parasitic life, we never knew. My consultant arrangements—what brought us to New Mexico, Corinne and I—kept me principally at Los Alamos and White Sands.

"Well. These agents—these men—they didn't threaten, you understand. Nothing so crass. Grief stricken at Corinne's loss, threats would have meant nothing anyway. The men simply emphasized the unthinkable consequences of my leaking the secret. One used the word 'traitorous.' I remember ordering him out. He just laughed and what could I do? I remember thinking of the Manhattan Project fellows back in the Dark Ages of Science at Oak Ridge and the University of Chicago and White Sands. I knew how they felt. I can't tell you any more. Not now. Not yet. My last clear—not very clear—memory is of the excruciating dilemma I felt I was facing. Fidelity to science? Fidelity to country? Were they mutually exclusive? Were my premises correct? Were the terms exact? What is science? What is one's country? On the horns of a dilemma Dr. Gault, what does one do? When it is the Devil or the Deep, what does one do?"

Gault said softly, "We know what you did, Doctor."

"I ran," said Craigie. "I hid."

"Not consciously. You must feel no blame. We all have a breaking point."

"No blame!" Craigie shook his head. "I suppose if we looked deep enough into motive, provocation, contributing factors, nobody could ever be blamed for anything. We are all innocent: Caligula, Hitler, Jack the Ripper."

"Albuquerque," said Gault. "The last place you remember is Albuquerque."

"So how did I get to Washington? Why? Why not back to Baltimore?"

"Just coincidence," said Gault, "but Albuquerque is where this epidemic is believed to have begun."

"The epidemic. Yes. Tell me about the epidemic."

"Oh, lord, Dr. Craigie," said Gault. "This late? Let it wait. Here, I'll give you a file to scan. It's all there in a nutshell, current mortality and morbidity reports, current summary from Dr. Blanchard's Epidemic Task Force in Bethesda."

"Blanchard?" said Craigie quickly. "Noah Blanchard?"

"Do you know him?"

"I taught him. Of course I know him. He's running this—what did you call it?"

"Epidemic Task Force. That's a title the President's press agents dreamed up to generate the public's confidence. It needs some, heaven knows. This thing is out of control—nothing ever before like it except maybe in 1918."

"Noah Blanchard! Dr. Gault, you get word to Noah Blanchard he needs to see me. I would call it urgent."

Chapter 17

Some people managed to extract a little stolen happiness even from the chaos and turmoil of the epidemic. Flight Nurse (Captain) Estelle Monroe of the USAF Aeromedical Service was one. From the co-pilot seat of a C-9A Nightingale evacuation transport which was flying across Oklahoma in the dark—two-man crew, five medical attendants, litter space for forty wounded soldiers—she lovingly admired the pilot's profile. They were on a southwest course, heading towards Tucson, having topped their tanks at Little Rock Municipal, Tinker AMA at Oklahoma City being closed by the epidemic. Ordinarily Major Bob Berry would have refueled at Blytheville or Barksdale, but all SAC and TAC bases were off-limits to transient aircraft. Nobody seemed to be sure why, although the air force was alive with rumors of impending combat operations against somebody or something.

Estelle could sit in the co-pilot's seat, because Captain Andy Anderson was drinking coffee in the cavernous passenger compartment with the medical corpsmen and the other nurses. Berry kept grumbling to her that it was a criminal waste of air force resources, flying a C-9A deadhead to Arizona just to pick up a doctor and his patient, but Estelle was happy about it. There was nothing she would rather do than this—fly through the night with her new-found lover beside her.

Major Berry hardly fitted the popular concept of lover. He was a bald, bandy-legged, thirty-eight-year-old officer with ten thousand accident-free flying hours. There was not a safer pilot in the Aeromedical Service and everyone knew it just as they knew he would never be chief of staff or probably even squadron commander. He was just a thoroughly professional transport pilot. It was what he did best. As an aviation cadet he had dreamed of becoming a dashing, glamorous fighter ace. Now his highest hope was to make lieutenant colonel before they retired him.

Estelle Monroe thought him dashing and glamorous as he was. She herself was a big, plain flight nurse, as professional in her field as he was in his, a thirty-year-old woman built for comfort and staying power. They were two specialists in an unusual, but essentially humdrum line of work. The only dramatic quality in their lives was Estelle's secret passion, which her pilot was too dutifully faithful to a bitchy wife to suspect. Casual copulation during overnight stops is fairly common in mixed aircrews, but people rarely made passes at friendly, horse-faced Estelle, and Bob never made passes at anybody.

Until last week—their most recent mission—when they stayed overnight in Montgomery. At midnight he scratched on her door in the Howard Johnson motel, maudlin drunk because of wife trouble. All he thought he wanted was friendly female sympathy, but one thing led to another, and Estelle had been in a state of guilty bliss ever since. He hadn't mentioned it, nor had they been away from the base since. Estelle hugged her memories to herself and hoped.

Below and beyond them the world stretched, totally black except for dim stars and a few pinpoints of yellow lights from farms and ranches. Four weeks earlier it

218

would have been spangled with the bright lights of small towns, but they were well west now where the epidemic had knocked out power plants. Estelle tried not to think about it. She thought about Monday night in Montgomery and tingled.

Bob said, "Who is this Dr. Green anyway? How does he get off ordering a C-9A all the way to Arizona for one patient? Where does he get that kind of clout?"

Estelle said doubtfully, "I think he's a cabinet officer—somebody way up in government anyway."

Berry glared out at the night. Away ahead in the distance reddish lightning flickered, low along the invisible horizon. Without warning he dropped his heavy right hand in Estelle's lap, gripped and squeezed her upper thigh. She thrilled in every ganglion. He said, "God, 'Stelle! I can't tell you—I don't know when I felt this way."

"I never have," she said weakly. "That's the God's truth. Oh, God, Bob, honey, please no. Don't try to unzip me. Not now, not here. I couldn't stand it."

"When we get back," he said huskily. "I don't care how late."

Her heart leaped. "You can't, Bob. Not in Washington. You can't take chances like that. Not in Washington. Your wife."

"What wife?" he growled. "She got the hell out yesterday. Took the kids and took off for Roanoke. To her sister's."

"Oh, Bob. I'm sorry. I didn't want to make trouble for you."

"You didn't do it. Moira doesn't know about—Montgomery. About us. Anything. That's the farthest thing from her mind. You don't have to feel responsible."

"She just got that scared? You told me she was."

"I don't know why she thinks Roanoke's safer. I don't think she's thinking. She's just running. Ever since a man up the street caught this Ulceration she's been like a crazy woman. Can't talk sense. I tried to make her get

219

vaccinated when I did—her and the kids. She fought it like a tiger. Absolutely in a panic. That's how I left her when we flew to Montgomery."

Skinny, brittle-talking, flashy brunette Moira Berry. Estelle could visualize her in the officers' club lounge, talking up a storm, acting snooty to flight nurses. I know a lot of pilots' wives resent us, but what right did she have to act superior? So you had hysterics, lady, and sent your husband off flying like that? Straight to my arms. Well, bless you, dummy. "I am really sorry, Bob," said Estelle. "It must be terrible. What will you do—move on to the base?"

"I guess so." He twirled a radio tuning handle and made a slight adjustment to the automatic pilot control. "Crosswind," he said.

After a minute Estelle said, "Sadie's moving out on me. She'll be gone by the time we get back."

"Is that right?"

"She's moving in with her intern. I guess he gets so little time off-duty with this epidemic crush at the hospital, they decided to spend it all together. Damned epidemic."

"Way I heard," said Bob, "people have quit shacking up because they were scared of catching this thing from each other."

"Not in my crowd, I'm happy to say."

Bob chuckled. "Think you could use a new roommate?"

Estelle's heart jumped again. Like a schoolgirl, she thought. No. Like a grown-up woman committing adultery and loving it. "If it's the right one," she said.

"I'd do my best," he said. For a while they said nothing, two people sitting side by side on the flight deck of an airplane boring steadily through the night, holding hands.

"We get to Davis-Monthan," said Bob, after a time, "we won't check in at Operations. This Dr. Green is supposed to meet us with his patient at the edge of the field somewhere. The Tower will tell us. They'll send a tanker out to refuel us. We're supposed to keep away from everything. And the word is maximum isolation for the patient once he's aboard. How does all that grab you, baby?"

"Sounds like we're breaking the Air Surgeon General's rule against taking epidemic patients aboard."

"I guess this Dr. Green can overrule the Air Surgeon General. Well, theirs not to reason why. Follow the last order first."

"As they taught me in basic training at Lackland."

"We're about an hour out," said Berry. "I'm going to try to raise the David-Monthan tower. Baby, don't go catching anything from this sick man. I'm planning to get real close to you from now on. You better go back now and tell Andy to quit trying to get into your nurses' britches, to get his ass up front. That's more lightning; could get a little bouncy over the Organ Range. Estelle—I hate to say this, but you know how it would have to be. If Moira decided to come back."

"I will take my chances, Major." She wriggled out of the seat, kissed his ear behind his radio headset, and went aft, a big plain woman in flying coveralls with a happy smile. Eat, drink, and be, she thought.

When they landed at Tucson a FOLLOW ME jeep, lighted back-end the only spot of illumination in the velvet-black desert night, led them along a taxiway to where a big helicopter, rotor blades drooping, waited on a hardstand. The jeep lights picked up the Mexican markings. Captain Anderson opened the Nightingale side door, hooked on the ladder, and dropped lightly down. A fat old man in a pale summer suit came up, offering his hand. From ground level the helicopter seemed to be a Sikorsky, probably an HH-53C.

"You're right on time," said the civilian approvingly. "I'm Dr. Green. Are you the pilot?"

"Co-pilot, sir. Captain Anderson."

"All right, Captain, first of all I got to talk to your head medic. I'd just as soon the rest of your crew kind of kept clear."

"As you say, sir." Andy looked back up at the nurses and corpsmen crowding the door. "Estelle, how about you coming down. The rest of you the doctor says please stay out of the way."

"Captain Monroe, Doctor," said Estelle, when she came down the ladder. "Chief Flight Nurse."

"I'm mighty glad to meet you, Miss Monroe," said Green. "Now both of you. This patient is Mr. Olvera. He has multiple fractures and has lost a great deal of blood from internal bleeding. He is comatose and has been for the last hour. The cause of his injuries is a thousand-foot fall down a mountain in his automobile. Specifically, a bus ran him off the road. A Mexican doctor and I put a couple of rough and ready plaster casts on him, but that's about all we could do. Now you've probably got plasma aboard and any other time I'd want a transfusion started first thing. For reasons there's no sense me trying to explain, that's contraindicated here. For the same reasons we can't risk any kind of medication that would tend to change his blood composition any way at all. Is that clear? You don't have to understand why, but is it clear?"

"Absolutely, sir," said Estelle crisply.

In the poor light Simon Green sized her up—a hundred and fifty pounds of solid woman on a big-boned five-foot ten; pale hair smoothed under her blue cap, a firm, competent manner. This one you would not have to tell twice. He nodded approvingly. "Two more things. Exposure to the patient must be held to absolute minimum. I'll explain if you want."

"We've all been vaccinated, sir," said Andy. "All hands."

"The Air Force require that?" said Green.

"No, sir. Volunteers."

"That's fine, but even so—minimum exposure, maximum isolation. But here is the most important thing. Our patient is in critical condition. It is in the very highest national interests that he arrive at the National Institutes of Health in Bethesda alive. The very highest interests. Questions?"

"Not a one, sir," said Andy.

"Good. You have a special care compartment on this airplane?"

"Yes, sir, Doctor," said Estelle. "Every Nightingale does—with special ventilation and pressure controls."

"First-class," said Green. "Excellent. Now let's get our patient out of the helicopter and aboard."

Incredibly, Luis Olvera opened his eyes and spoke. "Maria," he said, thickly. "*Agua*, Maria."

Simon Green said, "Nurse, a little fruit juice, I think, please. What unbelievable stamina this man has! I expect he's feeling dry-mouthed."

"Yes, sir." Estelle crouched beside the patient and spooned diluted grape juice between his dry lips.

The three of them were sealed from the rest of the world in the special care compartment. Olvera was receiving a glucose solution by IV, but that was all Dr. Green wanted to risk. His vital signs were good. Another hour would put them on the ground at Andrews AFB, where an ambulance was standing by. Simon Green had sent messages to NIH from Little Rock when they took on fuel. He was beginning to feel guardedly optimistic about Luis Olvera's chances of arriving alive.

"Absolutely unbelievable," he repeated. "Anyone else would have died long before."

"He's a carrier, isn't he, Doctor?"

Simon Green's eyebrows rose. "Where did you get that idea, young lady? Carrier of what?"

She smiled. "The epidemic disease, of course. I mean, it couldn't have anything to do with any other disease. Isolating him this way. And he doesn't show any symptoms of the Ulceration."

"Very intelligent," said Green. "But it might be best if you kept it quiet. Yes, we think he could be a carrier. We think he may be the original carrier."

"Oh, poor man!" she said, genuinely distressed.

"Terrible thing to have on your conscience, eh? Of course, he couldn't possibly have any idea, and anyway he couldn't possibly be called guilty of anything."

"Yes, sir, but still—"

"Um. But still. No, I certainly wouldn't want to be the one to tell him. You know, I believe he's trying to say something again."

Olvera moved his chin as if to say he wanted no more to drink. His brown eyes looked unfocused. He said, "Father, it was a good trip."

Simon Green looked at Estelle Monroe and put his finger to his lips. He bent down. "Tell me about it—son?"

"One good—client." Olvera's breathing quickened. "Albuquerque. Outside. Howard Con—Consolvo. Good, Father—going to be good—client. You will like—" His eyes closed.

Simon Green knuckled his mouth. There was a look almost of desperation in his face. Estelle watched him, baffled and a little alarmed. She did not think the patient should be encouraged to talk.

"Son," said Green softly. "Luis!" He whispered the name, but it was an urgent whisper. "Before Consolvo— before Albuquerque—whom did you see? Where?"

Again Olvera's breathing quickened. Estelle felt his pulse and gave Green a worried look. "Utah—Hethercote—"

"No!" whispered Green. "No, son. Before. Not after. Before Consolvo—Albuquerque."

"Oh." The brown eyes closed, opened, closed. "Before—yes. Wheelchair. Wheelchair man. Chemical plant. Alamogordo. Saw—saw Washburn. Not for us—"

Alamogordo, thought Simon Green. Washburn. Chemical plant. What does it mean? Something stirred in his mind. Chemical—Washburn. Sure. Like Dupont or Dow. Washburn Chemical. But Alamogordo? It was something to go after though. He bent down again. "Luis—Son—"

Estelle held her breath. This was wrong, all her training and instinct told her it was wrong, trying to make a patient in this critical state think and speak.

"Son—did you get hurt at Washburn—Alamogordo? An accident? Some little cut?"

"—knee—skinned knee. At greenhouse—"

"That's enough," said Simon Green. He mopped his forehead and Estelle saw that even in the air-cooled, pressurized compartment the fat doctor had been sweating. He had been as scared as she was.

She hoped the answers—whatever they meant—were worth the risk to the patient.

Chapter 18

Of the original ten-member Epidemic Task Force cadre only five remained—Lambdin, Badin, Hargrave, Russell, and Hattie Manger. Craydon, Ruffec, and Sue Berne were dead of Consolvo's Ulceration. Frank Weinstein and Ignatz Weinstraub had suffered nervous breakdowns and been hospitalized at Walter Reed. The five survivors sat at Walt Burrows's conference table, staring at each other. Fingering his peace pendant, Michael Hargrave said, "What's this gathering supposed to be in aid of, General Burrows? I've got more important things to do than sit around waiting for Dr. Almighty Blanchard."

"Everybody knows how important you are," snapped Hattie Manger, pushing her bangs back from her weary eyes. "You don't have to keep reminding us."

"Let him bitch, Hattie," yawned Ben Russell. "Nobody cares what Mike says. He doesn't mean it anyway. He just wants attention."

"Now, children," said old Duval Badin, "little birds in their nests agree." Of them all, thought Walt Burrows at the head of the conference table, only ancient Badin looked fresh and lively. He seemed to thrive on ceaseless work and little sleep. Maybe if you lived that long, you were bound to.

"My dear Duval," protested Lambdin, "pray, spare us your Louisa May Alcott homilies."

"Now take it easy, everybody," said Burrows. "Dr. Blanchard said he wouldn't keep you long. Here he is now."

"Sorry to call you off your jobs," said Noah, closing the door behind him. His voice sounded weary, his face looked drawn and gray, his whole appearance was that of a man on the ragged edge. Dobson was riding him too hard, thought Burrows worriedly. He'd better ease up. You could pile only so much on a man before he broke.

"I'll be brief as I can," Noah went on. "A couple of developments have come up you ought to know about. The first is that Simon Green—Dr. Green—suddenly turned up again. I don't suppose you even realized he was missing. Well, he was, and he had us worried. But it's all right. Turns out that he went off on his own to do some detective work. Everybody else had just about given up, but not Simon. He tracked down our elusive Luis Olvera, the missing investment counselor, and what's more he brought him back here to Bethesda. He's in an NIH hospital now."

"The epidemic carrier?" said Lambdin. "But that's marvelous!"

"The *suspected* carrier," Noah corrected. "We aren't sure he is yet, although the evidence keeps mounting. That's one of the things they'll try to establish at the hospital."

"Simon Green," said Walt Burrows, and chuckled softly. "Why that old rascal."

"He's not so old," said Badin.

Noah smiled. "Now, Duval, everybody's old, compared to you. Yes, Walt, old fat Simon did it—traced a rental car from Denver to a Mexican Indian village in the bottom of a canyon, and found Olvera in critical condition from a car wreck. It was an amazing piece of work."

227

"Tell me," said Lambdin, "does the man show any symptoms of the disease?"

"Evidently not," said Noah. "According to what Simon told me on the phone. But he is in extremely poor condition. Multiple fractures, concussion, loss of blood from internal hemorrhage, comatose. He's in Intensive Care with a prognosis less than favorable. Which is bad, bad news, not only for Mr. Olvera."

"Not being a medical man," said Badin, "how would they go about finding if he is a carrier?"

"Different ways," said Noah. "Controlled exposures—very risky—certain tests. First, of course, they have to keep him alive. And that may take some luck, limited as they are in what they can do."

Badin looked perplexed. The medical scientists nodded thoughtfully. Knitting his black brows, Russell said, "If he is a carrier, the vital need is to discover what antibodies in his blood make him immune."

"Right the first time," said Noah.

Michael Hargrave said, "What evidence is mounting that the man is a carrier?"

"Things Olvera told Dr. Green. He had semi-lucid intervals when he mistook Dr. Green for his dead father. In any case, young Olvera kept trying to give him a trip report—what he had accomplished by way of business. These are the facts Simon Green considers significant. Two days before Olvera saw Consolvo—the right incubation period—he skinned his knee, a possible entry of the pathogen into his bloodstream by which he became a vector. When Howard Consolvo scratched his arm—the famous scratch that developed into the first known case of Consolvo's Ulceration—Olvera bandaged the wound. Transmission of pathogen completed."

"Is that all?" said Hargrave.

Noah sighed. "Be patient, please. Incidentally, Olvera keeps praising Howard Consolvo to his father, calls him the finest kind of human being. I might say that was my impression too."

228

"That's right," said Ben Russell, giving him a curious look. "You did meet him, didn't you?"

"I did," said Noah curtly. "Lucky me."

Ben flushed. "Sorry. That sounded crass."

"No, no, Ben," said Noah wearily. "Not your fault. I'm touchy today." He grimaced and went on. "Olvera doesn't realize that Consolvo is dead, that there is an epidemic—anything. Simon told him nothing."

"I wouldn't have either," said Burrows. "A patient in Intensive Care, to tell him something like that could kill him."

"I can't see," said Hargrave, "that this so-called evidence proves anything. A skinned knee. A bandaged arm. Both on the word of a semiconscious man."

"I'll get to the rest, Mike," said Noah. "Before that, let's reflect on what we know about the causative organism—this purplish crystalloid spiculed pathogen: that it is neither true virus nor true bacterium; that it is anaerobic; that under ideal conditions it reproduces wildly. But what do we not know? Its source. Where it comes from. Nothing like it was ever known before. What could be responsible for it? Could it be the product of a chemical process—some bizarre effort to alter the nature of matter? There are petrochemical processes, remember, that have caused previously unknown viruses to appear. Could this be the result of some such process? Anyone?"

Hattie Manger said doubtfully, "If there were some chemical process you could connect it with, well, possibly—"

Russell and Lambdin nodded. Badin listened interestedly. Hargrave fiddled with his peace pendant. Walt Burrows watched Noah with deepening concern. "The last thing Olvera told Green then—" said Noah. "—It may be far-fetched, but think about it. Where did Luis Olvera skin his knee? At some kind of shutdown chemical experimental station outside Alamogordo. Very near White Sands, where the first nuclear detonation fused the desert into green glass. I don't say there is a connection. I do not know. I only know that Luis Olvera saw a man named Clavering Washburn two days before he saw Howard Consolvo. I know that Clavering Washburn is—"

"Good heavens!" exclaimed Duval Badin. "Is Clavering still around?"

"Excuse me," said Hattie Manger, "but should I know who this man is?"

"Hattie, Hattie," said Russell. "Everybody's heard of Washburn Chemical. It's like saying du Pont or Dow. Somehow I never thought of it as one man, though."

"If any major American industry is one man," said Badin, "it is Washburn Chemical. We don't produce his kind anymore. Nice boys from MIT and Harvard Business School with computers to figure the risks for them—they run the corporations now. But not always. Clavering Washburn! A natural force. A self-taught genius. Lord, how America turned them out once—men like Edison and Carver and Chrysler and Frank Lloyd Wright; innovators, movers and shakers—turned them out the way France did great chefs. No education— Washburn. Came out of the Florida phosphate pits. Self-taught chemist. God knows how many basic patents he holds. The Chemical Corps stuck two stars on his shoulders, and he helped us win wars. When guerrillas were lurking in jungle cover, he conceived a defoliant to expose them."

"That was certainly glorious," said Hargrave. "That was a boon for humanity."

"Young man," said Badin severely, "your remark is banal, puerile, rude, and irrelevant. It also bespeaks woeful ignorance of the climate of opinion of the time."

"Hear, hear," said Lambdin.

"If Clavering Washburn is out in the New Mexican desert blowing things up and mixing nasty messes," Badin continued, "it is in a good cause, and I would not be the least bit astonished to hear it. But I would have thought I would know about it."

"I don't believe any of it," said Hargrave. "Science for the People would certainly know if any chemical warfare experiments were going on out there. We'd probably have even closed them down by now."

"Please," said Noah, "let's get back to our subject. You would not find it inconceivable, Professor Badin, that Clavering Washburn could be engaged in some original chemical experiments of some sort for some purpose—probably bizarre?"

"If he is alive, I can believe it easily."

"And we agree that we cannot rule out the chance that this devilish killer organism could be the result of chemical experimentation?"

"Could be." Lambdin nodded thoughtfully. "Which is not to say that it is, of course."

"Of course. The thing to do is go out there and try to find out. Agreed?"

There was a murmur of assent. "And that," said Noah, "is exactly what I plan to do. The Center for Disease Control is assembling a team for me—toxicologists, biologists, chemists. We're going to Alamogordo as quickly as possible. We want to take soil, air, water samples—sift through whatever there is there."

"You're going?" Burrows frowned. "Does the President know?"

"He will," said Noah briefly.

Burrows started to speak, shook his head, started to speak again. Ben Russell cut in. "I'm surprised you said nothing about this television appeal for vaccine volunteers that these convicts are making tonight. You all know about it, of course. Don't you? My impression was that this was a highly positive development."

"It would be," said Hargrave, still stung by Badin's rebuke. "That's right down your alley—letting political prisoners, social and racial victims, take the risk of infection. You would like that, wouldn't you? I knew the hypocrisy would end. It always does. As always, we let the same underclass be sacrificed for the rich and privileged."

"Now see here," said Russell, "that's unfair and dishonest."

"You really are being very silly, Dr. Hargrave," said Duval Badin. "Dr. Russell's remarks were innocent and well-intended. You owe him an apology."

"I'm a lady," said Hattie Manger, "and I don't talk like this, but Mike's trouble is that he is a horse's ass."

Noah laughed, but to Burrows the laugh had a sour ring. "What a lot of jolly fun you all have down here in your hole. I wish I could spend more time with you. As for the convicts and their proposal, while I haven't given it much thought, my frank reaction is one of skepticism. Somehow I don't take much stock in that sort of altruism from Death Row inmates or lifers. Maybe I'm cynical. But I did a hitch one summer as an undergraduate at Joliet Penitentiary—a field exercise for a psychology class. That left me convinced that the typical prison inmate is often totally egocentric, incapable of living up to the responsibilities of citizenship, and ninety-nine times out of a hundred exactly where he ought to be for society's sake. So I don't have much faith in these noble convicts this evening. The President is optimistic, but not I. In any case, even if it worked out, it's just too late!"

Lambdin said, "That's an odd remark, Doctor. You speak as if there were some deadline."

Noah paused, licked his lips, and said, "Well, perhaps I didn't mean it exactly that way. But there isn't much time left. And we all know it. For one thing, we're nearing frost date in many parts of the country. People will start freezing. Now I must go. Thank you all for coming. I'll be back as quickly as possible. I hope Alamogordo pays off."

"See you half a minute?" said Burrows.

"All right," said Noah. "But make it quick."

When the others left, Burrows closed the door. "Now just what the hell is eating you?" he demanded. "Maybe nobody else caught it, but I did. You're like a bear in a hornets' nest. Is it something between you and Dobson? Are things that much worse than I realize? I don't have to be told everything, but are you holding back something from me you don't have to? I'm in this too, Noah."

"Damn right you are," said Noah. "Christ. I didn't want this job. Without you it would be impossible. No, Walt. It's—it's a hundred things—but right now I guess it's Kate mainly. Much as I hate to admit it."

"It bothers you that much, her going to Chicago?"

"I shouldn't let it, I guess," said Noah. "But yes, damn it, it does."

"You feel that she let you down?"

Noah tried to laugh. "Stupid, isn't it? But I do. No right to, I know how much she wants a big-time TV career. She doesn't owe me anything. But—I wouldn't tell everybody—but I was beginning to—well, think seriously about her."

"Nice lady," said Burrows neutrally. "Good-looking. Good company. I don't blame you."

"Ah, hell, she did me a favor by leaving. I'd be a rotten husband. Now, Walt, I can't violate a confidence. You understand that. But you put two and two together and—for God's sake, keep on these people. Don't let anybody let up. And keep in constant contact with Simon Green. He's got to find something in Olvera's blood—some antibody—something that will lead us to a cure or a different vaccine—and he's got to do it in a hurry. I can't say any more. But nothing could be more urgent. Nothing. Now I have to take off."

"Are you going to see the President?"

"Got to."

"Ten-to-one he won't let you go to Alamogordo. I don't think he should."

Noah gave the burly black general a steady, friendly stare. "He has no choice. He has to let me go."

"I don't think this is a good idea," said President Dobson. "I don't like the idea of you being out of reach. I would just as soon that you stayed here and let that CDC team go to New Mexico without you."

"Is that an order, Mr. President?" said Noah.

The President smiled a little. He looked far more relaxed, thought Noah, than when they were together last. Admiral Perrin must have managed to slip a Nembutal into his cocoa after all. "I'm not expected to have to give orders, Doctor. People are supposed to be glad to follow my suggestions."

"Mr. President," said Noah frostily, "in my judgment this is the most important thing I can to in the next twenty-four hours."

"Now why is that?" The President's voice sharpened "Are you more expert than specialists? Is there some technicality about this investigation that hasn't been explained to me, that I should know? Why do you have to go? As I get the picture—kindly correct me if I am mistaken—this Olvera fellow, believed to be the original epidemic carrier, now in a hospital, may have caught the disease during a visit he made to a closed-down chemical company activity of some sort near Alamogordo. *May* have. Is that it?"

Noah nodded. "Our reasons for thinking so are that Olvera—in his few coherent moments—told Dr. Green that before his contact with Consolvo he spent a day with a man named Clavering Washburn, who from my information appears to be—"

Dobson cut him off with a peremptory gesture. "I know who Clavering Washburn is. Anyone of my generation does. I did not know that he was still active. I was not even certain that he was alive. Is that all you have to go on?"

"Essentially, sir. But it's worth following up."

"Granted. But why you personally?"

"I feel that I should, sir," said Noah stubbornly.

The president rose abruptly and strode to a window to stare out. At the bottom of the brown ruined lawn, helmeted troopers with slung weapons patrolled the iron fence. On the sidewalk three protestors walked back and forth bearing placards reading NO VACCINE. Last week there had been a round dozen of them. The country was

234

running out of hope, thought Dobson. Even the lunatic fringe was giving in to apathy. "Dr. Blanchard," he said, "you are an exasperating man."

"I will resign, sir, if you like."

"What the devil is the matter with you, man?" The President had turned and was staring at Noah—for the first time ever, betraying genuine anger.

What is the matter with me, thought Noah. It's Kate, of course, but I can't tell him that. I'm ashamed to admit it to myself. Why should it matter that much? Why should her running out stick in my craw this way? "Sorry, Mr. President," he said. "You told me from the start that I must do as I thought best. I'm still trying to. I think it's best that I go with the CDC team."

"Let me get this straight. Your team of epidemiologists, biologists, toxicologists, what will they do down there? Sift the soil? Sample the air? Test the house-dust in the buildings? The water in the drinking fountains and the air cooling units if there are any? To what end? To look for some cell or bug or virus that causes Consolvo's Ulceration when it finds the right human host?"

"Essentially that, sir."

"But you've already isolated the organism! You showed me a picture of the spiky monster. Why do you have to keep looking?"

"Because, Mr. President, if this is the site of its origin, it might look and be quite different there. It could easily mutate once it entered human tissue—which is the only way we have seen it. Because we might find what it generated from. Because all those possibilities should be pursued in the hope of finding an effective treatment for the disease or a safer vaccine."

"Well," said Dobson, in a dissatisfied tone, "I don't understand the technicalities of all that, but I can grasp the principles. All right. So the investigation is worthwhile. But can't those CDC scientists do all that without you? Do you have to be there to show them what to do?"

"Put that way, sir, no. They don't need me for that."

"Then for heaven's sake, my testy friend, what for? Why do you insist on going?"

"I apologize for being rude, sir," said Noah. "Pressures, personal problems—but I still say I should go."

Dobson sank into his chair. "We are all under pressure. You would be less than human not to be, too. Don't apologize. Just explain why you feel this way."

"Mr. President, how much time is there?"

"Until what?"

"Until you pick up your famous red telephone and tell Tactical Air Command to start its neutron-bomb run on western American cities. Or SAC to launch preemptive strikes?"

The haunted look was back in Dobson's eyes. "I don't know. Everything now depends on factors out of my control—if there is a wide response to the TV appeal tonight for convict volunteers; if Dr. Green finds antibodies in Mr. Olvera's blood; if General Burrows's task force pulls some almighty rabbits in a hurry out of its research hats; if your CDC team makes a breakthrough at Alamogordo; and above all, how Moscow, Paris, and London respond to my propositions."

"A rough estimate of time, sir?"

"My God, Doctor," said Dobson softly. "If none of those last-minute possibilities pays off and the Europeans agree to my terms, why I can hardly delay Operation NATHAN HALE more than forty-eight hours."

"NATHAN HALE!" The irony of the code name revolted Noah. He had a sudden mental picture of Albuquerque writhing under neutron radiation. Nathan Hale indeed! "Within two days. God help us."

"Yes, damn it, yes!"

"I can't predict about Moscow," said Noah harshly. "I doubt that Walter Burrows's people can find fresh rabbits that soon. Olvera's blood does hold out promise, but he could die any minute and that would be the end of it. I don't look for miracles at Alamogordo. As for this convict thing, I'm skeptical. Even if it worked beyond our wildest dreams, every long-term prisoner in every prison everywhere heroically offering himself for the common good, the effort, the time, the security measures, all the logistical problems in testing and running studies on all those dangerous criminals without incurring intolerable risk to the public would require days, weeks. Finally, I don't have much faith in felons anyway."

"Maybe you are wrong about that."

"Nothing would please me more. Mr. President, I am trying to answer your question in a deliberately roundabout way. Why do I want to go to Alamogordo? Because of the time factor. What will happen to this CDC team if it is still there two days from now?"

Dobson looked alarmed, then irritated. "But they won't be. We will order them back."

"Mr. President, these aren't order-takers. These are independent-minded scientists, authorities in their fields, supreme egotists, utter individualists. If you don't understand that, then you don't know enough about investigative scientists."

Dobson smiled fleetingly. "I've learned a little about the ego and independent mind of at least one scientist, Doctor, thanks to you."

Noah dropped his eyes a second. "In any case, sir, take my word for this. We can tell that team anything we want. But if they encounter something at the Washburn site that intrigues their imaginations, piques their scientific curiosity, orders will mean nothing. The only way you could get them out of there in time would be a warning that every living thing on the ground where they stand would shortly be obliterated by nuclear radiation. Are you prepared to warn them of that before they leave?"

"Good God, man, you know I can't!"

"Then they'd better have a hard-nosed team captain who knows the danger, sir, and can be counted to boot their tails back aboard the airplane in time. That's my point, sir."

"And you had to go about proving it this way, I

237

suppose. Yes, I guess you did. You know me pretty well. I don't think I want to play poker with you, Doctor. You're too shrewd a psychologist."

"Never touch cards, sir."

"I would bet. Here. You'd better take this and scan it on the way to New Mexico. They dug it out for me at the Energy Department. Not that it tells us much." The President took a file folder from a desk drawer and tossed it over.

The cover read *Project Apache Candle*. It was an old file, Noah saw, dating from the third year of the Carter Administration. "I glanced through it," said Dobson. "Evidently one of those innumerable synthetic fuel projects the government funded back then. This had to do with some experiments involving certain varieties of desert vegetation. It's little more than an introduction. Doesn't even say what came of the project."

"Useful looking," said Noah cautiously. "It's Washburn Chemicals and undoubtedly the right location. Thank you very much, sir. It could be extremely valuable." That sly fox, he thought. Had this in his desk all the time and let me rattle on. Don't tell *me* who the poker player is. He holds 'em as close to the vest as I ever saw. "I'll leave now, sir, with your permission. They're holding an airplane at Andrews."

Chapter 19

The Intensive Care Unit of the NIH hospital where Luis Olvera lay in an oxygen tent in an array of tubing was a battleground with two objectives: to save his life and to exploit his rare blood in search of a new epidemic weapon. The objectives were contradictory.

Whether or not there were special antibodies swimming in his blood that could save epidemic victims, something gave Luis Olvera astounding vitality. Other men would have been dead days before. His X rays resembled jigsaw puzzles—fracture lines radiating through his skull, pelvis, clavicle, ankles, thigh bones and half a dozen ribs and vertebrae. He was still bleeding internally, probably from a ruptured spleen. His nervous system had suffered the shocks of rolling down a mountain ten stories high and of lurching for two hours down a mule trail. He had lain semi-conscious in a fly-infested native village and developed only a low-grade infection. The man belonged in the medical textbooks.

To complicate his handling was the suspicion that, as vector for the first known outbreak of the epidemic, he might be host to a particularly malignant strain. He had to be treated as gingerly as an armed bomb—the fewest possible ICU personnel coming near him, all taking maximum precautions.

In search of the unique property that made him immune to the pathogen, samples of his blood were subjected to minute analysis. No one knew what to look for—some unknown variety of defensive globulin perhaps; some undreamed-of potency of white corpuscles; something special in the clotting mechanism of his platelets; something so bizarre nobody had ever heard of anything remotely resembling it. They centrifuged his blood, broke it into components to be microscopically studied and chemically tested. They tried injecting it in different mixes and concentrations and dilutions on control cases of Consolvo's Ulceration victims in different stages of the disease. Ordinarily such experiments on living human beings would have been unthinkable. But the circumstances were desperate and the patients doomed. Simon Green closed his eyes and prayed, and ordered that it be done.

The old fat man, senior to everybody in the hospital by any definition, worked like a dynamo. Lest anybody forget it—he raged—the name of this game was how to stop an epidemic before it stopped us. God had restored this young man, and it would be a goddamn blasphemy not to take full advantage of His blessing. The doctors and nurses and lab technicians smiled or shrugged or were offended according to their religious bents, but they did what he told them and nobody let up.

The final complication was that time was running out on Luis Olvera. Not even his enormous stamina could sustain him forever. Slowly, in spite of everything, he kept sinking. There were many possible causes: accumulative results of shock; the persistent low-grade infection they could not halt; probable nerve damage in his spinal column; above all his massive blood loss. Whole-blood transfusion was demanded by every clinical standard. The chief of internal medicine urged it. Simon Green refused adamantly. "Good God, Dr. Green," said the chief, "he is dying!"

"Come in here, son," said Green, taking the chief into the office he had appropriated. "Doctor Braden," he said when the door was closed, "you think I don't care about that boy. Lemme tell you, I brought him out of Mexico. He owes me his life. You know how that makes me feel? He took me for his daddy. He held my hand all the way across the country in an airplane, calling me Father. You think I don't care about this boy? You think there's anything I wouldn't do to save him?"

"You know what will," said the chief angrily. "A-Negative whole blood. We've got it. I've had it cross-checked and matched. It's in our bank. We've got donors standing by, too."

"You can't be sure that would save him."

"You can be sure nothing will without it!"

"Dr. Braden," said Simon, "I guess I agree. But listen. How many people have died in this epidemic?"

"I have no idea," snapped Braden. "What kind of question is that?"

"Of course, you don't. Don't anybody. But it's millions and millions and so far we ain't a lick closer to stopping it than we ever were. This boy's blood gives us a chance. You know it well as I do. Some peculiar quality of his blood might get us over the terrible shortcoming of the vaccine, might save untold lives—save the country from a catastrophe."

"Might," said Braden, "might, might, might!"

"True," said Green somberly. "But show me something better than this *might*. Till you do, I don't see how to stop what we're doing. I don't dare take the chance of messing up his blood with a transfusion—not of the best-matched blood. This boy's blood is unique. We know it. We go diluting it, how do we know what we do to his special immunity? How do we know that we don't forfeit our one opportunity to save those millions of lives? How do you

241

compare his life to all those?"

"It's going to be academic in any case," said Doctor Braden stiffly. "He'll be dead before the day is out, in my judgment. And there goes your source for this elixir of life."

"No," said Green. "I ain't going to let him die."

"Well then! How else—? Oh. Oh. I see. Doctor, that's the most horrible, coldly calculated—"

"No sir, Dr. Braden. Calculated, but not cold. Not cold at all. It grieves me. But I don't see any choice. I'm going to keep doing what we're doing—pulling his blood and centrifuging it and giving him back the red cells and most of the plasma and that way keep him alive as long as possible. When we start to lose him—I know we will—I know it as well as you—we'll hook him onto a life-supporting system and keep him breathing after his brain is dead, keep him manufacturing blood and keep using it and testing it as long as possible."

"Until you bleed him dry." Braden gave Green a look of loathing. "Doctor, I may admire your logic, but I pray I never have to make a decision—I won't say immoral, I won't even say unethical—but—I see your mind is made up." He left, slamming the door.

"My friend," said Simon, as the door closed, "I didn't ask to make this decision. I only hope it's the right one. How am I going to ever know?" He heard his name being paged, a telephone call from General Burrows.

"I feel like a mole coming up here," said Walter Burrows. "I can't remember when I left that damn hole in the ground. Thanks for letting me come up. No luck so far on the blood?"

"It's frustrating, General. And there just isn't a whole lot of time left." Tersely, Simon explained the situation to Burrows who nodded worriedly.

"I came up, Dr. Green," said Burrows, "for a couple of reasons. Noah Blanchard asked me to monitor developments on Olvera's blood while he was gone, and I wanted to congratulate you on bringing that young man back from Mexico. That was terrific."

"It is courtly of you to say so, General," said Simon. "Noah gone? Where?"

"To Alamogordo with the CDC team inspecting the Washburn site you tipped us off to. I thought you knew."

"That's a surprise. What did he do that for? They don't need him. I'm surprised the President permitted it."

"My impression," said Burrows, "is that the president was opposed, but Noah went anyway. I was surprised, too. Lots of things about Noah surprise me right now. He worries me. All of a sudden he's out of character. About Alamogordo, he as much as said the President could like it or lump it. Something's eating Noah."

"He's under terrible pressure, of course," said Simon thoughtfully. "I'm not well-acquainted with President Dobson, but I doubt if he's an easy man to work for."

"The pressure's been on all along and Noah kept his cool. It was one of the things I admired about him. No, Doctor, it's something else. You could blame it on Kate's defection, but I think it's more than that."

"My dear General, you are full of surprises. What has Miss Kate done?"

"You don't know? Walked out on him in the middle of the night—flew to Chicago to go on that convict television show. He was as angry as I've ever seen him. But that wouldn't account for it all. He's no moonstruck lover boy."

Simon chuckled. "Noah? I should think not. Besides, the lady is a professional television reporter. It's her job. Why would this upset Noah so much?"

Burrows grinned. "I got the impression he was getting serious about her, thinking wedding bells."

"Noah Blanchard? Heavens, General. I assumed the relationship was not platonic, knowing Noah, but matrimony? Surely you are mistaken."

"I've been before," said Burrows, still smiling, "but not

243

this time. He as much as told me. Added that he'd make a rotten husband."

"Gracious. The pressures on him must have been greater than I realized, for Noah to contemplate matrimony."

Burrows laughed. "I thought you were a happily married man, Doctor."

"For forty years, sir. But I am not Noah. He told you he would go to New Mexico regardless? That the President could like it or lump it? In those words?"

"Not exactly, but that's what he meant—as if he had some leverage on the President."

"Such as what, General?"

"Strictly between us—sorry, I don't have to say that. We had a Task Force meeting, even more tense and argumentative than usual. Noah let something slip. He said time was running out."

"But it is, sir," said Simon gently. "Every day is a new disaster."

"He didn't mean that," said Burrows. "I know the man. I read him between the lines. He back-pedaled when he took him up on it, said he meant cold weather coming. But it was something far more urgent—some deadline for something. He knows things we don't."

"As the President's confidante, he should."

"Of course. And I'm not resentful and I don't pry. But I can worry. Conjectures come into my head and I get this awful sense of impending doom, even more than I've been living under."

"And you don't strike me," said Simon, smiling, "as a man given to vague alarms and nervous apprehension."

"I hope not," said Burrows ruefully. "Well, maybe I'm wrong."

"You may not be. I flew young Olvera back from Tucson on an Air Force medical airplane. Now, I don't know much about the military anymore—I doffed my soldier suit in 1945—but I noticed that we took on fuel at a civilian base, not a military one. The flight nurse said that all the fields with bombers and fighters were closed, nobody knew why, but her pilot guessed some big military operation was in the wind. The conjectures are obvious—and they scare me to death. Yes, I suspect Noah knows something we don't. And I think it's something menacing."

"There's always some poor joker who doesn't get the word," sighed Burrows. "When I was a captain, I thought if I made major they'd put me in the big picture. They didn't. Now I have two stars and they still don't tell me anything. Doctor, whatever it is Noah knows that we don't, it can only spell trouble. Let's pray you find what you're looking for in Mr. Olvera's blood."

"Or Noah finds what we need in Alamogordo."

"Or those convicts pull it off in their TV appeal. I think that might just pay off. Of course I grasp at every straw. What's your opinion?"

"Neutral," said Simon. "But timidly hopeful. I don't see how it could hurt. I am grasping for straws, too."

Burrows rubbed his face hard, seemed to ponder, to hesitate, after a pause spoke again. "Dr. Green, I've been reluctant to even bring this up. It's so crazy. It's so plausible and promising in one way—so weird and impossible in another way—it's had us—the three or four of us in on it—well, you tell me. You know, we get all sorts of crank calls. Can't refuse them. Somewhere there just might be some unheard-of genius who has a solution to all our problems."

"The one-in-a-million chance you can't afford to pass up, eh?" Simon smiled. "And you got a crank call that you're reluctant to tell me about? Tell me, man, tell me!"

Burrows shot him a quizzical look. "What if I told you Vincent Craigie wanted to talk to Noah?"

"Vincent—?" Simon shook his head. "My, my. You've been in communication with the dead. That is weird."

"Suppose I told you that no record exists of Vincent Craigie's death?"

"Nonsense," said Simon sharply. "He's been dead

for—? In any case how could you possibly know such a thing?"

"Coincidence, sir. Noah or I mentioned him by chance the other day, how useful a man of Craigie's qualifications would be to us just now. We both assumed he was dead. Then realized we did not know when or why. Out of curiosity we had the computer people check it out. No record. Vincent Craigie vanished from the scene seven or eight years ago. Just vanished. No record that he died."

"And now you think he's alive?"

"I don't know what to think. It could be a hoax, but it would be elaborate and pointless. Nor do I understand how a prankster—he would have to be a macabre one, too—could have all the information—Never mind. Here it is. A Dr. Henry Gault from St. Elizabeth's Hospital— the mental hospital—phoned most apologetically. An elderly schizophrenic patient who has been there for years—the time fits, let me insert—suddenly announces that he is Vincent Craigie. The identity—personality—the name they have known him by—was that of his grandfather. It's bizarre. I'm out of my field when it comes to abnormal psychology, but I suppose it could happen. The patient insists that the year is 1895 and—well, never mind that."

"Gault," murmured Simon, leafing through a medical register. "Here it is. There is a Henry Gault at St. Elizabeth's with, as you would expect, excellent credentials. Well, anyone could look that up. Sorry to interrupt."

"Well, now the patient announces he is Craigie. That his last memory is of being in New Mexico. That he had dealings with Clavering Washburn and it is essential he see Noah Blanchard—his former student—about the epidemic. There is more, but that was the essence of it."

"Good lord in heaven, General!" Simon Green leaped to his feet. "Do you have the—this mental patient? Is he Craigie? Why did you wait to tell me? Why this is—"

"Wait, Doctor, wait! Let me finish. Here's the

246

diabolical end of it. It could still be a hoax. Or worse. I was as excited as you, by then—we all were. We were going to send an ambulance over, or if Gault said Craigie shouldn't be subjected to a move, go to St. Elizabeth's ourselves. Gault was relieved by our reaction. I don't think he was really convinced himself. We arranged to go over and—wouldn't you know it!"

"Know what?"

"Ten minutes later, crestfallen, chagrined, Gault calls back. After ten hours sleep under mild sedation his patient woke up. Who is he? You guessed it. He is a man named Noyes. The year is 1895. Grover Cleveland is in the White House. Epidemic? What epidemic? If there is one, it's yellow fever and the first frost will end it."

"Oh—my—God," breathed Simon. "I can see why you hesitated to tell me. So where are we now?"

"That's what I asked Gault. The poor man. He blames himself for sedating his patient while at the same time insisting it could not possibly make a difference. Prognosis? Will he regain his identity? Who knows? Will it be the same one? Who knows? Is he really Craigie? It sounds like it, but again, who knows?"

"So near and yet so far," said Simon. "Who knows? But see here! You have people who must know Craigie."

"Duval Badin? I expect he would. I don't know if Gault will agree. It might not be wise, for the patient's sake, to expose him to strangers. Or people from his long-lost life."

"We have to try. You have to persuade Gault. We have to take any risk. This is too important. My lord, General, I'm letting that poor boy—well, never mind. I spoke my piece on that."

"They don't hire us for the easy decisions, Doctor," said Burrows. "And my guess is that the President— maybe Noah, too—is grappling with even harder ones. All right. I'll bear down on Dr. Henry Gault. The stakes are far too high not to."

"You might tell him that Noah will be back. That's the

time to bring Noyes-Craigie—whoever he is—to Bethesda."

"I'll do it," said Walt Burrows. "Count on me. I'll be in touch."

After Burrows left, Simon pondered. Craigie? Impossible! And yet? How could anyone make the Clavering Washburn connection who did not know? Suppose that fantastic intelligence still lived after all. What irony if locked away inside it was the vital knowledge for ending the epidemic. A split mind—a brain trapped in the past. It was a maddening conjecture. So near and yet so far—if true. How could it be true? But how could it not be?

"Doctor," said a young feminine voice. "Dr. Green."

Simon blinked and looked up. Framed in the door was a nurse. He did not know her, but she was one of the prettier young ones. I don't know their names, he thought, but I notice their shapes and faces. For all the good it does me. "Yes, Nurse?"

"Doctor, the old lady's insisting. We let her see him—from a distance—as you said. Now she's insisting on seeing you. She says you are personal friends."

"Oh. Of course. Miss Dalrymple." He had persuaded her to leave the Annandale office and move into a guesthouse on the NIH hospital grounds. It wasn't easy. The clincher had been that she would be near Luis if Simon found him and brought him there. "How much does she know?"

"I don't know, sir. Not much. We gowned and masked her and let her look in. All she could see was the cardiac monitor and the tent he is under. Will you see her? Do you want us to put her off?"

"No, no. It's all right. Where is she?"

"In the visitors' lounge. We tried to give her something to eat. She's been here hours. All she wants is to talk to you."

"She's a stubborn old woman."

"Yes, Doctor. And Dr. Braden wants to see you too. He was just waiting for your other visitor to leave."

"He'll have to wait. I'll see Miss Dalrymple." Simon sighed, pulled himself up, and lumbered around to the visitors' lounge. His feet had begun to hurt. It was always something.

When he entered she was sitting rigidly. She took hold of her cane to rise and he waved her back. "Miss Dalrymple. It seems a long time ago when we were in your office."

Her sharp eyes made him uneasy. "I thank you for bringing him home. I thank you for this good hospital care for him."

He nodded, not knowing what to say.

"He is very badly injured."

"It was a terrible accident," said Simon. "He has numerous fractures and other injuries."

"I heard," she said. "People don't pay heed to an old woman in a corner. I overheard that it's not the broken bones so much, it's the loss of blood."

"Well, that's part of it, but he also has an infection and probably neural damage. He is in grave condition, ma'am."

"I realize that. If you hadn't found him when you did, he could be dead by now. Isn't that so?"

"In medicine you can't be that positive, but yes, probably."

"So I thank you again for his life."

"Miss Dalrymple," said Simon miserably, "that young man is well worth saving. I was a battlefield doctor and treated brave young soldiers, but none braver than he. And I'll tell you something else. He was mostly unconscious, which is a mercy because it spared him pain. But when he was semi-conscious and talked to me, he told me things I needed to know—why, he took me for his daddy, Miss Dalrymple. He held my hand and called me Father. I won't forget that. I won't ever."

"But you're letting him die."

"Miss Dalrymple! I don't know who you've been talking to, but—"

"It's not the broken bones and the infection. I heard them talk. He needs a blood transfusion or he will die, and you won't let him have it. Isn't that right?"

"Miss Dalrymple, please."

"Is he a carrier of this disease? Have you proved that?"

"That's not something you can prove—or disprove—like two times two. But from the circumstantial evidence it looks like he is. That's why he's in isolation."

"Does that make him responsible for this epidemic? These people dead and dying, the country in this fix, is all that his fault? Do you blame Luis for that?"

"Well, not that way, ma'am."

"When you asked for help to find him—which I am eternally grateful you did—you said how important finding him could be. You said that what he could tell us about the source of the epidemic might be invaluable. Was that a lie, Doctor?"

"No, ma'am. I wouldn't dream of lying. Miss Dalrymple, the information he supplied is enormously useful. It might lead us to the cause and source of this disease."

"You don't blame him for the epidemic?"

Simon drew his breath. "Listen, Miss Dalrymple, even if he proves to be—as I think he is—the carrier, why it was innocent. He was a victim. And if he hadn't spread it, it would have spread another way. An organism that virulent, it won't stay bottled up."

"Then," she said, "he didn't do anything to be punished for? In fact, you owe him thanks."

"Yes, ma'am. I guess that's true."

"So why does he have to die?" she wailed. Without warning the old woman dissolved into tears, and Simon Green wanted to sink through the floor. Two nurses—they must have been eavesdropping—were there instantly. Without a glance at him they took the straight, frail old woman by her elbows and led her, limping, away. Green stalked out, muttering, and found Dr. Braden reading a chart at the nursing station.

"The ICU patient?" he said. "Condition?"

"Failing," said Braden. "Thready pulse, shallow respiration, blood pressure dropping. If you want that life-support system, we'd better hurry. I tried to see you earlier."

"Never mind that. Anything affirmative from transfusions of his plasma? Anything from the lab? From the epidemic ward?"

"Negative all the way, Doctor."

Simon Green, gentle soft-spoken man, crashed his fist down. "Goddamn it all to bloody hell!" he said as the nurses jumped. "I'm too old for this. All right. Two pints of whole blood. *Stat!* I'm sure you've got it matched and waiting."

"Yes sir, Doctor!"

"And tell a nurse to go tell that old woman what we did."

Simon Green plodded away, his feet aching furiously. Now everything depended on a schizophrenic, three condemned murderers, and what Noah Blanchard would find in Alamogordo.

Chapter 20

With a tailwind, the VC 140-B made Alamogordo in two and a half hours, giving the CDC team plenty of time to inspect the Washburn Chemical site and return to Washington by dark. If necessary, Noah told the specialists, they could fly back later for a follow-up investigation, but right now the President insisted on a quick appraisal. The team looked surprised and Maggie Eatonton, the toxicologist, almost protested, but thought better of it. Noah guessed he would have no trouble getting them all back aboard.

Flying in, the team had read the *Apache Candle* project file. It offered little—was essentially a prospectus seeking a government grant for research into new synthetic fuels—one of countless ventures during the Carter Administration's petroleum crisis. Unlike most, though, this came from a highly respected master of innovative chemistry. Clavering Washburn proposed to exploit useless flora native to the arid Southwest. His prospectus listed specific possibilities: converting the cellulose in woody trash plants such as greasewood, mesquite, and common sagebrush to usable energy sources by chemical processing, employing microorganisms similar to those in the digestive tracts of termites; producing fuel-grade methanol from worthless varieties of the *Agave* genus; and as a third and totally different approach, cultivation of the long-discussed, but never developed, guayule and jojoba plants with their well-known rubber and sperm-oil characteristics.

That was about all the file gave them. Anything more would have to be dug out, perhaps literally, of the mountainside near the Lincoln National Forest that Clavering Washburn had supposedly fenced off for his experiments. Maggie Eatonton wrinkled her freckled California nose at the project file and said to Noah, "From this you think we got an epidemic?"

"Beats me, Maggie. You're the toxicologist." Noah grinned at her, liking her rangy athletic figure and direct blue gaze. He also liked the discovery that, although Kate still rankled, a new woman had appeal for him.

"I suppose it's possible. Nobody dreamed that when they put vinyl chloride in plastics they were causing cancers. We'll see."

When they landed and taxied up to Base Operations at Holloman AFB, Noah saw to his dismay an official party standing at salute. He had no time for such foofaraw. As soon as the airplane door opened he was out, extending his hand.

"Welcome to Holloman, Mr. Secretary," said a thin, boy-faced brigadier general. "I'm Flickering, base commander. What would you like to inspect, sir?"

"Goodness, General," said Noah genially. "I don't plan to bother you at all. I need an hour or two with the local Public Health Service and then we'll get out of your hair."

"That's me, sir," said a straw-hatted civilian with a square sunburned face who had been standing in the background. "Herman Diehl. Your radio message caught me just in time. I was headed over to White Sands."

"Sorry to screw up your day, Dr. Diehl," said Noah. "We won't tie you up any longer than we can help. Are we okay on transportation?"

"No problem," said Diehl briskly. "We have my sedan

253

and a couple of Air Force vehicles General Flickering's lending me."

"I'd like to get going," said Noah. "Washington says we have to get back today."

"Dr. Blanchard," said Flickering, "could I have a word in private? Only a minute?"

"Of course, sir," said Noah, his heart sinking. "Doctor, introduce yourself to the team and get them and our gear loaded up, if you would, please. I'll be right back. Where to, General?"

"Over here is all right." Flickering walked him across to a strip of shadow cast by a hangar. As fighter wing commanders often do, he looked absurdly young, but his boyish face was haggard. "Mr. Secretary," he said, his eyes intent on Noah's, "would you kindly give me a quick rundown on conditions back east? We're at the end of the line here, completely cut off. How bad are things? All I've been told is to ground my airplanes and stand by for further orders."

Noah bit his lip. He looked off at the twin-tailed F-15s parked smartly along the flightline. He turned and squinted into morning haze through a frieze of cotton-wood trees towards the residential and administrative buildings of the base. This young fighter pilot, he thought, is charged by law with the safekeeping of men, women, children and millions of dollars worth of government property. We tell him to hold the fort and stand by. We don't tell him that inside of forty-eight hours, because of a damned epidemic we can't control, he and all his command may be exterminated by friendly airplanes. What am I supposed to say to him?

"I won't hand you any malarky," he said harshly. "Conditions are damned near as bad as they can be. But we're working like hell to get on top of this thing, and although the situation is desperate, I don't call it hopeless. We've got leads—I'm on one now. That's all I can say. You can tell your people, though, that they are not forgotten. We're doing everything we can to help them.

Just hang on. Do your best. That's not much, but that's all I can say. I wouldn't insult your intelligence."

Flickering's mouth was a grim line. "Thank you, sir. I'll pass that word. If the Pentagon asks, we've buried a quarter of the command, our hospital's full, we've lost a lot of medical personnel. But nobody has quit. Nobody's tried to run away. Not that I know where they would go. And we all realize that we're no worse off than the civilians in town. We'll stick. We'll stick it out."

"You bet I'll tell them," said Noah. "I'll tell the President too. Before this day is out. General, I—I wish I could say more."

"No occasion, sir," said Flickering stiffly. "As long as they know back there. Thank you for taking time."

It was not until Herman Diehl's gray PHS sedan had left the base and was driving towards timbered mountains in the east that Noah spoke. The team followed in an Air Force carry-all, its protective gear and equipment coming behind in a pickup truck. "How bad is the epidemic generally, Dr. Diehl?"

"Average, I suppose, twenty-plus percent casualty rate. Some places are far worse. We're coming to a settlement up here called Washburn where forty or fifty people used to live. Every man, woman, and child there died in three days, not one survivor."

"The whole *town?*" Noah whistled. "First case of that I've heard of. Washburn?"

"Named for the gent your message said you wanted to see. I think it was built for his employees to live in. They all left long ago. Just a wide place in the road, couple of stores, bars, a filling station. Or was. Now it's just vacant buildings."

"How close to the Washburn chemical works?"

"Down the mountain from it a few miles, I guess. Not that I've been up there."

"Have you met Washburn?"

"I never even heard of him until recently. I don't get out this way much. Besides I only came to Alamogordo last

255

year. I think he's inactive, maybe an invalid."

"Not to cross-examine you," said Noah, "but I'm bothered. Do you know when the epidemic hit this little town?"

"Oh, God," said Diehl. "Everything got hectic all at once. Seems to me I no sooner had an epidemic alert from Albuquerque than I heard that everybody in Washburn was dying. It was hit early, that's for sure."

"Now tell me this. Did anything unusual, unusual weather, any unusual natural phenomenon take place around Washburn in August?"

"Well, just Addie."

"Come again?"

"Hurricane Addie. Hurricanes don't touch this country, but Addie did—came ashore near Brownsville and headed for us. This is an arid land, but for once we got rain. Did we ever! Addie gave us two years worth in a day. Talk about cloudbursts and flashfloods. Water poured off these mountains. They say the arroyo cutting through Washburn had ten feet of water in it. Normally it's dry as a bone."

"A flashflood," said Noah. "And a short while later an epidemic that wiped out the population."

"Holy jumping Jesus." Diehl sailed his straw hat in the back seat and slapped his head. It was onion-bald and burnt brown as cordovan. "I never made that connection."

"It's only a wild guess," said Noah. "Is this Washburn we're coming to?"

"God, how could I have missed that?"

"You had no reason to suspect Washburn Chemical," said Noah. "Nobody did."

The country road widened and small adobe houses began to appear on both sides. Then they were in the main street of a block-long western hamlet: Conoco station, Last Chance Saloon, Nellie's Malt Shop, a liquor store, a general store, all forlorn as stage scenery in an abandoned theater. A culvert crossed a wide sandy arroyo, littered with tree limbs and brush washed down from the forested mountains.

"You suppose, by any chance," Noah pondered, "the water that came down that gulch was off the Washburn works?"

"We're about to find out." A hundred yards farther Diehl turned into a gravel road that began tacking up a mountainside in a series of hairpin turns, the air growing quickly cooler and beginning to smell of fir trees. Sparse stands of timber appeared, thickened, and became forest. In a very few minutes they climbed perhaps three thousand feet. "Nice up here," said Diehl. "Pretty soon now the aspens will be turning yellow. Well, well. What do you know? You suppose they'll let us in?"

The road was blocked by a chained, padlocked steel gate in a cyclone fence topped by barbed wire. A big weather-beaten sign, the letters dimmed by time, read: *Sacramento Mountain Site, WASHBURN CHEMICALS*. A small new sign hung from the chain: *Admission by Appointment. Telephone on Gatepost*. Diehl got out and went to the plastic box where the telephone hung, while Noah explored along the fence. Car engines ground up the road and the two following vehicles drew up and stopped. Six feet off the road, Noah found a fresh gully in the pine-needled earth under the fence and stopped to look at it, being careful not to touch anything. "Maggie," he called, "you might want to look at this. Bring a test kit."

She got out of the carryall, graceful of movement even in the bulky protective coveralls, and walked over, a box under one arm, pulling on gloves. "What have you got, Doctor?"

At the telephone Diehl was saying, "It's ringing but nobody answers. What do we do; break and enter?"

The airman who drove the pickup got out with a long-handled chain cutter. "You want that thing opened, sir?"

"Have at it, son," said Noah, and to Maggie, "I think

you might test the soil here where it's washed out under the fence." He explained his theory and she went to work. By the time the chain was severed and the big gates swung open of their own weight, Maggie was back in the road with a test tube that she held to the sunlight. She shook it and looked at it again.

"Verdict, Maggie?"

"I need more tests to be dead certain, but off-hand it's here. Abundantly. The color reaction shows the soil impregnated with anaerobic organisms, and they could very well be the Ulceration pathogen."

"So," said Noah softly. "The evidence grows. Might be smart if we all got into protective gear before going any farther."

"I'd advise it," said Maggie.

"How about respirators?" said one of the men.

"It's not supposed to be airborne," said another, "but there could be dust. I'd say have them handy."

The forest quickly gave way to a broad circular parkland lying between two arms of the mountain range. There was a pattern of gravel roads and a number of aluminum-sided buildings in the distance, all crystal sharp in the clear air. In the farthest distance, up under the dark belt of conifers growing down from the mountain peak, was a low white structure like a ranchhouse. Some of the aluminum buildings were windowless like warehouses, some seemed to be open-fronted sheds, some could have been offices or shops or for housing operations of any sort requiring workers and light machinery. Nearest of all were three greenhouses, all with numerous panes of shattered glass, presumably from hailstones.

"Let's look at those first," said Noah. "From what we know, the heart of this operation was botanical. I wish we had a botanist along. Well, it may not make any difference. Let's go, eh?"

The greenhouse they entered was humid and gloomy despite the bright shafts of sunlight through the broken panes. Under the impervious fabric of his coveralls Noah sweated. Pots and boxes of earth with desiccated remnants of vegetation in them sat on long low tables and shelves. There were small botanical signs: *Jojoba, Maguey, Mesquite*, each with its taxonomic Latin equivalent below. Maggie Eatonton stood beside Noah and sniffed. "Humidity, stagnant air, pot after pot of nutrient-enriched soil, no doubt. If I wanted to hatch out a fine crop of virulent microorganisms this would be a damned hard environment to beat." She started down an aisle, spooning soil samples from different pots and boxes, scooping others from the earthen floor.

"Maggie's going to be busy here," said Noah. "Let's get outside and divide up. We don't have a lot of time, remember."

Out in the open air, he went on. "Split up however you like. But let's cover this place, every building. Be on the lookout for recent run-offs of high water. Everything is beginning to point to contaminated material being washed down into that settlement, which would reinforce the possibility that this is where the epidemic started. Let's find out! Doctor Diehl and I will go up to that white building—it looks like headquarters, where the people live. Meet you here in one hour."

Diehl drove around on the perimeter road to the white building at the top. It was a two-story stucco with a porte cochere in front, where they parked and got out. Diehl rang the bell, waited, knocked, waited, shrugged, and tried the door handle. The door came open. He staggered back, choking. Then he turned and, clutching a column for support, began vomiting. From inside the house the pent-up air had come rushing out, loaded with the nauseating stench of Consolvo's Ulceration laced with the rotten-sweet pungency of ordinary putrefaction. Gasping for breath Noah fumbled with his respirator, managed to get it on, and by a great effort of will entered the house.

He found himself in an office filled with typewriter desks, file cabinets, and calculating machines, which were all covered with a film of dust. The air was icy. He heard the hum of the air-conditioning still running even though the hot days of August were over. He started opening windows to let fresh air in, and heard Diehl's voice, muffled by his respirator, "I'm sorry about that. I thought I was inured to the odor by now. But that was too much."

"You got the whole brunt of it. Look at the dust. How long do you suppose it's been closed like this? No bodies in here. Let's look farther."

Beyond the first office they came to a private office—an opulent, oak-panelled sanctuary for the chemical-industry tycoon whose last triumph this place was to have achieved. The walls were full of testimonials to his successes: photographs of lion-maned, giant-framed Clavering Washburn posed with every president since Herbert Hoover, in the uniform of a Chemical Corps general, along with the leaders of a nation's financial and industrial power spanning nearly four generations. Suddenly they saw the object of all this glory sprawled on the rug before them. The white-haired cripple lay a few feet from an overturned wheelchair, his hands outstretched and imploring, on his face the frozen look of horror that Clavering Washburn had known at the instant of death.

They did not touch him. He had been dead for weeks although, except for the distension of his abdomen, decomposition was not greatly advanced. One thing was clear. Whatever killed Clavering Washburn, it was not Consolvo's Ulceration. He was not the source of that unmistakable stench. That, they found in the two house servants. The old man lay in the kitchen, his white chef's cap still on his grizzled African head; his wife, hands clasped as if in prayer, in the small bedroom in the servants' annex.

Diehl and Noah left the house as quickly as possible. Outside, breathing pure mountain air gratefully, Noah said, "All right, Doctor, diagnosis, please."

The bald, sunburned man stared off to the west. The

vista was magnificent: violet mountain ranges, green forest sloping away, in the ultimate distance White Sands Missile Range swimming in haze. "An invalid confined to a wheelchair, alone in a house on a mountain except for two old servants, the nearest town where they might send to for help in the grip of a one-hundred-percent-fatal epidemic. The servants catch the disease and die. The master, totally helpless in his wheelchair, is left to die of—what?"

"A massive coronary?" asked Noah. "Stroke? Sheer terror?"

"The old-fashioned horrors? Why not, considering the predicament he found himself in?"

"I almost hope it was a stroke," said Noah. "Or a quick coronary. It would be horrible if he died of—say thirst?—trying to crawl to the bathroom or kitchen for a drink of water."

"Whatever he died of," said Diehl, "it will take an autopsy to determine, and nobody's got time for that, not in Lincoln County, New Mexico, in this epidemic. All I can do is send up a burial crew."

"I expect so," said Noah. "Well, I don't think there's anything more for us in there. Let's go see what the team has."

They held a council of war, sitting on the ground below the greenhouses. The CDC team had done its job. No organism had been found anywhere—not even in the fertile environment of the greenhouses—except in one shed apparently used to mix and process unknown ingredients. It held large vats, similar to those of a brewery, now empty but coated with a dry residual crust. In the earthen floor were traces of the organism that Maggie Eatonton had dug up from under the fence. Where they had struck gold, though—their Golconda, bonanza, veritable mother lode—was in a circular mound of grass-grown earth in the very lowest point of the plant complex, a kind of barrow.

"You wouldn't notice it in a million years," said Felix

Latour, the oldest team member. "It just looked like an innocuous natural hummock. If Carlos here hadn't gotten curious and gone exploring we'd never have tumbled."

Carlos McGinty, still in his twenties, sun-bleached as a tennis bum with his straw-pale hair clubbed behind, but a top-notch microbiologist, said, "Don't give me any credit. Deference to Maggie, I was looking for a place to piss."

"Viva la modesty," retorted Maggie.

"But there it is," said Latour. "As you suggested, a corner of the thing had washed away. Maybe there's an underground spring nobody knew about that overflowed when the deluge came. Carlos spotted it and yelled, and we checked it and oh, boy!"

"Oh boy is right," said Maggie with feeling. "It was redhot. Swarming. Teeming. The most intense concentration you could imagine. And from where it broke out, any contamination would inevitably wash down the hill to that gully and from there, no doubt, wind up in the arroyo at that village."

Diehl and Noah nodded at each other. "Okay," said Noah. "First-class work. Let's sum up. Let's see what hypothesis would logically arise from what evidence we have. Who wants to try?"

"How about this?" said Latour hesitantly. "Something went wrong in the mixing shed. God knows what. It certainly wasn't the sudden appearance of Consolvo's Ulceration, anything that dramatic. They couldn't have hushed that up, even if they were foolish or insane enough to try. All they knew was they had something unsafe. So they dug a sump to bury it in forever. I bet if we dared dig we'd find it sealed with concrete, bottled up against anything except a once-in-a-thousand-years cloudburst."

"Which broke it out and washed it down on Washburn village," said Diehl. "And I was too dumb to guess. Washburn was turned into a nest of epidemic vectors before they all died."

"Stop blaming yourself," said Noah. "You couldn't

262

have done anything about it. Besides Olvera had probably carried the disease out already."

"Back to my hypothesis," said Latour. "Workers got sick, maybe nothing more than a little rash, maybe something more serious, but would it be bad enough to close down the plant? I can't think so. Washburn wouldn't have hushed that up. He was a moral, honorable man. My opinion is that something else was responsible. I used to read about Clavering Washburn all the time, but a few years back he stopped being in the news. Not that I noticed at the time. You found him fallen from a wheelchair? Isn't it more likely that poor health—a stroke or something of the sort—six or seven years ago would have made him cease his operations?"

"Local gossip," said Diehl, "is that he was an invalid. I would call it a reasonable possibility."

"How about you, Maggie?" said Noah. "Sound plausible to you?"

"That trying to produce a synthetic fuel from exotic vegetation using chemicals could produce a toxic substance? It's the sort of thing that happens all the time in industrial processes. And they covered it up like a cat covering up a mess and said nothing to anyone. Perfectly plausible."

"I must protest the innuendo, Maggie," said Latour. "I repeat that Clavering Washburn had a reputation for the highest probity. The man could not possibly have suspected that this was a deadly substance."

"Is it conceivable," said Diehl, "that this slightly toxic substance, buried like that, could change? Could mutate? Turn into something deadly?"

"It is certainly not inconceivable," said Latour. "Multiple sclerosis is now suspected of being caused by slow-growing viruses. Who knows how tetanus spores grow in barnyard soil? Poor analogies perhaps, but certainly your guess is as good as any."

The squat, swarthy scientist named Solferino who had

never said a word in Noah's hearing burst forth astonishingly. In a high squeaky voice he cried: "There is an island in the Hebrides so polluted with anthrax spores no one dares set foot there; product of British biological warfare experimentation; we have mercury in the Delaware, arsenic in Lake Michigan, lead in the air we breathe! Our poor poisoned planet is dying from the radioactive waste materials we plunge into the sea and bury in our soil. But we must not blame high-minded, moral Mr. Washburn for creating a slow-ripening abscess on his mountainside. Oh, no! It is *progress*. It is *civilization*. It is too bad that Mr. Washburn killed twenty million fellow citizens and will kill more yet, but we must not blame him!"

An embarrassed silence ensued. Then Latour clapped his hands. "Great speech, Sol," he said genially. "They'll have to have you on the stage at the Science for the People's next symposium. But right now, we'd better get started cauterizing this hillside abscess of yours."

"Right," said Diehl. "I'll get on my radio and get a crew and earth-moving machinery started up. A couple of truckloads of quicklime and some carboys of carbolic, I should think—"

"A crew with shovels," said Latour. "You can't decontaminate that gully with heavy equipment. And they have to be dressed for it. Could you find enough men who've been vaccinated? I'd rather not let anybody on the job who hasn't been, if possible."

"We'll need tents too," said Maggie, "along with cooking and water purification stuff. I for one wouldn't go near that house until it's been cleared and fumigated, if then."

"Wait a minute here!" cried Noah, in sudden consternation. "What are you people talking about? We have to fly back to Washington today."

"Oh, come on," said Maggie. "That's silly."

"Really, Dr. Blanchard," said Latour, in a kind, but firm voice, "she's quite right. We've found the epidemic source. It must be eradicated. You know that. You don't need us for your report to the President. Why, we have the best part of a week's hard work here."

"But you can't!" said Noah desperately. "It's not—it isn't—you can't—it isn't safe for you to stay."

"Excuse me, sir," said young McGinty, looking at him curiously, "but this is what we do. Safety is beside the point. This is our work. And we know better than anyone how to protect ourselves."

"Well, you see," Noah began, and realized that even Herman Diehl's honest Dutch face was on him with an expression of perplexity if not suspicion. "Oh, all right," he said in sudden surrender. "I guess I can explain it to President Dobson."

"Why should the President mind?" asked Latour. "He should be delighted."

"Oh, he will be," said Noah cravenly. "All right. You're right of course, all of you. I'll just take the pickup and go back to Holloman in it. So long, thanks for the good job."

He shook hands quickly and rode away, leaving another half-dozen hostages behind. Less than forty-eight hours to go, he was thinking.

Chapter 21

The instant the chartered Lear jet—with Kate the only passenger aboard—lifted off at Washington National, remorse seized her. It was silly, of course. She was breaking no promise. She owed Noah nothing. She had certainly pulled her weight these weeks at the Fleur d'Or. She was only doing what she had planned to do ever since she smuggled out the note in Albuquerque. Why should she feel guilty? She ought to feel exultant. If Maury was right about his convicted murderer show—and Maury's instincts for ratings were usually infallible—by tomorrow she would be the hottest female in TV newscasting. When her contract expired in a month, all three networks would bid for her, with the sky the limit.

That in a month there might not be any networks nor much of anything else was an unpleasant possibility she simply would not think about. Noah and his white-smocked troop of scientists were sure to end the epidemic and bring everything back to normal. How they would do it Kate did not worry about. Although she had issued bulletins and run press conferences every day for weeks, the medical patter she'd used so glibly meant nothing to her. The most elementary principles of epidemiology eluded her. All she had was her childish faith that Noah's science would pull off some form of magic, and that she would soon be in New York or Hollywood, her name and face as familiar as the President's to millions of television addicts.

So why did she feel so rotten, sitting back here in solitary grandeur in a chartered airplane? Anybody would think she was in love with the guy.

The door to the pilot's compartment opened and a gangling young man came stooping down the aisle with a white cup in his hand. He had the same lank build as Noah, she noticed with a pang. "Have some coffee, Miss Petrakis," he said. "It's been in a thermos jug all night, but it's all there is."

"Thank you. I'm sure it will be very nice."

He sat across the aisle from her and peered out at the night, shielding his eyes from the cabin light. "Solid overcast and black as the ace of spades," he said. "It breaks up though, this side of Chicago. Don't worry if we stooge around in circles a little before landing—we'll just be waiting for daylight. No runway lights at Midway. But at least we can land there. O'Hare now, it's closed round the clock."

"Why is that?"

"Got no controllers in the Tower. It's been shut for a week."

"That's hard to imagine, remembering how busy O'Hare was when I left there."

"How long ago was that?"

"About the end of August."

The young pilot shrugged. "BTE—Before the Epidemic. That's like Before the Flood."

"Is everything around Chicago that shut down?"

"I couldn't say, Miss. We stage out of Madison. Things aren't so bad in Wisconsin—our part of it anyway. Of course, Charley and me—he's captain, I'm co-pilot—we have to pull our own preflights mostly. But that's no big thing. Chicago? I just don't know. We take a charter in now and then, always get right out again. But the city can't be entirely shut down, for your television station to hire us. I guess you're some kind of celebrity, huh, Miss Petrakis? Should I be getting an autograph?"

Kate laughed. "Nobody ever wanted one before. Maybe by tomorrow. You tune in GBC tonight and watch the 'Get With It' show. I'll be on it. With some pretty exciting news, I can promise you."

"We heard something about that on a nightowl radio show from Charleston, West Virginia, a few minutes ago. A plug for the show. Must be something pretty big. Something about the epidemic? Something good for a change?"

"The man I work for in Washington," said Kate, getting a small thrill from the words, "says every epidemic has to end—always has, always will. Otherwise there wouldn't be any people on earth. Historically, epidemics have run their courses and quit. Even the worst ones. But medical science, he says, is finding out how to stop them early. You'll see this epidemic stopped. Soon now. You just watch."

"That's the best news I've heard since I can remember, Miss Petrakis. I hope the man who said all that knows his stuff."

"Oh, he does, he does all right."

"He why you're going to Chicago?"

The coffee was lukewarm and stale, but sipping it gave her time to think. "Not exactly. He's in Washington."

"You're going back to Washington after? We'll stand by at Midway then. It's your airplane, you know, for the next twenty-four hours."

"Maybe I *will* fly back with you," said Kate slowly. "I'll let you know." That there was no hope of it made her want to cry which was the dumbest thing yet, simply the dumbest thing in her whole life.

The co-pilot took her cup and stood up. "Got to get back now. Nice talking to you. I'll try to watch your show tonight. Don't forget to buckle up when you hear the chime."

"I won't. Thank you for my coffee." Kate watched him go ducking forward, a younger version of long, lean Noah, and bit her lip. Why did it tear at her? She didn't love the man—never had. He was a ticket out of Albuquerque, so she wouldn't catch the disease or be gang-raped by soldiers. Sneaking into his bed that first night, she'd been horny as hell. He'd probably thought as the Malibu beach queen used to say, 'pay the guy off with a little nooky and let him go.' But no, she had wanted him badly. Besides, she had been frightened and lonely, and needed another human being to cling to. And it had been nice, although Noah was hardly the most exciting sack athlete she had known. Sweet and tender, though, and she'd enjoyed it. A one-night stand was what she'd intended until he'd seduced her the next day, damn him. So to be honest, I guess I did fall for him, she thought. A little bit. There aren't all that many tall mature masculine men around for a tall mature feminine woman.

I liked Washington, too, she thought—liked running his office, being a big shot, cooking his food, most of all, sleeping with him. That more all the time and then, goddamn it all to hell, Maury phoned.

The hell with Maury, with all those vain, self-centered half-men I used to know. Noah Blanchard is worth fifty of them. Caring about patients is a doctor's trade, but I never knew what it meant. Not until Noah would pull me to him in the night and pour out in anguished frustration the failure he felt because people were dying and he could not stop it. I didn't understand the technicalities, but I understood despair. I held his face to my breast and petted him and murmured meaningless sounds—the most motherly sensation I have ever felt. Crazy times there in those nights I thought I would marry him. I could have put it in his mind. He was guileless.

The night outside had gone pearly gray. Clouds shredded and raced past. The airplane was in a shallow incline. Why didn't I? thought Kate. Actually I think he was coming around to the idea himself. I could have just let it happen. You don't have to be delirious about a man to make a marriage work, not at my age. Not that I was ever delirious—or ever that young maybe.

Sunshine flooded the cabin. The airplane tilted round on a wing tip, and she saw Lake Michigan below, a hard rippled blue. Something chimed and she buckled her seat belt. I respected Noah too much, thought Kate. I wouldn't trick him, or let him trick himself. I was basically too decent, too honest. I've done lots of cheap things, but not that. Oh bullshit, Katie, she jeered. You wanted no part of it—doctor's wife, Winnetka house, all that middle-class bourgeois stultifying mediocrity. You're a liberated female—ambitious, talented, meeting and beating the world on your own terms. You're a New Woman. You're also an ego-driven, miserable harpy, she thought dully, daughter of a man-hating, soul-shriveled mother.

They taxied towards the terminal at Midway, a ghost airport where nothing moved but a black limousine driving out to meet them. The co-pilot put Kate and her bag in back, the stolid driver, a shotgun propped in the seat beside him, never budging. When the limousine door closed, he shot out of the airport and north on Cicero, eerily deserted in the bright morning, and turned on Adlai Stevenson Expressway towards the Loop, It was surrealistic—empty expressway, empty ground-level streets they flashed across, traffic lights winking green and red to no purpose. West of the Loop the driver headed north on Franklin and over to Wells, ignoring lights and signs. Kate saw the Merchandise Mart, whose central tower housed her studios, rising like a monstrous Babylonian ziggurat beyond the river. The sight of it gave her a premonitory sense of vague alarm. Then they were there under the overhang, river and flagpoles to her left, and to her surprise the driver was getting out to open the door.

"I take you up, lady," he said, his Back-of-the-Yards voice unexpectedly gentle. "Ain't safe alone." He led her through the tall doors, holding his shotgun like a bird hunter.

Waiting for an elevator on the silent ground floor, Kate said, "What's the danger—muggers?"

"Dis building," said the driver, "you see, lady, dis building's big as a whole town. Dis building's got nine hundred showrooms and all kinds wholesale offices and t'ings. T'ousands people work in dis building ordinary but—"

"Whoa!" Kate laughed. "I'm one of them. I work at the TV studio. I've been away, but that's where I work."

"Oh?" He looked at her. "Dey didn't say. Well, now, wid de epidemic see, de building's mostly empty. Bums and kids come prowling. I seen jig gangs here last night. Dey come prowling and stealing and robbing. What we need is cops in here, and dat's a fact. Here we are. I'll ride you up, lady."

He left her at the TV station on the twentieth floor. Kate stood looking about uncertainly. A month ago this was a busy place, people hurrying in and out, down hallways and through doors. Now there was not even a receptionist to greet her. Then Maury came bursting out, short, plump, smacking his hands in delight. She had never been so glad to see him.

"Kate, baby!" She bent for his kiss. "Great to have you back, kid. We're going to make rating history with this one, baby."

"My God, Maury," she said. "Who'll bother to tune us in? I thought people had given up on TV. It's nothing but stale re-runs."

"Who'll tune us in? You got to be kidding. _Everybody_, that's who. Everybody east of the Mississippi anyway."

"I thought everybody was dead practically."

"Don't sound so fucking negative. We got more viewers than ever. What the hell else they got to do? People scared to leave the house, scared of crowds, scared to screw. So they watch TV. And they'll watch this show, you bet. We put the word out. All-night long GBC affiliates have been breaking into broadcasts with spot announcements. Watch 'Get With It' for big epidemic

271

breakthrough! We'll have the biggest audience since Nixon quit. Kate, wait till you see these principals of ours. TV naturals. You know the black dude, he's famous— Olin Rodgers. Quarterbacked the Bisons to their best season ever and then the stupid son-of-a-bitch got messed up with drugs and killed a narc in a drug bust in Gary. Goddamn, we could build a whole show about Rodgers alone. Half the black football fans in the country still believe he was framed. Then there's this sneaky looking Indian devil named Hornbow I swear would slit your ears in a second. And finally the white guy, Balfour—a short blond country boy with muscles all over and shoulders out to here that the dames will swoon over. Three condemned murderers, Kate, all with eyes like snakes, ready to turn Good Guy on 'Get With It.' Baby, are we going to have a show, or are we going to have a show?"

"Where are these men?"

"Locked up in Studio Four. You want to meet them?"

"They can't get out?"

"Baby, they don't want to get out. They're here because they want to be. Besides the three guards that brought them are watching them. I tell you who you ought to meet. The governor sent along his prison psychiatrist, a clown named Poteau, to tell us what kind of personalities we're dealing with here."

"Maury," said Kate hesitantly, "it sounds like a good show, but I don't know. I get this creepy feeling. Maybe it's this big empty building with thugs crawling around in it, like that driver told me. I'm getting bad vibrations."

"Good God, Katie. What happened to you? You used to be a gutsy dame. The Merchandise Mart's safe as a fort. Hell, I'm living here. Most of us do. How could you beat it. With all the wholesale furniture showrooms, you could sleep in a different bed every night for a hundred years. We got the domestic-arts staff cooking meals. Best board and room in Chicago! Not that Chicago's so bad compared to some places. You wouldn't know in Washington, sleeping with the big Plague Czar."

"Cut that crap out, Maury."

"Touch a little nerve there, baby?"

"Screw you, Maury. I came to do a job, remember? Don't crack smart about my private life. I can make cracks, too, you know."

"Just funning, Katie. Don't get your bowels in an uproar. What do you want to do first? Interview the cons? Talk to the shrink?"

"I want breakfast first."

"That's where the shrink is right now, feeding his face, the slob."

"I'd like to get a peek at those convicts too," said Kate. "Isn't there a one-way window into Studio Four?"

"Sure. It's right on our way."

Standing in the corridor to the executive dining room, Kate looked in on the three prisoners sitting in the center of the big studio—Indian dozing, white man leafing through a magazine, black staring at nothing. Against the far wall sat three uniformed guards with guns in their laps. The Indian was slight and hatchet-faced with dusky skin and a red headband clasping his black hair. The white was towheaded and snubnosed with a country face made meager by his shoulder spread. Except for his enormous torso you would never notice him twice. It was the black who commanded the eye. Even clad in shapeless denims and puffy from prison fare his giant frame was impressive. Kate was no sports fan, but she remembered a photograph of that aquiline, bearded face laughing exultantly across the front page of the *Chicago Tribune*. To see Rodgers slumped in this despairing pose was to see a hero maimed, and her heart went out to him.

She said to Maury, "They *are* picturesque. Especially that poor football player."

"The cameras will love him," he chortled. "And don't sell the Indian short. That sinister cutthroat's going to come across like something out of your nightmare. He talks pretty good, too—he and the white guy both. So far Rodgers won't say anything, but I can open him up. If I have to, I'll jab it in about how he blew a million dollar career. I can get him talking."

"I'll bet you can, Maury. You're just the lad to do it."

He patted her rump. "Never mind the knife, kid. Just let Uncle Maury handle things. We'll go get you that breakfast and talk to the shrink."

In the dining room a middle-aged man with a mournful hound-dog face sat shoveling food in his mouth while a pretty brunette talked to him rapidly, making notes on a steno pad. Kate recognized her. Polly Magruder from the news department, a bright kid a few years out of Northwestern. At their entrance she started guiltily. "Why, welcome back, Miss Petrakis."

Kate gave Maury a derisive glance. "Always two strings to the old bow, eh? Hello, Polly. Nice to see you."

"Nuts, Kate," grinned Maury. "You didn't absolutely swear you'd come back. Dr. Poteau, meet Kate Petrakis, my regular co-host. Scamper along now, Polly. Thanks for standing in."

Obviously as disappointed as she was embarrassed, Polly stood up quickly. For the first time Kate realized that they were of a similar height and combed their dark hair alike. Maury might not have an eye for women in the usual way, but he must like the same type on his show. A lot of short men liked tall women, she had noticed.

"Polly," Kate said, "I'm truly sorry. He's a real bastard, though. I'm sorry you had to find it out this way. Better luck next time." Polly forced a smile, tucked the steno pad under her elbows and left.

Doctor Poteau ate busily through the exchange, hardly nodding when Maury introduced Kate. A fair-haired waitress came out of the kitchen. Kate ordered breakfast and slipped into the chair Polly had vacated. She examined the psychiatrist critically. His collar was frayed, his necktie stained, his double-knit suit ill-fitting. Probably the Indiana state penal system didn't pay its medical staff very well. Probably Poteau wasn't a very good psychiatrist if he was satisfied with such a job.

274

He mopped his plate with toast, gulped it, took a final swallow of coffee, and lit a cigarette. "Say, Doc," said Maury, sitting across from him, "Kate wants to know about these guys. Tell her the best way to draw them out."

"What's to tell?" The psychiatrist coughed thickly and scowled at his cigarette. "They're condemned murderers waiting to be electrocuted. They've got no hope, no money, no influence, no future. What more do you need to know?"

Kate nodded thanks as the waitress put bacon and eggs before her. "The point is, Doctor," she said, "we're not trained in criminal psychology. What we want from this show is a successful appeal for vaccine volunteers from among convicts everywhere—other people too—and Maury and I wondered what the best approach was for that. What is your advice? What's the best way to talk to men with no hope and no future?"

Poteau drew on his cigarette and coughed horribly. "Damn things are killing me," he said. "Could you be specific, Miss?"

"I was hoping you would be." She smiled. "Tell us about them as individuals, about their unique personalities."

"Can't be done," said Poteau. "Nobody gets inside these men to their unique personalities. They're locked away, covered over, hidden—maybe even from themselves."

Kate said, "Doctor, is that a generalization or does it just apply to these three?"

Poteau put his cigarette out and lit another immediately. "Everybody's got to die of something," he said. "Miss Petrakis, let's start this way. Take my word for it that no matter what these convicts tell you, don't believe it. Even if it is something you know is true. Because when they do tell the truth, they do it for a devious reason. Am I clear?"

"I guess," she said, sounding puzzled, "but why? Could you explain that?"

"You look like a high-class lady," said Poteau, "if you don't mind me saying so. I'll level with you. Murderers like these, men sentenced to death, they aren't like other people. Some authorities argue with that. What I say is, they don't have my twenty years' prison practice. They don't know. I do. Murderers are different from other people. It's baloney to say that everybody's a potential murderer. Not in our society, not under our social constraints. From three wars we've found out that most American soldiers won't even shoot at the enemy. They close their eyes and fire blindly, maybe in hopes that the enemy won't shoot at them. This is a known fact."

"What's that got to do with our convicts?" said Maury. "They talked pretty straight to me. They sounded sincere."

"They probably were," said Poteau. "By their lights. They probably told you what they thought was the truth."

"That's too deep for me," said Maury. "But hell, I don't care. Let them lie, long as we get a lively show. That's what I want."

"I thought what we wanted was vaccine volunteers," said Kate.

"We'll get them. Don't worry about that."

"I'm beginning to," she said. "Dr. Poteau's got me worried."

He smiled a little. "What I'm saying is, be on guard. Don't be taken in. These men are plausible liars. This is because they believe what they tell you. The truth they see is not your truth because they don't perceive truth as ordinary people do. They perceive a higher truth that exonerates them of blame. They cannot feel guilt. An ordinary person forced by circumstance to kill—say in self-defense or to protect his child—would still feel guilt, remorse. But these men, tried and found guilty and condemned to death by due process—and in our courts, with all the apparatus for appeal, the chance of an innocent man being sentenced to death is minuscule—these men have no sense of guilt. No remorse. Oh, they're

276

sorry they were caught. But for the murders they committed—not at all. Because the murders weren't their fault. They were the victim's fault, or society's, or God's. Egoism makes it impossible for them to acknowledge guilt. So they can't recognize the same truth as the rest of us."

"You mean," said Kate, "they're psychopathic personalities?"

Poteau stubbed out his cigarette and grimaced. "Ah, the little jargon words. When you say 'psychopathic,' you think you have defined something—solved the problem. The word means 'severely disturbed human behavior.' How many things fit that?"

Kate flushed. Poteau might be a better psychiatrist than she thought. "I apologize, Doctor. I know doctors resent lay people misusing technical language."

The psychiatrist chuckled. "I said you were a high-class lady. Now, while I can't probe their psyches for you, I can tell you how these lads landed on Death Row. If you know that, you know as much as anybody. You can slant your questions from that. Start with the Indian, Hornbow. Five years ago he was a law student, and leader of the campus Indian movement at Bloomington—Red Power, American Indian Movement, all that jazz. You remember how ethnic minorities were agitating back then. A Bloomington bank with an Indian name out of state history—Tippecanoe or Tecumseh, maybe—used a little cartoon Indian figure for its advertising: breechclout, bow and arrow, feather, harmless enough. But the Indian kids called it degrading. Maybe it was, and the bank probably would have apologized. But they busted in to stage a protest and got hustled to jail for disturbing the peace. It made the papers, the mayor got them released, and it would have blown over—only Hornbow got into some fire-water. There is physiological evidence of Indian intolerance for alcohol, by the way. He made public threats and charged back in. A nervous bank guard pulled his gun, Hornbow snatched it away and the bank

277

president got a bullet through the heart. Maybe it was accidental. But a prominent citizen was dead, there was premeditation, and you had a public fed up with protesting minorities, an Indian with no money, an inept public defender. Hornbow may not deserve execution. That's opinion. But he is indisputably guilty of causing a man's death, with only slight extenuating circumstances.

"Balfour now. This is a hick from the Indiana scaly bark ridges where they still live like Daniel Boone, same bucolic frontier culture Pretty Boy Floyd and John Dillinger and—come to think of it—Sergeant York came out of. Balfour was a soldier too, damn fine one. He didn't shut his eyes when he fired. Won a stack of medals in Viet Nam. Should have stayed in for a thirty-year man. Or gone home to plow his pappy's corn. But a city dame—if you call Logansport a city—got him, and he became an apartment-house super in a working class neighborhood. Fitted in well, drank with the boys in the corner bar, popular. Everything going for him—steady job, good wife, a little dough in the bank. Then one night after a beer too many he drove to the supermarket. Ran a red light—something. And a mean cop who hated hillbillies hauled him into the stationhouse. No witnesses. Balfour swears the cop started beating him, and all he did was defend himself. You've seen him, built like King Kong, and the Army had trained him to kill barehanded. So there was a cop with his neck broke which you don't get away with in Logansport. Balfour's got to die for it. What do you say to him? That you're sorry? Don't ask me.

"Rodgers now. He's the really pathetic one. Everybody knows his story. Lots of star black athletes—except for show business it's their main route up from poverty—but black quarterbacks? They're rare in the NFL. So Rodgers, a nice boy out of Grambling—yeah, yeah, I'm a fan—was Super Black who steered the Bisons to their best season in years. Idol of the Chicago Southside. Of every black football fan in the country. He had everything—money, glory, adulation galore. What does the stupid luckless bastard do? Caught in a drug bust, he panics and punches a narc, who dies. Most people think it was an accident—some that he was framed. Every black kid in Chicago does. Could be true. What I do know is that electrocuting Olin Rodgers—if they ever do—is a redundancy. He died in his soul a year ago. Most of the time he's virtually catatonic. How they penetrated his negativism to inveigle him into this vaccine volunteer scheme is a mystery to me. Maybe Hornbow put the Indian sign on him. Whatever that means. What do I know from Indians? I do know that Hornbow is the most complex and enigmatic personality of the lot. And dangerous. The other two are angels compared to that Indian. Well, Miss Petrakis, have I told you anything useful?"

"You told me enough to know that every one of them is more victim than villain. I feel deeply sympathetic to all three."

"Well, don't get carried away by it, is my advice," said Poteau. "The first thing you learn working with felons is don't let them snow-job you. They'll break your heart. According to the inmates, nobody on Death Row deserves to be there."

"I'm sure you're right, Doctor," said Kate. "But don't overlook one thing. Whatever these men ever did, they're willing to sacrifice themselves now for the rest of us. They are idealists, ready to die for others. Maury, that's the slant we ought to take."

"For Christ's sake don't get mawkish," Maury snapped. "This is a TV show, kid, not a revival meeting."

"Oh?" said Kate coldly. "I said this before, but I thought it was an effort to end the epidemic."

"Well, of course. That's the hook. But primarily it's still a show. Our show. Mainly we're after ratings. What about it, Doc? You think this appeal will work? You think these birds will really get a lot of volunteers?"

"I'm the wrong man to ask," said Poteau. "Being around cell blocks all your life makes you cynical. Maybe these three will save the country. But don't forget this. They're born losers, schmoes, schmucks. They all had things going their way, and they all screwed up. Why won't they screw this up, too? Then again, maybe the show will pay off like a slot machine. What do I know?"

"I think they at least deserve credit for trying," maintained Kate. "You ought to give them credit for that."

"Oh, I do," yawned Poteau. "I do indeed."

"How about you sitting in on the show?" said Maury. "For a fee, of course. That would be a good embellishment, their own psychiatrist adding comments."

"Not for me. Thank you, but no thank you. My wife's got a cousin living down by the Midway Campus she hasn't heard from since this epidemic started. I promised to look her up. If I can find transportation in this blighted town."

"We owe you that much anyway," said Maury. "Stick around until after the preliminary interview, and I'll try to scare up a car for you. It won't be long now."

"Many thanks," said Poteau. "I'll hang around. Miss Petrakis, good luck with your interviews. And stay skeptical." He lumbered out, pausing in the dining room door to light a cigarette.

By midafternoon Kate knew that Maury was right; the show would be a smash hit. The principals assured it. Although she had not rehearsed them, fearing that to do so would cost spontaneity, she had succeeded in loosening up even the indrawn Olin Rodgers to the point of speaking a few words, thanks to Turner Hornbow's persuasion. He alone seemed to be able to influence the fine-looking young black athlete. He alone could seem to penetrate that dim unfocused stare to get at the fine intelligence behind it. To watch the slight Indian lead the big, bearded black man along reminded Kate of Lennie and George in *Of Mice and Men*, although there was certainly nothing slow-witted about Rodgers. He was simply a man turned inward by torment.

Hornbow was a gifted, almost mesmeric speaker. With his glittering, obsidian-black eyes and compelling flow of diction—bookish, as befit a man who for five years had read lawbooks in endless solitude—he riveted attention to what he had to say. And although Balfour, by contrast, was fumble-mouthed, his direct and earnest colloquial style radiated warm rural honesty. Yes, it was a show that could not miss. And paradoxically, the more Kate was convinced of it, the less she believed it would accomplish anything. Somehow she couldn't envision an outpouring of felons eagerly volunteering to sacrifice themselves. Maybe it was Poteau's cynicism influencing her. More likely, intimacy with Noah had taught her to distrust glib solutions.

She might be wrong, though. She hoped she was. Listening to Turner Hornbow's persuasive pitch, she thought what a fine lawyer had been lost in that tragic struggle in the Bloomington bank. His candor won her instantly. He would not deceive her, said Hornbow, or pretend to be more altruistic than he really was. His reason for helping Balfour win volunteers was simple and selfish—for the sake of the Indian people only. There were millions of white and black and brown Americans, he said, and not even the worst epidemic would kill all of them. But there were only eight hundred thousand Indians. Unless this epidemic was controlled soon, they might be exterminated entirely. He would gladly sacrifice himself if it helped save his people. After all, his life was forfeited already, wasn't it?

The frank candor of it moved Kate. She glanced at Maury and was disgusted when he winked. Maury was a jerk, through and through. Nothing would ever change that.

Balfour took over then, talking in his slow country way. Maybe folks wouldn't think so, he said, but a man in a cell was still a man, still an American. He'd been a soldier once in a war. Well this was a war too, seemed like to him, and the country needed all the good soldiers it could get. Way he heard it, if the doctors didn't get healthy folks to test this here vaccine on, why the country was going to be licked. Maybe it was half-licked already, the way folks was scared to let them test that stuff on them. You couldn't blame them. Men and women with children to raise and jobs to do, they couldn't take that risk. But there was a whole big pile of healthy Americans that didn't have no children to raise nor useful work to do—five hundred waiting to die in the chair, thousands more in prison for years and years. That was what gave him the idea. He talked about it to Hornbow who talked about it to Rodgers, and they all agreed to this. They would all volunteer and try to get others, too. A con who caught the disease, well tough titty, but he didn't have much to lose anyway. And if he didn't, if he helped stop the epidemic, why, maybe the government or somebody would be thankful and shorten his sentence or commute it or something. But even if that didn't happen, that wasn't the main idea. The idea was that even lifers and condemned men were still Americans who had a right to be allowed to risk their lives for the country.

Once again Kate was genuinely affected, and once again Maury shrugged faintly and smirked. She began to detest him even more.

Then at a nudge from Hornbow the handsome young football player with a look of agony on his fine-featured face was talking. The words came out jerkily and in a monotone, almost as if he had memorized them. But Kate found them the most deeply affecting yet. Olin Rodgers, his voice so low she made a note to have them amplify his mike at air-time, said that he only wanted to get a message over to the kids of the country. Black kids. White kids. Any kind of kids. Look at him. Look what happened to him. It was what messing with drugs could do to you. Look at him. He hadn't even been a drug user. But he went with people who used them. He knew better, but he did it. Now look at him. So here he was. Glad to volunteer. Glad to do anything that let him tell the kids.

Warn the kids. He stopped as abruptly as he had begun. He shuddered and his dark brown eyes seemed to turn inward again. Kate could not say anything for a minute. She bent her head, unwilling to glance at Maury. If he had had that smirk on his face again she would have killed him.

The guards came and took the three convicts away. Kate nodded at Maury and walked out, wanting to be by herself. She went to a front office, looking south across the river at the taller buildings of the Loop. She glanced at her watch. Four hours to go. She thought she would take a nap and after freshening up get something light to eat. She turned and walked toward her office, just a cubbyhole adjacent to the one Maury used. On the way she went in to the women's lounge, but retreated hastily. Polly Magruder was there. She was crying, and Kate knew a pang of remorse. Poor kid. Her big chance, she thought, dashed away at the last second. Kate ducked out before Polly saw her, and in a chair beside the elevator bank saw Dr. Poteau sitting dispiritedly.

"You still around, Doctor?"

"I guess Mr. Murray forgot," he said. "Nobody seems to know about him providing a car for me. And frankly I don't have the nerve to start out across Chicago on my own."

"That man!" said Kate disgustedly. "You can't count on a thing he says to anybody. He's a phony and a liar and a—" All at once the seething conflict of emotion inside Kate boiled over. She was fed up with Maury's duplicity, with the artificial world of television entertainment, with the essential shoddiness of it all. People dying and Maury was playing a game with ratings. It was vomitous. Too late or not, she had to go back to Washington. "Wait here, Doctor," she said crisply. "You want to go out to the Midway campus? I've got a car and driver. Stick around a second."

She stormed into the women's lounge where Polly Magruder sat sniffling and dabbing her eyes. Kate seized

283

and shook her by the shoulders. "Snap out of it, you little fool! You want to do this show in my place?"

"Oh, my God," said Polly, eyes widening.

"Then do exactly what I say. Stay in here, out of sight, until thirty minutes before showtime. Then go tell Maury I split. You understand?"

"Oh, my God," repeated Polly and to Kate's irritation tried to kiss her.

Chapter 22

President Dobson hung up the telephone. "That was Blanchard," he said to Cohane, "talking on some airplane radio somewhere. They patched it through to the phone system. He's found the source of Consolvo's Ulceration—right where he predicted. An abandoned synthetic fuel chemical experiment in New Mexico. They're in the process of eradicating it now."

"You don't sound very joyful about it," said the secretary of defense. He was worried. He had not seen Dobson in four days and was shocked by his ashen cheeks and trembling hands. "I would have called that damn good news."

"It helps," said Dobson, "but it won't stop the epidemic. To do that you have to either exterminate the vectors or vaccinate the people. And the vectors are the people and they still refuse to be vaccinated."

"You know my advice on that."

"Sure. Pick the ones you can afford to lose and vaccinate them by force. It won't work, Charley. Not only for legal and moral reasons, but because you'd have mass rebellion."

Did he call me in to rehash all this? wondered Cohane. Why didn't he call Hiram Cawthorp, too? What's going on here? Look at his hands shake. I hope to God he's not cracking. "Another way to stop the epidemic," Cohane offered uneasily, "might be to find a sure cure."

"Simon Green thought poor young Olvera might help on that, but no luck so far, and now he may be dying."

"So where do we stand, sir?" I'm scared, thought Cohane. We can't keep on fiddle-farting around like this. We've got to take some kind of action—if not mine, somebody's. I still can't figure why he called me in.

As if reading his mind, Dobson said, "Obviously we can't sit and do nothing. We must act decisively. The threat from foreign nations grows more imminent. So I have acted. I made a bargain with the three major nuclear powers. You won't like it—I don't like it. But unless this television appeal tonight for prisoner volunteers to test the vaccine is successful I'm going to have to keep my end of the bargain."

"I'm beginning to dread hearing what that bargain is," said Cohane.

"You have to know what it is," said Dobson. "You're my Secretary of Defense. I already went over your head to Tactical Air Command to set the machinery in motion, even by-passed the Air Staff. Here's what I had to do, Charley." In quick, incisive language he explained Operation NATHAN HALE.

Cohane was staggered. "My God! They'll impeach you!"

"If I knew they would hang me, I would still have to go through with it. Blanchard reacted the same as you. I would too—any sane man would. But goddamn it, Charley, consider the alternatives! There just isn't any choice."

Cohane's mind reeled. He was a pragmatic man, little gifted with imagination, but he could visualize death raining invisibly on places he knew—the Juarez Bridge at El Paso, the Brown Palace Hotel where the Denver oil men met, the Mormon Tabernacle, the tawny pueblo-style buildings on the campus of the University of New

Mexico. The pictures whirled like a kaleidoscope, and his instincts screamed in protest. But the logical part of his brain recognized the remorseless logic of Dobson's decision. Charles Cohane covered his face a moment. "My God," he whispered. "What a price to pay."

"I looked at it every way, Charley. The one hope is this convict thing. Otherwise it's NATHAN HALE. Or nuclear warfare."

"It's up to prisoners? The whole country hanging on what a bunch of murderers and bank robbers decide to do? That's too much. Why don't we just vaccinate the bastards in their cells, sir?"

"Believe me," said Dobson, looking even more haggard, "I finally came to the same opinion. Laws or no laws. But there isn't time. Not anymore. We'd have prison riots that would take a week to put down. No, they have to be volunteers or else it's NATHAN HALE. In the end it comes down to this television program. Well, why not? Television has been the most powerful and pervasive force in the country for years and years. I want you here to watch it with me, Charley. There's nobody I'd rather have."

"I'm honored, sir," said Cohane.

Dobson managed a grim smile. "Thanks for not saying I told you so. You realize I'm finally taking your advice after all, don't you?"

"How so, Mr. President?"

"You said, be ruthless. Pick out people to sacrifice. I'm going to. The only difference is that I'm picking them geographically, not by social category."

"Somehow that doesn't make me any happier about it."

"I had a feeling it wouldn't, Charley."

After he talked to the President. Noah tried to radio General Burrows. He got through to him, but after that it was all static and dead breaks. Considering that Noah was four miles above the Ozarks transmitting to the Fort Smith airport tower, which was patching through to an

Arkansas Air National Guard MARS station, which was transmitting on to the Communications Squadron at Fort Myer for a final phone patch to General Burrows underground in Bethesda—it was not surprising, although still frustrating.

"—found *what?*" bellowed Burrows.

"—source—Washburn's Chemical works—source—eradicating—"

"Oh—good work—good—very."

"—much—not much—luck—Olvera?"

"—no luck—alive—nothing—" Suddenly Burrows's voice boomed clearly. "I read you now! Five by five! Do you receive? This is important. You said Vincent Craigie must be alive. He is. Or someone claiming to be. Patient at St. Elizabeth's. Schizophrenic."

"Craigie? Schizoid?

"Wait. It's not all bad. He remembered something. He remembered Washburn and the Ulceration stench. He treated—years ago—Washburn—same stench—"

"Goddamn it, you're fading!"

"—you—can't hear you—"

"Walt! Walt! Go get Craigie. I'll be there soon as—"

"Gone—gone—no can—"

"It's useless, Doctor," said the Jetstar pilot, turning the receiver controls. "Little Rock's gone. Maybe I can get Arnold to put your patch back through."

"Never mind," said Noah. "I heard what I needed. I heard enough. Let's just get to Andrews, the quicker the better. Make sure they've got a car waiting for me." Craigie! Vincent Craigie! Mentally ill. Good God. But if he remembered anything, even a mentally ill Vincent Craigie could be more valuable than a roomful of normal men.

Henry Gault weighed the possible traumatic damage to his patient from a ride through an epidemic-stricken city in the wrong century and decided the risk was justified. He need not have worried at all. Ambrose Alexander Noyes made the trip in total aplomb, evidently taking

288

Henry Gault's Oldsmobile for some appropriate nineteenth-century vehicle and scarcely glancing out the windows. It was twilight when they reached Bethesda, and he entered the bunker-like headquarters without comment. It was clear to Henry Gault that this strange schizophrenic could accept some anachronisms if not others.

They left the elevator six floors down, the orderly Perkins, wearing a suit coat over his whites, bringing up the rear. Walter Burrows was waiting in the foyer outside his office. He and the small, plump psychiatrist shook hands. "May I present my friend—"

"Ambrose Alexander Noyes, General," said the strapping, full-bearded man. "A pleasure."

"My pleasure, sir," said Burrows, with a questioning glance at Gault.

"And Perkins, our driver," said Gault.

"Thank you for coming by," said Burrows.

"What is your branch of Service, General?" asked the bearded man, looking at Burrows's green blouse with four rows of ribbons and braided *fourragère*. If he found anything odd in a black general, nothing indicated it.

Burrows blinked. "Why, Army Medical Corps, Mr. Noyes."

"I've been out of touch," smiled Noyes. "It's thirty years since I wore the uniform. It was blue then."

"Mr. Noyes was cavalry," said Gault.

"With Sheridan in the Shenandoah, I am proud to say. But that was long ago and of no interest now." Gault touched his elbow and they proceeded into Burrows's office. "What is the nature of your headquarters, General? Is this a military hospital?"

"Why, ah," said Burrows, with a despairing look at Gault, "it's a place for medical research into—ah—military health problems—epidemics."

"Epidemics. I remember. We lost more troops to camp fever than to Southern musketry."

"Of course," said Burrows, adding with great relief,

289

"this is Professor Badin, Mr. Noyes."

The ancient physicist, wispy white hair down his forehead, looked incredulous. "My heavens!" he said. "It *is* Doctor Craigie!"

The bearded man said, "You mistake me, sir. I am Ambrose Alexander Noyes of Baltimore."

Badin's eyebrows flew up. "I beg your pardon. Of course. An amazing resemblance. I certainly took you for someone else."

"Professor Badin," said Burrows hastily, "may I present Doctor Gault from St. Elizabeth's."

"Delighted," said Badin and led the psychiatrist aside in a casual way. "Sir," he whispered earnestly, "that man is Dr. Vincent Craigie. I would know him anywhere, despite the beard."

"I believe you," said Gault ruefully. "The trouble is making *him* believe it."

"General Burrows mentioned an identity crisis, but I never realized the extent. Why would he call himself by that other name?"

"Noyes was his grandfather, a paragon of the family, and, as a child, Dr. Craigie—it's difficult for me to think of him as Dr. Craigie—identified with him. He had a ready-made new personality when he required one."

"Is that a rather unusual sort of personality transference, Dr. Gault?"

"They're all unusual. But, yes, this has to be fairly extreme."

"What are the prospects of his regaining his old personality again? For that matter, why would he have lost it in the first place? I'm a physicist. The human mind is a great mystery to me."

Gault sighed. "To me, too. The more I learn the less I know."

"The beginnings of wisdom, they say."

"To try to answer your question, Dr. Craigie must have adopted his grandfather's identity—and his grandfather's century—because the life of Vincent Craigie and the time

290

in which he lived had become intolerable. It was something to do with work he did for the government in certain advisory capacities. He tried to tell me, but was too afraid, the one pure act of paranoia I have observed in him."

"Very, very curious," said Badin. "How does a metamorphosis like that come on? Suddenly?—like the cliché of the amnesiac not knowing who he is?"

"It can. Or it can be gradual, a gradual escape from reality as pressures accumulate."

"Is he going to stay lost? Is he coming back?"

"I agreed to bring him here, Professor Badin, partly because I understood that people like you from his old life would be present. I hoped that might help jar him back. But as you saw—"

"Perplexing," said Badin, "and, unhappily, so much may depend on his recovery. Ah. Here is our Chief. Hail to thee, Dr. Blanchard. I hear you scored a victory today."

Noah smiled wearily. Then he saw Noyes-Craigie and his eyes lighted. "It is! Even with beard! By the—! Dr. Craigie, sir, you don't know what a pleasure this is."

The bearded man looked at him blankly, shrugged, turned to Gault and said, "Really, this is getting to be a bit annoying. How much longer do you plan to stay here?"

The other men in the office exchanged quick, apprehensive glances. Perkins, who was drinking coffee with Sergeant Harrison in the back, straightened. Badin sized things up quickly and said, "I believe you were in the Valley with General Sheridan, sir. That campaign has always fascinated me."

"Really? What Department did you serve in, Professor?"

Badin smiled deprecatingly. "I regret that I was—not the right age. But wouldn't you say that General Sherman really learned his tactics from General Sheridan?"

Noyes looked pleased. "Strategy, sir, strategy. That was the strategy that broke the Rebellion."

Blanchard looked angrily at Burrows, then realized

that Gault was a stranger, and shook hands with him. The three moved to the side and conversed quickly. Noah said, "Now what triggered his memory, loading epidemic victims at the hospital?"

"At a guess, it was the stench that brought back his past. That's only a guess, Doctor."

"I see what you're getting at," said Burrows and flicked a finger. Seargeant Harrison was there instantly. "Your stinkpot," said Burrows. "Give us a quick whiff in here."

"Yes, sir," said Harrison and added, with a slight grin, "Hang on to your—nose."

Badin and Noyes-Craigie talked about the Civil War. Gault and Burrows looked uneasy. Noah stood glowering at the floor. There was a faint hiss and then the familiar, unmistakable reek of foulness filled the room, swelling tongues, churning bellies, making Gault retch audibly. "Damnation!" cried the bearded man. "That's it! That's how Washburn's people stunk. Where the devil did *you* come from, Blanchard?"

"*Apache Candle!*" snapped Noah. "Why did the government hush up *Apache Candle?*"

Vincent Craigie glared. "You've got it all wrong as usual. It wasn't *Apache Candle* they hushed up. It was the biological warfare experiments that went sour at Dugway Proving Ground. When those sheep died downwind—" A look of fear flashed across his face. "Damn it, Blanchard. You were military. You know I can't talk about that."

"Never mind what happened in Utah," said Noah brusquely. "I want to know what you did to cure Washburn's people. I know he called you in. What treatment did you use?"

"Ristocetin, blast your eyes! Ristocetin and zinc peroxide. Any first-year medical student would know. What makes you so stupid, Blanchard?"

"Ristocetin!" Noah struck his forehead. "Ristocetin, for God's sake. Who would have dreamed? Walt, phone Simon Green, we're coming right over. Harrison, for Christ's sake, kill that stink."

Harrison held a black spraybomb high. There was a sharp hiss as the sweet scent of narcissus nullified the stench. Dr. Vincent Craigie seemed suddenly bewildered. He glanced about uncertainly, then returned to Duval Badin. "The repeating carbine," he continued, "was the queen of cavalry skirmishes. The saber had been a joke, the revolver dangerous to horse and rider alike—"

Chapter 23

Heart pounding with nervous excitement, Polly Magruder hid in the women's lounge until exactly thirty minutes before "Get With It" was scheduled to go on the air. Then she went to Maury's office and knocked. He scowled up at her in the doorway. "Yeah, kid?"

"I thought somebody had better tell you, Mr. Murray. Miss Petrakis seems to have disappeared."

"What the hell you talking about?"

"The last anybody remembers seeing her, I guess, is over three hours ago, out by the elevators talking to that prison doctor. Somebody said she left with him."

"Left? Why? Where? Why didn't they stop her? Why didn't they tell me?"

"I—ah—I can't answer that, sir." Polly gulped. "Actually I'm not exactly sure who it was saw her. Actually I can't even swear she's gone."

Maury groaned. "Oh, she's gone all right. You can bet on it. I should have guessed. Damn slut; ran back to that frigging doctor. Well, that finishes Kate in this business. I'll see to that. What the hell do I do for a stand-in?"

He studied Polly standing before him: leggy, fresh-faced, brunette, looking almost like a kid sister of Kate. He'd been willing to give her a try on the show once. Well,

294

why not again? Maury looked solemn. "Polly, I could handle the show alone, but viewers are used to a man-and-woman team. I'd as soon keep it that way. Do you suppose you're up to filling in on this short notice?"

"Oh yes, sir! I wouldn't let you down, Mr. Murray."

"Maury," he corrected her. "If we're a team, you call me Maury." She'll work cheaper than Kate too, he was thinking. Dumb little bimbo probably didn't have an agent. "Okay, Polly. We'll do it like this. You just sit in Kate's place, and I won't mention her name or introduce you or anything. Let the viewers guess. As for the show, just follow my leads, pick up on my cues. You do good, I'll introduce you right at the end as my new partner. That sound all right?"

"Oh yes, sir—uh—Maury. Anything you want." The great brown eyes were so worshipful he momentarily wished he was a square john. This tall babe would do nip-ups for him.

"That's it, then. Trot your little ass over to Makeup and meet us on the set. Who needs Kate? Show could use some new blood anyway, hey, kid?"

With her heart thudding and a smile so fixed it made her face ache, Polly entered the studio past the three armed prison guards leaning on their rifles against the wall—hulking, brute-faced men in their billed caps and khaki pseudo-uniforms, it seemed to Polly. She resented the way they leered at her as she passed between them. But there were a dozen or so studio employees scattered about the theater seats of the studio and their friendly looks cheered her. A janitor she knew sent her a cheerful wink; two girls from the typing pool wiggled their fingers; and a news reporter clasped his hands over his head and shook them in a boxer's greeting.

Maury and the three convicts were already on the set, designed to suggest a farmhouse parlor in Maury's native Tennessee. He lounged in his famous wooden rocker with the convicts to his left sitting bolt upright in split-cane rural chairs, behind them a backdrop of imitation fieldstone fireplace and chinked-log walls. The Indian's dusky face was set impassive as a Mayan mask. Farley Balfour, despite his formidable shoulders, was clearly petrified with stage fright. Olin Rodgers, empty eyes staring out of his aquiline features, was a zombie. As a good Chicago Bisons fan, Polly could remember sitting in Soldier's Field, screaming her throat raw at Rodgers's backfield scrambling, at the bullet passes he hurled, at his razzle-dazzle play-calling. To see him like this, indrawn, defeated, a shell of a man, stabbed her heart with pity.

She sat down in the end chair beyond Balfour and gave his big thigh a reassuring pat. He started and gave her a look of dumb gratitude. The small act eased some of Polly's own tension.

In his glass booth the director began a countdown, and on cue Maury said, "Good evenin', good folks," in his cornpone, downhome accent. "I want to welcome you back to 'Get With It.' Like everybody knows, we been off the air, but we're back tonight with some real important guests that have got a proposal for ending this awful epidemic. One guest you're gonna recognize." The cameras moved to Rodgers's tormented face. "That's who it is! Scrambling Grambling Olin, the great Chicago Bisons quarterback. And the other two—in their own way—are important gents also. Mr. Turner Hornbow—" The narrow Indian face filled the monitor. "—a Mohawk-Huron who studied law at Indiana University. And we got us a decorated combat veteran of the Green Berets, ex-sergeant Farley Balfour." Farley grinned terrifyingly.

The cameras returned to Maury who waited a double beat. "Our three guests—" he resumed, "—black man, red man, white man—are members of the most exclusive, least desirable club in America, The Condemned. With about five hundred other men and boys—and a few women too, God help us—they sit in prison cells day after day, some of them year after year, waiting for the state to decide to put them to death. Five hundred, folks! That's as many as all the people in Lyles, Tennessee, or Kidron,

Ohio, or Bismarck, Illinois, maybe in the town you live in. That means people kept in unbearable anxiety, sane men and women judged unfit to live, penned up like hogs, waitin' for hog-killing time."

The camera panned on the convicts, even Balfour grim-faced now. Maury paused five beats. With the cameras back on him he said, "From that introduction you might expect us to talk about capital punishment, which is a controversial subject we will take up maybe another time. But tonight these fine, courageous, heroic men—no matter what the law says, they're fine, courageous, heroic men—are going to offer their own lives to save their country."

Intent on Maury's words, wondering when he would throw her a cue, Polly became vaguely conscious of distant unidentifiable noises. The studio was supposed to be soundproof, but she heard running and shouting and one or two gunshots. The small audience looked around, and Farley Balfour lifted his head in a puzzled way. The Indian smiled as if he knew something, but both Rodgers, staring emptily, and Maury, talking smoothly, seemed oblivious.

"These brave men," Maury was saying, "have declared war on the epidemic. Like good soldiers, they are prepared to give their lives if need be. Their leader was a soldier, our ex-Green Beret Sergeant Balfour—WHAT THE HELL IS THAT?"

A prison guard's rifle had fired, a deafening crash in the acoustic-walled studio. Light flooded in as the doors crashed open, and a wave of men—firearms brandished—knocked the guards down, beat them into the floor, and rushed the spectator seats to herd the studio employees ahead of them like sheep, all the time shouting: "Hornbow! Hornbow! Hornbow!"

Polly sat stunned. She saw Maury spring from his rocker yelling, "WHAT THE HELL IS THIS?" and saw Hornbow thrust him back. In the distance she saw the prison guards struggle up only to be beaten to the floor

297

again. She saw incredulity in the faces of Balfour and Rodgers. She saw now that the invaders were perhaps a dozen and a half men with dark Indian faces who pointed rifles and shotguns at her studio friends, holding them hands high along the wall and stripping them of wallets and watches. She heard the scream of a typist dragged down between the seat rows by a man in army fatigues. She stared up numbly as a hawkfaced man in a checked hunting shirt leaped onto the lighted set, a pistol in each hand, a knife sheathed at the waist.

"James!" cried Hornbow. "James Pigeonblood! By God, you pulled it off!"

Polly watched them embrace and pound each other on the back, heard the man in the checked shirt cry, "No sweat, Turner. Soon as we got your plan, we hot-wired a schoolbus and came up, the eighteen of us. A schoolbus! How about that? Here's a pistol for you. What about Ross Cutnose? Didn't he show yet?"

Polly looked toward the exit. She wished Kate was here. What would Kate do now?

"James, you mangy 'Pache breed!" cried Hornbow, taking the gun. "I knew I could count on you. This is the biggest thing for the American Indian Movement since seizing Alcatraz. Hell, bigger! No, Ross didn't show up. Screw him. We don't need Ross. I only thought he might raise an army of blacks to rush this place and spring their quarterback hero. But we don't need them now. Glory, glory, that ugly face of yours looked good busting in here."

"Man, you're still our leader," said James Pigeonblood. "Why wouldn't we rescue you? What now: lam out of here and hide you someplace?"

"God no," said Hornbow. "This is a million times bigger than me breaking jail. Wait till you hear. This is the beginning of the end for white men. This epidemic they got—wait till I tell you, James!"

Farley Balfour pushed between them. "Look here,

Turner," he said pugnaciously, "what the shit's going on? This wasn't the idea at all."

James Pigeonblood sprang back, cocking his pistol. "Never mind," said Turner. "He's O.K. He was in the cellblock with me. He and the black. They aren't enemy."

"If you say so," said James, thumbing down the pistol hammer. "Back off, friend," he said to Farley. "Don't bother us."

Farley ignored him. "Goddamn it, Turner! What you pulling? Who are these bums? What's happening?"

"For Christ's sake," said Turner impatiently. "Are you that stupid? Buddy, you got sucked in. For once, the Indian lied to the white man. Now keep out of the way. I've got important things to do."

At that instant Maury Murray came sputtering up again. "You son-of-a-bitch!" he squalled. "You son-of-a-bitch, you're ruining my show!"

Turner slapped him. Maury went purple, and with a womanish squeal he attacked. His make-believe world of television broadcasting was collapsing before his eyes, and now he was goaded past endurance. Not even the most brutal reformatory bully had ever called diminutive Maury a coward. He pushed aside Turner's nickel-plated .32 Saturday Night Special and from his full five-feet-five smashed his fist into the Indian's mouth, the final foolish act of Maury's life.

Hornbow stepped back, tasted blood from his split lip, and went mad. A puny white man had administered the ultimate insult to his Mohawk soul. He caught Maury by the hair, twisted his head back in full view of the cameras, and with thirty million horrified Americans watching, bored the three-inch pistol barrel between Maury's teeth and fired. The explosion jarred the audio system and bulged out Maury's eyes. Turner opened his left hand and Maury dropped. Polly could hear herself screaming as if from a distant room, as if it were someone else screaming.

Just then, Ross Cutnose and his two American Indian

Movement friends—Billy Two-Ducks, the Sac who headed the Northside Chicago organization, and John Hardy, the Cherokee from Oak Park—entered the studio. They had debated a long time about Turner's letter before reluctantly deciding to come to the studio. Believing that Turner's death sentence had been a travesty of justice, Ross was willing to help him escape, but Turner's proposal that he persuade black football fans to storm the television station to rescue Rodgers was preposterous. Ross coached in a black school, but he neither had that kind of influence nor wanted it.

"Good God!" said John Hardy, shocked. "You said this was a man of peace."

"I thought it," said Ross. "There has to be some justification for this."

Turner pointed the pistol at the three cameramen. His head was roaring. He saw through a blood-red haze. His Mohawk bloodlust was in full control. "Keep those cameras on me!" he snarled. "Keep the sound up. Indian people! Hear me, Indian brothers. I speak for the American Indian Movement. Liberation is at hand. The whites are finished. Believe me, brothers. I am Huron and the spirits of the Old Ones confide to me. Our time is at hand. The white man's time is running out. This great sickness is a sickness of the whites, sent to destroy the White hegemony. Indians are safe from it. Indians do not need that poison vaccine. Your red blood protects you."

"This bird is nuts," growled Billy Two-Ducks. "Where does he get off, spouting crap like that?"

Ross Cutnose looked bewildered. "In college he was the sanest of us all. I can't figure this—now what the hell?"

From behind, lowering his head like a bull charging from the chutes, Balfour roared: "Goddamn you, Turner Hornbow! You murdering miserable maniac! You gone nuts?" He clamped his hands on Hornbow's throat and began shaking him like a terrier with a snake. James Pigeonblood cocked his pistol, but Farley sent James sprawling with a thrust of Hornbow's body. Eyes fluttering, tongue protruding, pulled up on tiptoes, Hornbow still managed to twist his body around, push his pistol into Farley's groin, and pull the trigger four times. Balfour groaned, grabbed for his belly and, sank down. Still in his Mohawk frenzy Turner whirled, seeking another victim. He saw Polly staring up at him, mouth frozen in a great screaming O. He chopped her across the head, using the pistol like a tomahawk and Polly fell across Balfour, the two tangled and inert beside Maury's body. With a squawk of terror Olin Rodgers started out of his stupor and fled, running low and evasive as a broken-field ball carrier, across the studio, past the three Chicago AIM leaders, and out to the fire exit.

"Sweet Jesus," sighed John Hardy, "you guys can stay if you want. I'm cutting out. That's a homicidal maniac you want us to save. This is no place for me."

"You were wrong about him, Ross," said Billy Two-Ducks. "This bird belongs in a cell. Or the Chair. The AIM doesn't need anybody like this. Listen to him carry on!"

Turner was ranting again, wild-eyed and sweating. "Red brothers!" he exhorted. "Prepare to seize centers of power! Time is on our side. The white man is washed up. This is only the first seizure. We hold this building. We hold hostages. The whites dare not move against us. Brothers! Red brothers! Don't take his vaccine. Take his armories and radio stations and power generators and—"

James Pigeonblood had picked himself up from the floor. He stared uncertainly at Turner Hornbow, ranting among the bodies of his victims. He gestured. "Look, Turner. We can't hold out here. There's not enough of us. The cops—"

Out by the studio door Ross Cutnose reached his decision. "I was totally wrong," he said crisply. "Maniac is the word for him. I don't know what it's like, being on Death Row, but it made a maniac out of Hornbow. I thought it was all metaphor, that stuff he wrote about the

Old Ones in the smoky lodges. I thought all that Huron dream prophecy stuff he wrote was just high-sounding talk. But this violence—the crazy bugger believes in it. Let's get the hell out of here before the cops come." Shaking their heads, the three activists went without Turner ever knowing they had been there. Their purpose had been to rescue and smuggle him into Canada, believing, as had his followers during University times, that he was a victim of race prejudice. They had intended to explain that the old days of Indians firing Winchesters and waving signs were gone, that the Native American Rights Fund had discovered that Indian lawyers practicing in white courts—ironically the goal Turner Hornbow had first set for himself—was more effective than riots and shouting. Since Turner went to prison times had changed. Indians were winning mineral and fishing rights and millions of dollars in reparation for broken treaties. All this was what they had intended to remind Turner Hornbow about. But now they left him behind, disassociating themselves from the maddened Mohawk.

Behind them, James Pigeonblood's band of radicals was ready to leave, too. They would risk their lives to rescue Turner, but not to hear his insane mouthings to a television audience. With their loot, they gathered at the studio doors, waving to Pigeonblood. James was tugging Turner's elbow. "Come on, man," he pleaded. "We've got you broke out. Come on now. We'll hide you. Come on. You can lay low till—like you say—the white man is wiped out. But you can't stay here any longer. Every cop in town will be here."

Turner pushed him off, caught up in his fiery rhetoric. "Vaccination is a white man's trick!" he shouted. "Indians are already immune. The sickness is a white man's illness, a bad wind blowing for the white man out of the west . . ."

He pushed James Pigeonblood and his followers away impatiently when they tried to pull him away with them. He never saw their shrugs of despair as they gave up and fled before the police could arrive. He did not see the hostages melt away or the slipping off of the production crew. He never knew when the last camera stopped grinding, when the sound track stopped, when "Get With It" went off the air for the last time. Dominated by his maddened Mohawk soul, alone under the blazing set lights, Turner Hornbow ranted. At his feet lay the victims of his maniacal rage: Polly, Maury, Farley Balfour. At the far side of the studio where the doors stood wide the three khaki-clad prison guards lay across their weapons, inert where the Indian activist band of James Pigeonblood had left them for dead. Caught up in his tirade, made insane by five years of brooding in the imminence of execution, Turner Hornbow spouted his hate into a dead mike. He did not see the prison guard stir, did not see him crawl painfully to the last row of theater seats, did not see him level his rifle and take careful aim at the lighted set.

"Freeze, Hornbow!" the guard croaked.

Turner whirled, snapped the empty pistol, and the guard shot him between the eyes.

Chapter 24

Without warning, the television screen with Turner Hornbow spewing his venom, his face contorted, his arms flailing, went black. For a minute President Dobson and Secretary Cohane sat staring at it, as benumbed and shocked as millions of other American viewers. Then Cohane got up and turned the set off shakily.

"Well, there went that, Mr. President," he said. His voice cracked. "God save us. I suppose I was naive, but I never expected—the slaughter, the savagery—the sheer animal—no, animals are more decent."

"It's our century." Dobson bend his head. "Perhaps it came in with Hitler. Maybe the Russian Revolution. Atrocity. Terrorism. It's virtually standard tactics now. Maybe that Indian was a maniac, but those American Indian dissidents who crashed the studio, they looked sane enough. After all, what did they do that the IRA and the PLO and our own Symbionese and Weathermen and all the other revolutionary groups haven't done? The Chicago police will clean those pirates out, of course. but—Well, that was my last hope for postponing NATHAN HALE. The Europeans monitored that television broadcast, you can bet on it. Certainly their embassies did. You can imagine the messages flying back and forth right now. We look like a nation out of control, at the mercy of terrorists, an administration helpless. If I tried to temporize after that, what would the Europeans think? How would they judge us? What would they do?"

"I know there's no choice," said Cohane. "But shouldn't you at least convene the NSC?"

"The National Security Council and all the councils in the world won't make any difference. NATHAN HALE is a cold-blooded, criminal act. And I have to go through with it. I can't spread the blame. It's all mine. Right now I'm trying to get courage to take that phone out and phone Tactical Air Command. I'd rather cut off my hand." A black box on his desk buzzed and his secretary said, "I know your instructions, Mr. President, but I thought you might make an exception for Dr. Blanchard."

"Blanchard? Of course. Send him in." Dobson turned back to Cohane. "Blanchard has to be in on it. He's been in all along, as deep as I was. Hello, Doctor. How can you look so cheerful at a time like this?"

"I didn't realize it showed, sir." Noah grinned. "Maybe a little cheerfulness is in order. We have our first lead to a possible cure."

"Lord God of Hosts," whispered Cohane and crossed himself hastily.

Dobson gaped. "Something you found in New Mexico?"

"No, sir. It's been here all along, more than twenty years, Ristocetin. An old, forgotten, long-superseded antibiotic for staph infection."

"Risto—?" Dobson blinked. "I never heard of it."

"Ristocetin, sir. No reason you should. Most younger doctors haven't either. It was one of the original five antibiotics. Developed at George Washington University. Effective, except for bad side effects—inflammation and some kidney complications. Nothing to worry us if it cures Consolvo's Ulceration."

"But does it? My God, man, get to the bottom line!"

"Sorry, sir. I'm a little excited, I guess. We were only tipped off to it this evening. For the last three hours we've been subjecting it at Simon Green's NIH hospital to antibiotic sensitivity studies. The way you do that is to impregnate a disc with the antibiotic and give it twenty-four hours in a culture of the organism—"

"Jesus, Mary, and Joseph!" sputtered Cohane, "get to the point, Doctor! We don't want that clinical stuff. When will you know? Tomorrow?"

"Sooner. With luck. This organism reproduces so fast that it speeds up the sensitivity test. We may know enough in another hour to try the treatment on actual patients. Yes. By tomorrow we ought to be reasonably certain one way or the other."

"What's your gut feeling?" said Dobson anxiously. "Give it to me straight, Doctor. What's your judgment?"

Noah hesitated, then cast caution aside. "Yes, sir. Damn it, this time I think we've got something!"

"Glory, glory," said Cohane. "A miracle."

"Not quite," grinned Noah. "That's not my line of work. I'm no chaplain. Then again, maybe there was a miracle. A man we thought dead turning up alive—I guess that was sort of a miracle." He hesitated again, then plunged into a bare-bones narrative of Vincent Craigie emerging briefly from schizophrenia and how Craigie had treated Washburn chemical workers long ago with an unknown, putrescent—but certainly not fatal—skin rash, believed ancestor of Consolvo's Ulceration. Neither Dobson nor Cohane seemed quite as impressed, though, as Noah had expected. Maybe they took that sort of bizarre happening for granted. More likely it was that they were concentrating on something more important.

"I want the science attachés at the Russian, French, and British embassies read in on this immediately," said Dobson. "Better yet, Doctor, how about it if you took them in person to the NIH hospital—let them observe these tests for themselves? I think that's the quickest way to ease the pressure, wouldn't you say, Charley?"

306

"Hold up, sir," said Noah, alarmed. "That's a bit premature. All we have is what a mental patient told us. Not that I don't trust Dr. Craigie, knowing him as I did, but to bring outsiders in, foreigners—no, sir, I'd wait."

"Damnation!" Dobson exploded. "Wait is just what we can't afford. You remember NATHAN HALE, don't you? You know we're under the gun on it."

"I thought you were stalling that with your convict-volunteer appeal," said Noah. "Didn't it work out?"

Cohane gasped. "You didn't watch the show?"

"Watch?" said Noah, nonplussed. "Watch a television show? Who had time for that? I flew to New Mexico and back, I've been underground at Bethesda and stuck in a hospital ever since—what happened?"

"Lord, man! A debacle. A double-cross. A terrorist takeover. A band of armed Indian revolutionaries rushed in and seized the studio—took everybody hostage. There was fighting—murder. Why, they killed the man and woman show hosts right on camera! Now they're holding the building and—God, man! You're white as a ghost!"

Noah went dizzy. "Kate? You say they killed Kate? Kate Petrakis?"

The President said softly, "A friend of yours? We didn't know her name. A dark, pretty, very tall young woman."

"Kate," said Noah, sinking weakly into a chair. "Excuse me." He covered his eyes. "We were—close. Very. She's my—she's been running my office here."

"I am so sorry," said the President. "Is there anything I can do?"

"No, sir." Noah fought with himself, trying to master the grief and anger overwhelming him. "Well, yes. If I could get away—you can reach Burrows and Green at the hospital. They're on top of developments. Sir, I'd like an hour to see to things. If that's all right."

"By all means," said Dobson, his voice gentle. "Take all the time you want."

Driving through the dark and empty Washington

307

streets, Noah did not speak. Guilt, misery, incredulity, and bitter anguish consumed him. He had allowed her to leave, and now she was dead. Nothing had ever hurt him this much.

Gus drove up before the canopied silent entrance of the hotel. "You want me to wait, Doctor?"

"Yes," said Noah. "No. Come back in an hour." He got out and went inside. He was not certain of why he had returned to the Fleur d'Or. There was no other place to go, of course. It was where he had last seen her. How could he have let her go?

The dim-lit lobby was empty. In a chair in a corner, Henri snored. I'll pick up a few things, thought Noah, and get the hell out of here. I'll find another place to stay. Maybe with Walt Burrows. I can't stand staying here. He saw that the "Out of Order" sign still hung on the elevator door. He climbed the stairs to his suite. He turned the doorknob and walked in.

It was dark. He reached for the wall switch, but before his hand found it, a darker shape rose up. "Noah?" she said. Her voice sounded uncertain. "I had to. I couldn't stay. Can I come back? Is it all right?"

He heard himself laughing. It did not sound like his own voice or like any laughing he had ever heard. It was a discordant sound. "They said you were dead. The President said..."

"It was that girl. Polly. I got her killed. Noah. I had to come back. I chickened out. I couldn't stay. They killed her. And Maury. I saw it on television. Noah? Can I come back? Noah, I killed that child!"

It was as unreal as a waking dream. Noah took hold of her. He tasted tears when he kissed her. He wished his hard, exultant laughing would stop. This is hysteria, he was thinking. No. Joy. Relief. Disbelief. "All right, Kate?" It was almost a chuckle. "You're asking if it's all right for you to come back? Great God, I never wanted anything so much in my life!" He held her tight and swore he'd never let her go away again.

308

Chapter 25

Except for thirty minutes with Kate the night before—interrupted by a peremptory phone call from Simon Green summoning him to the NIH hospital—Noah had not lain down in thirty hours. In that time he had flown five thousand miles, uncovered the source of the epidemic and found a possible cure, had rung every change on his scale of emotions from despair to bliss. When he returned to President Dobson and Secretary of Defense Cohane at ten in the morning, he was so weary he stumbled on the rug.

"Sit down, man!" said Dobson sharply. "You look dead on your feet."

"Yes, sir." Noah sank gratefully into a chair. "It's worth it, though. I guess you can put the word out, Mr. President. It looks like we've got the answer."

Cohane clapped his hands. "You proved it? Ristocetin does it?"

"Started early enough, sir. That's the one hitch. It's effective only in the early stages. Of course, our experience is limited so far." He yawned. "Excuse me, please. Up all night. We only moved from sensitivity testing to trying it on patients about two o'clock this morning. As we gain clinical experience, maybe we can

309

make it more effective. But so far only patients with primary lesions respond." He grinned suddenly. "But I'll tell you this—in their cases it's fantastic—unbelievable. With Ristocetin—and zinc peroxide to release oxygen into the infected tissues—the lesions start drying almost at once. It's like those cases I've seen of spontaneous remission."

"Thank you, Dr. Blanchard," said Lloyd Dobson. His voice was husky. "Thank you for bringing this news to me." He dropped his head a moment, and before he looked up, blew his nose vigorously.

"Yes, sir," said Noah soberly. "I feel like that, too."

"If I follow you," said Cohane, "what this means is that, even if you can't help patients in advanced stages, the treatment takes the fear out of being vaccinated. Am I correct?"

"It certainly should," said Noah. "I don't see why it wouldn't. You vaccinate a hundred people, watch them a short while. It only takes a few hours, you know, for symptoms to develop. If they do, a quick treatment with Ristocetin. The others, the ninety percent, they of course are home free."

"We can prove this?" said Cohane cautiously. "You've cured people who caught Consolvo's Ulceration from the vaccine?"

Noah looked annoyed. "Well, no. We haven't had time, there aren't that many people catching Ulceration from the vaccine, because there aren't that many willing to be vaccinated. But there's no clinical evidence to suggest that Ristocetin would be less effective, regardless of the etiology of the disease. It's the same disease in every respect, whether you catch it from being vaccinated or from a source of contagion in the ordinary way. Believe me, Mr. Secretary."

"Oh, I believe you. I have total faith in you, Doctor. But I'm not a paranoid Russian. You might call it an unreasonable question, but it's exactly the sort they're apt to ask."

"Oh, my God," Noah breathed. "You know, you're right. That puts a crimp in it. This damn thing is like one of those Chinese box puzzles. Every time you open one there's another inside."

"Let's not borrow trouble," said Dobson. "We can't be sure the Russians would take that position."

"I bet they will," said Cohane. "I see it like this. We tell them we have this cure. Swell, they say. So before we start vaccinating good Russian citizens, prove we can cure the ones who catch the disease from it. If you can't, and if you still can't vaccinate your own people, then—to prove good faith—sacrifice those cities the way you promised."

"They couldn't be that unreasonable," Dobson protested. "Not even Russians."

"You know, sir, they might," said Noah. "What it comes back to is the same old snag. If Americans weren't afraid to be vaccinated, we'd have no problem."

"As we've all agreed on since the start," said Cohane testily. "What are you getting at?"

"It just occurred to me," said Noah. "You gentlemen were putting your hopes in a television performance by a bunch of jailbirds. It didn't work. Why not a television performance by a higher class of people? That might work."

"You lost me," said Cohane.

"Me, too," said Dobson. "Elucidate, Doctor."

"Mr. President," said Noah, "a fair question, sir. Do you trust Dr. Green? Do you honestly believe that he and his staff have found a reliable treatment for Consolvo's Ulceration if caught in the earliest stages?"

"If Doctor Green tells me that—if you tell me that—yes. I have absolute confidence in both of you."

Noah looked at him steadily. "Enough confidence to allow Mr. Cohane here, your right-hand man, to let himself be vaccinated? As I understand it, until now you've forbidden it."

"He's got you there, boss," said Cohane gleefully. "He's got you there."

311

Before Dobson could respond, Noah went on. "You expected those convicts to volunteer—you half-hoped that act would induce ordinary law-abiding Americans to volunteer, too. At least I think you entertained the hope. Well, excuse me, but if I were the average citizen scared to death out there, hiding in my house, I wouldn't risk my life getting vaccinated because of what some condemned murderers did. On the other hand, if I saw the President of the United States and his cabinet officers and some senators and congressmen and generals and admirals and a few bishops and board chairmen rolling up their sleeves—"

"Holy Moses!" roared Dobson and began punching buttons on his intercom box. "Get Lem Akins in here. Get my cabinet on the phone and put them all on hold. Get me—"

A spectacle without precedent appeared on network television that evening. In the Great Rotunda of the Capitol the influential figures of the land stood in line, sleeves rolled up, to be vaccinated. The President was first, followed by the Washington-based ambassadors of the major European nations. Then came the cabinet and the House and Senate majority and minority leaders. Archbishops and generals and board chairmen and sports and theatrical stars and even a university president or two were in line. It went on all night long.

The coal miners of Wansmere, West Virginia; the frightened blacks in the burnt-out ghettoes; the B'nai B'rith and DAR and Chamber of Commerce and Rotary and all the other organization members barricaded in suburban homes; Texas shrimpers and Maine potato growers and Oklahoma wildcatters and every class and category of American—watched and slowly grew persuaded. The network anchormen covering the spectacle reminded them that public health vaccine stations were open everywhere and round the clock. The rumor that Ristocetin was running short, they added, was un-

312

founded, but it might be wise all the same not to procrastinate.

A trickle became a stream, and a stream became a flood and by the first week of October the Center for Disease Control announced officially that the epidemic no longer existed.

Chapter 26

Indian Summer had lingered late in the Sandia high country. Snow might fly tomorrow, but this October dawn was blue-gold and fair. By mid-morning it would be as warm as June, but with the sun only peeping over the mountain the air was icy. Noah blew on his fingers, stiff from working the fly-rod, and shivered in his sheepskin coat. The smell of coffee boiling and trout sputtering in Pecos's skillet made his mouth water.

The camp was nine thousand feet up by the trout pond that Howard Consolvo kept stocked for when his kids came home. Noah could see a hundred miles across forested ranges. He hoped Herman Diehl down in Alamogordo was enjoying the yellow glory of the autumn aspens, and that General Flickering was getting his fighter wing back to operational readiness. Epidemic survivors everywhere were doing essentially that now—picking up broken lives and putting them back together.

Big Foot came wheezing uphill from checking the packhorses. He hunkered down on pine needles and picked up his story. Yeah, it was ironic-like, the way Doc Gutierrez went. Worked night and day in his epidemic ward without ever catching that Ulceration. Then one day, blooie! Grabbed his heart, squawked and keeled over. Cardiac arrest they said—that he plain worked hisself to death.

Noah agreed it could happen like that and grieved a minute for Nelson before thrusting him from his mind. There were so many to grieve for if he let himself go.

The first sun rays touched his face. Not everybody wanted the old life back, he reflected. Lloyd Dobson had formally announced that he would not run for a second term. He pled poor health, but Noah suspected that he did not trust himself for any more life-and-death decisions and was honest enough to step down. Simon Green was through, too. Noah chuckled. Fat Simon packing his duds to retire to Edenton, North Carolina, to do nothing ever again but tend crab pots. Walter Burrows was undaunted, though, getting a third star and taking over a major West Coast medical command near his father and sister. Noah rejoiced for him.

It was sad about Vincent Craigie. Two quick returns to the twentieth century and then evidently permanent refuge in the congeniality of his grandfather's time. Perhaps Craigie preferred it to feeling guilty for his role in those biological warfare experiments.

A wise black doctor at Cook County General had told Noah that Olin Rodgers was believed to be safe in Algeria. Black Chicago was happy about that. It shouldn't be, the doctor said.

Cheating the electric chair meant little to Olin. Inside where it counted, he had been dead a long time. The same doctor mentioned that Kate's understudy, who had been struck on the head by the barrel of Turner's gun had survived. Polly was undergoing trauma therapy for a severe concussion at Evanston Hospital. With luck she'd be back to work by Christmas. That made Noah happy, particularly because Kate had felt so awful about Polly.

Pecos handed him up a tin plate so hot he could hardly hold it. "Tell the little lady to wrap her lips around these vittles, Doc," he said. Cautiously Noah sampled a forkful

315

of rainbow trout minutes out of snow-water. He whistled, blew, savored. Nothing had ever tasted better.

When he went in the tent, Kate looked up tousled-haired from the double sleeping bag. He said, "Rise and shine, woman. After this you bring me breakfast."

"Why?" she said, taking the plate from him. "I rather like it this way."

THE CLAIRVOYANT
By Hans Holzer

PRICE: $2.25 T51573
CATEGORY: Novel (Hardcover publisher:
Mason/Charter 1976)

The story of a beautiful young Viennese girl whose gift of prophecy took her from the mountains of Austria to the glittering drawing rooms of Beverly Hills. She began to exhibit psychic powers at the age of four. Terrified of their daughter's "gift," her parents sent her to a remote school. As she moved from school to school and then from man to man, she used her psychic abilities to climb to perilous heights of fame and success!

Author of the best-selling Murder In Amityville

THE KESSLER ALLIANCE
By Thomas Horstman

PRICE: $2.25   BT51463
CATEGORY: Novel (original)

A devastatingly prophetic novel of what could happen to the world, if Nazi extremists remained unchecked and their forces overthrew the world. Munich, Germany is the focal point of events and the birthplace of Wilhelm Kessler, a youth who becomes fascinated with Adolph Hitler. Another youth, Leo Maeder, becomes a Catholic priest. The lives of these two men become entwined as a bizarre series of events shake the world, and nations convulse under tremendous economic, political and social pressures. Only one man knew of the diabolical plot, but no one would believe him!

DEATH OF A SCAVENGER
By Keith Spore

PRICE: $2.25   BT51465
CATEGORY: Mystery (Original)

Dr. Hugo Enclave takes on only the most clever
and cunning crimes, and is intrigued by those
considered unsolvable by the police. Enclave set
out to unravel the tangled threads surrounding the
death of Harland Rockmore, an investigator for a
law firm, whose body was found near his boss's
home after a scavenger hunt. Enclave moves
through a torturous labyrinth of murder, mayhem
and mystery to uncover a conspiracy aimed at
the White House itself!

SEND TO: **TOWER PUBLICATIONS**
P.O. BOX 270
NORWALK, CONN. 06852

PLEASE SEND ME THE FOLLOWING TITLES:

Quantity	Book Number	Price

**IN THE EVENT THAT WE ARE OUT OF STOCK
ON ANY OF YOUR SELECTIONS, PLEASE LIST
ALTERNATE TITLES BELOW:**

Postage/Handling

I enclose...

FOR U.S. ORDERS, add 50c for the first book and 10c for each additional book to cover cost of postage and handling. Buy five or more copies and we will pay for shipping. Sorry, no C.O.D.'s.

FOR ORDERS SENT OUTSIDE THE U.S.A., add $1.00 for the first book and 25c for each additional book. PAY BY foreign draft or money order drawn on a U.S. bank, payable in U.S. ($) dollars.

☐ **PLEASE SEND ME A FREE CATALOG.**

NAME_____
(Please print)

ADDRESS_____

CITY_____**STATE**_____**ZIP**_____
Allow Four Weeks for Delivery